Bola Borisade

My Number ONE Husband

WHITE
MEDIA
UK LIMITED

MY NUMBER ONE HUSBAND

Published in Great Britain in 2013 by

MEDIA
UK LIMITED
Glasgow, Scotland

A CIP catalogue record for this book
is available from the British Library

ISBN- 978-0-9926296-0-1

Printed and bound in Great Britain by:
Print-on-Demand Worldwide

Acknowledgment

I am indebted to the following for
their help and support:
To my wife, Yetunde, who
is always there for me.
To my son, Yemi,
who persuaded the members
of my family that they should
allow me to write.
To Faith, my typist,
who had to go over the script
several times.
To Joseph Adepoju,
who prepared the script
for publishing.
To all who believe
in me as a writer.

Bola Borisade

MY NUMBER
ONE
HUSBAND

CHAPTER ONE

Men called her the Emerald of Toro. No one who saw her failed to wonder at her beauty.

"No one should be this good-looking," they said.

Princess Alero, Toro's magnificent rose was a stunner. She was tender and delicate like the new palm frond and radiant as the rainbow. All the time, men came flocking around her. Princes and sons of the Lords of the land, were all panting to have her. But it appeared nature had deliberately sent Alero to the human world to make men unhappy, grieve their hearts, torture them with her beauty, display her tantalizingly before them like a lovely, ripe, delicious fruit, dangling temptingly and yet beyond the reach of the gardener. Alero was a beauty, the kind nature only sends down into the world once in a blue moon. You stare at her and your body is instantly aflame.

Alero was pretty but she had no heart. She had a sweet shape, but she had no emotion. She was captivating but she had no sentiment. She disliked men. She snubbed them. She spurned their advances.

She was cold, cold without any warmth inside her. Her lovely, shinning chocolate skin was an exhibit marked: "Look but do not touch," Her fine, beautiful lips were also exhibits marked: "Admire but do not kiss,"

Alero dazzled and mesmerized all young men, made them enjoy sleepless nights, raised up their blood pressures to high pitch, wounded their hearts, in the end opted for the convent. She knew her parents would never agree to such a crazy decision. She had therefore chosen this week when they were away in Lagos to secretly leave her home for the Convent of Holy Maria.
"God gives me a beautiful body. I am going to give the same back to him," she murmured as she wrote a note for her parents, stating as best as she could why she had opted to be a nun.

Prince Matete, her father, the heir to the famous ancient Kingdom of Toro, was one of the greatest Africans of his generation. Now 56, tall, handsome, and wealthy, he was born with a silver spoon in his mouth. He could afford anything money could buy and so Alero never lacked anything. He met Dora, Alero's mother years back in a wedding ceremony in Lagos and both fell in love at first sight. Six months later, they were married. A year later they had Alero.

As Alero walked quietly out of her house, she carried nothing with her except a handbag containing an additional dress. She didn't want to explain to the guards at the gate why she was traveling. Immediately she left the gate, she put on a veil to disguise herself.

She had enough money with her and therefore made up her mind to buy all the dresses and the materials she needed when she got to the Convent of Holy Maria in Ibadan. She had been there two times and she loved its serene and quiet environment.

A bus picked her up at Toro Square. Most of the passengers were women going to Ibadan Metropolis to buy materials for Christmas. They wore bright and lovely faces. All the remaining passengers were men, one of them, a reverend gentleman. The December morning was delicious, a cool breeze fanned Alero's face. As the bus surged forward like a concord, and its engine sighed quietly, the fascination of that morning adventure grew. Christmas was beckoning with both hands, just 48 hours ahead. The air everywhere smelt of festive mood. Everything showed a promise of a bright, lovely day in the making. All the women in the bus were from Toro. As the bus pierced through that morning warm, luxurious air in a buoyant mood, the atmosphere grew more and more electric. The women started to sing. Their choruses and invocative lyrics, woke up that day into a sudden brightness and Alero's spirit went into high gear. They had gone half way. The women had sung many songs and at last, appeared tired. Then, the reverend gentleman stood up to address the passengers:

"Good morning Ladies and Gentlemen! About another hour from now, we will be at Ibadan. I feel this is a good time to share with you few words of God."

"That crazy man, will you stop that!" bellowed a voice behind him, loud, and intimidating. The pastor suddenly stood rigid. All the passengers turned their attention towards the direction of the voice. The pastor also turned round, stared at the man barking angrily and queried: "Gentleman! What is the problem?"

The pastor queried a 'crazy' man and thus stepped on a cobra's tail. The man flew out of his seat, his eyes instantly turned red and glowed now like burning charcoals. He drew out a pistol from a black bag, put the same on quick firing. He was so frightening in his fury. Each passenger looked at him in dismay. A lunatic killed twelve passengers in a bus a week ago. That news was still fresh. The police were still looking for him. "Could this be the man?" Everyone stared at him, fear on his face.

The monster grabbed the pastor by the sleeve of his shirt. No one could move near them. Who dared raise a protest against a lunatic holding a gun. Everybody was shaking. Alero stared at the scene, open-mouthed. The monster shook the pastor violently, lifted him up with just one hand and then, threw him back into his seat. He was a Kilimanjaro of a man, huge and terrible. His eyes had a manic glimmer and he appeared to have swung into an orbit of pure insanity.

"Sit down and be quiet," he bellowed.

"I told you to stop talking. I never asked you to ask a question, did I?"

"No sir," replied the pastor, now frantic with anxiety. The eyes of the monster continued to send out fire.

All now stared at him, fearing what might be his next move. No one could predict a lunatic, and this terribly fearsome one because he carried a gun. But his face gradually softened as if all was over. But as he looked at the pastor's face again he screamed once more:

"I told you to stop because no one here is interested in your rigmarole. This place is not a church. No one wants to listen to your usual, old bickering. The world is already tired of it. My friend! Next time you do what you did, you will be in serious trouble. You are warned." Then turned he to the other passengers, surveyed their faces inquiringly, his lips twisted into a narrow, grim smile, as he spoke in a more friendly and gentle tone:

"Ladies and gentlemen! I did not allow the pastor to deliver his sermon to you because he started his speech with a lie. I hate a liar. I hate a liar with passion. I stopped him because I couldn't just allow him to feed you with his diet of falsehood and deceit. He greeted you: "Good morning," and that is a lie. There is nothing good about today's morning. To be honest with you, this is a bad morning. Very bad morning indeed!.

It is a bad morning because it is one morning you and trouble will meet face to face and look at each other's eyes. It is one morning, many of you will cry and wail. It is a morning of regret and sorrow. It is a morning you will all pray never to meet again." His eyes ran through the faces of the passengers once more, then bellowed:

"Boys! Take position!"

Four men, one from each angle of the bus sprang into action and brought out revolvers from their bags. All the passengers stared at them, shock on their faces.

"We are in trouble," stammered the woman next to Alero.

"Ruben! Action please!," screamed the monster.

Ruben, one of the four men, a bulky man with a wide chest, flew towards the driver, put the mouth of his gun on the driver's left cheek.

"Begin to slow down, we will soon turn to the left." Afar off, appeared an untarred road "That is where we are going," Ruben pointed to it. The driver, shaking with anxiety got there and turned the bus to the untarred road.

"You drive right down and stop where I ask you to stop." The driver drove down the dusty road for about two kilometers.

All the passengers looked around, fear on their faces. Alero first felt it was a dream. She made every conscious effort to wake up from that early morning, man-made terror. But she discovered strangely that there was no other world to wake into.

"Move on to the left and park," bellowed Ruben. The bus now stopped in the heart of a thick forest in a lonely, deserted road. Some of the passengers were now begging for mercy. Some just looked up, appealing to God for favour.

"If it is money you want, take money but don't kill

us," the passengers begged and begged out loud. Alero looked around, she could only mutter: "Jesus! Jesus!" The monster, the leader of the gang barked angrily again:

"Ladies and gentlemen! Can I have your attention please! Stop those yellings. If you talk and I catch you, you are a dead man. Now, listen to me! If you co-operate with us we won't harm any of you. If you behave precisely as I order, there will be no problem. I want to get over this operation in five minutes. You will come out of this bus one by one and through this very gate where I stand. No one must take his or her bag or any of his or her belongings out of the bus. Leave everything you carry on your seat. Secondly, you will take off all your clothes – everything you have on. I say everything: brassier, underwears, panties, I mean everything."

Three of the gun-men remained inside the bus. The monster and one other gun-man, each manned an entrance.

"Now, begin to come out," screamed the monster. The first woman who came out had put off all her dresses except her underpants. She was a massive woman. She had a queer shape – a protruded belly, a hill behind her which went for her buttocks, a heavy chest with two dangling gourds. The monster saw her and went wild. He fired several shots, one missing the woman narrowly. He intended to gun her down but the other gun-men appealed to him for restraint.

"I say put off every piece of dress. I know many of you use your private parts as your banks. I want to see you completely naked. I want your money. I don't need your ugly, smelling bodies. I give you two seconds."

The woman, shaking and panicking, put off her panties, then dashed into a nearby bush. Then came the next person, then the next person... then the reverend pastor. Alero was the last. She was shaking terribly. She stood up but fell on her seat several times. She was shaking violently that her legs refused to carry her. With a gun pointing threateningly at her skull, one of the members of the gang assisted her to stand on her feet, put off her dresses until only the knickers remained. The leader saw her and screamed once more. She hurriedly put off her knickers and rushed out of the bus into a nearby bush. The monster now took the key of the bus from the driver. He and the man at the other entrance now entered the bus and closed the doors.

Peeping through the window, the monster smiled for the first time.

"Ladies and gentlemen! The operation is over," he announced.

"We may possibly meet some other time again. Thank you for your cooperation. You are all wonderful people. We love you all," he said, as he waved to the passengers, then switched on the engine, and on that very spot, made a sudden U-turn with an incredible dexterity and terrific speed. He was a marvelous driver. The bus zoomed off, leaving the thirty passengers in the heart of a thick, dark, tropical forest.

CHAPTER TWO

Different shapes and sizes: mountainous men and thin, dry, emaciated ones like mosquitoes; the fine, beautiful women and the shapeless, ugly ones like hippopotamus, all in nude forms, stared at one another. Some young women covered their private parts with their hands, others ran into nearby bushes to hide. But all soon reconciled to the harsh reality and eventually put their shame aside.

Alero who hid inside some cassava plants gazed at the plants and their leaves, and they too gazed at her in dismay. She first took that morning drama to be a dream but she discovered now that it was no dream. When she could piece together her scattered wits, she found that she was still holding on to her knickers and brassiere and she hurriedly put them on.

On the dusty road, men and women stared at one another in lethargic horror. They were back in the original state of man in the biblical Garden of Eden. The eagles flying above, stared down at the men and women, screamed and laughed. The squirrels on nearby palm trees, ate their nuts, and giggled. The trees stared at them with empty eyes and smiled derisively. The nearby brook babbled and mocked.

The massive woman paced up and down in a queer grandeur. Her huge, dangling breasts and mammoth buttocks shook and trembled as if they had seen something fearsome. She wept, wailed and groaned at the same time.
"They took my 100,000 naira, my entire life-saving. Where do I begin? Where?" she queried.
"Stop crying and thank God for your life. What if they had killed you?" asked the pastor.

"Shu u u r up! Without money, what does life amount to? What is the worth of life if there is no money to feed and take care of the body? You say, I should thank God, what for? For losing my entire life-saving to armed robbers? Thank God for not protecting me when I needed His help? Pastor, I feel you need the service of a psychiatrist."

Just that moment, Alero emerged from a nearby bush where she had been hiding. In the bus, she was covered with the veil and no one recognized her. Now, the veil had gone and all the passengers suddenly stood rigid as they saw her. The knees of the women went down, and all men bowed as they chorused: "Your Highness!" Princess Alero smiled for the first time.

"Was Your Highness also in the vehicle that the armed robbers had just snatched?" asked the pastor.

"I was there. I put on a veil because I liked to travel incognito. Ladies and gentlemen, I am sorry for this unexpected, ugly event. But I must tell you that you don't need to keep on crying over spilt milk. What had happened had happened. Let us accept it as an act of God. Give me one person who will accompany me to the main road."

"Your Highness cannot go to the main road like this," one of the women objected.

"You don't need to worry about me. Let me go and arrange help for you. We cannot all stay here wailing and crying. That will not solve any problem. If we are here for a week, no one will know that we are here."

One man offered to accompany Princess Alero. They had now walked for about a kilometer when Alero stopped and looked at herself again.

"I, a princess, how can I appear like this by the roadside? What if I meet somebody who knows me? Why did I take such a crazy decision?"

She looked at her uncovered body, she felt like running back to the passengers but she remembered her promise and she resolved to go ahead.

As she got closer and closer to the main road, so also her anxiety grew. They had not got there, but they were so close now, and Alero was almost panicking. They got to the road at last. At this critical moment, courage failed her and Alero hurried to hide herself inside a small bush by the roadside.

"You stay by the roadside. Try to stop the on-coming

vehicles. I am sure one will stop for you," she told the man who accompanied her.

The man stood still. He stared at his nude body, shame covered him like a rag.

"Man! Try to put shame aside," he encouraged himself.
He prayed to God for favour. Finally, he summoned up courage and stepped forward. For about forty-five minutes, he tried all possible techniques to stop the on-coming vehicles, but none stopped for him. Each driver mistook him for a mad man. Each vehicle zoomed off at top speed as soon as the driver saw him. Who dared wait for an unclothed, mad man in the heart of a thick, gloomy forest? Gradually, he became frustrated. As he was about to leave the road-side, a beautiful Toyota car came on the scene, it was not speeding. The young man and the young lady inside appeared to be on a pleasure ride. They were young lovers on lovely morning adventure. They laughed, they argued, they giggled, they teased each other, they held each other and did several silly things. They were in their own world.

It was the young man that first saw him – a nude man waving ceaselessly, asking them to stop.
"Is this an apparition or a bush demon?" he queried.

When the car was not going to stop, the man jumped into the middle of the road and the driver froze with fear. For the first time, the lady also saw him and screamed: "Mad man! Mad man!"

The terrified driver quickly steered the vehicle to the left and zoomed off at top speed. For another ten minutes, the man made every conceivable effort to stop another vehicle, none stopped for him. As soon as each driver saw him, so took he the other way and zoomed off quickly. None was ready to stop and listen to a lunatic. What did he have to say?

"Your Highness! The people have refused to stop for me. Being a woman, perhaps, you may make a difference."

Alero stared at herself. She looked at her figure again and again, a celebrated princess, a woman of the people, the only female called by Toro people, the Epitome of Beauty, then came her fit again.
"Is it proper for me to stay by the roadside like this?" she asked herself.

But she needed to come out no matter what. She had offered to help and that help she must give. Reluctantly, she came out of the bush while the man took her position inside the small wood. She needed courage. She had to borrow one if she did not have one with her. Gradually that courage came. She waved to a vehicle, yet another, but none stopped for her. For fifteen minutes, no vehicle stopped.
At the time she was convinced that none would ever stop, a beautiful custom-made, new Mercedez Benz saloon car, appeared afar off and was drawing nearer. It was not on top speed and Alero waved frantically to it to stop "Please! Please!, I need help," she screamed. There were only two people in the car: the driver and a young man in his middle thirties, robust,

tall, well-built in a superbly tailored, three-piece suit. The man sat at the back seat. He was the first to see Alero. He stared at her intensely – a lady wearing only knickers. The figure he was looking at was more beautiful than any woman ever was. She was incredibly charming.

"Please slow down and stop! Who is she and what is she doing here?" he queried.
He knew that the lady was not a mad woman.
"No mad woman can be as glamorous as this," he mumbled.

"But why is she virtually naked? Why?" he wanted to find out. He stared at her again and again. Very straight, very slim, tall and very attractive. She was so enchanting and so fine, her dark hair abundant and her face perfectly shaped. She had a regal bearing and the delicacy of unmistakable nobility graced her sweet feature. Everything about her was elegant and electric. The car did not stop.

"Won't you help me?" she screamed again, her eyes moist with tears. She had the longest, and surely the darkest eyelashes the man had ever seen. Her complexion was exquisitely pure. Chief Ajai, the man at the back seat of the car, growled again:
"I say stop! Don't you have ears?" "No chief, I can't stop. The lady you are looking at is a bait"
"What do you mean?"

"This is the technique used by the robbers operating around here. There must be some armed men hidden in that bush behind her. We only have to stop and they will swoop on us."

The driver pressed the acceleration pedal and increased his speed, leaving the lady now wailing. Chief Ajayi looked back. He could not ignore the soft, wailing eyes of the lady he was looking at.

"Why must I abandon a woman in distress? My friend! That lady needs help – I say stop."

The driver now slowed down, then spoke to his boss:

"Chief, I have been in this business for long. This is my tenth year of driving. You are my third employer. I am a professional. I know this road. I know every inch of it and I know the characteristics of the miscreants who operate around here. What you are looking at, sir, is Danger."

"I don't believe you. The lady I am looking at has a genuine problem. She is not an ordinary person. She is too far from that. Everything about her, points to a noble bearing. She has a gorgeous, aristocratic carriage that is unmistakable."

"Chief! I can bet my life on it that she is planted there for a purpose. If not, what is her business in the heart of this forest? What is she doing where she stands? There is no broken down vehicle and so where does she come from? Drop from the sky? Why is she virtually nude, exposing all her beautiful statistics and the delicious curves of her buttocks? That she is very pretty, is a fact. But that is the kind used by robbers to attract the unwary."

"No, I don't believe you. I won't have peace if we simply zoom off without talking to her. Please, stop and turn round. I must go back and talk to her. I just must ask her some questions."

The driver stopped and stared at Chief Ajayi, dismay on his face.

"Chief! Why must we endanger our lives? Why should we engage in an adventure that will lead to regret? The men behind her will snatch this car and probably kill us in the process."

"My friend! Turn round the vehicle. If you are not willing to obey me, give me the key and get out of the car. I must find out that lady's problem."

The driver made a U-turn defiantly. He wore an angry look but that look changed into apprehension as the car approached the spot where Alero stood. Few metres to her, Ajai himself grew nervous for the first time.

"Assuming the driver is right," he murmured. The car now stopped at the other side of the road about twenty feet from Alero. Keep the engine running in case"…Chief Ajai whispered to the driver.

"Lady! Stay where you are, what is your problem?" he asked her. As Alero narrated her story, the Chief was watching keenly for any strange movement. There was none.

"Her story appears credible," he mumbled.

But just that moment, the bush behind Alero shook. Chief Ajai saw something that looked like a moving figure of a man. He froze. His eyes widened with fear. "Who is that?" he screamed.

He had an impulse to tell the driver to zoom off but something told him to exercise a little restraint.

"That is my partner," replied Alero.

"You have someone hidden in the bush."

"Yes, two of us came to the road to seek for help. The man in the bush is completely naked, that is why he hides himself there. We are 30 in number, the remaining 28 are about 2 kilometers from here. They are completely naked too."

"Let the man come out," ordered Chief Ajai, still looking at the bush with frightened eyes.

A tall man came out of the bush, nude. His hair was rough. He looked hundred percent a mad man.

"The robbers took away my clothes and bag," the man growled.

"I believe your story. But you still have to wait here while I call in the police."

While Chief Ajai was already convinced, the driver was not. He knew the whole story could still be a ruse and was not ready to take any chances. He did not make U-turn there, he drove for a considerable distance before he turned round the vehicle. Forty minutes later, a lorry load of policemen arrived at the scene together with the Chairman of the Local Government of the area.

Alero and her partner took them to the rest of the passengers, their story confirmed, the police swung into action while the Chairman of the Local Government hurried back to his office to arrange for dresses.

About an hour later, the Chairman returned and all the passengers put on new dresses and smiles lit their faces again, Alero wore the native "Up and down". It didn't have a perfect fit, even in it, she was a stunner. "True beauty is rarer than diamonds," the smashing beauty of Alero came up again in the new dress. Her figure radiated the usual glamour and indescribable charm.

Chief Ajai had been so much fascinated by her. He had waited all the while because Alero told him that she was going to Ibadan and that was where he too was going.

"Sweet lady! Now that everything is set, will you come with me?"

"It will be a pleasure, sir," said Alero whose smile was sweet and inviting.

As Alero came into the car, Chief Ajai started to survey her figure again. She was sweet and good-looking.

"Jesus! She is pretty," he mumbled.

"Which part of the city are you going?"

"I am going to the Convent of Holy Maria."

"You like to see someone there?" Chief Ajai asked, knowing for sure that this one with extremely pretty shape was not likely to be a nun.

"I am scheduled to see somebody there this morning."

Chief Ajai stared at her again. She had the longest hair he had ever seen, her complexion was just like that of a new baby.

"Alero! You will surely need some dresses when you get to Ibadan and perhaps some money too. Can you manage this?"

Alero counted the money, it was 10,000 dollars.
"What do I use this for? Is this not rather too much?"
Her gaze on Ajai was direct and unwavering.
"I am sure you will need it."
"No, I won't."
"Okay, keep it, when I come back, I will have what is left."

Chief Ajai did not pester Alero with questions, knowing the trouble she had gone through. They got to the Covent of Holy Maria, an hour later. The ground and the gardens were lovely. The landscape was filled with exotic plants and flowers. The buildings were all painted white and the paint shone brilliantly.

"When do you intend to leave here?" asked Chief Ajai
"I am not leaving here immediately."
"If I call in about a week, will you still be here?"
"Yes, I will surely be here."
"I'll see you then," said he, as he gave her his business card.

"Chief Ajai, I don't know how to thank you. You have been most wonderful."
"You don't need to thank me. I only count myself lucky to have been of service to a delightful lady like you."

Alero was not aware of it but her eyes were torturing Chief Ajai with their tenderness. The magic in those eyeballs would forever dazzle Chief Ajai as long as he lived.

CHAPTER THREE

Prince Matete and Dora, his wife, had searched for Alero in all the convents they knew, they couldn't find her. It was late in the night they got the information that Alero was in the Covent of Holy Maria at Ibadan.

They left Toro early in the morning the following day. By 9.a.m., they were at the gate of Holy Maria. It was 29th December, and there at the gate, they heard the angelic voices of the nuns. They sang with brio and might. Their lusty voices came out in perfect, rousing harmony. The song was gripping. Dora immediately identified the special tenor of Alero. She could not mistake it in a million voices.

"She is here. She is surely here," said she as she broke down in tears.

The words of the song were in Latin.

Adeste fideles
Natum triumphantes
Venite, venite in Bethlehem
Natum Videte

Regem Angelorum
Venite adoremus
Venite adoremus
Venite adoremus
Christo Domino

Translation

O come all ye faithful
Joyful and triumphant
O come ye, o come ye to Bethlehem
Lo! In a manger
Lies the king of angels
O come let us adore him
O come, let us adore him
O come, let us adore him
Christ, the Lord.

The melody was irresistible. The rendition was perfect. Waves and waves of melody drifted Prince Matete up and down and for some minutes, he was lost.

Prince Matete was a lover of music. He and Dora were asked to sit in the common room while a nun went for Alero. It was 10.a.m. when Alero was called in for them. She looked charming in her lovely, blue gown with white colour. She looked defiant and unfriendly as she approached her parents.

Dora could no longer control her emotion, she burst out:

"Alero! How could you do this to me? Why? You turned down all the advances of all prospective young men, you deprive me the privilege of having a grandchild. Why are you doing this? What is my offence?"

Alero only stared at her face; she did not say a word.

"Alero, won't you talk to me?"

Alero could not tear her gaze away from Dora's face but she remained dumb and stood there like a doorpost.

"Jesus! What has turned you to this? What?" screamed her mother.

Her father who had kept quite all this while suddenly roared:

"Go in and pack your load. You are leaving here and right now. You are leaving with us in that car." (pointing to the car).

"I give you just five minutes."

"Dad! I am above 21. You cannot take a decision for me. By my training, I am a lawyer. I know what the law says. The law does not permit you to order me around. I am a mature woman and I can decide on my own what to do. I have my life to live. I am afraid, I am not going to live it according to your Highness' dictate. You are bound by the law to abide by my choice and that choice has been made already. I am very sorry, I can't leave here because this is where I belong."

As soon as Dora heard these words, she screamed until she began to gasp, holding to her chest as if she was having chest pain.

Sister Lucia, the Head of the Covent, hurried to the scene. The anguish on Dora's face touched her deeply.

"I am afraid, you have to go with them," she told Alero.

"They are your parents. You need to have a kind of agreement with them; failing which you could kill this woman."

"Sister, I am not leaving here. Whatever happens, I won't leave.

The woman is my mother. I know her so well. This is just a drama. Leave me with them. I will sort out the matter."

"You feel you are able?"

"I am quite able."

Alero and her father had a long heated argument. When her parents finally departed at 12 noon, Alero refused to go with them.

CHAPTER FOUR

He had a fine, sturdy and powerful frame. Standing at 6 feet 2 inches, thirty seven year old Chief Ajai was honoured with a chieftaincy title only two months ago. He had two master degrees from an American University. He worked briefly for the Nigeria National Petroleum Corporation. He resigned his appointment there to start his own oil business. He first started with a chain of petrol stations across Nigeria. At 35, he bought his first oil field and went to Europe and America to shop for technical partners. His company after very many months of drilling, struck oil and since then, dollars had been rolling in millions from the black gold.

The day he saw Alero by the roadside, he was going to Lagos. He was scheduled to fly out that evening. He was on his way to Venezuela to perfect another deal on the purchase of another oil block in that country. He had investments in all major industrial nations of the world, estates and landed properties in many countries of the Middle East. He had been involved with many women yet he had refused to marry for a reason he only could explain. He was the world's most eligible bachelor.

"I have not met Miss Right," he always told his friends.

As his car was leaving the Convent of Holy Maria that morning, he knew he had met Miss Right at last. As the car zoomed off gently out of the convent, he looked back at Alero - standing straight, so slim, so deliciously beautiful, her long hair fluttering in the air, he felt deep inside him a rising passion. As long as he lived, he knew he could not ignore the magnets in Alero's eyeballs.

"Goodness! She has a pretty shape. She has a pretty smile. It is contagious too!" he sighed.

As his plane flew over the long stretch of the Atlantic Ocean between Lagos and Caracas, it was the picture of Alero that persistently came to his imagination. Few hours to the landing, he had a nap.

A nice, elegant Venezuelan lady checked his bag.

"Any other luggage?" she asked, a pretty smile on her face.

"No," he replied.

"You're welcome to Venezuela."

"Thank you," he replied.

In his lovely, executive suite in Hilton Hotel in Caracas, the haunting beauty of Alero did not leave him alone. Every minute, he could see her again. He recalled that he had never felt like this before. He had never had such a greedy lust for any woman. No woman had ever affected him the way Alero had.

"Jesus! She has the brightness of a rainbow and the cool fragrance of lily at dawn. She has hair, the colour of midnight," he sighed.
He could see the hair full of soft curls, the same now floating around her beautiful shoulders. She was extremely beautiful.

It was a week later that Chief Ajai returned to Lagos.
"You are taking me to the Convent of Holy Maria, can you still remember the route to the place?"
"Yes, I remember," replied the driver.

They got to the Convent two hours later. Alero's father had phoned her that morning that he would be coming to see her again. When Sister Lucia told Alero that she had a visitor waiting for her in the common room, she knew daddy had come with his usual troubles. She was ready to face him.
"I am not leaving here, no matter what," she mumbled, her face stern and uncompromising.

She entered the common room looking like a woman who had lost her patience. She wore a pugnacious look. She was bent on matching her mood with that of her father. But surprisingly, the person waiting for her was a different man. It was Chief Ajai. Alero saw him and heaved a sigh of relief. She smiled at him and Chief Ajai's spirit felt electrified. He hurried forward to embrace her. But just that moment, he observed that Alero was wearing the convent uniform and stopped, startled.

"Are you also a member of this convent?" he asked her, anxiety on his face.

"Yes, of course."

"You never told me. You only told me that you came here for a visit."

"That is true. I was not in a position to explain everything to you then, the mood and the situation did not permit."

Chief Ajai now stared at her, his confusion was palpable. The girl before him was pretty, perhaps the prettiest he had ever seen in his life, even in the uniform, Alero looked aristocratic, elegant and dignifying. She was not like any of the nuns, Chief Ajai had seen that morning. She was so different. She belonged to a different class and a different world. Chief Ajai looked at her again and again. She was intoxicating. She had a terrific shape and lovely eyes. As the penetrating, grey eyes of Alero was gazing at him, Chief Ajai blinked rapidly.

"How long have you been here," he asked.

"I was admitted into this place the very day you brought me here," she replied. She gave him her prettiest smile.

"Kindly give me a minute, I am going to bring that money," said Alero.

"Which money?"

"Your money."

But Chief Ajai pulled her back. He would not let her go "My dear girl, I am going to have no money. Please, listen to me. I come here for a very serious issue."

"And what about?"

Alero now stared at his face with frightened eyes.

"Alero, I am not sure whether you'll believe me. The moment I set my eyes on you, I so much loved you. I so much admired you. I came here this morning to let you know my feelings about you."

He paused and stared at Alero's eyes.

"I am here to request for your friendship."

He stopped and looked into her eyes again. Her look was more beautiful than the radiance of the enchanting Northern Italian plains at sunset.

"Though you have already joined the convent yet I will be unfair to myself if I don't tell you that I need you. I need you more than I can express by the power of words. You are the woman I have been looking for, for the past ten years.

What I'd experienced in the past one week after I left you showed me that I can't do without you. Alero, I want you to be my wife."

Alero looked at him with wide eyes as a narrow, funny smile played on her lips. Romantic words always sounded like music of annoyance in her ears. She didn't want to hear them. They made her sick and angry. It was true she had a pretty shape but her heart was colder than an iceberg. Words of love could not fire it back into action, the heat had gone. Alero stared at him: it took a moment for her to find her voice.

"Chief Ajai, I am very sorry. I am irrevocably committed to the convent. It's no use wasting your affection on me. Let me plead with you to reserve your love for a more

deserving lady."
Chief Ajai stared fixedly at her face.

"I am afraid, I am not going to do what you advise. Please, listen to me. You may not know it, but let me tell you one simple truth. God never did anything without a reason. Your glamorous shape and flawless complexion are not given to you for mere decoration. Your lush, glossy, super-smooth skin is created so because God wants it to be touched, felt and massaged by a male hand. God wants this your very fine body to be appreciated and loved. What nature has given you, it expects you to give out. It is given to you because somebody else needs it. God does not create you to be here, and you have no business here. Your beauty is not meant to be locked up in this cold, dreary prison, unseen, unadmired and uncherished. That is not the design of God for you. Please! Give the proposal before you a consideration. I know it is difficult more so when you have opted to be a nun. I am ready to wait for months, even years or as long as you want."

"Chief! You don't need to wait for an extra second.
I know how you feel but I am sorry, I can't be of help. As I said earlier on, I am irrevocably committed to the convent. That decision I had vowed never to change either now or in the future. It is a closed issue."

Chief Ajai stared at her face, then shook his head.
"Alero! I don't know why you opted to stay here, but even at the risk of sounding immodest, I must confess to you that God has so much blessed me. I can

provide that idyllic life any woman can conceive in her widest imagination. God has assisted me to amass a huge fortune at so young an age, and mind you huge fortune has no meaning, if there is no one to make use of it. I need a woman that I can cherish and pamper. I am looking for a woman that I can spoil. I have waited up to this time because I want someone I really love and I am so sure you are that woman."

Chief Ajai now stared at Alero's face pleadingly, his face promising the ecstasies of endless adventures, a world of holidays, parties, beautiful clothes, jewellery, cars, servants, super abundance and glamour, in short a new dawn, a new life and a new colour of sweetness. There was scarcely a woman under the sun who could resist what Chief Ajai was offering.

But Chief Ajai was speaking to a wrong woman. Although Alero looked breathtakingly beautiful and the Chief so much admired the gentle sway of her hips, her sexy figure and attractive back-view, yet she had no heart. Alero stared at the face of Chief Ajai, smiled and said:

"Chief, I have listened carefully to your speech but our worlds are so different. You may not know it, but I know it," she paused.

"I have been all through my life used to great abundance, riches and splendour. I have seen money and I have seen huge wealth but I am tired of them. They may have meaning to any other woman, certainly not to me. Money and huge wealth only make me sick."

This was what she wanted to say but stopped at the last moment. She did not want to appear arrogant. But just that moment, Prince Matete, Alero's father entered into that common room.

"Chief Ajai! Just a minute! This is my father," said Alero who now hurried to meet a tall man in his fifties. Chief Ajai stared at her as she hastened forward.
"My God! How can a lady be so adorable and yet so cold?" he queried.

"Good morning Alero."
"Good morning, daddy."
"Your mother was admitted into Saint Stephen's Specialist Hospital two days ago. The doctor said she is suffering from cardiac problem. Her condition is not improving rather it is getting worse. She is very anxious to see you. Alero! Let me warn you, if that woman dies, I won't forgive you."

Alero was about to speak but her father did not give her that opportunity as he turned to Chief Ajai.
"I saw you talking to Alero as I was coming in."
"That is true, sir."

"Good! I don't know whether Alero is your friend. But whatever she is to you, help me appeal to her to leave this place, and come back home. Her mother is seriously sick and she is the only person who has the medicine for her cure. The poor woman had done so much for her. As a grateful child, it is only normal she does for that woman the only thing she is requesting from her. She wants her to give her a grandchild. I am sure this is not the place where she can meet that demand. Very many good suitors are pestering her for marriage but she is not prepared to marry any man. I don't know the kind of sickness that makes a woman behave like this. Strange! Just too strange!"

Turning now to Alero, Prince Matete warned in a violent language of a man that was helpless.
"You this cruel, heartless and unfeeling hag, if you kill my wife, God will request her blood from you."

Then turned he round and started to walk away. Prince Matete eyes were moist with tears.

CHAPTER FIVE

For about a minute, Chief Ajai and Alero stood there staring at each other. Chief Ajai did not know what further thing to say. But he spoke at last:

"Alero! I had never met your father, not until today. I had only read about him. You have a wonderful father. Prince Matete is one of the few men of character in our nation. You should be proud that you have such a great father. Alero, an adage says: 'the voice of the people is the voice of God.' When many people say the same thing or reason the same way – you are probably listening to the voice of God. I won't say more than that. Your parents say you need a man and without prejudice, I share their view hundred percent. I know your mind is already made up but for God's sake, open that mind if only for few hours and consider the proposal before you. Your daddy was crying when he was leaving. It's not a good thing to make an old man cry. It is not nice to wound his heart. Alero! For an old man to be crying, it is a serious matter. You must lighten the burden in the heart of that old man. It is a must. Now Alero, can I ask you a question?"

"Yes, what is it?" Her eyes wore a bottomless sorrow.

"When are you going to see your mom?"
"I will find time to see her within the next one week."

Chief Ajayi stared curiously at her face.
"Daddy only came here to act a drama and he acted it so well. But I could see through him."
"So you don't feel the situation is as bad."
"Definitely not."
"But try to see your mom soonest; you never can say."
"I will."
"Alero, I must be going now. I will try to see you again, may be after a week. Bye for now."

Alero did not leave for home immediately. But three days later, an SOS arrived.

"Mom's life is in danger. Come immediately."

She left the convent the following morning. But that decision came too late. Mom slumped into a coma twelve hours before her arrival. And she would remain in that condition for a long time.

Alero arrived in Toro and hurried to the hospital. Dora was in a special ward. As Alero walked down the corridor, she observed that everywhere was unusually quiet.
A pretty, slim, smiling nurse rose to attention as Alero entered the room where Dora was. "We've been expecting Your Highness since yesterday."
"I was tied down by few things which needed to be tidied up."
Immediately she saw Dora, she stood there, rigid.

Dora was unconscious. She lay on her bed completely oblivious of all things going on in that room. Alero stared at the body of Dora again and again.

"When did it come to this?"

"It happened just yesterday," the nurse replied.

Alero stared at Dora again, she could not move her legs, her hands or any part of her body. Hardly could Alero imagine that things could turn out this way. Her decision not to marry any man was in her view, a very trivial issue.

"Why should mom take such a trifle to heart? What is in it? Am I the first woman to be a nun? Those who are nuns, don't they have mothers?"

A catena of such questions came up in her mind as she stared at Dora. She recalled her last visit to the convent and the way she cried while holding on to her chest. She stared at her again, the anguish on her face so much touched her now.

"Why didn't I see the seriousness of this matter when she talked to me? Why did I fail to observe that I was killing her little by little? She so much loves me, why should I do this to her?" she asked herself, her cheeks now wet with silent tears.

For hours she sat by Dora's bed. Even when she went out for fresh air, she soon came back again. A times, she would cry during the dark hours of the night, alone looking at her. So many nights she remained awake crying unto God to change the situation. Surprisingly, Dora's condition never changed.

The doctor looked at Dora one morning then stared

warmly at the face of Alero and said:

"There is hope," he said.

"Are you sure?" asked a confused Alero.

"That she will come back to consciousness is very high."

With those words of assurance, Alero kept on hoping.

"If she comes round what do we do to ensure that she doesn't relapse into another coma again?"

"Your Highness! The answer is partly in your hand."

"How?", she queried.

"Before she went into a coma, all she kept on muttering was: 'All my friends have grandchildren, but Alero denies me the joy of having one. She hurts me so badly. Why is she so cruel to me? Why?'

Those were her questions and she repeated it over and over again. It was a painful sore in her heart. I tried all I could to appeal to her but I couldn't just remove her pain. If she comes round and learns that you are married, her depression may disappear. She may even start to be on the road to permanent recovery. If what takes her to this condition is no longer there, she may recover."

"There are over 150 nuns in Holy Maria. None of them dropped from the sky. They all have mothers. But none of the mothers behaves like Dora; my mother. This is a peculiar behaviour, I can't understand why".

"Your Highness! Don't forget you are the first born and you are also a woman and a princess. Your mom must have been dreaming of the day she will hold and carry your baby. If her friends are already playing with their grandchildren, then you don't need to be surprised at this kind of behaviour. Remember, traditional African women love children a lot. You can't blame her for what happened."

Now, Alero seemed prepared to do all what she could to ensure that Dora recovered. That day, she began to have a second look at Chief Ajai's proposal.
"Mom must not die. I must do something quick to save her life. She must live and I must find a way of removing her pain. I owe her that obligation as a daughter."

CHAPTER SIX

I t was two months later. A lot of things had happened during the short period. Alero had pulled out of the convent. God works in a mysterious way. The mother of all surprises had happened. It was so mysterious to Chief Matete himself. Chief Ajai and Alero had become husband and wife. For many years, Alero snubbed all prospective young men. Her reaction to romance was cold. Talk of love in her ears, she would immediately become wild. Now, the warmth was back. Just watching Alero and Chief Ajai for ten minutes, one would recommend them as the best couple in town. Lovely and ebullient, Alero had strangely regained all her feminine features.

Only one thing still spoilt the joy of the moment, Dora's health continued to be a source of worry. Her health continued to zig-zag. One time, she would be so close to consciousness, the following day, her conscious level would drop sharply again.
"There is hope," the doctor never failed to assure Alero.

One Friday, Chief Ajai and Alero stood by Dora's bed, both looking morose. Alero was frantic with anxiety because Dora was gasping.

"We have done all things possible," said the doctor "but her condition seems to be deteriorating fast in the last forty eight hours."

At 11a.m. that day, Dora's chest started to shake in an erratic manner. The breathing was gas-assisted but the chest kept on shaking all the same. By 12 noon, the shaking started to grow weaker and at 12.39 p.m., Dora's heart suddenly stopped.

"Doctor! Doctor!" Alero shouted. The doctor hurried to the scene, examined his six-month patient and said in a quiet, sober voice:

"I am sorry, we've lost her."

"I kill her, I kill her at last!" screamed Alero. She wept sore. Her husband and the doctor held her between them. Chief Ajai told her:

"You are not the one who killed her. That is how she is destined to die. No matter how we try, we cannot add a second to her life."

All Nigerian newspapers carried the notice of Dora's obituary. Various television stations inundated the air with the funeral announcements. It was a celebration of an icon.

Then came the day of the burial. From all parts of Nigeria, all roads led to Toro. This small, ancient town in the South-Western Nigeria became an El-Dorado, beckoning to everyone.

"I have never seen such an armada of cars," said a sixty year old man. That day, the quiet, serene air of Toro abruptly changed its vibe as thousands of horns woke up this tranquil, sleepy town from its mid-day slumber into an instantaneous buoyancy. The deafening sirens of many State Governors aroused the entire community and ignited an instant fire of poetic wails. Honourable Ministers, Senators, Captains of Industries and Commerce, I mean the teaks, the mahoganies, the Irokos, the Obeches - mighty men of Nigerian politics and eminent men in oil business from Africa, Europe and Americas had arrived in Toro.

The road leading to the church was strongly secured. There were policemen to hold back the crowd that had gathered to watch the dignitaries arrive.

Dora Matete's body was carried in a beautiful casket made of costly mahogany wood decked with gold. The church service was brief. The bishop preached the sermon...

"Jesus said unto her, I am the resurrection and the life: he that believeth in me, though he were dead, yet shall he live, and whosoever liveth and believeth in me shall never die."

The bishop stared at the faces of the members of the congregation. Prince Matete looked up for the first time. He wore a black agbada with dark glasses. Princess Alero looked down, she was too sober and too sad. Her father had promised never to forgive her for the death of his wife but what he saw in the last few weeks before his wife's death, made him change his mind. Alero was so remorseful. He could appreciate now that she acted out of ignorance.

"The life of our sister - Dora Matete was short, but it was great," said the bishop.

The graveside ceremony at Wasimi cemetery was also brief.
"Unto God's gracious mercy and protection, we commit you. The Lord bless you and keep you. The Lord make His face to shine upon you and be gracious unto you. The Lord lift up the light of his countenance upon you and give you peace now and forever – Amen."

As Alero watched her mother's body being lowered into its final resting place, she broke down and cried bitterly.
Chief Ajai held her.
"You've cried enough. It's time to take heart."

As Alero and Chief Ajai left the cemetery, Alero brightened up. Nigerians are peculiar people. They never take their grief home. They leave it at the graveside. And perhaps this is one of the reasons people call them the happiest people on earth.

The entertainment of guests took place at Toro Square, at the center of the town. The service was handled by a 5-Star Hotel from Lagos. It was beautiful. It was a different Alero that appeared at the venue. Hilarious and cheerful, she had changed from a sad, gloomy woman into a happy, ebullient person. As the guests were being entertained, the dancers took the floor. A popular band from Lagos was on the bandstand. It was Afro-music. The music had a gripping melody. The beats were infatuating. There were about twenty people on the dance floor. In the midst of the dancers was Alero. She wore a colourful "iro" and "buba" made of expensive lace materials. All eyes were on her. All eyes just stayed glued to her. None could look elsewhere. Alero was such a terrific dancer and a delight to watch. Alexander the Great, was a highly talented warrior, Pele had a gift for football. Cicero had a gift for eloquence, Picasso had a gift for painting. Alero had a wonderful gift for dancing. Nature crafted her legs, moulded her hips and built her soft, delicate frame for that art. Rocking her body with royal ease, swinging her hips with princely elegance, her motions were graced with regal dignity. Her steps and the music had amazing rhythms. The gyration of her sweet, beautiful body matched with the beats. The beats and Alero were in love. Watching her dance, was like taking a sweet, irresistible wine. Alero was too sweet and too intoxicating.

The tempo of the music grew higher and higher until its melody was almost approaching the unbearable limit. The band leader went wild. He abandoned his microphone, picked up his gangan-talking-drum, and with that drum, began to extol and praise this most terrific Princess of Toro. The gangan-talking-drum spoke out. It spoke out loud:

"Alero! The beautiful Princess of Toro.
The morning sun with the golden rays.
The lovely Rose with the sweetest fragrance.
The great wonder from the Creator's mould.

The pearl of beauty on whom the Great Creator had to spend some extra hours in order to make an excellence of perfection.
A lady who is as innocent as the dove and yet electrifying as the thunder.
The elegant Princess that kings and princes are panting to have.
Alero! The Emerald of Toro, the Epitome of Beauty.
It is you I call, please answer me!"

The drummer hit hard his talking-drum. Really fierce and violent strokes. The drum screamed, and screamed – pouring out more and more poetic eulogies. Alero caught fire. She shook and rocked her elegant, princely body alluringly.

To say Alero was beautiful was to accept that one was in short of the appropriate adjectives. She was too hot, just too hot for comfort. Her face was radiant like the Hawaiian sunset. Her smiles were not only sweet, they were warm and contagious. Her figure was sparkling and lovely like the first rays of the sun on the Nigerian Mambila Plains.

Standing before her and wearing a flowing *agbada*, was Chief Ajai, her darling husband. A huge, tall, robust, nice-looking man, Chief Ajai was one of the latest nou-veau riche who had suddenly shot into limelight in the African Oil Business.
To appreciate one's wife while dancing in the public, the Nigerian culture expects the husband to give her money that is appreciable, and he must do so by putting the currency notes one by one on the woman's

forehead. Chief Ajai opened his beautiful leather portfolio and brought out one hundred thousand naira and started to put the notes, one after another on Alero's beautiful forehead. For many minutes, his hand went up and down until a hill of naira notes was erected around Alero's body.

The tempo of the music quickened. The band leader was bent on getting Chief Ajai drunk with his beats. He hit furiously on the gangan-talking-drum and the drum screamed out calling Chief Ajai hundreds of appellations and exhuming his numerous achievements and various historic exploits of his noble ancestors. For very many minutes, it went on recounting his many titles to fame and reverence:

"Ajai!
The great giant before whom great and famous men fade into pygmies.
The noble husband of Princess Alero.
The huge mahogany that towers above all and sundry
The great skyscraper among men
The huge elephant that shakes the African Business Circle like a mighty storm
The oil guru whose presence generates tremors and earthquakes in the Third World Chamber of Commerce and Industry.
A dazzling oil magnate, a business wizard, a genius among geniuses."

The gangan-talking-drum continued to pour on Ajai torrents of encomiums and a frightening deluge of appellations. For several minutes, it went on decorating him with a long, unending chains of titles and honours. Chief Ajai soon got intoxicated with this sweet wine of praises. He moved to the band leader and started to "spray" him with 1000 naira notes. When he exhausted the one hundred thousand naira in his hand, he went for another one hundred thousand. Like a drunkard who had lost his reasoning power, Chief Ajai went on spending. All the drums sounded high. The gangan-talking-drum became crazy. It talked and talked and talked – praising, extolling and applauding this wealthy, super-rich, prodigal son. But the talking- drum did not stop talking. The dance went on, growing hotter and hotter with each passing minute.

CHAPTER SEVEN

I, Mayo Williams, stood there watching this show of vanity. I stood in the midst of the spectators looking at Alero and Chief Ajai - eyes wide and angry. I stood there, motionless and unbelieving. I had made up my mind to watch this drama secretly without drawing attention to myself. But that was gradually becoming impossible for me now, as strong, uncontrollable tremors were cruising through my body. It was a bright, warm evening but I stood there shivering while my heart was pounding at a frantic tempo. I was wailing and crying inwardly but as a man, a famous person in academia and a celebrated scholar, I knew it was improper for me to cry in the public.

"Is the picture before me real or is it just another fantasy created by the strange devices of human imagination?" I asked myself.

I looked at the man, and then the woman, again and again, my eyes glittered with rage. My eyeballs rolled violently in their sockets like the eyes of a raving lunatic. The dance of Alero and Chief Ajai set my body on fire and the burning heat was becoming more and more unbearable with the passage of each minute. But as the bodies of Chief Ajai and that of Alero moved apart and came together to the rhythm of the music, and in a growing frenzy of passion, my agony went into a climax and I almost screamed out like someone in anguish.

"How long can I bear this? How long can I endure what I am looking at? Jesus! How long can I stand this galling sight? Why has the world chosen to persecute me like this? Why? Why?"

It seemed I heard a voice:

"My friend! You are not the only one being persecuted. Many belong to your class." Then I remembered the story Wale, my friend, told me only yesterday.

Wale and his wife had retired to bed that night after listening to the news from the Nigerian Television Authority Network Service at 9p.m. It had been a strenuous day for both. The wife, Angela, 35, a slim, tall, pretty woman, a Finance Graduate from University of Lagos worked for a Commercial Bank in Marina, Lagos. Wale who had MBA from Pace University, New York City worked for NICON, a most reputable Insurance Company in the city. Theirs was a warm, luxurious four-bedroom bungalow in Surulere District of Lagos Metropolis.

At 1.30a.m., the gate bell rang. Its incessant and irritating sound woke the couple from sleep.

"My God! Who can that be at this time of the night?" Wale grumbled as he lifted up his head from the pillow and rubbed off sleep from his dizzy eyes.

"Perhaps one of the neighbours needs help or something," the wife whispered.

"That is most likely," said Wale as he flew out of bed and hurried into the living room. He put on the light, drew the curtain on the window to one side.

"Who is it?" he queried. There was no reply. He peeped through the window, and that moment, he saw some strange figures. He rubbed his eyes once more to make sure he was not seeing double pictures. He could see very clearly now. Five men stood at the gate.

"Who are these?" he queried silently.

"Gentlemen, can I help you?" he said, raising up his voice.

"Come and open your gate. I give you one minute to do so. Comply quickly and live. Delay, then, you are as good as dead. If you delay and we have to assist you to open the gate...Man! It won't pay you."

The man shook his head to drive home his point. His two eyes were red. Fire and thunder were coming out of his face. It was a face that had never known kindness or mercy for ages.

"If you delay, I warn you, the consequences will be grave. If you love yourself, comply quickly. If you have a gun, you are warned in your own interest not to shoot. If you do, we will bring this house down with a grenade," he paused.

"Look at it! Don't you see it?" asked the man as he dangled the grenade so that Wale could see it clearly.

"Please, don't mess around. Don't play any funny game with us; if you do, we will wipe out your entire family; wife, children, relatives, if you have any."

Wale stared at the men dazed; totally dazed. He was so terrified that his fingers began to vibrate.

"Wale! Who is it? What is happening?" asked Angela from the direction of the room.

"Darling! Trouble has come," he replied.

"What kind of trouble?" queried Angela as she hurried out of bed into the sitting room. The couple conferred within seconds. They knew that the five men behind their gate were armed robbers. Four had rifles; the one who seemed like the leader carried a sub-machine gun. To refuse to open the gate could be an open invitation to war; to open is trouble indeed! But if they did not open, the hoodlums would open the gate on their own, and then the main door, and hell would be let loose thereafter.

"Darling! I will go and open for them, and negotiate."

"Wale! Don't open! You want to negotiate with armed robbers? People who are already drunk with cocaine or marijuana? What kind of negotiation will you do with mad people?"

"If we don't open, they will open the gate and the door on their own and thereafter kill us. I will go and open."

"What! Don't open yet," pleaded Angela as she tiptoed

silently to the telephone box and dialed nervously the police number.

"Hello, Hello! Is that police department?"

"Yes! This is Nigerian Police. Can I help you?"

"Armed robbers are in my apartment. I speak from No. 3 Martins Street…Hello, Hello," the line went dead. Angela shook the phone box violently; it was now as dead as dodo.

"Oh my God," she cried.

"Man! You are playing with fire. You have exhausted the one minute we gave you. This is your last warning," screamed an impatient, angry voice behind the gate. And Wale remembered that moment the couple who did not open their door for armed robbers on time and were shot just a week ago. He read it in one of the dailies.

"Man will not die two times;" he told himself. He went to the main door, opened it, walked nervously towards the gate and opened it. The leader of the five-man gang gave him a hard slap on the face. Wale fell down only to rise up quickly.

"Have that for your delay! Stupid man! You have no business delaying our operation. Get inside;" he roared.

They marched Wale in at gunpoint. He and Angela were ordered to lie face down with guns pointing to their skulls while the remaining three robbers ransacked the rooms, their wardrobes for money and jewellery. About thirty minutes later, the three robbers came out of the rooms.

"Colonel! We found only two thousand naira in their wardrobe!"

"Two thousand naira! An amount not enough to fuel back our vehicle!"

"You buffoons!" he removed his left foot from Wale's neck for the first time.

"Where do you keep your money?"

"Sir, we don't keep money at home."

"Where do you keep it?" he screamed.

"In the bank."

"How can you live in this kind of sumptuous apartment, and yet have no money with you? How? Who asked you to live here?"

"My place of work arranged this place for me and paid for it."

"You are a bastard!" the gang leader landed another hard slap on Wale's face.

"Your place of work puts a foolish man like you here? And that place of work is not charitable enough to put adequate money in your pocket, just in case you have some emergency visitors as you are having now? Well, that place of work will find money for your undertakers."

"Captain! Shoot him and put his body in that corner. I am tired of this rigmarole!"

"Please! Please! Don't kill my husband. I am just 35, don't make me a widow so soon. Please, take anything you like from the house;" screamed Angela.

The Colonel turned to Angela.

"Woman! You have jewellery?"

"No, I don't have, but you can have my dresses and shoes if you like."

"We neither need your dresses nor your shoes. We only need jewellery and since you don't have, I'll better take what you have. Captain! Tie up the husband."

One of the three men brought out a strong rope; tied the legs of Wale together; then tied the hands together and further tied Wale's body to a three seater-chair, and there, before his eyes, the Colonel started to rape his wife! After he had finished, and the robbers were about to leave the apartment, the Colonel walked briskly to Wale.
"Look at you! I thought that I was in the home of a civilized and well-cultured gentleman. I was expecting you to say: 'Thank you for a job well done' or didn't you watch my performance?"

Wale only stared at him.
"You must be a most unappreciative animal; a brute," he said as he gave Wale another slap.

That moment, the sound of the police siren came on the air. It was drawing nearer and nearer. The robbers rushed out of the house, jumped over the fence and escaped.

As I looked at Alero dancing before Chief Ajai, I appreciated now what Wale went through. Experience, they say, is the best teacher. As I looked at the man and the woman, my heart missed some beats and my legs shook like the vibrating cheeks of a man suffering from severe cold. As Alero swung her beautiful hips enticingly before the Chief and her delicate, slim body gyrated to the music in a manner that would make the strongest of the male species grow dizzy with passion, a huge avalanche of anger started to build up inside me until it was impossible for me to contain the surging, violent hurricane.

There was a touch on my shoulder.

"Gentleman, are you all right?" asked the man who touched me.

"Yes, I am quite fine."

"But you seem restless and highly agitated. Are you sure you don't need help?"

"No, I don't. I am only disturbed by what is going on here."

"Disturbed?"

"Yes."

"By this show?"

"Yes."

"That is strange." The man looked at the band and the people dancing and exclaimed:

"Good music! Fantastic dance! The show is so good. It enlivens my heart. Are you saying this highly delightful performance makes you sick? What kind of person are you? How can anyone be disturbed by this kind of lovely, merry show? How?"

"I cannot but be disturbed. The pretty woman you are looking at, dancing before the Chief, is my wife!"

"Your wife?"

"Yes, my wife."

The man stared at my face, confused.

"Man! Are you sure you are in your right senses?"

I stared at his face. He could see I didn't take kindly to the question.

"Gentleman! Please pardon my rudeness. I only talked that way because the man and the woman dancing are Chief and Mrs. Ajai. They are husband and wife; don't you know that? You say the woman is your wife? How?"

"The Chief you are looking at is a robber; a brigand who has stolen another man's woman. The woman is my own legitimate property; not his. She belongs to me."

As I spoke, my anger suddenly rose up sharply like a violent angry tide. If it were somebody raping my wife under my own eyes, the ordeal would have been less severe. The agony would only last a few minutes. But I was facing a trauma of a different nature. The woman, who had made a vow to be mine forever had been commandeered by a rich desperado. Watching the Chief and my woman having their pleasure was most unbearable. My brain seemed now to be spinning round. I felt a surge of bitterness in every tissue and cell of my body. Now, my mind began to unravel the long catalogue of agony and pain I had gone through. I tried to keep myself under restraint but I didn't know when I exploded:

"So this is the man who stole Alero! This is the man who lured Alero away with his money! This is the man responsible for all my pains and headache! This is the man who destroyed my dream, my life, my destiny, and my vision! This is the man…"

I remembered that moment that I had my double-barrelled gun in the boot of my car.

"Thank God! This is the time to deal with this rascal once and for all. This matter must be settled here and now. It cannot be postponed till any other time. Gun down the Chief. You have a good case. You may suffer for some weeks or months in police custody but that doesn't matter. The court will eventually say that you have been provoked;" something told me.

I hastened to my car. I opened the booth and grabbed my gun.
"This is a good scene and this is a good situation to end this long, cruel drama. Man! You mustn't miss it," some instincts whispered to me. But that moment, I heard another voice:

"Mayo! Do you need to kill? Kill because of what? Kill because of a woman? Kill because of mere dirt and rubbish in a human form? You want to be a murderer? You? Son of Williams? With all your wonderful credentials, laurels and intimidating achievement? I think you owe the world and yourself more than that."

I held on to the gun, stood frozen to that spot, hands now shaking and tears streaming down my cheeks. And that moment, the affairs between Alero and me started to roll back before my eyes. I could see all the details, those details all over again!

CHAPTER EIGHT

I can now recall that this long story started in January, 1953. I was seven. Mom said I would go to school and I didn't love the idea. I had been told by a man of God, living near our house, that God, one Great Being, living above the sky, would always grant one's request; if only one could pray to Him, and sincerely believe that He would do it. Now that I had a problem in my hand, I looked up and began to pray. I prayed hard and I believed that He had heard me. It was unbelievable - most unbelievable, what I dreaded most, I mean that day of inquisition, still came one morning and I was to go to school.

"How?" I queried.

I was asked to pray and I prayed. I was asked to have faith, and I had faith. "What is happening? Is the Great God I offered my prayer to no longer on His throne? Is He gone on leave? If not, why has He refused to grant the earnest and anxious desire of a small, innocent child? Why?"

These were my questions as mom and I went down the street that morning. It was very cold. The harmattan wind was blowing and I was feeling very uncomfortable. We soon got to the "Land of Sorrow" which Toro people called the CMS School. And there, mom handed me over to one huge hyena: a fierce and grim looking man called Mr. George. He lost his wife that morning and he had come directly to the school from the funeral ground. That was my guess because I had never seen a face so gloomy and bitter. He looked like a man carrying the collective sorrow of the entire universe on his shoulder. His face, dark, hostile and morose would make the Devil himself stop at a distance. He looked one hundred per cent a man one would see and run. "Why did mom hand me over to this kind of man?"

In the class that morning, all my previous fears about school were confirmed. When I stood up, Mr. George asked me to sit down. When I sat down and seemed to be enjoying myself, he asked me to stand up. Each time, what he asked me to do was the exact opposite of what I loved to do.

"What kind of place is this?" I grumbled.

Within thirty minutes, I was bored stiff. Then I went to Mr. George.

"Sir! I'd love to go out and play on that lovely lawn outside. I'd love very much to be in the sunshine."

"What?"

"I said I love to be in the sunshine."

Mr. George stared at me, open-mouthed. My audacity must have seemed to him most incredible. He was suddenly filled with cold fury.

"What do you take this place to be? Your private home?" he screamed. "It is not yet break-time. Go and sit down, my friend. And mind you, don't make any further trouble or else…" His eyes glittered with rage and he fixed those eyes on me for a long time as a sign of warning never to come up again to trouble him.

When I was eventually released from his prison at 1.40p.m. that day and I was allowed to go home, I said:
"Never again! I will never…never show up in this place no matter what."

When the hour for school struck the following morning, I did what so many oppressed people would have done in similar circumstances, I took to the small wood behind our house and hid myself behind an acadia tree. It was nearly half an hour before I was retrieved from the place.
"I am not going and I won't go," I protested violently.
"You will go and you have to go. You have no choice in this matter!" exclaimed my mother.

Angrily, I rolled on the ground, then rose up, kicked the floor violently and screamed loudly. I only stopped crying when a little girl, about my age, came from the blue and held my hand.
"Stop crying. We will go together," she told me

The girl, called Alero, was to become the most important feature in my life after that. In fact, with effect from that morning, my entire life changed and started to revolve around her. Out of the blue, came Alero that cold morning like a warm, friendly sunshine and I warmed up to her at first sight. Though a small girl, Alero was radiant as a new dawn. Her dress was elegant. A touch of royalty could be seen from her beautiful features. She was seven but her language was imperious and authoritative. As she spoke, I immediately knew that she was someone who must be obeyed.

I stared at her. Jesus! She had lovely eyes. My anger and complaint about going to school strangely evaporated. I did not know why. Her touch was soothing and friendly. Whatever she wanted, I was prepared to do. Wherever she wanted to lead me, I was ready to follow. Whatever command she gave, I was ready to obey. I so much liked Alero. Two young women wearing beautiful costumes and costly beads, stood behind her. I understood later that they were her attendants.

I had seen very many girls of my age in Toro but no one was like Alero. As she held my right hand that morning on our way to school, I looked at her again and again. The more I stared at her, the more I discovered that I couldn't have enough of her. Alero was so adorable. That afternoon, as we came back from school, with Alero holding my right hand, we must have presented a funny picture to our mothers who stood together watching us with broad smiles. "What an amusing pair!" they said.

I lived with my mother in a small bungalow in the center district of Toro. The next house was that of Prince Matete, a mighty storey building with a unique design, no doubt the prettiest house in Toro and the surrounding villages. Surrounded by ten acres of well-tended and beautifully maintained lawn with flowers in a riot of colours, Matete's house was a Garden of Eden. The house, big, solid, impregnable like a medieval fortress, had a breath-taking beauty. Prince Matete was Alero's father. Everyone knew Matete to be a great man. Many feats were credited to him by the local people. He was held in awe by all. No doubt, this made Alero, his daughter have such a great impression upon me. Besides this, Alero was a beautiful girl. She had beautiful dresses. Everyday, she appeared in a new, colourful dress. She was such a delight to behold.

Daily, we went to school and came back together. We soon became great friends. We could not do without seeing each other. She became a permanent feature in my life, a vital component of my everyday routine, and soon the one I could not do without.

It was almost two months since I met Alero but that short period of time appeared like many years. Everyday, I always looked forward to the time the big iron gate of the Garden House would open and Alero would come out. I was always anxious to see her. Her face had a softness that I liked. The rays of her astonishing eye-balls were like the first rays of the December sun, bright and inviting. I so much loved them.

During the weekend, Alero always came out of her Garden House to play with me. As a rule, two officials in uniform always accompanied her. They would stay at a distance, never coming so close to disturb our play. But they were always around.

I remember now that each time Alero came out, she always put on a new gown and each gown was specially sewn and tailored to fit. They were all British products. I never saw her in one gown two times and I began to wonder how large her wardrobe would be. In a period when girls and boys walked barefoot in the streets of Toro, Alero had more than 50 pairs of shoes. She was so fashionable.

She spoke in few words, and spoke as if there was a specific limit on the number of words she must speak per day. Words came out of her mouth most of the time in poetic rhythm, but I was not sure whether she was aware of this. Her steps were calculated and measured. I loved so much the way she stepped. It had a peculiar beauty and a touch of class. In behaviour, in walking, in talking, Alero was a princess, and never less than a princess.

I must admit, whenever I saw Alero, I always grew green with envy. Whenever she came to play with me, I never failed to survey her body and compare it with mine. I had many spots and scars on my legs and palms due to mosquito bites, accidents and the strokes of the cane, I regularly received at school. It was impossible to live in Toro without having some spots. Strangely, Alero had no spots. Her palms and legs were spotless. Her skin was smooth as glass. Her skin seemed as if it was daily massaged by butter and honey – glossy and super-smooth. My God! She had a lovely skin.

Whenever she came out of the Garden House, the attendants hovering around her, were always watching out for her safety. They gave Alero nothing-must-touch-her attention. They also worked with nothing-must-scratch-her-skin kind of passion. They treated her like a raw egg which must be handled with care. Alero was tender and delicate. But she was a glamorous Princess all the same. For any slight change in her mood, the attendants would query:

"Your Highness! Are you all right? Does your Highness want to go home?"

Her ladies always encumbered her with numerous courtesies. Anything she wanted, they always looked for it quickly and gave it to her.

"Why is the world so anxious to please this little girl, and this little girl alone? Why is everyone so anxious to meet her demands? Why is she venerated like an idol? Why has she become a little god which everyone appears so desperately anxious to worship? Why has God showered on her so much favours? Why has He created her so differently from the rest of us? Why has He decorated and decked her with such terrific beauty? Why?"

As a child, I always asked these questions privately but I never had any satisfactory answers to them. And so one day, I took the matter up with my mom.

"What kind of girl is Alero?" I asked mom.

"She is a princess,"mom replied.

"Who is a princess?," I queried.

"A princess is a daughter of a king."

"Prince Matete, Alero's father is not a king, is he?"

"No, he is not. But he is heir to the throne. When the present king dies, he is the one to succeed him."

"Mom, I like Alero."

"I like her too. She is a very adorable princess."

Even in those early years when we were little children, I liked Alero so much. As a pretty, sweet girl, I admired her. As a Princess, I envied her. All what Alero represented to me was glamour. She was royally made.

CHAPTER NINE

N ow, our friendship grew stronger by the day. In the last one week, Alero always came to play with me without her attendants. My home had become one of the few privileged places she could go to alone. One day she came to play with me and Alero, Tinu and Mewa (Tinu's sister) and I played the game of hide and seek. It was thrilling. Alero used three pieces of cloth to cover the eyes of the three of us and then went into hiding.

"You can open your eyes now," she shouted.

I knew where the voice came from. I would fetch her out in a matter of seconds. But we searched and searched and searched, Alero seemed to have dissolved into the thin air.

"Has she gone home?" the girls asked me.

"How am I to know?" I replied, but Tinu tried to find out from one of the security officers at the gate of the Garden House.

"She is yet to come in," he replied.

Just that moment, it occurred to me to look for Alero

inside my own house, and there she was, behind the main door.

"Don't move! Don't just move! I have caught you," I shouted.

Alero, came out to embrace me.

The embrace of a princess could be so sweet. That, I knew that day. Mom had embraced me several times. But it was certainly not like this. Alero's hands were soft and feminine. Her touch seemed like the touch of a velvet, so smooth and so pleasant. Her caressing fingers gave me a kind of pleasure I had never experienced before. Her body contact was delicious. My Goodness! I liked Alero.

It was yet another day. We would not be going to school because we had our mid-term holiday. After my breakfast, I was the first to be out of the house. I looked around, I did not see any of the three girls. I looked at the huge iron gate of the Garden House, praying secretly in my mind that that gate would open and Alero would appear. I longed to see Alero. I loved to hear her voice – that thin, sonorous, beautiful voice. I loved to look at Alero's face - that face that ever seemed to beckon and invite. I loved to stare at Alero's lovely dimples which made her face look so fine. I loved to hear her laugh. Princesses had their own peculiar way of laughing that I so much admired. My imagination was still traveling and going round and round when suddenly the gate to the Garden House opened and Alero appeared. I was so excited.

"Mom was not going to allow me to come out and play with you."

"Why?" I asked her.

"Going out to play with Mayo cannot be everyday affair. You saw him yesterday, didn't you?"

"Yes, I did."

"Why today again?" she asked me.

I didn't know how to answer her question. I only said: "Mom! Please! Please!" then stared at her face.

"Don't keep late there before you come back home."

"I won't keep late," I promised.

"I stared at Alero. I so much liked her. I so much liked her dress.

She wore a white gown with green stripes. She also wore a pair of green shoes. Her hair was long and brought together dexterously at a point behind her back. I always wondered whether her maids had any other job other than adorning her.

Alero was still talking to me when Tinu and Mewa appeared. Out of sheer excitement, I asked the girls: "Can we start the game of hide and seek?"

"But we had that yesterday, can't we go for a different game?" asked Alero.

"Okay, we will play police and the thief," shouted Mewa.

"No! … No! Who wants to be the thief? Certainly not me," exclaimed Tinu. It was later agreed that we'd have a marriage ceremony.

Tinu was 10. Alero, Mewa and I were born the same year. We were 7. We treated Tinu as our big sister. As our undisputed leader, she now took over.

"Please, come," Tinu beckoned to Mewa.

"You are getting married to Mayo and we have to prepare you as a lovely bride."

"No! … No!", I protested.

"Why?" Tinu asked me.

"I am the one to choose the girl that I like to marry, I have seen people getting married but it was the man who always chose his woman. Permit me therefore to make my choice."

Tinu now stared at my face intrusively.

"And who is your choice if I may ask?"

"Princess Alero is my choice."

Tinu burst into peals of laughter, then stopped suddenly.

"You! You! You want to marry a princess," pointing to me accusingly as if I had committed an unpardonable crime.

"You are the greatest clown in this universe, do you know that?" she asked as the corners of her mouth twitched with a narrow, scornful smile.

I stared at Tinu's face, confused.

"What have I done wrong? What is my offence?" I asked.

"A son of a mere commoner wishing to marry Her Royal Highness, the Princess of Toro!
Doesn't the idea sound ridiculous to you?"

"It may sound ridiculous to you but it doesn't sound so to me."

"Mayo! Please, listen. By traditions, a Princess must marry a Prince or at worst marry the son of a top ranking chief and I am afraid you are neither of the two."

"I don't have to be either."

"You feel so?" a mocking smile played on Tinu's lips

Her scorn stung me like a poisoned arrow. Her derision hurt me badly and I felt like crying.

"You must not cry," something told me.

"Why should a girl make you cry? Don't you know you are a man?"

I have been told by my mother not to cry before a girl. "You must always be a man," she never failed to tell me.

I made up my mind not to cry though I was not sure whether my eyes were not wet already. I braced up. I was ready to defend my stand as I sent out now my first salvo.

"Tinu! Have you forgotten what we learnt in our Sunday School class?"

"And what about it?"

"How Esther, an orphan, a poor girl from a very poor home and a slave, married King Ahasuerus, the then ruler of the world? What of Michal – a Princess, the daughter of King Saul of Israel? Don't you remember her?"

"What about her," Tinu queried, raising her eyebrows and smiling for the first time.

"King Saul, her father agreed that she could marry David, a poor shepherd boy."

"Mayo! What a good lawyer! You have argued your case so beautifully. You are simply marvelous," she shouted.

For some seconds, Tinu stared at me in awe.

"But we still have a hurdle before us."

"And where is that hurdle." I asked her.

"I need to find out from the Princess whether she likes to marry you. She needs to give her consent, don't you feel so?"

"O.K. Go ahead," I told her.

"Tinu now smiled infectiously as she now turned to Princess Alero. Her eyes surveyed slowly Alero's exquisite figure, admiring now every curve of that little, wonderful body; then she asked:
"Princess, will you marry Mayo?"

Alero first stared at my face, then a narrow, mechanical smile came on her lips. The smile didn't seem to give any hint of approval. I stared now at Alero's face like a pupil about to hear the outcome of the end of the year examination. I was tense. And my tension grew more and more as Alero just smiled but refused to talk. We were small innocent children but I liked Alero so much. I admired her more than any other person in this world. What she would say gave me so much anxiety. I looked at her face virtually begging her with every fibre of my being to say yes. This was a mere child's play, and at best a fun, but I was dreadfully tense because I wouldn't be happy if Alero turned me down. I stared at her face intensely. For many seconds, I stared fixedly at that face.

"Will she reject me? Will she say no because I am a son of a commoner?"
My heart was thudding inside me. If she said 'no,' that wouldn't be the end of the world. But her 'no' would hurt me badly. It would hurt my ego. It would shatter my pride and make me feel unhappy. I was not even sure that I was not going to cry.
"But what will she say?"
I stared at her face expectantly. But Alero chose to keep

mute for a reason best known to her.

"Your Highness! Will you marry Mayo or not?" Tinu asked her again, smiling.

"Yes, I will," she replied, beaming out a contagious smile.

"Bravo! Mayo! Aren't you lucky? You are going to marry a princess. Wonderful! All your friends will envy you. The world itself will celebrate you. Now that we have got the bride and the groom, what else are we waiting for?"

Tinu now beckoned to Alero.

"Princess, please come nearer."

Alero walked to her. Within me, I was excited. I felt on top of the world. I felt a kind of triumph inside me as if the princess was going to marry me in the real sense of the word. I so much admired Alero and the significance of the fact that she did not reject me was not lost on me.

Tinu now turned to Princess Alero.

"Mayo's bride! Can you sit down? Mewa and I will have to weave your hair in a special manner. We are going to make you look really sweet. We want to make you look like a real bride before we present you to Mayo, your darling husband."

Alero now sat on a small stool and right away, the two girls began to weave her huge hair into a pyramid. Tinu looked at my direction.

"Mayo, you are not supposed to stay with us. You have to leave us. When your bride is ready, we will bring her to you."

"That is okay," I told Tinu as I left the three girls. I walked for about 20 metres and then stayed under a big tree. While waiting, I felt I should prepare a place where the bride would stay on arrival. Since my home was made of red sand, it occurred to me to build something similar for Alero, my bride. In no time, I moulded a miniature house made with red sand. I looked for some sticks which now served as the roof. I looked at the house, it was beautiful, I was quite happy with the structure that I put in place. In my estimation, I had been a good architect and a good construction engineer. I was sure Alero would commend me for my effort.

Now, I looked at the girls, they too had finished their preparation. My bride was ready. Alero's hair, weaved into a pyramid shape, gave her a stunning look. My God! Alero was a small angel. The two girls held her in between them as she approached now in regal splendour. She approached with slow, measured steps. Princesses could be really adorable and Alero was really lovely. She had a very fine shape. She winked at me and gave me a shy, innocent smile, I communicated back to her with the eye, saying to her that she was really sweet. As she drew nearer and nearer, her face continued to talk to me. I could not decode all the messages but I knew that it was all a language of love. I felt very proud as I inspected each step of hers in a leisurely fashion.

"We present to you your lovely bride," said Tinu and Mewa as they handed over Alero to me. I looked at Alero, my beautiful bride, it was a dream come true. I took her hand, soft and feminine, I felt so excited.

Then Alero stared at the faces of the two girls, then at my face and said:

"Before these girls who are our witnesses, I promise that I will always be your bride."

With excitement burning inside me, I also stared at Alero's face and said:

"I also promise that I will always like you." Then I sprang forward excitedly.

"Come on, Alero!

This is the house we are going to live in," pointing to the miniature house. No real husband in the entire human history could feel as proud as I was. I was happier than the angels living in the heavenly places. But Alero looked at what was supposed to be our new home, then stared at me, and then burst into tears.

"Alero what is the problem? Why are you crying? Don't you like the house?" I asked her, holding her two pretty hands. She tore herself loose from me and queried:

"You mean, this dirty, smelling, ugly shack is what I will live in as your bride? How do you expect me to live in a house like this? No flowers, no lawn, no fine shrubs, nothing of beauty – a princess to live in a mud house?"

And without warning, Alero sprang forward, kicked at the labour of over forty minutes and demolished it within seconds.

"What the hell are you doing?" I queried? A demonic rage had entered into Alero. In anger, she picked up the sticks used for the roof of the house and threw them away. Alero might not like the house I built for both of us but she certainly had no business destroying a structure I had expended so much labour and time on. I was furious, I was a child and I behaved like one. I couldn't explain what really happened. In the heat of my anger I temporarily lost my sanity and I forgot the fact that the girl before me was a princess. It happened before I knew what happened.

I gave Alero a slap on the face, she also gave me a hard slap on the face and the next moment we were fighting. Tinu rushed in quickly to separate us but Alero's gown was slightly torn during our scuffle.

"How dare you tear my gown?"
It was that question that woke me from my temporary madness and I became sane again.
I looked at the torn gown, I was afraid. I wanted to be swallowed by some invisible elements or at least be anywhere but not there.
"How will I explain that I tore the gown of Her Royal Highness? What excuse will I give for slapping the princess - the one everyone including our teachers virtually trembled before her? What demon had gone into me? What madness had gone into my head? This was the work of Satan. But why should I permit Satan to possess me?"
The questions came in torrents. I was in trouble. I had done what no one should ever dare to do. With tears raining down Alero's eyes, she picked up her belt from the floor and started to go away. She only needed to get home in that condition and security officials would come down and pick me and my mother. We would be going straight into the police custody. Our ordeal would be terrible.

Whichever punishment would be meted out to me for my folly, I did not dread as the threat given by Alero:

"I will never come here again to play with you. Never." She emphasized each word very carefully to bring home to me the seriousness of her resolve. I had boxed myself into a corner.

Alero had been my best friend. She was the closest person to me, apart from my mom. Every morning, we always went to school together. In the afternoon, we came back from school together. She had become part of me and I part of her. Her friendship had become one of my necessities of life. I needed her like the flowers need the rains. "How am I to do without her? Can I afford to miss her?" I asked myself.
I knew I could not.
I ran after her with tears on my face.
"Alero, I won't fight you again. I made a mistake. Please, forgive me. I want you, please, don't leave me," I screamed.
"Never call my name again. I am not your friend. Do friends fight?" she asked me, while cleaning her face with the back of her palm.
"No," I replied.
"Then why did you beat me?"
"I never intended to beat you. You know how much I like you but anger made me behave foolishly. I am sorry. Please, please, forgive me."
The appeals fell on deaf ears. She would heed none of them. She quickened her steps. I ran after her, held on to her and tried once more to appease her. I stared at her face again and again.

"Alero! I am sorry. I won't do it again."
"No!…No!", she yelled hysterically as she tore herself
from me.

"Alero! Don't leave me. Don't leave me, please," I
pleaded. She only flashed a sad look at me and
hastened her steps, I knew now that the battle was
already lost and I broke down, screaming.
"Alero! Tell me, you won't leave me…Please!"
I stared at her and I groaned now like someone about
to go into a fit. And really, I was close to a fit level.

Just that moment, Alero's eyes suddenly took a new
colour and she stopped. She stood transfixed to the
spot. One part of her wanted to move on, but another
part could not leave me there wailing. Anger and pity
fought inside her. Rage and compassion struggled for
the control of her heart. For some seconds, no one
could say which one was going to win. She stared at
my face; her eyes gazing intensely at me again and
again. There must have been a power in my wailing
eyes that had suddenly become an arrester. The rays
flashing out of those eyeballs must have evoked a
sort of pity that so much touched her now. With
tears still running down her cheeks, Alero walked
back to me. She lifted her tear-stained eyes to mine,
and then put her arm around my waist and pulled me
closer.
"Mayo! Stop crying. I won't leave you," she exclaimed.
I was still crying. Tears were still coming down her
own cheeks, as we held to each other.

"Mayo! Stop crying! I say I am not going to leave

75

you," she said pleadingly as she cleaned the tear from my eyes with the edge of her gown and then stroke the hair at the back of my head soothingly; just like an elderly woman would do to a crying child. Tears from her swollen eyes still came down in drops. The pain I inflicted on her still burned and lingered on; but that pain she endured now with princely dignity. Her passion to ease my pain had taken over. Her agony, she was prepared to bear but mine, she was determined to remove.

A sweet, contagious smile lit her sad face, her pain and agony now gave way to a strange warmth. What a lovely, tender creature she was! My God! I have never seen such a wonderful little angel.

Within minutes, her sympathetic look and melting eyes dissolved the fog of misunderstanding between us. The fight was over. The next moment, Alero and I were sitting together again playing as if nothing had happened. That turned out to be the last time we ever quarreled physically on any issue. For after that incident, this little bride of mine and I understood each other so perfectly. Believe me, the love shown to me by that lovely sweet, innocent, small girl that day touched the deepest part of my heart. I swore, I would never live a day without remembering it.

But something happened when Alero and I were fighting. Just as Tinu moved in to separate us and Alero picked her belt from the ground and was on her way home, a distress call came from the direction of Tinu's house

"That is grandma's voice. My God! What's happened to her? I hope she has not broken her legs," exclaimed Tinu as she raced towards her house and Mewa raced after her.

But about ten minutes later, Tinu was back. She met me and Alero talking and giggling.
"You mean the two of you are still here? How?"
"Alero! I felt you had gone home."
"No, I haven't gone yet."
"You mean you have settled your quarrel – or what happened?"

We both stared at Tinu's face and smiled

"Okay, I can guess what happened. You have settled your quarrel. Mewa had given out your secret, she told me that you so much like each other. She told me that you are not just husband and wife in a drama, that you are real husband and wife."

CHAPTER TEN

As days lengthened into weeks, and weeks into months and months into years, so also Alero grew more attractive everyday. At age 10, she had become the central figure in the CMS Primary School. A Princess, Alero was the best dressed pupil in CMS school. Good-looking with a pretty face, she was the envy of all her colleagues. Every pupil wanted to be with her and be seen with her. She became the center around which all activities of CMS school gravitated. She was the sun of our little solar system. Being around her was a pleasure. Walking with her was a great delight. But I was closer to her than any other person.

I soon became jealous over Alero. But when does jealousy cast its print upon the innocent mind of a child? When does a child begin to develop possessive instincts? When does he begin to nurture a feeling not to share something special he has with another person? As Alero and I became close friends, I discovered that I didn't like to share her friendship with any other pupil. I wanted to have her to myself. I cannot precisely say when I started to nurse this rather strange ambition. But it turned out to be a mission impossible. For as a pupil, Alero was simply desired by all.

Mr. Balogun was the school bandmaster. He loved rumba, a Cuba Negro dance that became so popular in Nigeria in the early 1950s. Every Friday, between 1p.m. and 1.40p.m., we always had rumba. Alero and one boy called Coker were the best rumba dancers in the school. Coker was a son of a High Chief. He was also neat and well dressed. The families of Alero and Coker belonged to the exclusive upper class in Toro and this showed in everything.

That Friday, Mr. Balogun asked Coker and Alero to come out to the stage, and there they danced to the admiration of all. Alero stood on the same spot, she stood in regal splendour but all the movable flesh on her slim pretty body shook admiringly. Her princely, magnificent frame rolled up and down, sending waves of regal glamour and delight to the on-lookers. I had never seen such a fantastic dancer. Coker also caught fire; he twisted and gyrated like the legendary Michael Jackson, turning himself into all manners of shapes. What a wonderful pair!

"My God! This is marvelous!" exclaimed Mr. Balogun
"They danced like professionals versed in the art," screamed the headmaster.
"These ones will certainly go places;" exclaimed Mr. George.
"Fantastic! Superb! The steps and the motions are

just too magnificent. Look at Alero, There is something quite regal about her;" exclaimed yet another teacher.

When they finally stopped, a loud burst of applause went on for many minutes.

Everybody was so happy. But I was not. I was in a fury. The dance made me feel sick. It made me feel extremely uncomfortable. I must confess; I was envious of this special advantage being enjoyed by Coker. I was somehow apprehensive of being displaced by this boy who was becoming rather too close to Princess Alero, my own bride. I felt he was constituting a threat to me over what I considered to be my own legitimate property. I could not say what I was losing but I felt terribly jealous.

I had wanted to voice out my objection to the dance but I did not know how to go about it. As Alero and I walked home that afternoon, I did not talk to her. She talked to me, I didn't answer. I was cold. I was also very angry.

"Mayo, what's the matter? Why are you so cold?"

"Nothing," I replied.

"Won't you talk to me? Won't you talk to your bride? Or have you got another bride so soon?" Alero tried to tease me.

"Nothing is wrong," I answered.

"I have been talking to you and each time you answer with a monosyllable. Am I a radio station that talks without a reply?"

"I don't know."

"Why don't you know?" she screamed.

"Alero, listen to me," as I was now ready to speak.

"You have been dancing with Coker, I didn't talk."

"What if I dance with Coker, what does that mean?"

"I don't know what it means; but listen to me, and listen very carefully. If you ever dance with Coker again, I won't play with you."

"Why?"

"Don't ask me why. Just be informed that I am not going to play with you any more if you ever dance with Coker," my voice now imperious and forceful.

"Did I ever request to dance with Coker?"

"I don't know," I replied.

"But you should know. And you know. You certainly cannot run away from the fact that it was Mr. Balogun who asked me to dance."

"I don't care, I don't want to know anything about the person who asked you to dance. That is your own cup of tea. Just know that I won't play with you if you ever dance with Coker again."

Alero stared at my face; she couldn't see what I should be angry about. From that point until we got home, we didn't talk to each other.

Another Friday came at last, and another rumba session. Mr. Balogun invited a guest, Mr. Aina, from another school to come and watch the rumba session of that day.

"When you see them, you will see dancers at their best. I have never seen such wonderful little angels in my life. Their motions are superb, magnificent and yet natural. You will doff your hat for them;" he said.

The drum beat and another exciting moment started again in CMS School.

"Princess Alero and Coker will open today's rumba

session with a powerful demonstration dance," said Mr. Balogun, and there was a loud applause.

Coker hurried to the stage but Alero hid in one corner of that room and didn't come out.

"Princess Alero! Where are you?" asked Mr. Balogun.

Alero did not answer.

"She is here," shouted some pupils.

"Will you come to the stage?"

Alero looked at my face. Naturally, my look was stern and unfriendly. She was in a great dilemma.

"Princess! What is wrong with you? Will you come this way?" shouted Mr. Balogun now growing impatient.

Alero came out, her face was dull and uninviting. She looked like a sick person and danced now like an eighty year old woman who had bad legs. The glamour, the gaiety, the magnificence were absent; her body was there but her mind was so far away. It was obvious to everyone that this small girl was not ready to dance. Mr. Balogun screamed and shouted, but it was a bad outing!

It was several years later when I reviewed the scene of that afternoon that I appreciated how much loyalty Alero had shown to me.

CHAPTER ELEVEN

I can't remember precisely now how long Alero and I spent together in those early years. The period seemed so long but highly exciting.

My mother had to move to daddy's house, and so, one evening, she called me and said:

"We are leaving here tomorrow."

"Why? And where are we going?"

"We are going to your father's place."

"I don't want to go there. I can't leave here. I like to be where I can see Princess Alero and play with her."

"We are not going too far from here. You can always come back and play with Alero anytime you like."

I shrugged, then kept quiet, showing that mom could please herself. I was not pleased but it appeared there was no amount of protest that could change mom's decision. With our departure, Alero and I saw each other mostly in the school but as days, months and, indeed, years rolled by, our interest in each other did not wane in any way.

Alero so much liked me and I liked her with passion.

It was in her company that I found my greatest joy, she too confessed to me that: "Whenever I don't see you I always feel like a sick person."

We had interacted over the years as children. We had grown to know each other so well. But that year 1958, I started seeing Alero in a different form. We were in our final year in the primary school. We were 13 and we had become teenagers.

Hitherto, Alero and I had played together and at times quarreled, I scarcely appreciated then that there was any much difference between us. Now I began to see the difference. I began to see Alero's feminine features. She had blossomed into an adorable young lady. Her pointed, roundish, beautiful breasts pushing against her gown, had started to send romantic signals to me. The honey on her lips seemed to be inviting me even though I had never kissed any girl before. Her hot hips began to engage the attention of my eyes more than necessary. The extraordinary smoothness of her skin appeared to be saying: "Come and touch me." Jesus! Alero had become a different girl.

At that young age, Alero showed a vivid promise of a great beauty in the making. Her frame looked so pretty and enchanting. Her figure was slim, tender and delicate. Her eye balls were large and bright. Her palms were slender and shapely. Her fingers were long and lovely. Her neck was fine, her nose was pointed like that of a Fulani girl. Her mouth was moderate and her lips were neither too thick nor too narrow. She was a darling of both teachers and pupils.

For the first time, I discovered that I was being fascinated emotionally by Alero and I found myself looking at her face time and again, searching for the magic of those eye balls. Surprisingly, Alero's beauty never palled on me once, the more I looked at her, the fairer she grew by the passage of each day. Strangely too, as I was being fascinated by Alero so was she being fascinated by me. She too started to like me emotionally, the way she had not done before. Whenever I looked at her and her eyes caught mine, she always winked at me. Through making faces to each other, Alero and I started to exchange messages of love. Through amorous glances, we started to exchange secret communications. With the eyes, Alero began to talk to me and send love codes which I and only I could decode.

Mr. George and his colleagues made the CMS School a small hell. Any slight offence, Mr. George always rolled out his canes. He caned us with such fury and wreckless abandon that I hated going to school. If one pupil was spared from canes, that was Princess Alero. No teacher dared do anything to her other than respect. She was an idol worshipped by all.

I wouldn't be telling you the whole truth, if I said I hated going to school. While the canes repelled me, the presence of Alero pulled me back at the same time. Alero was a pretty girl. Her fine shape was a magnet that continuously drew me to school.

Her attractive figure acted like a magnetic force. It always invigorated my cells and my nerves and helped me to bear all the tortures and the pains of the CMS School. Her sweet face always seemed like the coming of the sun after a long, dark, cold night. Mere winking at me acted upon me like magic. The signals from her big, amorous eyeballs always dispelled my fog of gloom and despair. Her tender, delicate body was a love elixir. Her shy, innocent smile lit our class like a bright, powerful electric lamp. I just loved to be with Alero.

Mr. George's strokes of the canes were everyday ritual. They were sure to come as the sun after the dawn. Whatever happened one could not escape two or three strokes of the cane everyday.

But after receiving the strokes of the cane, Alero always came to me during break time when every pupil had left the class for one outdoor activity or the other. She would help me to rub and massage my swollen palms.

"God will punish Mr. George for what he did to you. I hate him. I hate his guts," she would tell me. The soothing massage from Alero's tender, feminine hands always gave me such delicious pleasure which I daily looked forward to.

While my punishment did not make Alero happy, strangely I always prayed secretly to receive some strokes of the cane in order to qualify for the soft, caressing wave of pleasure, rippling through my body whenever Alero's hands gently and lovingly touched my palms and pressed on the hard muscles of my shoulders. I just liked her infectious touch. It kept my body alive.

As young as we were, we both knew that we felt an intense affection for each other. We never spoke about it, but deep inside us, there were those inner feelings and emotions that connected both of us together like a mysterious, invisible chain. It was one of my most thrilling moments.

CHAPTER TWELVE

Fola, a short, strongly built boy of 14, sat next to me in our class. As I returned from a lunch break one afternoon, he was crying.

"What is the matter?" I asked him.

"I have been searching for my English Grammar Book for the past one hour, I can't find it."

"Have you searched all the desks in the class?"

"Yes, I have;"

"Have you spoken to all the pupils whether anyone took it by mistake?"

"I have, but no one claimed to have seen it."

"Are you really sure you brought it from home?"

"What type of question is that? I did an exercise from the book only a few hours ago. This is the exercise;" he showed it to me.

I stood there, confused.

"Who then could have taken the book and why?" We were unable to unravel the mystery.

"Somebody must have stolen it;" said Fola.

"Do you suspect anyone?"

"No, I don't."

"What will you do now?"

"I don't know. I am confused. I can't tell my father, he is a hot-tempered person. He will almost beat life out of me."

"If you aren't going to tell the person who can give you the money to buy another book, how do you solve the problem?" I asked him.

Fola's face was lit with a strange, mischievous smile as he moved closer to me, put his mouth near my right ear and whispered:

"I am going to steal the grammar book of another pupil."

I almost jumped out of my chair.

"No, you can't do that."

"Why?"

"It's not right, you know that, don't you?"

"Why is it not right?"

"Because the Bible tells us not to steal. God, our Father and our Friend in heaven does not like a thief. If you go and steal, He may refuse to be your friend. Have you forgotten the sermon of the pastor, the one he gave during the Children's Day?"

"What about it?"

"He said we young children must never allow God to turn His face from us even for a minute because we will be in trouble."

"Mayo! That is enough. Please, save me the rest. I know you well. You are more religious than the Pope. But this is not a religious matter. If you love to be a pastor, go to the church. Since we are not in the church, please keep God out of this. And really, He has no business in this particular matter. You don't need to involve Him in an issue that doesn't concern

Him. This is a purely human affair."

I stared at Fola's face, puzzled.

"You say your affair does not concern God? Is that possible?" I asked him.

"I say this matter does not concern God and I mean it, but if you insist on bringing Him into it, I will have to ask you some questions and you must answer them."

"What are your questions?" I asked him.

"Where was God when someone came here to steal my book? Where was He? Since He is the Almighty and knows all things and can do all things – why didn't He prevent the thief from stealing my book? Why couldn't He save me all these worries? When the thief was planning to steal my book, God did not intervene. When he was in the process of carrying out his plan, God did not intervene. When he stole the book, God did not bother Himself. Now I want to steal another pupil's book, you say God will be annoyed. Why should He? What is His concern in the matter? When the whole issue started, He did not show any interest. When the thief stole my book and went away, He only looked the other way. He didn't do a thing. What justification has He now to come in when I want to steal? If He did not bother himself earlier on, why now?"

"Fola, you've got it wrong."

"How?"

"Just listen to me! Contrary to your view, God bothers about all issues including this one. Our pastor said: 'God will never force anyone to do His will.' God creates each human being and allows him to have his own free will. For example, God wants all human beings to worship Him; but many people worship rivers, stones, idols or the devil. Much as He loves all to worship Him, He will not compel people who worship other gods to worship Him by force. That is not His style. You are at liberty to worship whom you want to worship. In the same way, God cannot force a thief not to steal. God wants everyone to be humble, but he will never force a proud man not to be proud.

On this issue, God knows what is going on. What is going on bothers Him. But the pastor said that God always waits patiently till a matter comes to an end. At that very end, you will face His judgment. Since He knows that the issue will end up with him, He is always prepared to exercise patience. And that is what you misinterpreted to mean that He doesn't bother. He does."

"Mayo! When did God hire you as His attorney? You have argued His case so beautifully. His style is so clear to me now. But having said that, my original problem still remains. Tell me! How do I get another grammar book?"

"I don't know but whenever we have a problem that we cannot solve the pastor says we should tell God."

"So you want me to tell God."

"Precisely."

"And you feel He will do something?"

"If you believe that He will, surely He will."

That afternoon, we had story telling under the fig trees behind the school buildings. It was one exercise

Fola and I always looked forward to. Surprisingly, Fola was absent from that day story telling. When the lesson came to a close, I looked for him, I couldn't find him. But about ten minutes later, I saw him coming from the direction of the classroom.

"Where have you been? We've been all over the place looking for you."

"I went to the toilet," he replied. A suspicious smile lit his face.

"What is funny?"

"Nothing;" he replied.

Not long, the school bell rang, announcing that lessons had finally ended that day. We all trooped to the assembly hall. Few minutes after that, the school came to a close. I was so happy. Between then and the next morning, I would be free from the claws of the hyenas of the CMS School. I won't hear the angry barking of the Alsatian Dog. That was the nickname we gave Mr. George.

Hundreds of pupils in joyous moods trooped out of the assembly hall into their classes to pick their bags and began to go home. I was excited that work that day had come to an end at last. I ran to my class, bubbling with ecstasy. But I got there only to find Alero surrounded by four other pupils. They all looked morose and sober.

"What is the problem?" I asked

"Somebody has stolen Alero's English Grammar book, she can't find it," replied Mewa.

"My father will smack me. He will say I am very careless and you know I am not," said Alero as she was crying.

I stood rooted to that spot, nervous and angry. I knew this was Fola's handiwork. I knew he was the one who stole the book. I had no doubt in my mind.

"So this was what he had gone out to do when I was looking for him. I asked him not to steal, in spite of the warnings, the devilish boy had gone ahead." I murmured. I felt very bad.

"I can't leave Alero wailing and crying. I am going to tell her the person who stole her book."
"But that won't be right," something warned me.
"Why not?" I asked.

"It will be a breach of trust. You cannot betray another man's confidence – don't you know that? It will bring more problems than the one you intend to solve."

For some minutes, I stood there rigid, staring at Alero, not knowing precisely what to do. I was in a great dilemma. Gradually, I moved closer to her and took her in my arms. I couldn't endure looking at Alero crying. I wanted to behave like a man but strangely my emotion failed me and I discovered that drops of tear were also coming down from my eyes. With my wet eyes, I talked to Alero.
"Don't cry," I told her.
"Daddy is not going to smack you."
"He will," she sobbed.
"I assure you, he won't. I have prayed. It's going to be well."
I tried all I could to calm her. I stared at her, for one

strange reason, Alero was now so fine and more attractive in her sorrow. With drops of tear coming down from her eyes, her dimples became so fine, her face became much lovelier than any other time I knew. In her distress, what made Alero so much a charming, young lady, came out now in the superlatives. Beauty, spell and sorrow mixed together – the three blended into magnetic, melting eyes, making Alero so angelic, so bewitching and yet so innocent.

I met Fola the following day and I took him to one corner, anger on my face.

"Why did you do what you did?"

"What did I do?" he asked me.

"You stole Alero's book. You disappointed me."

"Who told you that I stole her book?" matching his anger now with mine.

"Please, stop that gimmick. Don't try it on me. I am so sure you stole her book. I asked you not to steal, didn't I?"

"Yes, you did."

"And why did you still go ahead to steal it? After all those pleadings? After I seriously begged you not to do anything terrible?"

"Cool down, my friend! Yes I stole Alero's book. You aren't Princess Alero, are you?"

"Please stop that! Even if you decided to steal, why Alero's book?"

"Why not her book? You are neither her brother nor her relative - what is your own in the matter? Tell me!"

"Alero is my friend."

"But you never told me. Look here, do you want me to steal the book of a poor pupil whose parents may not have the means to replace it on time? Alero's father is a multi-millionaire. What is the cost of a grammar book to him?"

"And was that the reason why you stole her book?"

"Precisely."

"You are a funny character."

Alero brought a new grammar book to the class that morning. She was all smiles and sunshine. I looked at her beautiful palms and her lovely, straight legs, my passion ran riot. I just liked Alero. Her skin was like a polished ivory: smooth, cool and flawless. As we were about to sit down in the class, she looked at my direction and flashed at me one of her infectious smiles. She spoke to me with the eyes. Her messages were capsuled in form of facial codes. I was still trying to decode them when our teacher entered into the room and all attention now turned to him.

During the break-time that morning when all pupils had gone into the field to play, and only three of us remained in the class, Alero came to me, sat on the desk behind me, put her pretty hands on my shoulders, then scratched my hair soothingly and whispered:

"Mayo! Aren't you going to ask me what happened when I got home yesterday?"

"That was what I was about to ask you."

"Daddy did not quarrel with me. It was mom who was very angry."

"Why?" I asked her

"I told her that all my girl friends did not cry when I was crying but that you were the only one who cried."

"That shows how much Mayo likes you," she said.

"I know he likes me a lot."

"But princesses do not cry in the public. I have told you about that several times, haven't I?"

"Yes, you have," I replied.

"If I have told you, why did you cry? Why did you break the rule? Why couldn't you observe the formal etiquette and decorum expected of a Princess?"

"Mom, I am sorry. I did not know when my emotion snapped. Again, when I remembered that dad would not be happy with me..."

"Even with that, it is bad enough for a princess to be crying before her subjects," mom insisted.

"Mom. I won't do it again."

"Please, never repeat such thing," she told me.

"Is that all?" I asked her.

"That is all. But Mayo, I was going to ask you a question."

"And what is that?"

A narrow, sweet, smile lit Alero's face. She traced my face with her big eye balls slowly, and methodically, then queried:

"When you saw me crying, you also broke down and cried. Why did you cry?"

"I cried because I felt bad that you were going to be blamed for an offence you never committed. You were not careless yet you would have to take the blame for carelessness. You were put into trouble, yet you committed no offence. That made me feel bad. I must confess I did not know when I started to shed tears."

"You imagined that my dad would punish me – wasn't it?"

"Yes, you are right."

"And you did not want me to be punished?"

"No, I did not."

"From your eyes, I could read how you felt. I knew you would have willingly surrendered yourself to receive the punishment due to me. Am I right?"

"Yes, you are right."

"Mayo, I saw how you felt, but I am sure you have not confessed the actual reason why you were crying. I know you. If it were Mewa who lost her book in a similar circumstance, and she was crying, you would not have cried. I am not even sure whether you would have paid her any attention."

"That is true. If Mewa were the one crying, it would have meant nothing to me. In fact, I would have looked at her face, smiled and walked away".

"Mayo, I am happy you admit that."

She now turned her amorous face on me again, her big eyeballs now mesmerized me with energy. I was so young, and she also so young, but Alero's charms started to seduce me. She looked like an angel. Her sweet, innocent face was so pretty as she spoke:

"If you won't confess the truth why you were crying, I am going to tell you that truth because I know why you were crying."

"Why was I crying?" I asked her.

"You were crying because the girl involved is your bride."

Then I stared at her face and smiled. She winked infectiously at me, and said: "you were crying because you did not want your bride to be punished."

"Why should I? What is the essence of being a groom if one cannot protect the interest of one's bride?"

"That is the real issue. And why are you trying to run away from it?"

I stared at Alero, a pleasing smile lit my face. I knew she caught me this time. For a brief moment, we did not talk, only our faces were probing each other. I was staring at the world's loveliest and sweetest girl. But Alero soon broke the silence.

"When you saw me crying, I knew you were going to cry."

"How did you know?"

"I know you so much. I know how much you like me. I know your feeling for me is so strong. I know you cannot endure to see me cry. As you saw me crying, I knew what was going to happen. I knew you were going to cry and I was happy you did not disappoint me. I must also let you know that I like you so much. I must confess that I like you even the more for what you did. Why won't I like you? I know how passionate you are about me. You made me feel that I was not alone. You always make me feel that we are together and that you are always there for me. Among all my friends, you are the only one who always makes me feel that way."

I felt so tall that Alero could appreciate my little support. "And candidly what have I done to earn the kind words she spoke about me?" I asked myself.

"Mayo!"

"Yes, you want to say something?"

"No, I only wish to find out something from you."

"And what is it?"

"I know you like me a lot, but will you always like me?"

"Of course, yes."

"Will you always be my friend, even when I offend you?"

"Believe me sincerely, I will always be your friend."

"Mayo! You know a time I can be violent in my anger, particularly when I am annoyed, you want to promise me that you will still like me in spite of such weakness?"

"I like you the way you are. Even with all your faults, I like you still."

"Mayo, I want to tell you something, I have never told you before and I cannot tell anyone besides you."

"And what is it?"

"You want me to tell you?" her eyes opened wider and they became so charming.

"I felt you said you were going to tell me."

"As long as you like me, as long as you are my friend, do you know that I don't care about anything else in this world."

Wao! I suddenly felt as if I were not in control of myself. Alero's words made my brain run riot. Believe me, I had never heard anything so beautiful in my life. And coming from Princess Alero, who I so much admired, and who everyone venerated like a goddess, I felt intoxicated.

CHAPTER THIRTEEN

We were told one Monday morning that Mr. Moore, the school supervisor, an Englishman, based at Ado-Ekiti, the Divisional Headquarter, would be visiting our school. From the minute that announcement was made, the school put on a different aura. There was perfect silence everywhere. All our teachers suddenly looked morose and tense. It was as if a brigade of an enemy force was about to overrun the CMS School. I began to wonder what an hyena of a man Mr. Moore would be.

"Why is his impending visit bringing so much apprehension? Why are all our teachers trembling when he is yet to appear? What is he coming to do? Why is panic everywhere?"

I became very anxious to meet this official of the British Imperial Majesty who was yet to appear and yet the earth was already shaking. I felt so curious to see Mr. Moore's face and find out what kind of man he was.

I did not wait for too long. For around 10.a.m. on Thursday, a black Hillman drove to a halt in the front of the school, and a tall, white man came out of it. We knew that moment that the long expected visitor had arrived at last. Our teacher was the first person to see him. He signaled to us to sit erect. The headmaster, Mr. Adamu hurried out of his office towards the visitor, shook his hand and greeted him with a sort of reverence we had never seen him give to anyone. A narrow, mechanical smile lit the face of the visiting generalissimo who looked proudly at the hurriedly cut lawn and the neat environment, staring at the scenery like the victorious General surveying a recently conquered territory. Mr. Adamu led the way and the generalissimo swaggered into the headmaster's office. A terrifying, suffocating silence suddenly enveloped the entire school.

The visitor sat but Mr. Adamu remained standing with his two hands locked behind him as if he were on trial.
The silence everywhere thickened. Our class was adjacent to the headmaster's office. A thin wall of locally made mat separated the two. The same had one small hole very close to the very spot where I sat and from that hole I could see clearly what was going on.

The visitor brought several photographs out of his portfolio, looked through them, picked one and then handed it over to Mr. Adamu.
"What's going on here?" he asked.
Mr. Adamu held the picture, looked at it fixedly, stunned and speechless for a brief moment. He looked like someone who could not believe his eyes.
"Mr. Adamu, I say what's going on in that picture?"

"It is a child's naming ceremony, sir," he replied.

"Who is the mother of the child," the visitor queried.

"The woman carrying the baby in the picture," replied Mr. Adamu.

According to Yoruba traditions, the father of the child normally sits by the side of the mother during any child naming ceremony, since you are the man sitting with her in this picture - do I then assume the woman is your wife?"

"No sir," Mr. Adamu replied.

"Why are you sitting together? What is the connection?"

Mr Adamu mumbled his answers and I didn't get what he said.

"I put it to you that the woman is your wife," affirmed the visitor.

"No, sir," replied Mr. Adamu, his voice came up sharply. The visitor smiled cynically, gave three other pictures to Mr. Adamu and a letter of petition written by somebody. Mr. Adamu cast a quick glance at the pictures and then read through the petition. As he read through, his eyes gradually turned red.

"With the three pictures I had just given to you and the facts in that letter of petition, Mr. Adamu, are you now willing to concede that the woman is your wife?"

Mr. Adamu began to make some explanation.

"Mr. Adamu, I won't listen to that rigmarole. I don't want to hear more lies; just answer my question with either yes or no," the visitor suddenly raised his voice. Mr. Moore's face showed that he was fast losing his patience.

"The petition is a mere allegation," reacted Mr. Adamu.

"Mr. Adamu! Do you still say this is a mere allegation

despite the preponderance of facts in this letter? Oh my God! You are not prepared to admit your guilt and it makes me feel really sad. I feel highly disappointed Mr. Adamu that you can be treating your own career like this. Call in the Assistant Headmaster."

Mr. George entered the room and Mr. Moore turned to him.
"Please, take over the running of the school immediately. Mr. Adamu has ceased to be a member of staff."

The visitor stood up and walked into his car. The car soon roared into life, and in a minute, Mr. Moore was gone.
Later that day, we got through the grapevine that Mr. Adamu was fired because he had taken a second wife, an offence considered to be a very serious one by the CMS Authority; the owner of the school. I was at sea. I couldn't understand the rationale behind such a punishment. My father had four wives. If Mr. Adamu has only two – what is bad in that?" I queried. I knew that the Odofin, a high chief had sixteen wives. And the Oba had over twenty.
"How do we now accuse someone who had just two of any greed? What strange standards are the CMS Authority trying to enforce? Why is that body intruding into Mr. Adamu's privacy?" These were the questions I addressed to my mom immediately I got home.
"Adamu's offence is a very serious one," she told me.
"Why?"
"The only system of marriage the white man recognizes is one man, one wife. A man who decides to work for a white man, must obey the white man's rules. He who

pays the piper dictates the tune."

"What a peculiar kind of people are white people! What are people with strange customs and traditions!," I told mom.

The school had not fully recovered from the hurricane caused by Mr. Moore's visit when the week came to an end. The fact that it was a week of forced silence and a period when all the girls were asked to wait everyday to clean the classrooms after school hours, made me and Alero see less of each other. But as we trooped out of the school that afternoon and breathed a free air again, I felt very anxious to see Alero. I felt as if I saw her last almost a year ago. I wanted to look at her face, I wanted to admire her pretty, big eye balls. I wanted to look again at Alero's fine, straight legs and her tender, delicate palms. I wanted to touch her fine, shining skin which always seemed as if it was daily massaged by honey and butter.

I looked anxiously through the crowd.

"Has Alero gone home?" I asked.

Bravo! There she stood behind a flower. I hastened towards her. And immediately her eyes caught mine, she flashed at me her usual, nice, contagious smile and all my cells came alive.

"You this troublesome boy where have you been?" she asked me.

"I went to the classroom to pick my bag." I did not tell her that I was looking for her and that turned out to be a costly error.

I looked at Alero's face, her countenance suddenly changed and I didn't know why.

"Let us go," I told her as I held her hand. In the whole length and breadth of Toro CMS School, I was the only person privileged to hold the hand of Princess Alero. Not even a teacher enjoyed this rare privilege. Tell me! Why wouldn't I feel proud?

I stared at Alero as we walked down the road. She looked sad.

"You aren't looking bright today, what is the problem?" I asked her. Alero only stared at me but refused to talk.

"Alero! I say what is wrong with you?"

She stared at me again but would still not talk

"Won't you talk to me?" I screamed.

That probably triggered her off and she burst out:

"Once upon a time, I was your bride. You wouldn't leave this school without me by your side. I am afraid that situation has changed now. Mayo, when last did I see you? When last did you talk to me?. Even at closing time, you did not bother to wait for me anymore. You always abandoned me and went home. You always disappeared before the girls finished their cleaning of the classrooms. Whenever I looked around, I discovered that you had already gone home. I can see that you don't bother about me these days. Then she stopped, looked at my face and asked – "Am I still your bride?"

Alero's countenance was misty with emotion and she was about to cry.

"Alero! Why do you talk like this? Mr. George asked

all the boys to leave the school premises and go home and leave the girls to do the cleaning. I wanted to stay and wait for you but there was an order from above that I shouldn't. For the past three days I have been anxious to see you. And that is the reason why I made up my mind never to go home today until I see you. I was searching for you in the crowd when you saw me. Alero! You know that I like you. You can't deny it that I like you more than anyone in this world. Now, Alero, why are you quarreling with me? Why are you making me unhappy? What is my offence?" She stared at my face and kept mute.

"When I saw you, I had been looking for you for more than five minutes."

Alero smiled for the first time as she now asked:
"Did you want to tell me something?"
"No, I just want to see you, look at your face again, no more."
"Now, you've seen my face, what next?"
"Yes, I have seen your face. You are pretty. You are beautiful. You are lovely. All the time, I am just thinking about how much I like you."

She winked at me. She rolled her big eye balls. Young as Alero was, she knew what button to press to display her feminine power and she pressed those buttons now. Various amorous signals flashed from her eye balls and I became suddenly electrocuted. I had never seen her face in that kind of posture before. My entire structure seemed now to be crumbling under its radiance.

I held Alero's hand and we started to walk down the road. We walked arm in arm, listening now to the rhythm of each other's breathing. The touch of Alero's delicate, fine hand was thrilling. That touch was communicating various amorous signals to me. We soon passed through a small wood and came to a brook. None of the women who came to the brook to fetch water with their clay pots, was there that afternoon. We looked around, we saw no one. We were alone. In that heat of the tropical afternoon and under the shade of some mahogany trees, in the quiet solitude, Alero stared at my face and I stared at hers. Love was talking through all my cells and tissues but I didn't really know how to express the same by my words. We stood looking at each other and occasionally looking at the sparkling, clear, clean water of the brook before us because this was where Alero and I would have to part and each would take a different route home.

I stole a look at Alero's face again. That face was dazzlingly lovely and had not stopped to fascinate me. "Why has Alero become such a tormentor? Why is it that I enjoy no peace whenever I don't see her? Why is she so beautiful?" These were the questions in my mind as I stared at Alero's magnetic eyeballs.

I did not want to leave her. She also stared at my face curiously. She too did not want to leave me. For long, we were staring at each other's face. We did not talk only our love was talking. Our burning passion for each other was sending out now hot and sweet lava of love.

"Alero! I remember now that I wanted to tell you something," as I finally broke that afternoon silence.

"What is it?" she asked me, her eyes turning now with slow relish towards me.

"Hu n un un, it is something I have always loved to ask you. It is one issue that is often bothering my heart?"

"I say what is it?" she asked. There was a disarming smile on her face.

"I imagine that one time, one moment, one boy would want to take you away from me."

She stared at my face curiously.

"You said one boy would take me away from you - isn't that what you said?"

"Yes, that may probably happen one day."

"And you believe that? Don't you trust me?"

"I trust you."

"If you trust me, why should that ever cross your mind?"

She stared at my face for an answer.

"Well, I don't know."

Alero surveyed my face with a slow, understanding smile and said:

"Mayo! Nobody can take me away from you."

"Are you sure?" I asked her.

"I am sure or do you want a proof?"

I was yet to answer her question when Alero suddenly sprang forward, pulled me into her embrace, her lips met mine and her tongue went into my mouth - probing all directions and exploring the secrets of my mouth and sending fire of excitement as it went. It was too much for me and the thrill was too delicious. I had embraced Alero many times when we were much younger, but it was certainly not like this. I did not feel anything then. But there was a wondrous sweetness now in the heat that came to me from Alero's body. That was the first time, I would kiss a woman and also felt her warm embrace. The whole episode lasted about twenty seconds but it seemed like an experience of a thousand years. As we later stood there staring at each other, I didn't know when I exclaimed:

"You are sweet; you are charming. No one can take you away from me. I will contest and fight for every cell of this your lovely, pretty body."

Alero smiled shyly.
"There will be no reason to fight anyone because I am not going to leave you. You have chosen me as your bride, isn't it?"

"Yes, it is," I replied.
"Then I promise, I will forever remain your bride."

She stared at my face again. I also stared at hers. Alero's face was incredibly beautiful. Her lovely eye balls rolled enticingly in their sockets as she turned those large amazing eyes on me. The rays from those eyes were becoming too intoxicating. Alero drew me closer and whispered quietly into my ear:
"I am the yoke, you are the albumen.
Together nature had destined us.
The snail cannot do without its shell.
The eagle cannot do without its feathers.

The ship cannot do without its rudder.
The moon cannot do without the earth.
The tongue cannot do without the mouth.
The vowel cannot do without the consonant
So also, I cannot do without you."
Wow! I burst out in a yell of delight. I had never heard anything more beautiful in my life. That Alero told me that she could not do without me, suddenly got me drunk with excitement.

I stared at Alero's face, the charming adorable Princess of Toro. She had an extraordinary grace around her. She had an extraordinary beauty too. A glamorous princess but whenever she was with me, she never carried the toga of her royalty with her. She always became an ordinary girl. It was that kind of girl that spoke to me now as Alero whispered again:
"Mayo, you may not believe me but I have to tell you all the same that something always tells me that God created me for you. I still remember now how I heard a voice on the way to the brook one day which said:

'I have created you for Mayo and no one else.' I looked left and right, I saw no one. What I say, does it sound strange to you?"
"No, it does not."
"Why not?"
"It doesn't because something I cannot equally explain always tells me similar things. For example, one voice in my dream talked to me few weeks ago and said:
'Among the world's women, I am going to give you Alero.'

Alero! Aren't you too surprised by this too?"

"No, I am not."

"Why are you not?"

"I am not surprised because what both of us are experiencing only confirm what one man of God said recently."

"What did he say?"

"He said that everything God created was created to solve a problem. For example because of the problem of seeing, God created the eyes, because of smelling, He created the nose, because of hearing, He created the ears, because of walking, He created the feet and because of …"

I sprang forward quickly, drew Alero closer and whispered to her right ear, "…and because of Mayo, He created Alero."

My words sent a rushing thrill through her and she screamed like someone who had won a million dollars in a popular lottery. She held me by the waist and stared at my face and said:

"Come on Mayo! Let us talk about some other things. You remember I too was looking for you, you haven't asked me why?"

"Why?"

"I want to give you something." My eyes opened wider.

"And what is that?"

"Look at him. Don't be too anxious now," she warned as her eyebrows rose and fell in a manner that made her face look so irresistible. Looking at her was very arousing. I was going to grab her and kiss her now that I had been introduced into the mysterious science of kissing but I stopped at the last moment as I saw her putting her hand into her bag, brought out two beautiful ripe mango fruits and gave them to me. My brain ran riot. Nearly everyday, Alero had been showing to me the practical demonstration of her love for me.

"What else do I want? What else do I want God to do for me that He has not done already?" I asked myself. I felt so proud.

"The celebrated Princess of Toro, the one everyone venerates and adores belongs to me as a fruit tree belongs to the gardener," I muttered.

A man who had stumbled on a rich field of gold could not have been happier than I am.

CHAPTER FOURTEEN

As I walked home that afternoon, there were springs in my steps. I looked again and again at the beautiful fruits that Alero gave me; my spirit was elated. My heart thrilled with excitement. The fruits could not cost more than a few pence but the difference was that they were gifts from a Princess. That made them so priceless and special. That Princess Alero showed and demonstrated that she so much loved me, made me feel happier than the angels living in heavenly places.

Now, I could appreciate that there was nothing more powerful than the bond of love. As I admired the fruits and looked at their fleshy skins, I made up my mind to surprise Alero the following Monday by giving to her the biggest and the most delicious apricots she had ever seen.

❀ ❀ ❀ ❀ ❀ ❀ ❀

Pa Richard's residence which lay down the corner, was a stone's throw from our house. He had a beautiful orchard of mango, pear, orange trees and apricots of special species. They were nurtured by some agriculturists and they had very nice taste. The fruits were now ripe for harvest. But the orchard was fenced round by a high wall making it virtually inaccessible to any external intruders. Pa Richard, a veteran of the Second World War who claimed to have fought the Japanese under the British Brigadier Wingate in Burma, Borneo and the forests of Indonesia, lived like a hermit in a small bungalow inside this orchard. His wife died before he returned from the war, and since the couple had no child, Pa Richard naturally transferred all his affection to his fruits which he guarded so jealously. But his hoarding of the fruits ended that day.

I had invited my three friends Fola, Tunde and Dada to join me under the acacia trees behind our home. The four of us had become so intimate in the last few years.

"Boys! There is an important assignment to do," I told them.

"When and where?" asked Fola. He was a dare-devil kind of character. There was no evil his brain could not conceive. He looked at my face desperately anxious to hear what I had to say.

"The apricots of Pa Richard are ripe for harvest. You know how delicious apricots are?" I asked.

"Slightly bitter but sweet, a blend of sweet and bitter but extremely tasty," said Fola.

"Good!

Pa Richard's apricots are of special breed – fleshy, succulent and very fat. We only need to sneak into his orchard and pick as much as we want and come back home to enjoy ourselves.

I have thought hard in the last few days on what can give us an exciting game. Something told me this morning that no other thing can provide a good sport than going into a no-go area, and my mind went straight to Pa Richard's orchard. No one dares go to Pa Richard's orchard; that is the story everywhere. Whenever the man roars, everyone trembles. He is an ex-soldier; he is an atomic bomb. He will explode and destroy people and houses. The man has become a small god. I want us to demystify this old, famous, veteran and derobe him of his toga of invincibility and arrogance. I want us to take the extraordinary off him and show him to the world that he is just an ordinary man after all. I have always believed that the art of doing the impossible is what makes a man. As young boys, I feel we must have the ambition of doing the unusual, I mean something exceptional and unique."

"Mayo! I love you for that statement," said Fola. "I love new things. I love new adventures. I love to break rules. I love to break traditions. I love to break new grounds. I love to do what others consider impossible. Mayo! God bless you. We are going to Pa Richard's orchard."

For the next one and half hours, we rehearsed our plans over and over again until we mastered it to the minutest details. Tagged "OPERATION SILENCE RICHARD (OSR)," its critical features were: speed, accuracy and surprise. Operation Silence Richard went into action that Friday at exactly 5.30p.m.

According to the plan, Fola and I would climb the tree

115

and pick the fruits. Tunde would gather them into a sack. Dada would stand at about twenty metres distance from the tree towards the direction of Pa Richard's house, watching carefully the movement of the old man. At his approach, Dada would give a signal. Tunde would rush to the wall, throw the sack containing the fruits over it; lift himself over the fence and escape. Those on the tree would jump down quickly, the one who alerted and the two from the tree would run into three different directions towards the wall; jump over and escape. I had never seen a programme so brilliantly executed.

'Operation Silence Richard' was a great success. That evening, the movements were mathematically precise. They were so beautiful. I recalled that I was still aiming for a fruit when I heard Dada's voice, "IT IS TIME FOR THE EAGLES TO FLY!" That was the signal saying Pa Richard was coming. I jumped down from the tree and landed softly like a cat. Fola landed few seconds before me and I saw the four of us dashing like missiles towards the wall. Pa Richard shouted on top of his voice:
"Stop there! I say stop!"

Shouting has no arresting power; we didn't stop. Who dared stop and wait for an ex-soldier?

I ran desperately towards the wall, the old man charged furiously behind us. I remembered that two metres to the wall, I flew and held on to the top of it. A second after, I sat comfortably on the top of the wall. Pa Richard was about six or seven metres away. I did not bother to jump down from the wall. Why should I miss the marathon race of a sixty-year old man and this for free?

"Run! Run Pa Richard, Run!" We started to hail him. I stretched out my right hand, getting ready to shake the hand of this old veteran, the famous Victor of the Swamp of Burma. It must have occurred to him that a sudden dash forward would perform the trick, and he dashed forward, my leg escaped his grip by a split of a second. I sprang like lightning and landed softly behind the wall.

"Pa Richard! I am a shadow; No one catches a shadow. No one can hold the wind. No one can bind darkness and make it its prisoner. No one ever holds water in a basket. Never. No one can embrace a mirage. You can never catch me."

"May evil spirit torment your mother. May thunder strike you dead. May demons and bad spirits continue to molest your peace. As you have tortured an old man, may all of you die of torture and torment," the angry man barked.

I could hear his ranting as he walked back to his house. While his anger and complaints continued, we smiled home with our fruits.

The following day at 5.p.m., we were back in Pa Richard's orchard. The old famous veteran of the Second World War, the great jungle fighter of Burma, had murdered sleep and Pa Richard shall sleep no more. There was one and only one narrow path he could take to the apricot trees. As we sneaked into the garden that evening, we tied three ropes across this very path in three places and at three metres interval. The bushes all along the narrow, winding path were waiting to be cut and the three ropes were hidden inside them so cleverly that no one could suspect they were there.

"Yes! The traps are set. We are now battle ready." I told my colleagues.

Today, we were more confident than we were on our first trip. We were already on the top of the tree when we heard the roaring of Pa Richard.

Pa Richard charged out as a lion charges out of his den, fierce and ferocious.

"It's time for the eagles to fly," shouted Dada.

The warning sent a chill through me. I didn't know why. Fola and I had planned behind the two other boys not to jump down from the tree immediately. We wanted to watch Pa Richard.

"Whatever happens, the traps are there... They can't fail us," assured Fola.

But as Pa Richard charged out, no one could wait for the violent hurricane sweeping everything as he approached. We jumped down from the tree and took to our heels. Pa Richard's voice suddenly changed, he bellowed. The bull raced angrily after us. I heard his heavy footsteps behind me. They appeared like the steps of three or four elephants on top speed. The veteran was a good sprinter.

"I am done for," I muttered. "I have taken a wild and stupid gamble."

That second when I almost froze with fear, there was a loud crash. I first jumped up and then spun around to see what was happening. Pa Richard was lying face down. I waited and stared at him. Then he looked up, saw me staring at him, my lips now lit with a mischievous, derisive smile. The scorn on my face stung him like a poisoned arrow. My effrontery baffled him.

Boiling, his face radiating a rising anger, he sprang up quickly.

"Boy! You are in trouble." He was desperate now to catch me and he knew no matter how I ran; he would level up with me before I got to the wall. But I knew why I stopped and waited. My confidence was based on something unknown to the veteran. Pa Richard rushed forward in a frenzy of impatience into a carefully laid up trick. The second rope seized his legs. The force of his movement was so great that the rope broke into two. The old man staggered like the drunk, trying desperately now to maintain a balance and suddenly ran into the third rope and came down heavily.

We were already on the top of the wall watching this old soldier who had now become that evening entertainer. The four of us burst into a huge prolonged laughter.

"Good for you Pa Richard! Good for you!"

"Pa Richard! Don't just stay there lying down. Rise up and give us more dramas. We are enjoying your show. Stand up, give us more entertainment," I told him.

The old man remained on the floor for several minutes. He stayed there in a thick cloud of humiliation. He closed his eyes and took deep, anxious breaths. Later, he raised up his head, stared into space, his face sad and gloomy. Never in his life was he so humbled. Trembling with anger, the man finally rose up and walked away.

CHAPTER FIFTEEN

I t was late in the afternoon on Sunday when we struck again. Fola and I climbed the tree and the other associates took their positions. There were two robust, fleshy, ripe apricots on the top of the branch on which I was and I made up my mind to pick them.

"They are the ones I am going to give to Alero on Monday;" I decided within myself.

For over ten minutes, we were on the top of the tree, feeling so relaxed, unmolested and unperturbed.

"Boys! What's happening? We haven't heard the bellows of the bull today?" I said.

"The bull is not at home," replied Fola.

"That will be a serious matter."

"How? How does his absence disturb you?"

"There will be no entertainment. There will be no fun."

"How important is that? We neither come here for fun nor entertainment. We are here to pick fruits and we have got so many; the sack is already full," exclaimed Fola.

"I prefer the funs to the fruits. Pa Richard is a fantastic

entertainer. I can pay a million pounds to watch his performance any day. I want something to enliven my spirit."

I am afraid, your spirit will need to enliven itself today; Pa Richard is not at home."

"There is one aspect of the man I find so intriguing," exclaimed Tunde.

"And what is that?"

"The man always talked so much about his exploits.
He was a guest of my father one day. He talked for almost three hours, all about himself. The talk centered on his various exploits in the Eastern campaigns during the Second World War. All his listeners that day were illiterates; men who had never gone outside Toro in their lives. Speaking about Burma, Indonesia, Malaysia – all strange names many thousands of miles away, Pa Richard seemed to all the men who were listening to him like someone who had just landed from the moon. They all stared at him spellbound. With relish, he went on from one story to another:

'I remember one night in a village in Burma when I fought single-handedly with twenty Japanese and I subdued them…' said Pa Richard.

'Or another day when I led a brigade against the enemy force in the swamp of Borneo. My God! What a day! What a battle!'

'Or one memorable morning when the enemy forces encircled us in the Island of Iwo Jima. My white officers were fretting and shaking. But our enemies regretted. I gave them hell. That day, Brigadier Wingate decorated me with a medal of bravery…'

"That is great!" said my father.

"That is more than marvelous," said another man

"The great son of Apampa, the Victor of Kiriji War, we do not expect anything less from you. Your father was a great warrior. We know that you will live up to your father's reputation wherever you find yourself," said yet the third man.

Pa Richard walked arrogantly up and down before his friends, hands in pockets, chest out, head standing perpendicularly on his neck, looking morose like a man who had lost his patience, the self-acclaimed conqueror of the Japanese, the Victor of Iwo Jima, the most gigantic soldier of modern time, swaggered before his admirers, so pleased with himself."

"And they all believed the braggart?" asked Fola.

"Why wouldn't they believe him. In any case, he was the only one who got to Burma, Malaysia and their likes. The other men weren't there."

"What he told your father and his friends were mere fabrications and lies from start to finish. I met one ex –service man just a week ago. The same told my father that Pa Richard was not a soldier. He never took part in any of the battles. He was never so near any battle-line as to hear the sounds of guns. He said if he'd heard the sounds of mortars and tanks, he would run into hiding. He said Pa Richard was just a common cook in the kitchen."

"A cook?" I asked in disbelief.

"Yes, a cook," replied Fola.

"My Goodness! A cook masquerading as a veteran of Second World War? Boys! Why are we running from a cook? Why are we running from a common rat pretending to be an hyena? Why are we running from a lizard that pretends to be an alligator? It is insulting that we had been running from an ordinary cook since all these days. As from today, I am not going to flee before him. I am going to wait for him and let him call down fire and brimstone, if he so desires," I asserted.

Just that moment, there was a stir. I heard a movement below. I stopped talking suddenly; then looked down. Somebody was standing under the tree and my associates were now running desperately now towards the wall. I felt suddenly dizzy.

"What is happening? Who is the man standing below? What is his mission? Pa Richard is not at home and no one lives with him – where comes this other man? What does he want in Pa Richard's garden?"
I stared at him again and again. Just that moment, I realized with a thrill of terror that the man standing below was Pa Richard!

"What? How did he get to where he is? Why did Dada fail to give the usual signal? Who and what alerted my colleagues?"

There was no one to answer these series of questions. Pa Richard had for once behaved like a soldier and he had laid an ambush for us and I had walked into it. I stared at the bull and the bull stared at me; his face now a whirlwind about to tear off half of the earth in its fury. His chest heaved up and down like a landscape experiencing heavy tremors. His body furious and wild like a volcano about to erupt and overturn a whole city in its rage and anger. My heart was thudding inside me. For a moment, I was dizzy with fear. With horror written all over my face, I stared at him.

"What can I do now?" I asked myself. My mind was reeling with various options.
"Come down, my dear boy;" said Pa Richard.
"Justice has finally caught up with you at last. There is no escape route for you, just come down." The tone was of pure relish and triumph. I stared at him, but remained where I was.

"Boy! Are you deaf? I say come down!" he thundered in a loud, dreadful, intimidating voice, his mood furious and impatient. Man will not die two times. Now I made up my mind to face the bull. I stared at Pa Richard, unmoved and unperturbed. I did not come down. I sat down as if I did not hear him.

"Boy! If you are a bird, you can fly but I am afraid, you have no feathers. You can't fly away. You have no choice than to come down. Come down and take your punishment. I am going to make you a public example. I am going to teach you a lesson you will forever remember. But note, the more you keep up there, the greater your punishment. You have a choice to come down right now."
I stared at him with burning concentration and insolence. Then I smiled; it was a smile of disdain. Suddenly, I let out a huge roar of laughter.

He looked left and right for the person laughing because he did not believe that I was the one. When he saw no one, he looked up again and asked:

"Boy, are you the one laughing?"
"Yes, I am the one," I replied.
"What is amusing?"
"Big, old man! It's you. You amuse me a lot."
"What? You say I amuse you?"
"Yes, you do because you speak like one famous, foolish, old clown that I know."
"Me a foolish clown?" he asked with an imperious voice; his face emitting fire.
"Yes, you are a clown."

Pa Richard stared at me again, his fingers trembling now with anger.
"Me? Me, a foolish clown?" A demonic rage welled up inside him and ran out of control.
"Old man! I have no apology for saying what I said. You are a foolish clown, a very big one at that."
"You are in serious trouble. Now come down!"
"Assuming I choose not to, what will you do?"
"I will force you down and right now."
"You! You!" I pointed to him. "Old man! You think too much of yourself."
"Me?"
"You!"
"This one has gone crazy. Who fathered this kind of child? From whose womb came out this wayward offspring?"

"Old man! Don't say anything about my parents. I

have been very charitable to you so far. I have been so patient listening to your rigmarole. I know you are an ex-soldier; a tough and no-nonsense man. But today you will also know that you are not the only man of steel. Now I command you, leave that place."

"Which place?" he queried, surprise on his face.
"I say, leave where you are standing, and leave there quickly."
"Me?"
"Yes! Keep moving. I give you only five seconds. If you don't leave where you are, you will blame yourself."
"Me?" he asked again, puzzled and unbelieving.
"You! Old man! You will have enough regret if you don't behave precisely as I command you. You are warned."
"My God! What is happening? What is the world turning to?" he muttered.
"Boy! If I don't leave; what will you do?"
"I will do a thousand things."

That moment, I threw at him one big unripe, apricot. It was a heavy fruit and it hit him hard on the shoulder blade.

"Ye! Ye! My God!" The old man screamed loudly as he held on to his shoulder, and danced up and down in agony like a masquerade. I followed that quickly with another fruit, which hit him at the back of his neck.
"Ye!… Ye!… Ye!…" he let out another loud scream.
"Old man! Look here! I am not up here for a joke. Leave that place! You have been warned." Pa Richard

held on to his aching neck. He was groaning in serious pain. But he still stood on the same spot. I had never seen such a stubborn, old man. I wouldn't want to, but now I had to play my next joker, and if that failed, then I would play the very last one; that is, bring out my catapult and finish the job. I was prepared to fight this battle with everything in my arsenal.

"Pa Richard! Your very last warning! Leave that place. I say leave if you really value your life. This place is neither the swamp of Burma nor the Island of Iwo Jima where you were a legend. I warn you, you are playing with fire."

That moment, I threw the biggest fruit, a heavy, unripe apricot at the bald head of Pa Richard. The throw was dead accurate. It hit him hard right at the centre of his head, which looked like the ugly, arid surface of the Sahara.

"O pa mi o!" (Meaning: "he has killed me") shouted Pa Richard, as he suddenly let out a loud agonizing scream. He fell down and convulsed for several seconds like an epileptic patient. Then the body became stiff. I stared at him in alarm. The old man's body lay there rigid. I could see he was unconscious.

"My God! I have killed the old man. I am in trouble … real serious trouble. What do I do now?"

"Boy! You need to get out of here pretty quick. Run; don't wait! If the police catches up with you, you are in for a serious trouble. Run! I say run!" something warned me.

"My God! I never intend to kill Pa Richard. I only

wished to scare him off." I looked right and left, there was nobody in sight. That meant nobody would know who killed the old man. It would be several days before his stinking body would be discovered. I felt a great pity for him. I was very unhappy that the old, innocent man should die defending what legitimately belonged to him. I felt really bad that I was the instrument used by Death this time around.

I descended hurriedly from the tree, and about six feet to the ground; I jumped and landed on a heap. Wasting less than a second, I sprang forward and leapt in the air like the tiger. Then, something happened. Some unknown hands suddenly gripped my legs in the air and I fell down. I turned round. Alas! Pa Richard had resurrected from the dead. Horrified, I stared at him unbelievingly; just like Mary staring at the resurrected body of Lazarus. For some few seconds, I was so dazed that I could not think of anything. Pa Richard's face broke into a grin, terrifying smile.

"My dear boy! You are going nowhere. You are a terribly wayward and unruly character but you can't beat me in this kind of game. You may know a few tricks but you are meeting the master of the game. I had been in it for long. You had fought me with everything you have. Now the real battle is just starting."
He pounced on me. I struggled with him for about two minutes. He gripped my legs so hard that I knew further struggle was out of the question. I was in trouble.
"You are in for it. An antelope that goes to relax in the

den of a lion never goes free. The rodent that takes his siesta in the bed of a cobra should blame no one for his folly. The dog that invites a lion into a duel cannot but have enough regrets. The hen that goes into the house of the fox to eat some corns had invited trouble and she will surely get it. I know justice will catch up with you one day but I never know that it can be so soon."

Pa Richard wore a savage look, his angry voice rose up and fell like a drowning wind in a storm. He brought out a chain somewhere near the tree, chained my two legs together; then my two hands and lastly, chained me to the tree. Then, he moved closer and whispered softly to my left ear:

"My dear boy! You can now relax and enjoy yourself. Pa Richard, the cook, is going to prepare a real, delicious dish for you. It's bye for now."

Soon after he left me under the tree, Pa Richard went home. The time was around 5.p.m.

"How long will he keep me here in his garden? Will he abandon me here overnight under the terrible harmattan cold?" I guessed he would not.

I examined the locks of the chain in my hand and fought desperately to set myself free. The struggles were futile. My mind wandered to my three associates who had now abandoned me to my fate. Somebody said that in the period of adversity, friends normally melted away like snow in the morning sun. I could see the truth behind that saying very clearly now. Suddenly I remembered Alero, then a smile came on my lips.

"My previous plan will still go on as scheduled." I exclaimed. "We have more than enough apricots in the sack taken away by one of my colleagues. I will select few beautiful ones from them and give them to Alero on Monday. It's going to be a surprise package all the same."

Now I became excited. I didn't feel depressed anymore. I imagined how pleased Alero would be when I gave her the beautiful fruits.

"Wao! Big fleshy, lovely, succulent apricots! Mayo! Where did you get all these? I haven't seen these species before!" I could imagine Alero now asking me such questions. I could see Alero now in my mind's eyes, giving me that special, infectious smile. I could see that wondrous sweetness, that magnificent tenderness that made Alero such an enchanting Princess. Now I felt so good.

Having spent about twenty minutes sitting down and resting my back on the apricot tree, in this airy and lovely prison, I started to doze. Some minutes later, I slept. How long I slept, I did not know, but I woke up suddenly hearing the sounds of some approaching steps. I looked up. I saw Pa Richard walking towards me.

"What does the old man want again?" I queried.
"He must be coming to release you," something suggested to me.
"Release after about an hour? That sounds great! It will be fantastic." I said excitedly. I recalled now that old people are always very kind to children. With that discovery, I became hopeful that I might be out of my chain earlier than expected. Inside me, my heart was jumping up. A thrill of excitement was cruising through my veins. I stared at my chain, I said:

"It's all over at last. Thank God for all his mercy. I had imagined that my punishment would be much serious than this."

But as Pa Richard drew closer, I perceived that he was carrying a whip. My eyes opened wide with fear.

"What?" I queried. I closed my eyes, opened them and closed them again, and took deep, anxious breaths. My heart beat fiercely, my fingers now trembling. Horrified, I stared at Pa Richard as he approached furiously and with increasing impatience, looking like an angry demon whose face showed that danger and destruction waited in his hands.
"No sane person will flog a 13-year old boy with this type of leather whip Pa Richard was carrying. No one can be so cruel," I muttered. "But how sane is Pa Richard? How merciful can be a man who has no child of his own?"
A mixture of fear and alarm came on my face as this

terribly frightening monster drew closer.

"Boy! I am going to teach you the greatest lesson of your life. By the time I finish with you, not only will you daily remember this day, you will have become a very sober and sane person."

Then came the first lash! I jumped up but the chain rigidly held me in position.

"Ye! Ye! My God, I am dead!" I screamed loudly. The whip hit me like a stab from a hot dagger and removed the outer layer of my skin. The pain was most unbearable. Too cruel, just too cruel.

My body was gyrating, contorting into all manners of shapes when the second lash came stinging so hard and biting like the bee.

"Where are you, God? Are you listening to me? Help me; please help me!" I cried.

"God did not ask you to steal nor did He ask you to insult an elder; did He?"

"No!...No! He didn't."

"Then, leave God out of this. Don't get Him involved in a matter which least concerns Him. In any case, God cannot answer you. His ears are not open to the cry of a thief and an unrepentant miscreant like you."

Now, I was sure that I was going to die. He gave me twelve strokes in all. When he had pleased himself, he set me loose, opened his gate for me and asked me to get out of his compound.

For two weeks, I could not go to school. I was all the while on my sick bed. My parents refused to report the matter to the police. Since this was a punishment, I received in a stealing expedition; they felt it was a punishment well deserved.

My three friends did not know precisely what happened. I told mom not to disclose to any of them my experience should any of them decide to check on me at home.

CHAPTER SIXTEEN

I was so sure Alero would look for me. But I didn't want her to see my bruises. I did not want her to see me in my naked, ugly condition. I did not want her to know what happened. She just must not see me as I was. "How do I explain to her?" I asked myself over and over again. This was an ugly episode, and it was better to keep it to myself. So during the two weeks I kept at home, I relocated to grandma's house.

"Don't tell Alero where I am. You may tell her that I have traveled with my uncle. You may tell her that I have gone on a trip. You may tell her I had gone for the survey of my father's farm. But don't tell her what actually happened. Never tell her where I am," I told mom, almost begging.

"Alero came here many times;" Mom told me the night I was back. "Mayo has traveled and he is not yet back," I told her. "On Saturday, I mean yesterday, she came three times. She was desperately eager to see you. She would not tell me why but I knew there was something in the air! I didn't know what it was. I looked at her, there were tears on her face."

"What's wrong?" I asked her.

"Nothing ma," she replied.

"She was not happy and I began to wonder why. Have you taken anything from her that she wants to have back?"

"No, I haven't?"

"Why was she crying then?"

"Mom, don't worry yourself about that. You don't understand."

"What is it that I don't understand?"

"Mom, I say don't worry. I will see Alero in the school tomorrow."

"You'll better see her."

I was in school early the following day. It was a bright, lovely Monday. The sun came out early and in a radiance that wooed every heart. I recalled that all the days I kept at grandma's place, there was no second I did not remember Alero. Everyday, my whole frame quivered with expectancy and longing to see her again and drink from her soul tempting glance and large luminous eyes which when they dazzled, I immediately became Alero's willing slave.

Today, I was going to see her. That alone made me feel so excited. There were springs in my steps. I was yet to see her but I was already drunk by the sweet imagination of her presence. As I walked towards the

CMS School that morning, my spirit soared like an eagle. Happiness surged inside me like a violent ocean tide. I got to the school and looked anxiously for Alero. She was not one of the early arrivals. When that morning session started, Alero had not arrived and I began to wonder why.

When the school closed in the afternoon, Alero was yet to surface. Why? I didn't know. The barometre of my happiness dropped below the zero point. As I walked home, I was not in a pleasant state of mind.

"Cheer up, boy," I began to encourage myself.
"Alero will be around tomorrow. Your agony has a time limit. It will only last another twenty-four hours. You don't need to be downcast, my friend!"

"Mayo! Mayo!" I just heard that moment a soft, lovely, feminine voice calling me from behind. I turned round.
"Bravo! Alero is around after all!" I screamed. But why was she not in class? Where was she? Where was she hiding? For God's sake, where had she been to? She just must explain to me where she was." I wore a pugnacious look. Alero certainly has a case to answer. I stood there stern-looking and belligerent. My mind was still going over the various questions I would ask her when I realised it was Mewa who was now hasting towards me. She looked like someone who had an important message.

"Alero and I were looking for you on Friday. Where were you?" she queried.
"I was in my grandma's house. I had been sick for sometime," I replied.

"Where is Alero? Do you know where she is?" Those were the questions I wanted to ask her but my spirit told me to let her finish first. In fact, Mewa had started talking and I had to wait.

"On Saturday, we were in your place, Alero and I went to your house three times that day alone. She was so anxious to see you. When we couldn't find you and she didn't know where and how to contact you, she broke down. For minutes, she was crying. I tried all I could to console her but she would not. Mayo! Why did you do that to her? Why must you make her cry? Where on earth were you? Alero wanted to inform you that she was leaving the school."

"What?" I asked as my eyes opened wider with shock.

"I say she is leaving this school."

"And why and where is she going?"

"She is not just going, she had already left for Accra."

"Accra, Ghana or where do you mean?"

"Yes, as a matter of fact, she left Toro for Lagos on Saturday around 3p.m. in her aunt's car – and from Lagos, I understand she and her aunt would travel on a big ship to Accra, the capital of Ghana. She told me that she was going to Accra to live with the said aunt. I understand that her aunt's husband works at the Headquarters of West African Examinations Council in Accra."

I stood there rigid while my burning eyes gazed at Mewa curiously.

"Can her story be true?" I asked myself, now confused, and unbelieving.

"Don't just stand there staring at me in surprise. For two days, Alero looked frantically for you; she couldn't find you. She wanted to talk to you; you were nowhere to be found. Now, you are staring like a man who has missed his way in the Sahara."

I still could not believe Mewa but whatever it might be worth, I blurted out.
"Did Alero give you her contact address in Accra?"
"No she didn't."
"How soon is she likely to be in Toro again?"
"I am not sure of the time. She told me that she would probably not come back to Toro for a long time."
I erupted in a peal of laughter. I knew Mewa was up for a game. I was sure this was a cock and bull story - It was a mere drama, but a drama of a fool.

"Mewa! Are you sure you are in your right senses? How do you want me to believe all what you are saying? Do you think I am a fool?"
"You may believe or you may not. That is your own cup of tea. Why do I need to waste my precious time, talking to you in the first place?" she asked in anger as she started to walk away.

I knew Mewa was acting a script in a drama
I knew she would only walk for some distance, then turn round and scream:
"Mayo! I was only trying to tease you. Your Alero is at home." But as she walked down the road, Mewa never looked back. She got to the end of it, turned a bend and disappeared. I was not moved. I knew she would hide for some minutes behind a wall and later

reappear. I stood on the same spot, waiting for this lovely clown but she never appeared again.

I walked down the street. I was going to fish her out from her hiding place but I discovered strangely that she had gone!

"Is it possible that Alero has gone to Ghana?" I asked again and again. I decided to find out. I hastened to Alero's house. I met her mother right in the front of her home. I greeted her and just as Alero's name was coming out of my mouth, she looked at me inquiringly and said:

"She left Toro on Saturday for Accra. Didn't she tell you that she was traveling?"

I stood there frozen. For many seconds, I stared at her in stony silence.

"Mama! You mean Alero has gone?" I asked, when I finally found my voice.

"Are you saying, she didn't tell you about it?"

"I have not been at home for sometime," I stammered.

"Oh, that is the reason. She is gone to Accra to live with her aunt."

"Mama, can you give me her address?"

"I am sorry, I don't know her address yet. The aunt is arranging a special elite school for her. She is going to be in a boarding school and she makes me understand that only she, her guardian, will have access to her in the place. If for example, I decide to write her a letter, it will not be delivered to her. The letter will only be sent to her aunt, her guardian. When I eventually know the address, if I give it to you, it may serve no useful purpose because if you write her, the letter may not be delivered to her."

"Mama, when is she coming back to Nigeria?"

"I don't know, may be three or four years. Her aunt only comes home once in a blue moon."

I stared at her open-mouthed. My confusion was greater than that of a man who had lost his way in the Amazon forest.

"Mama! Thank you," I stammered when I finally recovered from my shock.

"Extend my warm regards to your mom, my boy."

I walked down the street devastated, too confused and too bewildered to take a breath. I was miserable. In the blink of an eye, my entire world had changed. The bottom had fallen out of my life. Soon, I got to one popular bridge near our house. There, I stopped. Enveloped in a thick cloud of sorrow, I stared at the water below and moaned:

"My Alero has gone to Accra."

I rolled that sentence in my mouth over and over like a dog rolling a big bone which it was finding it difficult to swallow. Now, sorrow held me motionless. For several minutes, I stood there choked by emotion. Later, I observed that I was crying.

"But why should Alero fly away like a dream? Why should she vanish like a vision in the night? Why must she abandon me when I need her most? Why? … Why?"

CHAPTER SEVENTEEN

Alero and I had been together, grown up together in the quiet, and lovely district of Central Toro. In those early and critical years, together we shared each other's pains and joy. Daily, we walked to school facing the human hyenas and lions who were our teachers, comforting each other in times of trouble, nursing each other's bruises and holding each other when our steps faltered. Together, we shared ideas, forged common commitments and resolved to face the future.

We had become so close, much closer than people connected by blood. I was the bone; Alero was my flesh. She was the snail; I was the shell. We had vowed that nothing except death would separate us. That was our promise to each other. I never knew that a force, greater than any of us but not death, could do as much.

I liked Alero with all the cells of my being. She was not just part of me, she was my life. She was the flesh of my flesh and bone of my bone. She was my missing link; the vital component without which my chemistry was not complete. She was the button that switched on my human machine, the key that opened the door to my heart. She was the grease that eased all my joints without which my engine would ground to a stop. She was the one that animated my soul and spirit. For example, it was her look that always enlivened me and put my spirit on a high gear. It was her smile that gave me all the sunshine I needed. It was the radiance from her luminous eyeballs that got my body warm and heated during the morning cold. She was simply everything to me. But apart from this, Alero was an embodiment of love, a fountain of affection, a soulmate in time of trouble. Alero was the only sincere friend that I knew. With Alero, life had meaning; without her, life became one long stretch of impenetrable gloom and regret.

For weeks, the memory of Alero's departure from Toro pestered me like a bad dream. It tormented me like a stubborn demon that refused to leave. It pained me like a terrible sore that refused to heal. The fact that I did not know where to contact her subjected me to a mental torture, which I could scarcely cope with at that time and age. Nobody, not even my mother visualized the depth of the wound that Alero's abrupt departure from Toro had inflicted on my heart. It was like depriving a drowning man his only life-saving jacket. It was the cruelest act I had ever experienced in life. Let us face it and let us reason together, what business did Alero have in Accra? What training did she need that she could not get in Nigeria and had to go to Ghana to get? What was the basis for her movement? If indeed she was crying, and it was true she was crying while looking for me, my guess could only be that she was not pleased to go! Why was she forced to go against her will? Why is the world so cruel? What is our offence?

For some strange reason, I kept on believing that Alero would not stay long in Accra. When she didn't see me for a long time, I guessed she would probably fall sick and her aunt would have no choice than to send her back home. Day after day, my faith in this hope grew stronger and stronger. So, day after day, I kept on hoping that one time, one moment, Alero would suddenly turn up in Toro again and calm my agitated nerves. I strongly believed that there would be a knock on my door one day and I would ask:
"Who is it?" and the reply would be:
"It's Alero."

Strangely, that moment never came. It was a wish, an imagination that never became a reality. Alero had just mesmerized me, raised up my passion to its peak and then disappeared. But in that breath of time, Alero had seized my heart and had gone with it, leaving me an empty carcass, now helpless and in despair.

My next few weeks were full of pain. But there was one particular day that stood out among those various days of my trial. It was one Tuesday in the second week Alero left for Accra. I sat under the shade of a huge fig tree behind our house. There, Alero and I often retired to play whenever she visited me. I looked at the stone she always sat upon. I recalled now with nostalgia the way she always spoke to me – her sweet, lovely diction, her charming, Lagosian accent. It seemed as if I were looking at her face again, those big eyeballs, winking as if asking me to come nearer. Suddenly, I became aware that I was in a trance. Now, I felt like seeing Alero. The passion to see her was so strong and unbearable. I did not know when I started to write:

My dear Alero,
The Beautiful Rose of Toro,
The real piece of beauty,
The breath of freshness.
The eyes that speak love.
The one more beautiful than any woman ever was,
Though brilliant yet shy and innocent.
Full of ideas but humble to a fault.
A friend to own and a confidant to trust.
A beauty to behold and manners to emulate.
The only one possessing the magic drug,
that can mend my broken heart.
My soul and flesh cry for you.
When will you be around?
To calm my troubled heart.
And tell me as of old,
that you are still for me.
Alero, my bride, living beyond the ocean.
My beautiful darling, living o'er the sea.
How much I long to see you again.
And behold once more the wonder of your eye balls.
Alero! Remember that it is your presence that gives me life.

And your support that makes me feel so good.
With your absence, I feel, weak and powerless.
Alero, my joy,
How sweet your name is?
I will continue to call your name.
Till the music of your name,
refreshes my broken heart.

I did not know that I was crying. My sorrow was deeper than that of a condemned soul marching into hell, and that sorrow weighed me down like a dreadful fatigue. My anguish seemed like that of a man asked to proceed into an electric chair. I could hear clearly now the groaning of my heart. I could hear the bitter lamentation of my soul. I could hear the agonizing sobs of my spirit. I could hear the weeping of my flesh. I could hear the wailings of my cells and tissues – all now crying with no one to comfort them.

CHAPTER EIGHTEEN

It was almost three weeks now that Alero left for Accra. I didn't know that my mother had been watching me all along. I was surprised one evening when she called me after dinner and said:

"I have been observing you in the last three weeks or so, I can see that you are not as active as before. You look morose. That you are unhappy, I can see that very clearly. Though you did not tell me directly. I know you love Alero so much. I know how much she means to you. I know she is your best friend. I know her absence will affect you and it has affected you a lot. I was imagining that with time, you would get over it, forget about her and become your normal self again. But this has not happened. I feel it is time to call you and tell you some motherly truths."

"And what are these truths, mom?"

"Alero is a Princess."

"Yes, I know that."

"She is so different from any other girl."

"Yes, I know ma."

"Thank God that you know so much. Then you can as

well add to your knowledge that she can only marry a Prince or a son of a High Chief. Unfortunately, you are neither. You and Alero do not belong to the same class and because you don't, she cannot marry you, no matter how you try. The class problem is there waiting for you at the end of the day."

"Why are you saying all these?" I queried.

"Because I want to tell you the truth."

"And that is not the truth, mom."

"Mom stared at my face in surprise and then queried:

"What then is the truth?"

"You want to know the truth?"

"Yes, I want."

"If you want, then listen to me. I am not a Prince. Neither am I a son of a High Chief nor do I pray to be one. I never in my life aspire to be any other person than myself. I want to be me. But one thing I am sure of is that Alero is going to be my future wife. That is the truth. Any other thing, don't believe it, don't listen to it; don't entertain it in your mind because it is not the truth."

A narrow, mocking and mischievous smile lit mom's face.

"My dear son, why do you build your castle in the air? Why are you suffering from self-deceits? Why can't you be realistic? Tell me! Who will give Alero to you in marriage?"

"Mom don't worry about that yet. We have not gotten to the river. When we get there, we will know what to do to cross it. Alero's parents cannot give her to another man. They dare not."

"What will you do if they dare?"

"Mom! That cannot happen. Not here on earth. There is no reason debating something that I know is not going to happen. Please be informed that Alero cannot accept any other man. I am too sure of that."

"Has she given you a promise?"

"Of course, yes."

"And you are so foolish to rely on the same?"

"What then should I rely upon?"

"Don't you know that both of you are little older than children and what you call love is mere infatuation?"

"Mom, that is not true."

"Even when you disagree with me, the fact still remains that the two of you have very many years ahead; Alero's passion may change along the line; don't you know that?"

"Mom! You are a liar. It cannot."

"Assuming it does?"

"Get thee behind me Satan!" I screamed.

"So I have now become a devil?"

"Yes! Because the devil is a liar and mom you have been telling lies; a lot of them this evening."

"My dear son! I love you. Your problem is my problem and that is the reason why I am saying all these. Alero's parents will change her mind along the line. They will tell her that she must be properly married. That is, she must get married to a man of her class."

"Mom! I have heard too much of this class problem, can you save me the agony of it now?"

"I am saying all these in order to make sure that you cut your coat according to your size. I don't want disappointment for you in matters of love. It can be traumatic. It can be extremely unpleasant."

"Mom! All these problems and disappointments are products of your own imagination. They will never happen. You don't need to worry about them. Why must you spend time and energy thinking about such things?"

"Good Heavens! I say all these because I know much better than you do. My dear son, what do you think Alero to be – an ordinary lady? She is not a commodity that anyone can go to the market, pick from the shelf and purchase. She is a precious jewel. She is a girl of class meant for men of class. She is not a toy that all men play with; she is the golden egg that all behold and admire. She is not everybody's woman but a prize that great and men of honour will have to compete fiercely for to possess. She is not a football that can be kicked up and down by any foot. She is the golden trophy that the greatest of all great men will get at the end of a fierce and well-contested match. She is not a cap, which can be worn by any head. She is the crown meant for the heads of kings and princes. She is not a woman just for any man. She is destined by her birth for a man of substance. She is a woman of class. She is a prize."

"Mom! I have heard you, your points are so beautiful but you are still so wrong. Alero is mine. Nothing here on earth can change it. She is destined to be mine, that I know so much, and the same she equally knows."

Mom fixed her eyes on me for a long time. She didn't understand what gave me so much confidence on this issue. She must have been baffled by my faith. Then, she spoke slowly, picking her words:

"My dear son! Only one thing can make Alero marry you," she stared at my face now.

"Have you found at least a reason? And what is that? What is that condition?"

"If you can conquer the world. If you can have the world under your feet."

"How do I conquer the world?"

"You don't know?"

"No, I don't."

"Then, I will explain to you. There are men who are great and eminent lawyers. There are those who are famous men of letters. There are great men of knowledge. They are held in high esteem even by kings and princes. Such men are those who have conquered the world in their fields. If you can become one of such great people, then Alero may not be too difficult to get."

"What you are saying in effect is that I must be a star if I want Alero - isn't it?"

"Yes, you get what I am talking about. But as a star, you must not stand out only, you must stand alone like the great oak tree in the savannah that has no rival."

"Mom! I am going to be a super star then. I am going to excel. I am going to shine much brighter than all my colleagues and contemporaries. I am going to shake the world. I am going to have Alero. I cannot accept a situation where Alero will have to be another man's wife. Not here on earth. Never. Whatever needs to be done, I will do it. I assure you of that, mom."

"Yes, you have contacted the fire and the passion

needed for the challenge. If you don't allow it to go down, then you will have Alero."

"Thank you, mom."

As I said those sentences, I suddenly experienced peace in my system. My God! This was a mind that had known no peace for many weeks. Now, I had got a clue to my problem. I had got the medicine for my sickness. Now, I made up my mind to shine for the great prize, the most wonderful Alero, the great and charming princess of my dream. With effect from that day, I planned my work meticulously and concentrated good attention on my work. Not long, the results began to come in. Within two months, I was on top of my class. At the end of that year, I gained admission with scholarship to one of Nigeria's most prestigious secondary schools – Igbobi College, Lagos. In the entire history of CMS School, Toro, I was the first pupil to perform this great feat.

CHAPTER NINETEEN

I arrived at Igbobi College Lagos, one beautiful evening. I can still recall the day - a warm, lovely evening. That day, all the new students gathered in the huge assembly hall, which people called the Hall of Fame. It was in this hall we were given a rousing welcome as new Igbobians.

"Look at the wall and see the pictures of great Africans who had passed through this college," exclaimed Mr. Adinnal.

I stared at the various pictures in awe: great politicians, renowned educationists, famous journalists, great scientists, and men of distinction in various fields. Hall of Fame was really a museum of famous people. Mr. Adinnal stared at my face and then asked:
"You want to be like one of these great men in the pictures?"
"I want to be greater than all of them." I replied.
"Oh that is a great ambition. You will need to work really hard then."

Mr. Brookes, an Englishman, was our class teacher - a

tall, handsome young man. He was one of the recent products from Oxford University.

"What is your name?" Mr. Brookes asked the nearest boy to him as we gathered in Class One that first Monday, after our arrival at the school.
"Bode James."
"School?"
"Methodist School, Marina, Lagos."
"That is a good school."
"Next boy – what is your name?"
"My name is Lanre Ajai."
"Your school?"
"St. James School, Oke-bola, Ibadan."
"That is a famous Anglican School. Beautiful."
Then, Mr. Brookes turned to me.
"Your name?"
"My name is Mayo Williams."
"Your school?"
"CMS School, Toro."
"Where is Toro?"
"Toro is in Ondo Province of Western Nigeria."
"What?" he queried.
"I said Toro is in Western Nigeria."
"It can't be. I have never heard of such a name. It certainly can't be in Western Nigeria," he protested.
"It is there." I insisted.
"No! It is not there. You can't be right. Such ugly name can only come from Abakaliki Area, no other place."

There was a huge burst of laughter. For many seconds, rumblings went from one end of that room to the other. I stared at Mr. Brookes' face blankly. Abakaliki was then a notorious district in Eastern Nigeria where innocent people were reportedly killed every now and then. I didn't want to be associated with such a place. I therefore raised up my voice in protest.

"My friend! Don't waste your breath. I know Toro is in Abakaliki. Its no use entering into a debate with me on the issue."

Mr. Brookes strangely claimed to know Toro more than I who came from the place and since it appeared that there might be no end to the argument, I opted to keep quiet.

"But how does Toro sound so ugly to Mr. Brookes? Does he have any problem with his hearing? Is Toro not one of the sweetest of all names?"

After Mr. Brookes had written the names of all the pupils in his register, he turned to me again. This time, he stared at me inquiringly. His eyes fixed on me with such heat and malignant concentration that I grew nervous.

"Where do I seek protection?" I queried silently.

"What does Mr. Brookes want from me?" I couldn't guess.

"Abakaliki boy!" he screamed suddenly. I looked left and right for a strange figure, Abakaliki Boy, who had entered into the class. I saw no one. I then stared at Mr. Brookes's face, confused.

"You are the one I am calling," he pointed to me.

"That is not my name," I told him.

"That is the name I have chosen to call you and I am afraid that is the name you'll bear henceforth."

All the other students erupted in a roar of laughter.
"I am sorry sir, I am not going to accept such a name."

"Your protest is noted but please come out, pick up that duster on the table and clean this chalk-board for me."

I stood up in rising anger. I picked up the duster. My face and my steps were protesting loudly, but Mr. Brookes only stared at me. He didn't appear to bother about my private feelings. His face wore an arrogant and contemptuous curiosity which made me feel highly uncomfortable. Then he smiled. I couldn't see what was funny.

His subtle, derisive smile appeared to be growing into a scorn and all my cells rose up in revolt. I felt like screaming aloud.

"Abakaliki Boy!" he screamed again.
"Since you are the one who comes from a bush school, you just must accept to do the donkey job. I can't call on any other student. It won't be fair on him. Look at all the other boys – they all come from famous and reputable schools."

I didn't know which yardsticks Mr. Brookes was using to grade the schools under reference - but if I could accept that I came from a bush school - "Why do I need to be baptized with a new name? And why Abakaliki Boy?"

What was worse, wherever I moved after that day, the name Abakaliki Boy always rang behind me.

"Stop that! I say stop it! I won't have more of such nonsense," I screamed at a boy one morning.

"Abakaliki Boy!" yelled yet another voice. As I tried to turn and look at the one growling, another voice calling Abakalliki Boy roared from my left. The more I tried to shake off this unwanted toga, the more people threw it back at me. Within a few days, no one remembered my real name anymore. This was the first irritation Igbobi College presented to me. Everyday, I was in a state of war. I wore a pugnacious look. My eyeballs shone like a red, hot oven. My nerves were up. But this only emboldened my tormentors to put in more efforts. Gradually, I began to realize that anger and fury would not do the job. They had only escalated the situation. Then, I resolved to tame my anger into patience. After all, what cannot be escaped must be endured. I decided to accept my new name. I took it as a necessary cross that I had to bear. Gradually, I began to see that there was nothing so bad in Abakaliki Boy. I could appreciate now that there was even something sonorous in the name itself.

"Abakaliki Boy!"

"O yes!" I would reply with a sweet smile on my face. One afternoon, I was addressing the class:

"Audience, please, I say listen to your beautiful Abakaliki Boy!" There was silence everywhere. My classmates surprisingly discovered now that Abakaliki Boy had become a new menu I very much relish. Now, my tormentors had no further weapon in their arsenal. I had just disarmed them of the potent weapon of intimidation in their hands. I could see now that I had been very foolish raising all the previous protests and wearing forlorn looks for no reason. There was really nothing to protest about. What is in a name after all?

I was lucky that I did not allow this irritation to dampen my spirit. I never lost focus. I never forgot the great mission of my life which is to shine like the star, to excel in what I did, to perform the spectacular and, at the end, to possess the beautiful Alero, the Great Princess of my dream.

I resolved to be on top of my class. I worked hard. I made up my mind to break all available academic records. So, right from the first day, I started as if my colleagues and I were running a competitive race. I pushed ahead. I pressed towards the mark of excellence. I drove myself hard, not for any personal fame or reward but all for ALERO – the charming Princess of Toro, whom I was determined to possess.

Time ran with supersonic speed. We soon got to the end of the second term and we had a major examination. A week after the examination, Mr. Brookes hurried into our class one afternoon. As he stared at my face and I stared at his, I wondered what he was up to again.

"Should I prepare myself for a new name or another session of torment since this has become Mr. Brookes's pastime?"
I stood erect, eyes open, ears alert and fully ready to match Mr. Brookes word for word and weapon for weapon, if the need arose. Suddenly, he asked me:
"Which primary school did you attend?". I stared at

him curiously.

"Mr. Brookes, why are you asking that question? I am sure you asked me this same question eight months ago and I remember giving you an answer. Why are you revisiting the same question now?" that was how I wished to react.

But something warned me to tread a less aggressive path. I just found myself replying:

"St. Peter's School, Abakaliki."

"Oh, No! I am not joking this time. Where really is your school?"

"Mr. Brookes, I am not joking either. I am from St. Peter's School, Abakaliki."

"Oh, don't be funny."

"Mr. Brookes, when I told you the name and location of my school eight months ago, you never accepted them. You said they were in Abakaliki. As my teacher, how can I claim to know better than you do?"

A narrow, infectious smile lit Mr. Brookes face.

"My boy! I think you are right."

He beckoned me to come nearer. I walked towards him. He pulled me into his embrace and hugged me affectionately.

"You are a wonderful boy. I must apologize to you. I must admit that you come from a great school. You have not only come first in your examination, you led in virtually all the subjects. You broke all the records. This school is very proud of you. I had also checked the results of last year's entrance examination to this school and I discovered that you led and had a scholarship. You have proved your point beyond any reasonable doubt. You are surely a product of a great school and obviously from a great town. Or, what other evidence does one need?"

From that day on and until I came out of the college, Mr. Brookes became my best friend.

CHAPTER TWENTY

We were going on holiday that morning. I had been away from home for eight months. I longed to see Toro, my small, delightful town again. I loved to see my mother.

I remembered Alero. How I wished to see her again! How I wished to behold her lovely face!

"Will I get information about her when I get to Toro? Or has she forgotten me completely? It has been very many months now – why couldn't she make some efforts to contact me?" I queried.

I had phoned for a taxi. As that taxi now drove to a halt in the front of my dormitory, I saw a student hurrying towards me. It was Gabriel, one of my classmates.

"Mayo! You have a letter here." He gave me the letter and I looked at it; the envelope had a Ghanian stamp.

"Only one person knows me in Ghana", I mumbled. With trembling hands, I tore open the envelope only to be greeted with the long awaited message from Alero.

"Just yesterday, I was informed that I came first in my examination, then Mr. Brooke's historic embrace, now a letter from Alero! All within 24 hours! God! This is too much for me," I exclaimed.

St. Theresas Girls High School,
Cape Coast, Ghana.
2nd August, 1960.

My dear Mayo,
I am sorry that I couldn't write you earlier. But everyday,
every hour and every minute, I think of you. It was Mewa
who gave me the information that you are now at Igbobi
College, Lagos. Mewa wrote a letter to me and since she
did not know my address, she gave the letter to my mom.
My mom sent the same to my aunt and my aunt sent it to me.
From the letter, I got your address. How are you? I am sure
you are enjoying your new place. I also enrolled as a student
here eight months ago. St Theresas Girls High School is a
mission school. Its rules are so strict. I had to smuggle out
this letter because we are under strict instruction not to
write anyone except our guardians.
Do not attempt to write me. I will always write whenever I
can smuggle a letter out of here. If you don't hear from me;
no matter how long, don't worry. Just know and believe
that Alero, your bride, is quite fine. Just yesterday I
composed this poem for you:
Distance can be an obstacle.
But in love, distance matters not.
Mountains, rivers, valleys, seas and their likes are great
physical barriers.
But true love goes through all of them,
To deliver the message of affection to the loved one on the other
side.

And today I send my whole heart to you to keep.
Time and season may change.
The tide may change its direction.
The river may change its course.
The leopard may change its spots.
The earth may change from its orbit.
The Pampas may relocate from Argentina.
The Amazon may relocate from Brazil.
Christmas may change from December 25.
But you will forever remain,
The constant stanza in my daily song.
It's your loving bride,

Alero.

It was ten months later that Alero wrote me again. In all my six years at Igbobi College, Alero wrote me seven letters. I slept and woke up with them. They were like precious diamonds which shine brighter and brighter every day.

All my years at Igbobi College were the most exciting in my life. We usually woke up around 6a.m., had the morning prayer, then attended classes up to 1.40p.m. We were back in the classes again between 3p.m. and 4p.m., had our dinner at 6p.m. and went to bed at 9p.m.

Academically, I was leading my class. A commoner who would marry a Princess must perform the extraordinary and I decided to perform the extraordinary. I pursued excellence as if I was prepared to die for it.

My passion to have Alero drove me on. The obsession to possess the Princess of Toro gave me no rest. Day and night, I pressed on like a runner bent on obtaining nothing less than gold in the Olympics. In my dream, in my imagination I could see ahead of me – the beautiful Princess, Alero the great prize, I would obtain at the end of day.

The years were running. I scarcely noticed them. Alero continued to write but she never showed up in Toro. But I was sure that one year, one month, one day, we would meet again.

CHAPTER TWENTY-ONE

I t was now 1965. I was already in my final year. Our August holiday that year coincided with the traditional OGUN FESTIVAL, the most famous festival in Toro. It is a great traditional carnival that attracts many people from all parts of the nation and abroad. I had missed this great cultural show, the peak of glamour and splendour of the kingdom of Toro. But that year, I was going to watch it again. I felt so excited as I was now hurrying to Toro, the land of ancient romance and beauty.

That Saturday, the festival started with the "Irogbala"- the traditional dancing round the palace walls by the princes, princesses, chiefs and barons of the kingdom. The local historian said that this great dance started in 25 B.C. when Alaworo, the Great, entered into the ground alive, never to be seen in the land of the living.

Alaworo, a brave warrior and a great king of Toro Kingdom, was dearly loved by his people for his bold deeds and generous heart. He was a man of adventure.

He spent most of his time conquering rebellious tribes that kept on molesting the peace of his kingdom. He had been absent from Toro for seven years and was returning from one of his long, military campaigns. The excitement that he was going to see Toro again had been building up in his system in the last few days. That excitement suddenly reached a fever heat now.

As Toro came into view, Alaworo was filled with unbearable joy. He hurried forward as if he were going to embrace and kiss this beautiful damsel of the Savannah as he exclaimed:

"My beautiful Toro, the land of ancient beauty, the curious museum of mystery.
A land whose magic charms has dazzled men of all ages.
How are you?"

The fringes of Toro glittered under the early morning sun, and from the distance, it appeared as if Toro, a glamorous damsel was beckoning to Alaworo with a warm, radiant and delicious smile.

Alaworo's heart was racing with excitement as his spirit kept on turning now on the same axis of joy.
"What a wonderful day! I feel so happy," said he.
The king's horse galloped excitedly, its mood almost matching that of its rider.

Just that moment, His Royal Highness and his party were suddenly awakened by a huge noise coming from Toro. Then came a growing roar. The king stiffened.
"What noise is that? Is an enemy force attacking Toro?" he queried, now rooted to the same spot.

His men stared at one another blankly. But one quickly spoke up:

"Your Royal Highness! What I am hearing is a happy, hilarious noise. It seems like a noise of people celebrating, certainly not that of war."

"I think you are right. I can hear it now more distinctly. It is an excited noise. But what festival do Toro people celebrate at this time of the year;" asked the king.

"You Highness! I can't remember any, August is not a month of festival in Toro."

"What then can be the reason for this growing roar? Even if a hundred couples are being married at the same time, the noise and excitement cannot be as much as what we are hearing."

A large portion of Toro had come into view and right at the center of the town, they could see sea of heads.

"Men! Let us stop here. Let somebody run quickly and find out for me what is happening."

A soldier gave a salute and dashed forward on his horse towards the crowd. As the soldier was running back, so also an excited crowd was rushing to meet their king. But the soldier outran the crowd and soon got to His Royal Highness.

"Your Royal Highness! A coronation is on," said the soldier.

"Coronation?"

"Yes, Your Royal Highness."

"Somebody had already seized my throne in my absence? Is that possible? Can anyone be so mad?" his face suddenly turned red and furious.

"I never imagine that we will still need to fight one more battle before we enter Toro."

"Your Highness! It is Apa, your son, who is being crowned."

"You mean my son has been made a king by the people?"

"Yes. Your Highness."

"Why?"

"The people felt that Your Highness must have perished in one of the wars. They said they had waited for seven years without hearing from you and they naturally concluded that a tragic incident might have happened to Your Highness."

The king stood still, and then sighed deeply.

"If that is the case, I can't enter Toro," he said.

"Why Your Highness?"

"According to Toro's traditions, two living kings of Toro must never see each other. It is an abomination. It is a taboo. It is a sacrilege."

The people stared at the king's face, confused.

"Your Highness! How do we resolve the problem then? What do we do?"

The king smiled grimly and said:

"There is nothing to worry about," said he

"Your Royal Highness! You say we shouldn't worry?"

"No, you don't need to."

"Why?"

"Because it is time."

"Which time, Your Highness?"

"Time to leave you. Time to depart. I have finished my course. I have completed my task. I have accomplished my mission."

167

Suddenly, the king turned round his horse, now backing Toro, he started to run away. All the warriors, the chiefs and the people started to run after him.

"Your Highness! Where are you going? Please wait! You don't need to go away. You don't need to leave us. We love you."

But the more they spoke, the more his horse increased its speed. A chief called Asaba riding a white horse, a fantastic rider was the one who eventually caught up with the king, stopped him and held on to his flowing gown.

"You must return to Toro. It is your home. You built it; it is your place. You cannot abandon it. Where else do you want to go?"

"No, I cannot and I won't."

"Why?"

"I am sure I had told you the reason. Two kings of Toro must not see each other. You know that. I cannot defy an age long tradition. By virtue of my position, I am supposed to know better than that. Let Apa reign. That is the will of the people and that will, I must respect."

"Your Royal Highness! What is going to happen to you now? What do you intend to do?"

"I already told you that it is time for me to depart."

"Your Highness said so but I love to know where exactly Your Highness intends to go to."

"You want to know?"

"Yes, Your Highness."

By this time, a multitude made up of the soldiers that were accompanying the king and other indigenes of

Toro had caught up with them and gathered round the king and Asaba. Bewildered, they could not move near the king but were watching the Royal Highness and Asaba in the short dialogue.

The king smiled grimly as he came down from his horse. He walked a little distance from Asaba, then raised up his left foot and pointed it to the sky. There was a flash of lightning. The ground under the king quaked and convulsed angrily and suddenly caved in. There was a huge noise and then a huge thick smoke. In a blink of an eye, the Great Alaworo went into the bowel of the earth, never to be seen again in the land of the living. By the time the smoke fizzled out about two minutes thereafter, a mighty rock, steaming granite was standing at the spot where Alaworo was last seen. In unison and as if it had been rehearsed, the people roared: "Kabiyesi, Alaworo, the Great!"

That event happened over two thousand years ago and the people of the ancient kingdom of Toro have never failed to commemorate this event every year. The celebration always lasted seven days. Each day, the ceremony became more and more exciting until it finally reached its peak on the seventh day with the great dance - THE DANCE OF THE QUEEN.

I, Mayo Williams, watched this great festival last eight years ago. That year 1965, I was going to watch it again. And as I left Igbobi College, Lagos, now hurrying to Toro, I was full of excitement. Toro had recently got a new king and I knew this would certainly add a new colour and glamour to the festival that year.

CHAPTER TWENTY-TWO

London, 1964

Jennifer Adams hurried out of the taxi like someone who was five minutes late for an important engagement. She pressed the door bell and then waited. There was no response. She looked at the door and pressed the door bell again and again. There was still no response. She remembered she phoned mom and dad that she would be arriving home that afternoon. She was expecting to go straight into their warm embrace on arrival. As a new LLM graduate from London School of Economics and Political Science, she had imagined how excited her parents would be at seeing her.

"Are you in the right apartment?" asked the taxi driver.

"Yes, of course."

She pressed the bell switch again. Growing restless but feeling concerned, the taxi driver asked again:

"Are you quiet sure you are in the right place?"

"Very sure. You can go. Thank you."

"How do you expect me to leave you in this cold when

the door has not been opened for you?"
"Don't worry. I will manage. There is no reason to delay you any further because this is my home and my destination."

That moment, Jennifer saw a small note at the left hand corner of the foot-mat. She picked it up. The note read:
"Jennifer! We are sorry. We are off to Dundee, Scotland. We will be back tomorrow by the first train. When we are back, we will explain to you the reason for our impromptu trip. Take the key from the usual place and try to enjoy yourself. Cheers!"

Jennifer picked the key from a flower pot in the front garden and went in. She switched on the television. There was a beautiful documentary on Mongolia on Thames Television and she settled for it. After spending six hours watching television, she became bored. She recalled that Angela, her friend and Henry, her boy friend, had invited her to a night party in Bromley Continental Hotel, Kent, that evening.

"I can't make it. I had promised my parents that I would spend the night with them."

Now the parents had chosen to go elsewhere. Jennifer phoned Angela:
"My parents have gone to Dundee; do you mind if I join you at the party?"
"Jennifer, that will be great!" said an excited Angela.
"I will be with you in the next forty minutes."

Jennifer arrived at the party at 9p.m. Bromley

Continental Hotel is located in a quiet suburb of Kent. Its tasteful, cool lighting made the hotel so beautiful. Jennifer could feel the delicious aroma of a loving evening.

"Nice you made it," said a radiant Henry.

"Jennifer! With you around, we are going to have a wonderful night," exclaimed Angela.

Just that minute, a tall, black gentleman joined them, and Henry became highly excited.

"Jennifer!, Meet Maxwell Alade, my friend, a Nigerian and a classmate. We both finished a few days ago with PhD in Political Science from Oxford."

"Jennifer! It's nice meeting you," said Maxwell who smiled benignly at the stunning, beautiful Rose in her mid-twenties. He surveyed Jennifer, the slim, pretty Jamaican lady with an intellectual face. He looked at one of her legs that came out of her skirt, straight and lovely and he loved her at first sight. Jennifer also had met many men but took to Maxwell Alade the very moment she was introduced to him. He had everything she was looking for in a man; an intellectual, a PhD holder from one of the world's most reputable universities, tall with athletic frame, with huge shining hair and wearing a three piece suit that fitted him so beautifully.

They were in each other's arms almost all night as they danced and danced. By the time they were parting the following morning, it was as if they had known each other for several years. Three months after that historic meeting, they were married at B&C Registry in London.

Prince Maxwell Alade, who left the Nigerian shore for Britain at the age of five, came from a royal family in Toro. Toro, an ancient Yoruba Kingdom founded by Alaworo and consisting of about fifty villages had a brilliant and inspiring past. His father, Samuel Alade, a rich monarch wanted his son to have a British education. Maxwell was sent to Britain at an early age and had his primary and secondary education in London. Thereafter, he proceeded to Oxford where he obtained a Doctor of Philosophy in Political Science.

Six months after their marriage, Jennifer and Maxwell Alade arrived in Lagos, Nigeria. Maxwell took up a teaching appointment as a University Lecturer in one of the higher institutions in the city. Jennifer set up a beautiful law chamber. Her office in 2121 Marina, one of the most sumptuous streets of Lagos Island, directly faced the lovely water of the Atlantic Ocean. They lived in an elite accommodation in the quiet Ikoyi Island, the haven of the Nigerian millionaires.

The young couple became the talk of the neighbourhood. Strolling down the street arm-in-arm, playing the game of hide and seek in their pretty compound, dancing on the lawn in the evening, they were a beauty to watch. Then something happened, and their entire way of life suddenly changed.

His Royal Highness, Samuel Alade, the reigning King of Toro, the father of Prince Matete and Prince Maxwell, died suddenly. Prince Matete who was the heir to the throne, conceded the throne to his younger brother because of health reasons, so , in February 1965, Maxwell Alade became the 152nd King of Toro in a colourful coronation.

The new king had spent barely six months on the throne when Toro began to celebrate the famous annual Ogun Festival in 1965. The festival had been on for six days. The last day – the seventh, was the day of the Great Dance – The Dance of the Queen.

Go to the restaurant, visit the brook, talk to the woman in the street, it was this dance that was on every lip.

"Will the dance hold?" asked Bada.

"It is most unlikely," replied a palace official.

"That will be terrible. The dance has never failed since Toro was founded over two thousand years ago. Why should it fail now? Why should the new king cancel it?"

"It is a pagan dance. I don't want it. Rubbish – fascinating rubbish!" the king called it, according to the palace official.

"Who put this kind of ignoramus on the throne?" queried Bada.

"I beg your pardon! The king is well read. He has a PhD from a British university."

"My friend! We are not talking of the white man's education. We are talking of native education that makes one become knowledgeable in the dos and don'ts of his own land. The man is going to land this kingdom in trouble because of his ignorance. The chiefs have just left the palace, trying various arguments to persuade him to change his stand. I am told he has so far refused to shift grounds on this particular issue. He is so stubborn and impossible. Who put him on the throne? Who?" asked an exasperated Bada.

"Who put him on the throne is not the issue now. That the kingdom will face terrible consequences is my worry."

According to Toro traditions, the Queen normally rounds up the yearly festival by dancing before a huge crowd in the Palace Square. It is not just a dance. It is a great ritual. It is a dance that links the dead with the living. It is a covenant dance. It is a measured, calculated and mathematical dance with specific steps and motions. It has a rigid pattern. Time changes, weather changes, climate changes, rivers change their courses, human beings change their ways of life but this dance never changes. It remains unchangeable as the sun and the moon overhead. It is unalterable as eternity.

Toro people call it the Dance of Death because if the Queen misses her steps, she is a dead woman.
"I am a Christian. I can't allow my wife to take part in such a pagan dance. Count us out of it," said the king.

"Your Royal Highness! The Queen cannot escape this dance. It is a must. It is a duty. It is an obligation; she dares not fail to honour. If she refuses, the kingdom will have many troubles. The gods will be angry in heaven and they will unleash their anger on our people."

The king stared at the faces of his chiefs and screamed:

"You are all liars. I don't believe you. I have no belief in your gods. What you are saying is a mere bundle of rubbish. If there is no dance, and your gods want to make trouble, my own God will take care of them. Let your gods go to hell."

"Your Highness! Don't play with fire. It is on record that two Toro Kings who asked their queens not to dance in the past paid for it with their lives. Go and find out. We love you and we cannot look on while Your Highness wants to endanger his own life. You are warned. The gods of Toro never joke with people. They are like fire, they burn. This dance is the thing that guarantees the good health of the kingdom. Without it, we will all face the wrath of the gods."

"Gentlemen! Enough of that! I can't take in such stuff because I can't see the logic."

"Your Royal Highness! We are talking of spiritual matter. Logic has nothing to do with this. To an educated person, a spiritual matter seems like foolishness. We are not surprised that you can't see the grave implication of what we are saying because you were not reared up in our culture. But as your chiefs, we will be failing in our duty if we allow Your Highness to put his fingers into a burning fire. The gods will blame us."

"I don't give a damn about your gods. They cannot remove a single hair from my head. They may be everything to you – fine. But they are nothing to me.

You say they will bring down volcano and earthquake; let them try. Let them unleash their hurricane and tornado. They may even shift the earth from its orbit; that is their headache. You believe so much in their power, I have no quarrel with you on that. You are free to believe anything you want to believe. That is your own cup of tea. But me, I won't succumb to your intimidation. It is mere rubbish. My wife will not take part in any pagan dance. Please, regard my verdict as final. That chapter is already closed and no one must open it again." The king suddenly rose up.

That moment, Jennifer came into the room.
"Your Highness! You don't need to pick up a quarrel with your chiefs over a trifle. You are a manager. You are a leader. As a manager, you are the greatest servant of your people. You are here to serve. You are a public servant. Don't miss that point. You are on the throne because of these people. You are a man of the people. You don't belong to yourself anymore. Now, as for the dance, I am going to dance. What is in a dance that is causing so much furor?"

"My dear! You don't understand. My late father had spoken to me about the dance. It is not an ordinary dance. It is a deadly dance. Though I did not so much believe him, I want to distance myself from it."
"Deadly dance? Why? How?"
"I am told that if you dance and you miss your steps, you will die."
"And you believe that?"
"I don't totally believe but I don't trust these people."

177

"Darling! Forget about death. And let us forget about my person. If they say the dance is so important to the health of the kingdom, I don't see anyway out of it. For the health of Toro kingdom, I am prepared to dance. I am ready for it. Don't worry – nothing will happen to me. I know my God. I trust him. Let us even for the sake of argument assume that the dance is a deadly one, the words of God in Psalms 23 says:

'Yea, though I walk through the valley of the shadow of death, I will fear no evil, for thou art with me...'

"Darling! I say I don't want the dance;" screamed the king.

"Your Highness! You don't need to get unnecessarily agitated on such trivial matters. I am told that nothing had happened to the queens who took part in the dance since the last three decades. Nothing is going to happen to me. I am so sure about that. They will teach me the steps and the motions. I am told it is a measured, calculated and mathematical dance. The queens who had taken part in this dance before now were mostly illiterate women. If they didn't find it so difficult, why should I?"

"Darling! I don't trust these people. I don't want anyone to play any trick on me. They appear to me as a people who can play some funny game."

"Darling!" Jennifer patted the king on the back. "Have your peace, there is no problem."

CHAPTER TWENTY-THREE

Today was the day of the Great Dance – the mother of all events. I accompanied a chief, a distant relative to the king's square where the Great Dance would take place: The dance of a popular barrister, the dance of an LLM holder from University of London, the dance of the Queen of beauty, the dance of the Number One Lady in Toro Kingdom. Nothing had generated greater curiosity and no event had caused a greater hysteria and anticipation in Toro.

"It's going to be a spectacular show but I must confess that I am not feeling comfortable about it;" said the chief.
"Why?" I asked him.
"I am afraid for her."
"Why are you afraid?"
"My spirit tells me that something will go wrong. I have a premonition that Jennifer will miss her steps."
"And if she does?"
"She will die."
"And you too believe such a thing?"

"Yes I do because it is the truth. If anyone tells you something to the contrary, don't believe him. This is not an ordinary dance. It is a deadly ritual. The queen who missed her steps in 1879 died in her sleep at exactly 12.00 midnight that day. Another who missed her steps in 1901 also died in her sleep at exactly 12.00 midnight that day. Yet another missed her steps in 1933, she also died in her sleep at exactly 12.00 midnight that day."

"Couldn't all these be mere coincidences?"

"Three women died, each after she danced and missed her steps. Though different days, but at the same hour, the same minute, in the same manner. If they were coincidences, aren't they strange coincidences? Don't you think Queen Jennifer's case can end up in a similar coincidence?"

That moment, I recalled that my father told me that he personally witnessed how the queen died after missing her steps in 1933. He told the story with such details that I knew its accuracy was not in doubt. For the first time, I too began to entertain some fear for Jennifer, the beautiful, innocent, Jamaican lady with lovely, beautiful skin who had chosen to engage in a pagan dance that might soon put her life on the line.

I stared intensely at Jennifer, a charming 24-year-old woman with nice frame. She was tall, slim, ebony black, a kind of woman that Nigerian young men call 'figure 8', tiny waist, sumptuous hips, big, nice busts with pretty face and huge hair. She was an extremely beautiful queen.

She stood in a central location. She stood there in deep silence, looking straight, her head standing at an angle of ninety degrees upon her graceful, beautiful neck. She stood there frantic with anxiety. As I stared at her, and for a reason I didn't understand, my apprehension kept on growing. I wondered whether all the coachings given to Jennifer would guarantee success in this dance that was totally strange to her culture. Anxiety weighed me down like a man carrying a heavy load on his shoulders. Jennifer stood there like a criminal who had just got a death sentence; staring now at the guillotine, tense and nervous. She stood there motionless and lost to the world while the eyes of over twenty thousand spectators focused intensely on her. Like gladiators in Ancient Rome, about to fight some hungry lions, bowing and saluting the spectators and saying: *Morituri te Salutamus"*, that is, "We who are about to die, salute you." …

This woman who was about to play chess with death, stood there alone, a deserted shack in the wilderness, companionless, forsaken, enveloped in eternal silence; nothing but silence. Did she volunteer to undertake this dance because of the love she had for her husband or as a result of her royal obligation to Toro Kingdom? Whatever it was, it was certain that she was not totally aware of the grave danger she was about to face.

From the upper ridge of her breast to the ankles, the

body of Jennifer was covered with a white cloth. But all the remaining parts including her face were painted in a leopard colour. From a distance, she looked like a stationary leopard, waiting anxiously for a prey. There was perfect silence. Any moment from now, the drums would sound and Jennifer and death would start to play the game of chess.

Afar off and sitting on a beautiful chair on a high platform was the king of Toro, nervous, anxious and frightful. He focused intensely on Jennifer, his Queen, apparently praying that the dance of that year would turn out well.

A magician wearing a load of amulets paced up and down before the Queen, whipping the air to ward off bad spirits, uttering silent incantations to the gods to appease them to show favour to the Queen.

"All gods and goddesses of the land, you must support your daughter in today's dance. Alaworo, let this ritual turn right. Let the dance of your daughter be acceptable unto you. The sixteen elders who founded the kingdom of Toro, you must accept your daughter's dance today. The thousand demons of the Sacred Oro Forest, you must accept this dance."

The man went up and down, restless, his face hard and grim. Now the Chief held my hand and indicated to me with the movement of his eyes that the dance was about to start. I stayed there in great impatience. My anxiety did not last a long time because the drums finally sounded.

I stared at the Queen as she lifted her right foot

forward, then the left, her feet moving with careful slowness and caution. The steps highly calculated, methodical, mathematical and precise. All eyes focused on her in a breathless gaze. She danced towards the northern end of the pitch and then danced back. The movements were like the slow motions of the tiger: silent, soft and soothing as a whisper. Asa stared at her, not winking not shaking, rigid as a pole.

Finally, Queen Jennifer came to the end of the pitch, stopped and then remained motionless, waiting now for the verdict. Fear suddenly gripped me and I began to sweat. Now is the hour. I could hear the rapid, frightened breathing of many people. The huge general noise was now swallowed up by sudden silence. The silence gradually became deafening.
Asa, looking stern and morose kept silent for almost three minutes; then suddenly, he exclaimed: "Yes! Yes! I can hear you! Yes! Thank you." Then he spoke:
"The gods say they have rejected the dance because the Queen missed her steps."

The cool, happy, serene atmosphere suddenly changed into turmoil. Jennifer stared at Asa in disbelief. She stared at him with frightened eyes. Dismay beamed out of every face. The king stood up quickly and hurried to the scene.
"What?" he screamed.
"The gods had not accepted the dance." Asa further asserted. The king suddenly exploded:
"You are a liar. Don't play your monkey game with me. Go over the steps again."
"I have done that already. I have done all what I

should, but the verdicts of the gods remain the same;" exclaimed Asa.

"I put it to you that you are a blatant liar. That verdict is not from any god."

"Whose verdict is it?" queried a bewildered Asa.

"Your own personal verdict," the king roared.

"You must accept that dance. You just must accept it. You have no choice in this matter."

"I cannot, and I won't."

"Asa! You dare not act contrary to what I tell you. Be wise and do not put up any unreasonable opposition or else your hands will be in the lion's mouth."

"Your Highness can do nothing to me. I am performing my legitimate duty as stipulated by the law and the traditions of the land."

"I am the law. I am the tradition. I determine when both will not apply. And be informed that both stand suspended with immediate effect. And now the verdict of your gods is overruled."

"What?" queried Asa.

"No one argues with the king;" screamed an official.

"You say you have overruled the verdict of the gods?"

"Precisely," replied the king.

"Sacrilege! Abomination! Eewo Orisa! No one ever quarrels with his head and decides to cut it off. Never. No son ever quarrels with his father and gives the father a slap. No earthly power can issue a warrant of arrest against a heavenly body. It is beyond the power of any policeman to arrest an angel. So also, no king here on earth can overrule the verdict of the gods. The physical cannot overrule the spiritual. It is the law of nature that whatever the spiritual decrees, the physical must do. It must comply with it unquestioningly. We human beings are mere pencils in the hands of the gods. They can use the pencils to write whatever they like. Whatever the gods decree cannot be debated. It can never be challenged or changed. That decision is final."

The king stared at Asa's face and queried:

"Have you, Asa, become a god?"

"No! Not all. I am only a priest. I am the gods' agent here on earth. The gods had told me their verdict and it is my duty to convey the same to the queen faithfully. And this is what I had done."

"Asa! It is either you have a bad hearing and could not hear the gods clearly enough or you are a blatant liar. No gods asked you to say what you said."

"Your Highness! How do you come to that conclusion?"

"Because I know."

Asa stared at the king's face, confused.

"Now! Asa, listen to me.

If really your gods talk to you, then convey my words to your gods that their verdict is not acceptable to me, and look here, I give them two minutes to retract that verdict, failing which you, I say you (pointing to Asa), their agent, will be in trouble. Tell your gods that a new fish has entered the pool and a new era in Toro has started. No priest, no gods shall dictate to me. I am the king. I will rule and I will reign. You and your gods had dictated to the past kings of Toro and you had got away with it. I will like to inform you that your era has come to an end."

"Your Highness! Don't allow too much learning,

pride and emotion to becloud your reasoning."

"Asa! Are you talking to the king like that?" screamed an official.

"I am sorry but I need to warn and warn very seriously too, that the king should not draw a battle-line between himself and the gods; that will be a most hazardous thing to do. It is a dangerous venture. Without fear of contradiction, I must say that Your Highness has no business here. Your portfolio does not cover this schedule. It is a matter clearly outside your jurisdiction. It is outside your constituency. Your action is therefore ultra vires!"

The king smiled grimly and said:

"This one has gone crazy. He has lost his senses. He will need the services of a psychiatrist.

Arrest him," screamed the king.

In a minute, the king's bodyguards surrounded Asa, his hands chained behind him and was bundled out of the arena. The huge crowd dispersed in confusion. As Asa was being led away, he roared:

"Tell your king that he will have enough problems even before this day closes. Before this day passes away, he will have enough regrets."

"Move on," screamed Bawa, the king's bodyguard. Bawa pushed Asa with both hands. He was in no mood for Asa's rantings.

The priest of Toro great gods, a man whose words were laws, the venerated patriarch, a man who always heard from the gods, a supernatural being, was being pushed by unholy hands. Asa had never seen any thing more sacrilegious. He stared at Bawa, his face radiating a growing contempt.

"He that god wants to destroy he first makes mad. Your

186

king is mad. This is the highest level of insanity;" screamed a bewildered Asa.

"Keep moving! We are not interested in all those bickering."

They were now at the entrance of the dungeon.

"I am sorry for your king. He is the most foolish ruler ever to preside over the affairs of Toro."

"Push in the buffoon and close the door!" screamed Bawa.

The journey from the eminent position of a judge to that of a degraded, lonely prisoner in the dungeon took just a few minutes that Asa could scarcely believe what happened.

CHAPTER TWENTY-FOUR

Asa had been fasting for the past three days. He was to break his fast after the queen's dance by 6p.m. that day. He was now tired and hungry.

He heard some footsteps and stood up. It was Bawa, the Chief Police. He opened the door to Asa's cell and walked in.

"Asa! Are you still hearing from your gods?"

Asa only glared at his face.

"Or have they stopped talking to you?"

Asa didn't utter a word.

"Didn't your gods warn you that today is not going to be a happy day and that you would get into trouble? Or they too did not know that a great palaver was in the offing? You have kept three hours in this dungeon and I begin to feel that if your gods are really what you call them; they ought to have released you from here. Or have they gone on holidays?"

Asa stared at him in contempt but did not say a word.

"Asa! Now on a more serious note. I am here this time

as your friend. You are tired and hungry; you certainly need food but we have been instructed not to give you anything. I have thought things over and I feel it is time I should tell you some home truths. If you remain stubborn, you are going to die here. And mind you, there is no need to. The king said you should pronounce that the Queen's dance was all right. My friend! What is difficult in that? Just say that sentence and you are out of trouble. Why are you punishing yourself? Why will you die before your day? Even if the gods tell you that the dance is not all right, why can't you comply with the king's directive and save your own neck from the gallows?"

"I am a priest. If a priest no longer tells the truth, who will?"

"Asa! That truth will lead you nowhere. It can give you nothing except trouble. It may in fact lead you to an untimely grave. I know you are afraid of your gods. But you'll better fear the king more, I mean the god you can see than the ones you cannot see physically. This is a no-nonsense ruler. Don't put your neck into the guillotine. Cooperate with him and say what he asked you to say."

"I can't say what the gods did not tell me. I don't have a personal verdict of my own," replied Asa.

"Asa! I am afraid; you will remain here for long. I pity you."

"Man! I don't ask for anybody's sympathy and you don't need to show me one. If it is the will of the gods that I should die here, let it be. I have no regrets."

189

"Asa! You sound so bold. But let me tell you that you haven't seen anything yet. The king said the rodent and the snake cannot live together in the same hole. He also said you and your gods will have to relocate because he cannot tolerate any of you around here. There is, however, a more serious issue than that; I mean a more immediate issue: you will be thrown into the refuse dump tomorrow. I mean the dump into which the people excrete. You will be lowered into it and only your neck and head will be above the dirty pond. Maggots and germs will be dancing on this your big, bald head. Be reasonable. It is time to apologize to the king and retract your verdict.

Asa! This is a new king. This one was brought up in Britain and knows nothing about your so-called culture and traditions. Time has changed. I am only asking you to change with the time. And if you don't, time will leave you behind. And I am afraid it won't be funny. You have no choice in this matter. If you are wise, you will do exactly what the king asked you to do."

"I won't!", Asa spoke up. "I can never change the verdict of the gods. I haven't such powers. I am a mere agent."

"Asa! You will have many regrets and please do not blame anyone," roared Bawa as he closed the door and started to walk away.

"Bawa! Just before you go."

"Have you finally changed your mind?" asked Bawa.

"What nonsense are you telling me?" queried an unrepentant Asa. I have been patient listening to your foolery and that of your king. Your king is playing with fire. By midnight today, he will know who is superior - he or the gods. He is threatening fire and brimstone now. Let him try. When a young child insists on playing in a forest of prickles, it's no use dissuading him. When he comes back from the place, he will relate his experience. Experience is always the best teacher. He says he will expel me and the gods from his kingdom. Let him go ahead. We will soon know who is the real owner of the land." Asa shook his head, stared at Bawa's face, then smiled and said:

"Go Bawa! Tell your king that the die is cast."

CHAPTER TWENTY-FIVE

The clown feels he can play his usual monkey game with me; he will know that he cannot," said the king as he put his arm around Jennifer's waist while taking a stroll in the palace garden.

He stared at Jennifer again, he so much loved her shape.

"Darling! Don't mind that rascal; no evil can happen to you. We are covenant children and do you still remember the covenant of God as He says it in Psalms 91?"

"Please remind me," exclaimed Jennifer

"He says:

"Because thou hath made the Lord, Which is my refuge, even the most High, thy habitation, No evil shall befall thee, neither shall any plague come near thy dwelling."

"That is a good one," said Jennifer as she smiled shyly for the first time.

When the king finally got to his room, he assessed the situation again. He had been told that those queens who missed their steps in the past usually died in their sleep at exactly 12.00 midnight.

"I don't believe that missing one's steps in any dance can kill anyone. But assuming there is some truth in the conjecture of these fools, I can find a way round it. I will organize a night party for today. No one will sleep. Jennifer will not sleep. The thought of her dying in her sleep will not even arise. I can block all possible loopholes and that is what I am going to do. I will show the jesters that they might have outwitted the past kings of Toro; they cannot succeed with me using the same trick. They will see that they are not dealing with amateurs this time."

"Who is there?" the king suddenly roared.

"It's Saba, Your Highness."

"Saba! You will send messages to all my chiefs, barons and dignitaries of Toro Kingdom and inform them that I am holding an all-night party tonight. I want everyone to be there. The party will start at 9p.m. Dispatch the horse-riders quickly and alert the kitchen."

The king sat on his throne. Queen Jennifer had never been more beautiful. She put on a royal robe of maroon colour. Costly jewels adorned her beautiful neck. Her face was sweet, her figure was queenly and magnificent. Although the notice was too short, all the men and women that mattered in Toro Kingdom and beyond were at the party. Dr. Harry Boyd, the Medical Superintendent of the Government Hospital at Iddo and his wife, Melody, came at 10p.m. Dr Boyd had known the king in their days at Oxford. He and his wife paid the normal homage and were conducted to their seats.

The police Band which came from the Divisional Headquarters, 30 kilometres away entertained the guests. Its rendering of Sha-Sha-Sha, a Jamaican version of Jazz was superb. The king and the queen took to the dancing floor.

"My God! This is a wonderful pair. They are superb dancers," exclaimed Melody.

"Africans really excel in dancing. It is their natural field;" said Dr Boyd.

When the king finally retired to his seat, he smiled benignly at Jennifer and said:

"Darling! How are you?"

"I am fine. I have never felt so wonderful in my life."

"I am happy to hear that the queen feels so good. I will make Asa and his group appreciate the value of education. There are too many superstitions all over the place. When the clowns see you tomorrow, hail and hearty, they will know that their so-called gods cannot kill a fly. They will realise that their gods are no gods. They will know that ours is the Omnipotent God, all other gods are mere creations of human imaginations."

The night was tantalizing. The band was good. The food and drinks were abundant. The guests really enjoyed themselves. The king kept watching the clock; it was 11.00p.m.

"Just one hour to Asa's zone of death," he muttered.

He looked at the clock again at 11.30p.m. The clock continued to tinkle and he watched it now from time to time. As 12.00 midnight drew closer and closer, his anxiety began to grow.

"There is nothing to fear," something told him. "What if the clowns are right? Remember those queens who missed their steps died at exactly 12.00 midnight. It is on record, and history cannot tell lies," another thought pestered him.

"I know Asa and his cohorts cannot be right," he told himself forcefully. But much as he made good effort to exercise control over what seemed like fear, he discovered that his anxiety kept on growing; for a reason he could not explain.

Soon, it was 11.50p.m. Jennifer and Melody were arguing on an issue on the lawn of the palace ground, each holding a cup of champagne. They were so lovely to watch.
"The poor woman had forgotten everything about Asa and his 12.00 midnight zone of death. And that makes the situation really good. Jennifer is not having any anxiety. I thank God for that," said the king.

It was 11.58p.m. and the king began to follow the second hand of the clock with his eyes and with growing apprehension. It was 11.59p.m. He looked at Jennifer; she was looking so good and radiant as ever. Then came 11.59p.m. 10 seconds. Then came 11.59.30 seconds … 11.59.40 seconds … 11.59.50 seconds. Jennifer stood there; talking and gesticulating like a brilliant teacher before her students.

"Yes! I have outwitted those fools," said the king

excitedly. But that excitement suddenly evaporated because just that moment, there was a stir as Jennifer suddenly screamed:

"Help! Help! I say Help!" In a second, she slumped and fell flat on the ground. A terrified look appeared on Melody's face as she rushed forward quickly to raise her up.

"What is the matter?" she asked.

Dr Boyd hurried to the scene, took Jennifer and laid her flat on the lawn. She was gasping as if she was short of breath. The doctor tried various methods to assist the heart which was now working erratically but short of assisting it with a mechanical device, the situation seemed hopeless! There was commotion among the guests and dignitaries. The king, confused and dumbfounded, stared at Jennifer in disbelief.

"I have to rush her to the hospital at once. Melody! Please, bring my car!"

But before the car arrived, Jennifer's condition went out of control. Her heart beat rapidly and suddenly stopped.

"What?" the doctor queried. He shook Jennifer's body; gave her artificial respiration. It was of no use! He examined her again and again.

"What's happening?" a bewildered doctor queried. For almost five minutes, Dr Boyd kept on trying various methods to resuscitate Jennifer.

"She is dead;" he finally pronounced.

"What?" screamed the king.

The king took Jennifer in his hands, shook her repeatedly.

"Jennifer! Jennifer!" he shouted. The body was rigid and stiff.

"My God! Where are you? Where are you, God?
Can this be true? Is it true? Is this just a dream?
No! No! I say No!".
That moment, the king just had a prick of the needle
in one of his arms. Dr Boyd signaled to three palace
officials:
"Please! Carry the king into the palace and lay him on
his bed." In the next moment, the king was asleep.

The entire kingdom was in deep mourning.
Representatives from all towns and villages far and
near came to grace the burial on the following day.
The casket was the most beautiful the people had ever
seen. Jennifer was dressed in her barrister's suit. She
looked so serene and sweet as if she were just sleeping.
The king wore a black suit with dark glasses. Palace
officials stood on both sides of the monarch. He still
did not know whether Jennifer's death was still a
dream or not.

Pastor Francis preached the sermon. It was a brief
but colourful funeral ceremony:
"God giveth and God taketh away. Glory be to the
name of the Lord." It was a short sermon. "The life
of our sister was short but glorious." That was the
theme of his sermon.
As Jennifer's body was being lowered into the grave in the
cemetery behind the church, the congregation sang:
"Alleluia! Alleluia! Alleluia!
The strife is over, the battle done:
The victory of life is won

197

The song of triumph had begun
Alleluia!
The powers of death have done their worse
But Christ their legions had dispersed
Let shouts of holy joy outburst, Alleluia."

The king still maintained his composure but when the congregation sang:
"On the resurrection morning
Soul and body meet again
No more sorrow, no more weeping
No more pain."

The king could no longer bear the sorrow. He burst into tears.

Jennifer came from a very wealthy home in Kingston, Jamaica. She had a lot of jewellery. While she was being lowered into her grave, the king said:

"Bury everything with her. She owns everything. I can't stand a situation in which another woman will use them. What type of souvenirs will they be to me? Let my Jewel go with her jewellery."

By 11a.m., the funeral service was over. Beautiful and special concrete slabs were made to cover the grave. Having sealed up the tomb, the congregation dispersed.

CHAPTER TWENTY-SIX

Asa was sitting in one corner of his 8' by 8' cell when Bawa, the Chief Police, opened the door.

"Jennifer is dead," he told him.

"When?"

"Yesterday at 12 mid-night."

"I knew it would happen like that. Jennifer died when she missed her steps. Although she did not collapse and die on the spot, all what she spent after that were mere extra time. The soul departed from her body immediately I proclaimed the verdict of the gods. I believe what has happened so far will teach your king a lesson that he is fighting a force greater than he. I told you people that the gods are consuming fire. No one jokes with them and goes unpunished. There is no greater fool today in the entire Toro Kingdom than our king. He has only seen the tributary. He has not got to the main river yet. Tell him that the gods say he himself has only seven days to live."

"What?" queried Bawa.

"I say he has only seven days. He will soon join his wife. That one is as sure as death. He has insulted the gods and the gods are angry with him. But the gods are kind beings. They are ready to forgive him if he is ready to apologize and thereafter tread the path of sanity. But I know he is an arrogant person. His western education has put on him a toga of pride. And that is what is going to destroy him. But if he can humble himself, forgo his pride, dance before the shrine of Alaworo, the great Toro god and apologize publicly to the gods, he will live."

"His Highness to dance before a shrine?"

"Of course yes. He will put off his flowing gown. He will only have the pant and the singlet on and dance under the full glare of all his subjects. If he does this, he will live his full life. His reign shall be prosperous. The kingdom of Toro will enjoy an unprecedented peace. That is the verdict of the gods."

"You want me to tell the king this message?"

"I feel you are his officer and friend. If you love him, you'll better tell him. Let me repeat myself to your hearing, he has only one life jacket, and that is — to dance before Alaworo shrine. But if he is too educated and too sophisticated to do that, go and buy his casket because he would surely die within seven days. He will die like his wife and he will go down in history as the first king of Toro who dies because of his folly."

Asa spoke with such righteous indignation and fearful certainty that Bawa left the place trembling.

The king fixed his eyes on Bawa for a long time. Then, he laughed a weathered, dry laugh. Suddenly his eyes glittered with rage as he exclaimed:

"You mean I should go and dance before a pagan shrine?"

"Yes, Your Highness! Just for the safety of your life!

The priest says if you refuse, then Your Highness has only seven days to live."

"And you believe such foolery?"

"Your Highness! The man told me earlier on that Queen Jennifer would die at 12.00 midnight and that had happened already. Your Highness! Please don't toy with the man. Do not toy with his words. On this issue, I advise that we have to stoop to conquer."

For some minutes, the king looked on, he did not talk.

"I won't dance before a shrine. Never. What does Asa feel I am?" the king suddenly spoke.

"Your Highness! You don't need to take offence on this issue."

"Shut up!" The king suddenly roared.

"I will never dance before a shrine. If the God I am serving cannot protect me; that is his business."

"But Your God has not protected Queen Jennifer even though she believed so much in Him. Your Highness, let us be careful with the man."

"Bawa! I will rather die than dance before a shrine. That will not happen. Not here on earth. No circumstance, no condition, no situation can make me dance almost naked before any shrine. Tell Asa to get ready all his arsenals for the battle ahead. I am not going to shift an inch of the ground to him. I am still in a state of mourning. After forty-eight hours, I will have time to deal with him. The snake and the rabbit cannot live together in the same hole. Asa and his gods cannot exist with me in this kingdom. One will have to leave for the other. And I am sure; they are the ones who will leave."

CHAPTER TWENTY-SEVEN

At the outskirts of Toro, in an uncompleted three-bedroom bungalow, Faithful, a 27-year-old-automechanic stood in a dark room. He paced up and down, wearing an impatient look.

"They ought to have been here by now. The boys are not good for this kind of business. And this is another proof. Anyone who does not have respect for time is a misfit."

His anger kept on rising. He peeped through the window; no one was in sight. His anger shot up sharply. But just that moment, he had some, approaching footsteps. They were Honesty's.

"Just strolling into this place ten minutes after the scheduled time? What do you people think you are doing? And where is Christian?"

"He is coming up right now."

"Boys! I can't condone this kind of indiscipline."

"Faithful! We are sorry. One customer turned up when we were about to start off."

"I have heard that kind of story over and over again."

"This will be the last time."

"Please, let it be. We are already late. Without wasting further time, let us get to business." Faithful stared at the faces of his colleagues and asked:

"Didn't you boys see the queen's casket when it was being lowered down into the grave?"
"We saw it. It was very beautiful."
"I was told that the casket is filled to the brim with jewellery."
"That was precisely what we heard too."
"That casket will fetch half a million pounds in the provincial headquarters," cut in Honesty.

"It can't be less," affirmed Faithful. "If we can take possession of the jewellery, we will sell them for nothing less than 10 million pounds. We will bid poverty farewell forever and join the exclusive class of Nigerian rich men. We will leave this kind of business to the younger ones that are just coming up. We will not need to spend sleepless nights looking for whom to rob. We will no more risk our lives on dangerous adventures. Like multi-millionaires in Lagos, Port Harcourt or Kano who terrorize people with their highly expensive cars: Limousines, Mercedez Benz etc, we will also become oppressors. We will join the arrogant class of intimidators who drive through Nigeria's streets with sirens and set people stampeding into different directions at their approach. We will ride through the streets with dispatch riders in front. We will not need to be looking for the beautiful ladies in town; it will be their duty to look for us. Men! We will live like the barons and princes of the land."

"Faithful! That is enough. We are taking possession of the jewellery. Nothing shall stop us," said Honesty.

"Good! You have caught the mood and the passion necessary for this business. But boys let me sound a note of warning. As we are planning, certain people are likely to be planning for the same jewellery too. We are not the only tough boys in town. We need to move fast. We need to beat any possible rivals arms down. This is an opportunity of a lifetime. And this kind only comes, perhaps once in a lifetime. If we miss it ..."

"Stop that! Don't say that sentence again. How can we miss it? Why should we miss it?" queried Christian.

"Boys! We dare not because we have no reason to," affirmed Faithful, the leader of the three man gang that posed as auto-technicians in the afternoon and operate as armed robbers at night. They had been in a flourishing, armed robbery business for the past three years and they were already masters of the game. They rode beautiful cars and lived in reasonable comfort.

"We must move fast. We need to move fast. But it is 3.20p.m. Boys! We can't go to the cemetery now. We can only go there when it is dark," said Honesty.

"No fool can go there in the afternoon," added Faithful.

"The earliest time we can get there is 12.00 midnight."

"Faithful! That will be too late."

"What is too late? Do you want us to go there when people around are not asleep?" asked Christian.

"Some others could be there before 12.00 midnight."

"You don't need to have high blood pressure because of that. We can lay an ambush in the small bush along the path leading to the cemetery as from 10p.m. Whosoever goes there before us will not escape," said Honesty.

"I feel, I buy that idea," exclaimed Faithful. That is a master stroke."

"Men! I have been in this business for sometime."

CHAPTER TWENTY-EIGHT

Inside the grave, the magic portion on the skin of Queen Jennifer had been losing its effect six hours ago. It was now two minutes to 12.00 midnight. Queen Jennifer opened her eyes; she saw nothing but a thick darkness. She was sure she had been sleeping. She was sweating profusely. The heat was unbearable.

"Darling! Why has the room become so hot?" she queried as she tried to turn her body and embrace her husband. She found that she was hemmed in on both sides.

"What? Where am I?" she queried. "This is certainly not a bedroom. And what is it?"

She noticed that she was lying on her back, and inside what seemed like a cage.

"Why am I here? How did I get here? Who put me here and why?"

The heat was growing more and more suffocating and Jennifer knew she just must get out of the present enclosure in the next few minutes; if not, she would be a dead woman.

"But how did I get here? Who put me here? Why am I put in a cage?"

She did a brief mental recall. Her last memory was when she and Melody stood discussing on the palace lawn. She recalled now how she had a sudden pain in the heart.

"What happened after that? Could it be that I fainted?" Gradually it occurred to her now that she must have died and perhaps buried?

She examined the cage. She observed that it was a wooden cage.

"Am I inside a coffin?" she queried
She suddenly panicked.

"Help! Help! I say Help!" she shouted. She kicked the casket with all the force she could muster.

"Help!" She screamed again. Her voice vibrated through the huge grave where the casket laid. She kicked the casket now screaming on top of her voice. She listened with all her might but she heard no sound. Two minutes after that, she was losing her breath and was finding it difficult to breathe. She struggled hard but the air in that enclosure was not just enough for her. A moment later, she could perceive she was growing unconscious again. She started to gasp. About five minutes later, Jennifer's body appeared rigid. She went into a coma

Five hundred metres away, Faithful, Christian and Honesty were lying in ambush in a small bush south of the cemetery each with AK.47 in his hand. They had been waiting for the thieves who might wish to go to Jennifer's grave. But they saw no one. It was almost 12.00 midnight.

"Men! I feel we have waited enough. It is time to move," said Faithful.

"The cemetery is fenced round by barbed-wires," whispered Christian.

" Yes, I know that and I have a wire-cutter here with me."

"That is good, but I forgot to tell you that two security men occasionally parade the cemetery at night."

"I also know that. I have a silent revolver with me. If the men are on parade today, I am sorry for them. The Pastor will pick up their dead bodies tomorrow morning. My Friend! I am in a no-nonsense mood. If my mother is there on parade, she is a dead woman."

The three men soon got to the cemetery. The moon was full but was hiding its face behind a thick cloud. Everywhere was slightly bright. There was no guard in sight.

"They must be inside that small house," said Christian, pointing to a small rectangular building.

Faithful tiptoed towards it and suddenly kicked the door and it gave way. The guards woke up from their sleep with shock.

"If you scream for help, you are all dead men," pointing his gun at the men.

"But if you cooperate, you have nothing to fear. Now lie down flat. Put your faces on the floor and cover them with your hands. No shaking; no movement of any sort or else I'll shoot,"

"We will cooperate," said the two shaking men.

Faithful stood a few metres from them pointing his gun menacingly at the men.

"Boys! Move into action," he screamed.

Honesty and Christian hurried to Jennifer's grave. The king had made a 10' by 10' by 6' grave for Jennifer and himself. The extra space was waiting for him whenever he was ready. The slabs covering the grave were bought from a local block-making industry and the edges had not been permanently sealed off.

"Our job is going to be very easy, much easier than I had anticipated," said Christian.

Carefully, they removed four of the slabs and below them was Jennifer's casket. The two men descended into the huge hole before them and brought out the casket into the open.

Christian unscrewed the lid of the casket, lifted the lid up and there before them was Jennifer, serene and beautiful. Her body lay there as if she were still asleep. Honesty lifted up Jennifer's right hand and removed all the golden bangles, then lifted the left hand, removed the bangles.

"The body is still very warm," said he.

"That is strange. She was buried at 11a.m. yesterday. I mean thirteen hours ago.

"Shei! This is a beautiful woman," whispered Honesty.

"No matter how beautiful, she is dead. Man! We are not here to appreciate any beauty. We are here strictly on business."

"That is true but I am imagining how this one would respond in bed. She is too fine."

"Honesty! Don't be silly! Face your business."

Honesty lifted up Jennifer's head and Christian began to remove the necklace. The two stared at the costly diamonds and exchanged delicious smiles.

Jennifer first felt a touch on her neck; then on her right palm. Her eyes opened gradually. She saw two people on her; one holding her head. She closed her eyes and then opened them again.

"Who are these? What are they doing to me?" she wondered. She remembered she was feeling very hot sometime ago and was screaming for help.

"Has help finally arrived at last? Have these ones come to rescue me?" she queried. She stared at the men; they were tall, hefty giants but complete strangers. The two men could not see her eyes in the dark.

"Look at the legs, there must be some expensive chains there," said Honesty.

"Who are you and what are you doing?" Jennifer's sonorous voice asked.

The men stood frozen. They knew they heard a voice but were not sure where it came from. Certainly it could not be from the dead woman before them. And they turned round for the speaker.

"I say, who are you?" asked Jennifer whose body began to rise up. There was a startled silence. The two men paralyzed with shock, stood glued to their positions, a mixture of fear and alarm on their faces. Honesty was the first to shake off the stupor, and he screamed:

"Ghost! Ghost! Hey Ghost! We are in trouble!" The two dropped the jewellery in their hands. They could not pick their AK.47 as they fled in different directions jumping over the fence.

Faithful heard the noise of commotion, and then saw his two associates dashing away on top speed, shouting … but in that confusion he did not clearly understand what was going on.

"What is the matter?" he queried. He looked round; he did not see anyone. The boys could not be running from policemen because he did not see anyone around.
"Have they seen a python?" He had heard that one huge python used to live very close to the cemetery. Some claimed to have seen it on several occasions.

"Has the python appeared again?" But he remembered that each had AK.47, and then queried: "Why must they run away from a python? I have always doubted the ability of these boys. This shows clearly that they are not up to the task and I will have to fire them."

That moment, the moon peeped out behind the cloud and the surroundings became clearer. Faithful saw the boys when they were bringing out the casket. He saw them opening the lid. He now stared at the casket again and suddenly stood frozen. He saw someone sitting inside it. He looked at the figure again and again.

"This is a human being. This is certainly a woman."

Now the figure appeared to be moving and the hands were now arranging the hair on the woman's head. Faithful needed no one to tell him now that this was what the boys saw. That moment, the figure appeared to be rising up in her flowing gown.
"Ghost! Save me God!" Faithful screamed as he flew over the fence and fled.

The guards heard of the commotion. They heard the sounds of people running. They looked up; Faithful was no longer in his position.
"I suspect the policemen are around," whispered the first guard. He tiptoed to the door and tried to pull it back gently until he closed it.
"What are you doing that for?" asked his partner.
"We might get killed by stray bullets in case of a shoot - out between the robbers and the police."

"Then lie down quickly. You don't need to stand up. It is by standing that you can endanger your life."

CHAPTER TWENTY-NINE

Queen Jennifer looked left and right; her surrounding was frighteningly quiet. Various tombs now stared at her. The graves sent a chill down her spine. Horrified, she stood up quickly. Every tomb and every stone cried out:

"Where are you going? You can't leave us." Jennifer could swear that she heard those sentences so clearly. That moment, she saw the Pastor's house afar off and started to run towards it. She would not allow the spirits of the dead people to drag her back into the grave. As she ran, she could hear a thousand steps behind her. She increased her speed as her barrister's flowing gown dazzled under the rays of the shinning moon. Her heart beat so fiercely; she soon got to the door of the pastor's house. Her heart was pounding. She wanted the door open quickly before the pursuing spirits caught up with her. She pounced on the door and knocked furiously, terror on her face. She looked back again and again. If it were possible for her now to dissolve through the keyhole and get in quickly, she would have done so.

It was the banging on the door that woke up Pastor Francis. He first sat up on his bed. The banging continued. He stood up quickly, took his lantern, opened the door to his room and walked angrily down the corridor, towards the main door.

"Darling! Who is it?" asked Hannah, his wife who had already woken up.

"I am yet to find out." Pastor Francis hastened his steps.

"Am I not entitled to some rest? What business has anyone in my house at 1a.m.? What kind of life am I in?" The questions came in torrents.

"Sorry! You have to wait till tomorrow morning if you want me to attend to you." That was what he made up his mind to tell the intruder. Then, came again the violent knocks on the door.

"Who is it?" asked Pastor Francis, wearing a pugnacious look.

"It is Jennifer," a voice replied.

"Pardon!"

"I say, I am Jennifer."

"Jennifer?" The lantern almost dropped from Pastor Francis' hand, as he suddenly stood rigid. He knew only one Jennifer and that one was dead and buried yesterday.

"This may be another Jennifer," his mind quickly suggested to him. "The person behind the door must surely be another Jennifer whom you are yet to meet. My friend! You don't need to panic." He summoned up courage and then asked:

"Which Jennifer and from where?"

"I am Jennifer, the Queen," she answered.

"Jennifer What?"

"I say, I am Jennifer, the Queen."

His already rapid heart beat accelerated as he screamed: "Jesus! The ghost of Jennifer had come to visit me. What have I done to deserve this?"

His eyes burning with embarrassment, he bellowed: "Jennifer! I am not the one who killed you. I have no hand in your death. Why must your ghost come to torment an innocent man? Why are you here? I only assisted in your burial and that is my duty as a pastor. Jennifer! Now listen to me!

The dead cannot visit the living.
No!
Never!
The words of God say those who die must continue to take their rest until the day of resurrection. You evil spirit, go back and take your rest.!
Go back to the cemetery!
You have no further business with the land of the living!
You have completed your task!
Go! I say, go!
May God rebuke you!
May the fire of the Holy Ghost consume you.
Go back to the land of the dead.
Go and never come back."
"Pastor Francis! It is true I was dead, but I have risen up. I am now alive. Please open quickly, I don't like the atmosphere outside here. It terrifies me."

"You terrible spirit, listen to me!
You cannot enter here.
This is the home of the living.
This is a forbidden territory.

The dead and the living cannot transact any business together.
Never!"

Something suddenly switched on Pastor Francis and he erupted in a strange voice:

> *"Chiro ma ma ma*
> *Chiro ma ma ma*
> *Chima ye ye*
> *Ma ma su ra do*
> *Ma ma pa pa ye ye*
> *Ma ma su ra do*
> *Ma ma ko mu ni ca do*
> *Ma ma su ra do..."*

For over a minute, Pastor Francis was speaking in a strange tongue. But he suddenly stopped, jerked and moved back as Jennifer banged the door furiously again.
"I say open for me. Please open!"
"You mean you are still there?" queried Pastor Francis.

"My God! This must certainly be a stubborn spirit. Whatever you are, I take authority over you. God has ordained me to do this job. He called me to work in his vineyard. I did not call my self. God has no other choice, He must give me a back-up. You spirit behind the door, in the name of Jesus, every knee should bow. Be it things in heaven or on earth or below the earth. I therefore command you in the name of Jesus to leave my house and go." The banging suddenly became more violent. It seemed as if the unwanted visitor had gone crazy.
"I say open," Jennifer screamed.

"You mean you are still there?" screamed a bewildered Pastor Francis.

"Jesus! I am in trouble. What do I do now?" But just that moment, Pastor Francis remembered Psalm 35 and he burst out:
"Plead my cause O Lord with those that strive with me.
Fight against them that fight against me.
Take hold of the shield and buckler and stand for my help.
Draw the spear and stop the way against them that persecute me.
Say unto my soul, I am thy salvation.
Let them be confounded that seek after my soul.
In particular let this terrible spirit behind my door be confounded
Let the angel of the Lord chase it away now."

Jennifer was hearing all the rantings; she could not understand why Pastor Francis, a man of God, could not open his door for a woman in distress. She stared at the cemetery, it seemed as if men were sitting on the various tombs and were now pointing at her. She screamed loudly.
"I say open for me. I need help ... Open!" the Queen screamed more loudly.

Pastor Francis's wife, Hannah, had been hearing all the altercations and was wondering what was happening. She hurried out of her room.
"Darling! Who is the person? What does she want?"
"It is the ghost of Queen Jennifer;" Pastor Francis whispered to his wife.
"And what about her ghost?"

217

"It is the one behind the door. It is the one knocking and pleading that the door be opened unto her."
"That is impossible. How do you arrive at that?"

"Pastor! I say open for me?" Jennifer screamed hysterically again. She saw over one hundred figures rising up from the graves behind her - and they were moving nearer and nearer. She could no longer stand the dreadful sight. It was most unbearable. She looked back. The various tombs were howling. Her body stiffened and it appeared she would soon go into a fit.

"In the name of God, please have mercy, open for me," she cried.

"My God! You are correct. That is her voice. That is certainly the Queen's voice;" Hannah yelled in dismay. She stared at her husband's face in bewilderment. "That is it. She is surely the one behind the door. Darling! Come this way (pulling the husband now towards herself). Let us go up to our room and lock ourselves in. Let's go in quickly."

But Pastor Francis would not leave the corridor.
"Darling! I hate burial ceremonies. Haven't I warned you not to take part in it anymore? Now we are in trouble. The ghost of Jennifer has come to torment us. Where do we go now? Who will assist us to drive it away? I warned you about the inherent dangers when you informed me that you had the calling of God to go into full time ministry. I do not intend to die now and neither do I wish to be a widow. God what do we do now?"

The sexton, a 60-year-old man who was a guest of Pastor Francis had been listening to a growing roar outside his room; he opened his door and hurried unto a dismayed couple.

"Pastor Francis! What is the matter? Can I help you?"

"Sexton! It is Jennifer's ghost! It is behind this door."

"Jennifer?"

"Yes, Jennifer, the Queen."

"That is impossible."

"What is impossible?" Just that moment, that midnight silence was torn into two by Jennifer's scream.

"I say I am not dead. I am alive, please, open for me," a voice bellowed behind the door and the speaker at the same time shook the door furiously.

"She will pull down this door and where do we run to?"

"Pastor! Is that what is scaring you? How can you be fooled so easily? That is not Jennifer's voice."

"Whose voice is it?"

"I don't know. But that is certainly a man's voice; not that of a woman.

Was that the one who called himself Jennifer?"

"Yes."

"That is a mere pretender. The person behind the door is a clown."

"Are you sure?"

"Sure? How can you be easily deceived by a mere impostor? Can you still remember your sermon of last Sunday?"

"What does my sermon have to do with this?"

"It has a lot to do. In that sermon, you said over and over again that:

Some of you are cowards. When you hear the

movement of a cockroach in the night, you scream for help. As sons and daughters of God, where is your faith? God says that you should be bold and courageous. How many of you have courage when problems come?"

Those were your own words. Weren't they?"

"Yes, they were."

"The impostor behind the door wants to make fun of you and has decided to visit you at night pretending to be Jennifer and find out how you will behave. Pastor Francis, the Apostle of Courage, has failed the test of courage." The Sexton stared at the Pastor's face; then said: "The man has decided to test you and you have failed his test."

Pastor Francis stared at the Sexton's face, confused.

"Now, Pastor, I am going to open the door and get ready to laugh."

The Sexton went towards the door, drew the bolts and opened it suddenly and there before him was Jennifer, the Queen in the same barrister's regalia in which she was buried yesterday. The Sexton fell down and fainted.

Pastor Francis fled towards the direction of his room upstairs.

"God! Save me! Save me! I am in trouble. Save me!" His deafening yells in that quiet hour of the early morning could be heard two kilometres away. He climbed the staircase quickly and screamed loudly.

"Hannah! Hannah! Open for me! Open quickly!"

When Hannah would not open the door to her room on time, the Pastor quickly mounted the window, jumped down from a height of fourteen feet and escaped into the bush.

CHAPTER THIRTY

For some minutes, Jennifer stood there confused. "Ha! Ha! Ha!", she heard some people laughing behind her. She spun around with frightened eyes but she saw no one.

"It serves you right," said a voice but Jennifer did not see the speaker.

"Come back here. You belong to us. You can't abandon us; no matter how much you try. You already had the taste of our friendship. You partook of our communion. It is now too late to desert us; just too late," said another voice.

"Too late! Too late!" re-echoed a thousand voices from the tombs. Jennifer turned round, horror on her face, ran quickly down the road, terror staring at her from every direction. Her heart palpitated as she heard her own steps running after her. The more she ran from the terror of her own making, the more desperate the thousand spirits running after her became. She was soon outside the Vicarage. She negotiated a bend quickly and soon got to the main road. After another ten minute run, she got to the palace, a mixture of fear and alarm still on her face

After resting for a few minutes, she decided to make an effort to enter into the palace.

"What am I to do?" she asked herself. She did not know. She did not want another commotion and so she decided not to mention her name this time. She knocked at the gate.

"Who is it?" queried a voice.

"It's me," she answered.

"Who are you? Haven't you a name?"

"I am Maria." That was the name of one of her maids.

"Maria!? When did you go out and where are you coming from at 1a.m.?"

Jennifer did not answer.

A grumbling gateman hastened towards the iron gate before him, complaining profusely as he proceeded, his face stern and morose like one poised for a fight.

"Maria! You have no business disturbing me at this hour. As to where you are coming from, I am afraid; you have an explanation to make."

In annoyance, the man opened the gate suddenly and before him was Jennifer. The baton fell from his hand; he opened his mouth and let out a huge scream, then he turned round to run, but first fell down, then rose up quickly and fled.

"Ghost! Ghost! Queen Jennifer's Ghost! Help! I say help!" he screamed. His yelling tore into shreds the deep silence of that early morning and suddenly woke up the sleepy palace into a midnight shock and turmoil.

In a moment, people were stampeding out of their rooms.

"Where is the ghost?" asked the three palace guards who first joined the gateman.

"Look! It's the one coming," pointing to a figure in a flowing barrister's outfit, approaching from the direction of the gate. The men saw a figure of a woman, but stood still. As the figure moved closer, it became clearer that it was certainly that of the Queen. For some seconds, they stood there, open-mouthed, alarm on their faces. But as Jennifer drew closer, all the men started to back away.

"Gentlemen! Wait! You don't need to run away from me. I am not a ghost," shouted Jennifer. But the men would not wait. When she attempted to walk faster towards them, the men fled in different directions. Men, women were stampeding into their rooms, closing their doors.

The head of the Palace Guards screamed at one of the officers:

"Run quickly for Adala, the magician. Tell him that the palace is in distress. He should hurry. He is the one to handle this. We need a powerful magician to drive this terrible spirit back into her grave. I have heard this told in stories but I never believed it. This is most unbelievable. This is strange. It is an abomination. What have we done to annoy the gods? What is our offence?"

The king had woken up from his sleep and was listening to a growing roar outside his room. Just that moment, one of the palace officials rushed in.

"Your Highness! Trouble has come. We have seen the ghost of the Queen."

"Pardon!"

"The ghost of Queen Jennifer is right here in the palace. We've seen it."

"Ghost?"

"Yes, Ghost, Your Highness!".

"Where did you see it?"

A female figure standing by the door suddenly spoke up:

"You haven't seen any ghost. I am Jennifer. I am not a ghost."

The king stared at Jennifer, now standing by the door and in the same barrister's costume she was dressed when she was being buried the previous day. He suddenly stood frozen, transfixed to his bed. He stared at the ghost as it came closer and closer, horror on his face.

"Darling! You don't need to panic. I have woken up. I am not dead," said Jennifer as she moved closer still.

The king ran and hid behind a palace official, and the palace official held on to the king; both shaking and screaming for help.

"Go away! Terrible monster! Go! You have gone to the land of the dead. You have no further business here. Go!" screamed the king.

Darling! Be reasonable! I say you are not talking to a

ghost. This is me. This is your Queen Jennifer. This is your own Jennifer. I am a human being."

Jennifer tried to explain herself. But as she drew nearer, the king yelled and convulsed like an epileptic patient.
"Go! I say go away."

Jennifer now stared at the king fixedly as if she would jump on him at anytime.

"Help! I say help!" the king let out a huge scream. He could not bear the sight before him.
"What is all this?" shouted Jennifer who suddenly sprang forward and held on to the king. The king went into a fit. But the magician was just in time to save the situation. Pointing a cow horn with many amulets and talismans to Jennifer, he roared:

"You terrible spirit! I command you to leave here now. All lower principalities automatically bow before the higher ones. Therefore, you must humble yourself before me.
All animals humble themselves before the lion.
The day a rat sees a cat; he must run for cover.
The day an antelope sees the tiger; he must run without looking back. When a child goes into a bush of nettle, he rushes out of it quickly and runs .
I command you – run!.
Run back to your grave.
This place is not your abode."

The magician suddenly saw over a thousand stars as a hard slap landed on his face.

"Ye! Ye! Ye! She is attacking me," he scrammed but Jennifer followed up quickly with another slap, and yet another. The horn dropped from Adala's hand. He could not pick it up as he ran down the corridor and fled. The king took the opportunity of the scuffle to rush out of the room and escaped into the garden. In a minute, the corridor was deserted, leaving Jennifer standing alone. There was silence everywhere.

But Jennifer soon parted the thick silence with her scream:

"Your Highness! Can't you understand? Do I look like a ghost? Does a ghost have a physical body? Two people cannot suffer from deception; it is either your reasoning is impaired or mine is impaired. But I know I am normal. Come and touch me. Look at my face! I am not a ghost. And this can be verified."

Then Jennifer began to narrate the whole story. When the people and the king eventually got to the cemetery and saw the open coffin on the lawn, they could piece the whole story together. There and then, the king apologized to his queen, embraced her and the mourning suddenly turned into a carnival.

CHAPTER THIRTY-ONE

A sa woke up this morning completely oblivious of the new development in the palace. Hands in his pockets, he paced up and down in his cell; so pleased with himself.

"The death of Queen Jennifer is a golden opportunity for me to talk tough. I will harass the king to submission. I will make him crawl on the ground before me. I am going to reduce him into a mere puppet. I will become a god to him. When I ask him to sit down, he will sit; when I say, stand up, he will stand. I will make sure that he is just a king in name. All powers, I will exercise. This is the privilege enjoyed by all Asas through the ages. No one can deny me the same." He laughed loud, then shook his head proudly as he began to recount his various appellations:

"I, the wind, no one can hold,

The tiger that catches its prey and devour it all alone.

The all-consuming fear, which dread itself sees and flees.

Yes, that is my name." He beat his chest and laughed hysterically, then exclaimed:

"Only those who don't know me enough may try to toy with me. The king has not seen anything yet. That cocky, arrogant, power-drunk victim of western education thinks he can rubbish the customs and traditions of the land. He has started to learn his lessons in a bitter way."

He looked out of the window, watching the rising sun over the blue Gidigidi Hills in an explosion of colours then exclaimed:

"I have harassed Bawa, the Chief Police to submission. Next to him is the king. Before this day closes, he will be inside this my pocket," touching the right pocket of his trousers.

There was a huge roar. Various sounds of gangan-talking-drums woke up the palace this morning from slumber into an unexpected, growing hilarious mood. A carnival was on. Asa looked towards the direction of the palace and stood rigid. He stood for sometime in apprehensive silence.

"I can hear the beat of gangan-talking-drums. Gangan drums are used for celebration. What are these people celebrating? Celebrating the death of Queen Jennifer? How?" he queried.

Now, he looked up towards the palace again with frightened eyes. The palace is supposed to be mourning, but what I am hearing seems like a thousand voices of joy. How? Why? What is going on?"

His eyes fixed on the palace now with a burning heat. Then came another huge explosion of joyful shouts. Then came a continuous huge roar and a song of over a thousand people:

228

"Ewo ni a ni yo si?
Ewo ni a o ni yo si?
Bi a se fe ko ri
Beena lo ri
Ewo ni a o ni yo si?"

Meaning:

"Why won't we rejoice?
Why won't we rejoice?
The way we desired.
That is how it turns out to be.
Why won't we rejoice?"
"Why are they rejoicing? Rejoicing over the death of Queen Jennifer? What is happening?" That moment, the door to Asa's cell was flung open and Bawa came in.
"The king will love to see you?" said Bawa.
"When?"
"Right now."

When Asa arrived at the palace, the people shouting and singing had left for the town. Their huge, lusty voices were already swallowed up by the long, winding road facing the palace. The palace wore its usual sober look. Asa was greatly relieved.

"Those joyful shouts are not from here. Certainly not. I really have nothing to worry about;" he mumbled. The audacity and insolence that had temporarily left him, returned.
Asa looked stern and morose as he approached the king.
"Here I am, Your Highness;" said he, defiant and

uncompromising as he now stood proudly and stared at the king's face.

The king stared at him but internally he was boiling in fury. For some moment, he didn't talk.

"Your Highness! Bawa says you need me. Do I take it that Your Highness has finally changed his mind and you have decided to do what the gods asked you to do?"

"What did they ask me to do?" the king queried.

"Your Highness will have to dance at the shrine of Alaworo. You will apologize to the gods publicly for insulting them. If you refuse to do this, then prepare to die. You have just six days left. The gods gave seven days' notice of death to Your Highness yesterday. One day has gone already. I have asked Bawa to tell Your Highness all these." He stared fixedly at the king's face.

"Your Highness! You need to take quick action. Delay may be dangerous." The king drew himself up to his fullest height, now an intimidating goliath poised for a fight; then suddenly roared:

"I will never dance before the shrine of your gods. Never. Count me out of it."

Asa stared at the king's face confused. Then his lips parted giving out a narrow smile mixed with amused contempt.

"Your Highness! Then prepare your will since you have less than a week to live. Buy a good casket because I am sure you will need one. Then, tell your people to get ready for your funeral ceremony. You should get in touch with your undertakers and let them begin to make necessary preparations."

"You are a liar;" screamed the king. "Your gods are stupid, powerless and lousy gods. I have told you that if they make trouble, my God will deal with them!"

Asa burst into a huge laughter and stopped suddenly like one acting a drama. Hands akimbo and contempt written all over him, he asked:

"Your Highness! Where was your God when your queen slumped and died? Where was He? Was He on leave? Has He gone on sabbatical? If He is capable of saving you, why didn't He save your queen? Your Highness! Why do you deceive yourself? I had warned you but let me warn you again – Do not play with fire. Do not walk into a burning furnace."

"Asa! This will not be the first time you will threaten with fire and brimstone. Enough of that! I have summoned you before me not for another theatrical show. I have no time for that. I have a visitor who wants to see you."

Then the king looked to the right and screamed:
"Bawa! Go and bring the visitor."
"Long live, Your Highness."
Bawa went in and in the next moment, a woman dressed in a flowing, dazzling barrister gown appeared. She was Queen Jennifer. Pointing to her, the king queried:
"Asa! Do you still remember this woman?"
Asa and Jennifer exchanged bewildered glances. Surprise held Asa motionless. He stared at Jennifer, confused and unbelieving. The spectacle before him

was too incredible. He stared at her again and again, open-mouthed. There was a long pregnant silence during which time Asa stood transfixed to that spot, completely immobilized by shock

Finally he spoke:
"I am too sure that the woman before me is the twin sister of Queen Jennifer. She can never be any other person. Jennifer, the Queen can never come back to this world. Never! She is dead and she will forever rest in her grave. The river never flows up-hill. A dead lion never holds a meeting with a living one. Jennifer can never have anything to do in the land of the living. Impossible!"

"Asa! Don't deceive yourself. Jennifer has no twin sister. You are looking at Queen Jennifer, not any other woman. Your gods killed her. She was dead and buried. But my own God woke her up. I told you that your gods are mere, lousy, powerless gods. You did not believe me then; but you can see the proof for yourself now. If your gods kill this woman a thousand times, my own God will raise her up each time. That is how powerful my God is," said the king.

For some minutes, Asa stood there, confused.
"Bawa!", screamed the king. "Asa will need time to sort himself out. Take him back to his cell."

Back in his cell, Asa looked at the walls, then at the floor, then queried:
"Is the woman I saw the true Jennifer? If so, how did she wake up? Is this a fiction? Am I dreaming? What's

happening? Here in this dungeon, I saw the long procession accompanying Jennifer's casket to the graveyard. I heard the lugubrious wailing of people and the funeral dirges of mourners rendered in touchingly emotional voices. I heard the groaning of the aged and the agonizing sobs of the youths. I heard the sober voice of Pastor Francis when he said: 'Ash to ash and dust to dust' I saw the huge masses of people departing from the graveyard when Queen Jennifer had been buried. Then my questions:

How did Jennifer come back to life? How did it happen? Couldn't this thing be a trick? The woman I saw just now could as well be Jennifer's sister even though the king said she was Jennifer, the Queen. But again, the woman looked hundred per cent like Queen Jennifer."

Asa was so confused. The more he thought on the issue, the greater his confusion. Finally, he spoke:
"Since I don't know the truth about this matter and I am not sure what may be its final outcome, I'll better prepare myself ready for the worst."

Bawa came in that evening to see him.
"Asa! You will surely keep this night in your home if you can apologize to the king. You tender your apology this minute, the next minute you are out of here.
Why don't you save yourself all these troubles? Why are you unnecessarily stubborn?"

"I have not committed any offence. What am I to tender apology for? The king asked me to reverse the order of the gods, and that is not only impossible, it is beyond me."

"Asa! These gods whose verdict you cannot reverse killed Queen Jennifer but the king's God woke up Jennifer from the dead. It is clear to any reasonable person that the king's God is superior to your gods. You need to acknowledge this and tender your apology to the king. This is my advice to you".

Asa remained defiant. But as Bawa was about to leave Asa called him.

"Bawa! I have a request."

"What is it?"

"I want to see Ewete, my eldest son. Will you be kind enough to allow him to see me?"

"When do you want to see him?"

"Tonight."

"I will send for him right away. He will surely come to see you."

"You are so nice, Bawa."

"Asa, I am not personally happy to continue keeping you here. I want you to take my advice. There is still an opportunity for you to settle this problem with the king. You shouldn't throw away your golden chance. Tell His Royal Highness that you are sorry and this matter will immediately come to an end. The king is a highly understanding person."

"Bawa, I cannot do such a thing. I have not committed any offence – what am I going to be sorry for? You want me to take my orders from your king. That can never be. All the generations of Asas never take their orders from human beings. They take orders from the gods, why should my own be different? Why should I invite the wrath of the gods on my own head? Why?"

"But the king's God has just demonstrated to you that He is superior to your gods. Why can't you admit this and swallow your pride?"

"Bawa, I don't believe that there is any superior God to my gods. Not on this earth."

As Bawa finally left Asa that evening, he planted two secret agents in the rooms adjacent to Asa's cell. He wanted to know what Asa would discuss with his son.

Ewete came an hour later. He greeted his father and Asa smiled grimly.

"My son, I have sent for you because I don't know what may be the end of my stay here. I want to prepare my mind for the worst but I know and I believe that the worst is not going to happen. Even if I die, the institution of Asa must not die. And so, this is the time to hand over to you the age long secret which the generations of all Asas had kept for over two thousand years. I have kept it sacrosanct and you must keep it the same way. All the generations of Asas rule this kingdom. The kings are only there in name. We exercise all the powers. We make all kings do whatever we want. This is why we are venerated like gods. Our words are laws. Our pronouncements are decrees. All Asas always tell the people that whatever they say are orders from the gods and they must be complied with unquestioningly. Ewete, I want to inform you that we Asas never hear anything from any god."

"What?" asked Ewete who suddenly sat rigid.

"Yes, we do not hear anything from any god."

"When you made a pronouncement that the queen missed her steps, are you saying you were not relaying the order of the gods?"

"No. I was not. The pronouncement was purely my own. No god asked me to say so."

"But after you made the pronouncement that the gods did not accept Queen Jennifer's dance, the woman died mysteriously at midnight that day. Who killed her?"

"The gods were not the ones who killed her. Her death was a purely human device. The verdict I gave was not dictated to me by any god. No god talked to me. To tell you the truth, my son, I don't know whether gods talk or do not talk. I don't even know whether gods exist or they don't."

"My father, are you sane? I mean, are you in your right senses?" asked Ewete

"Son, nothing is wrong with me. My senses are functioning properly. I am not sick. I am mentally balanced. Since it is time to tell you the truth, then listen to the truth. Now, I don't want to be interrupted. Just listen to me very carefully. Jennifer's body was painted in a tiger colour before the dance. The painting was completed by 12 midnight. The paint has certain composition that would make her slump and die twenty four hours later and the same acted with precision. If there would be any variation, it is a question of about a minute or less than that. For any queen we want to spare, we normally use another chemical substance to paint her body and thereafter return the verdict that the gods accept her dance. The two substances are white in colour, no one except the initiated can tell the difference between the two. The two substances are kept in two separate pots in the right corner of my room: one in a small pot and the other in a big pot. To kill any queen you must use the paint in the small pot, to spare the life of any queen, you must use the one in the big one. The question you may wish to ask me is: Why do we have to do this? We do it in order to make all people fear Asa. We do it so as to check the power of the king. We also do it in order to prevent the king from becoming a monster like the current one we are having. We do it to ensure that real power lies in the Asa's family. No more.

When this new king who came from the United Kingdom was installed, I immediately observed that he is a stubborn and proud person who will not submit to ancient rules and traditions. I therefore decided to teach him a lesson. I made up my mind to kill his queen in order to demonstrate to him the powers of my gods. I painted Jennifer's body with the paint taken from the small pot and so Jennifer slumped and died twenty four hours later. The victim always appears like the dead, but she is not dead. The paint only weakens the heart of the victim to a level that it will appear as if she is no longer breathing. But twenty hours later, the effect will start reducing little by little, and four hours after that, the victim can recover and wake up, if she is not immediately buried. But we always insist that the victim is quickly buried by telling the people that any delay will result in the death of the king. My son this is the secret of Asa's power."

"My father, I have listened to you very carefully, I was tempted to stop you half-way but I changed my mind. I wanted you to say all what you love to say."

"You wanted to stop me? Why?"

"Because the secret you have so much dwelt upon has no relevance anymore. It has no use. It has already lost its value."

"How?" Asa queried. "Ewete, you are my eldest son. You will be the next Asa. Do you say the source of power of all Asas, the thing that will give you all the powers to rule, has no value to you?"

Ewete burst into a huge laughter.

"My father, I can never be the next Asa because the post of Asa had been abolished already. The secret you have just unfolded to me has no use anymore. I don't need it. The situation has changed."

"Look here, my son. No power on earth can abolish the post of Asa. Even the gods cannot do so. Impossible."

"My father, but you have just confirmed now that the gods are mere make-believe. Which gods are you now talking about? The king cancelled all pagan festivals, all pagan rituals, all pagan titles throughout the kingdom yesterday. Instead of pagan rituals, he has substituted Christian crusades."

Asa stared at Ewete's face, confused.

"My father, immediately the king cancelled all the rituals and pagan titles, the people trooped into the streets jubilating. My father, you are today alone. All people have deserted you. All the chiefs had gone with the king. The chiefs who should bring 10 sheep and 20 goats to you yesterday, did not bring them."

"What?", queried Asa.

"They didn't. They said time had changed. I haven't told you, the greatest news of all."

"And what is that?" asked Asa.

"Chief Nana, the Deputy Chief Priest, your assistant, renounced his pagan title this morning in a colourful ceremony."

"Ewete! Stop that! Why do you speak heresy? Heaven and earth will pass away, Chief Nana can never change his belief."

"Father! Heaven and earth have not passed away yet Chief Nana not only changed his faith, he was baptized at 11a.m. this morning by Pastor Francis and given a new name Joshua. His wife, the Chief Priestess was also baptized and took a new name, Ruth. Pastor Francis had appointed Chief Nana, the new sexton of the new CMS Church. The new sexton was the one who rang the big bell that summoned evening worshipers to the church at 5p.m., four hours ago. My father! Things are changing at a baffling speed."

"Chief Nana – a sexton?" screamed Asa.

"Yes," replied Ewete.

Asa looked up in dismay.

"Father! Since the post of Asa has been abolished, you are already out of job. You will have to look for something else to do when you are out of here. Not that alone, the shrine that serves as your office had been bulldozed by a caterpillar between 2p.m. and 3p.m. this afternoon."

"Stop that! No man, however, mad can do that. That is sacrilege!"

"Father! A bulldozer had already leveled the place. No building, no tree, no relics stand up there now. The land had been allocated to a new Christian Church, and I understand that the foundation of the new church building will be laid tomorrow morning. The king is moving like a whirlwind".

Asa could no longer control his fury. His body was shaking.

"The king told the people that your gods (Asa's gods) are cruel and merciless gods but his own God is a merciful and benevolent God. He said your own gods killed Jennifer but his own God woke Jennifer up from the dead.

All the people hailed the king as they chorused:

'The merciful God that woke up the dead is a superior God, and that is the one we will serve.'

My father, your season is gone. Your era has ended. You just have to admit this. The tide has changed. For you to be relevant, you must flow with the new tide. If not, you will be consigned into the dustbin of history. Chief Nana knew when to call it quit. Discretion is the better part of valour. I will say it is time to call off the fight. No matter the effort, you cannot win. The forces against you are too formidable. Why not seize the current opportunity and change like your deputy?"

"Never! I will never do such a thing. No Asa in history did the same."

"My father! What did Asa in history have to do with what we are talking about? Has any Asa faced this kind of situation you are facing now? Why then do you need to compare yourself with any other Asa?"

"No matter the situation a lion cannot accept to eat

the grass like the cow. The eagle cannot descend from its lofty height and become a bird that scratches the dust like the hen. A cat can never become the servant of the mouse. Never!"

"And so what will you do?"

"Ewete, I don't know what I will do."

"Father! Think about it till tomorrow. I will see you early tomorrow morning. Think about what to do. But always remember that change may be bitter but there is no shame in being part of a change."

When Ewete finally left, the two secret agents took the tape of their recorded speech to Bawa. The tape was played to the king.

"God! This kingdom had been deceived by charlatans for so long. Asa will go to jail for this. We already have enough facts to nail his coffin. Tomorrow morning, charge the case to court."

At 7a.m. the following day, Bawa hurried to Asa's cell. He opened the door. The old man lay on the floor face down. He was dead.

CHAPTER THIRTY-TWO

I, Mayo Williams, had witnessed several Ogun Festivals but that of August, 1965 was different in its glamour and magnificence. The death and resurrection of Queen Jennifer Alade (nee Adams) was one incident Toro people would also remember for a long time. It was one event I could not easily forget.

I had enjoyed every minute of my holiday in Toro. It was now time to go back to school I couldn't remember one day I felt happy leaving Toro, and as usual, I was feeling unhappy. My mother would have loved me to stay longer but it was time to go back to school.

As mother and I walked down the street towards the center of Toro where I would join the big bus going to Lagos Metropolis, we both looked sober and morose. For long, my mother did not talk. I stared at her face; I could see the agony of a mother. She was with me all right, but there was a far-away look on her face. The streets had woken up, they all stared at me; their faces flashing at me silent sympathy. The trees all along the road also looked at me with burning eyes. They giggled at one another. Their leaves swayed this way and that way and I could hear their soft voices saying: "goodbye for now." As we got to the end of the long street, and descended a slope, the valley before us was waiting anxiously and it embraced us with both hands. Just few metres away was the haughty River Iregun that divided Toro into two. Even that early morning, she was singing again. Her choir day and night, year after year, sings continuously in an endless harmony, giving melody to this famous ancient town. I cast a quick glance at its water and the water, cool and sober, looked at me with a wry smile.

The eastern sky had flushed into fire; now dressed in a cloud of purple. The sun, a bright–looking Romeo, soon came out of the cloud, winked infectiously at Toro. But this beautiful Juliet was just waking up from a long, deep slumber.

I have always loved Toro; one of Nigeria's prettiest towns, the sweet lady of the Nigerian Savannah. She is a centre of culture, a meeting point of the past and the present, a land having its root in the ancient but whose face had been touched by the entrancing paint of modernity, a museum of mystery, a custodian of traditions, a land of alluring landscapes whose charms had dazzled men and women of all ages. That is the noble place of my birth. As I went through the various streets, now almost certain that in the next one hour, I would leave the warmth and gaiety of Toro behind, my spirit was down.

We finally got to the town's square only to learn that

the bus that would take me to Lagos would not arrive until ten minutes or so. But just around that time, the bus drove to the town's square and came to a stop. The passengers started to come out. They were mostly indigenes of Toro and the surrounding villages who were working in Lagos and who had come home for the weekend. They wore flashy dresses. Lagosians are highly fashionable people. I looked at their trendy; beautiful outfits. What lovely people were Lagosians!

Suddenly, this fascinating scenery took a dramatic turn. I had heard of people who engaged in day dream and who could turn the product of their own fertile imagination into a vivid, real and fascinating picture. "Am I daydreaming? Is the picture before me real or am I staring at the product of self-created fantasy?" I asked myself. What I was looking at seemed like the back-view of someone I knew intimately. It seemed like the back-view of Alero. I blinked rapidly. The blood was racing through my body.

"But Alero is in Accra, Ghana. There is no indication that she will be in Toro at this time. If she is coming to Nigeria, I will be the first person to be informed. And there is no information to that effect," I spoke within myself. The back view I was looking at was so fine. The skin was delicate as a newly born baby's cheek. Its nice, smooth chocolate complexion seemed to be desperately inviting a touch. The lady who had been in a bending position all this while gradually stood up in full, regal splendour. And before me, stood the most glamorous lady I had ever seen. I stared at her fixedly, and just that moment, I could no longer mistake

Alero, the Princess of Toro even though we saw each other last six years ago. I stood suddenly still and unbelieving. My pulse ran out of control as we both stood rigid, immobilized by surprise.

"Mayo! I am sure it is you," she screamed as she dropped her bag and rushed forward in a frenzy of impatience towards me. In a moment, we fell into each other's arms. For minutes, we stood there glued together and crying like little children. I could not remember how long we were in each other's arms crying. As Alero held me tight to herself while her pointed breasts - soft, warm and provocative, caressed the secret of my chest, I found Alero's body most intoxicating. The touch of Alero's delicious, lovely skin pumped honey into my cells and I felt charged with electricity.

I stared at Alero, a sweet lady with sparkling eyes. I looked at her skin – flawless and shining. She seemed like one heroine of legend. I so much liked her. As we stood knitted together and listening to the rhythms of each other's breathing, I felt a thrill of excitement, just the same way as Mungo Park, that famous British explorer felt in July 1795 when he saw the long - sought - for majestic Niger at Segu, glittering to the morning sun.

My mother stood under one shed staring at us. A lady beckoned to her friend and said:
"Come, just come and see the greatest spectacle of the year: Toro's most celebrated and glamorous Princess wailing in the arms of a young man!" Going

to Lagos was now out of the question. Leaving with the big bus was no longer a priority. It had become everything for Alero and Alero for everything.

After that long embrace, I picked up Alero's bag and we started to walk towards her home. But a young boy, a relative, helped me with the bag. As Alero and I walked down the street, hand in hand, I stared at her. She had become ripe like a beautiful fruit waiting to be plucked and fresh like the lily by the riverside. Her hair was heavy and black and the same was coiled dexterously at the nape of Alero's neck. Her breasts had developed into full size and they thrust up and down invitingly as she walked. Her lips were soft and sensuous, saying a million things at the same time. Her thick eyelashes gave her face such an exquisite feature. Alero was pretty.

"Alero! You are so beautiful," I told her.

"Mayo! You have also become a dazzlingly handsome young man. I had surveyed your features over and over again. Am I safe?"

"How?" I asked her.

"How many rivals do I have among the flashy, beautiful Lagos girls?"

"Rivals?"

"Yes," she replied.

"I don't know of any."

Alero opened wider her big eye-balls, stared at me and said:

"You must be wondering why I didn't tell you that I would be around?"

"Yes, you are right."

"I never knew that I would be coming to Nigeria until yesterday."

"Really?"

"Yes, Mr. Peters, the husband of my aunt has a meeting and some other business transactions to do at the office of the West African Examinations Council in Lagos. My aunt insisted on accompanying him and I too refused to be left behind in Accra. We arrived in Lagos by air yesterday and since they will not return to Ghana until next week Friday, I got permission to quickly dash to Toro because I guessed you will be here. My confidence was greatly reinforced when I got to your college and the gateman told me that the boys were still on holidays."

"You were at Igbobi College?"

"Yes, of course," she gave me a slow, pretty smile, then raised up her eyebrows.

"Don't tell me that you don't know that I have been dying to see you."

"I know how you feel."

"It's nice that you know," she smiled sweetly. She rolled her big, beautiful eyeballs. Jesus! She was so irresistible. She stared at my face. Her gaze was unwavering and intense. Her eyes seemed to be probing mine inquiringly. Suddenly, she stopped, faced me directly, held me to herself again and then exclaimed in a voice so touchingly emotional:

"Mayo temi nikan!" which translates:

"Mayo that belongs to me alone. How are you?"

"It has been so rough without you being around," I replied.

"How is your school?" I asked her. She looked at me; a narrow, gentle smile lit her lips.

"Nice, beautiful place", she replied "The teachers are all nuns. Very pretty things. If you see them, you will wonder why such lovely roses should opt for the convent. I must confess, some of them would have been proud and ravishing queens in some European palaces.

My college itself is attractive. When I arrived there, its attraction for me was so strong. There are well laid-out roads and beautiful buildings in a well tended and nurtured 60 acres of land. There are beautiful flowers in riot of colours at every turn. It is a rich, luscious, proud ground. Even the biblical Garden of Eden would see it and immediately grow jealous. But the rules are so strict. Every minute, one feels as if one were in a maximum prison. But that really is not a problem. I could cope with it. My real problem during my first year was you. I remembered you every minute. Your absence made me feel homesick." She stopped then stared at my face, put her pretty, slender hands on my shoulders, then said:

"You know that you have been my only friend. You were the closest to me and the only person who knew me intimately. You were the one I had been used to from my cradle; the only one that filled my world. It was in your company I found my greatest joy. It was your voice that sang to me on our way to school and warmed me in the harmattan cold. You were the only one who knew very well my anatomy and the various elements that made up my passion and why I behaved the way I did. I always believed that you understood me more than I understood myself. And because you took time to study and know me, you were the only one who knew how to handle me. When I kept quiet,

248

you were the oracle that knew what was going on in my mind. When I smiled, by just looking at me, you knew why I was excited. When I was unhappy you were the only one who knew how to charge my battery and regulate my emotion and put me on a high mood. Naturally, I loved to be with you all the time. But my father pounced on me, bundled me out of the country.

Without you, life suddenly became empty. I found myself like a fish out of water. It was my first most unpalatable experience."

"You want to say daddy forced you against your wish?"

"Don't pretend that you don't know my father. What can a thirteen-year-old girl do when a man like my father had made up his mind? Perhaps if I had seen you, you would have provided me with one or two tricks to avoid the journey. I know you would have invented or devised one trick or the other but you were nowhere to be found. Up to the very last minute, I was sure you would show up, but you did not. I was crying all through the journey and I cried for days. Where were you? Where in particular were you hiding when I was looking for you? And why did you do that to me? Even if I had offended you, I never believed you could be so cruel to me. What was my offence?"

"You never offended me. I was only out of the house, and I was out because of you."

"Because of me?"

"Yes! Because of you!"

"How?" asked Alero staring at me curiously.

"It's a long story but I will only give a summary of it. The day we saw each other last, I mean before your journey to Accra, you gave me some mangoes. Do you still remember?"

"Yes, I do. I can remember that day vividly, even now."

"Good! That day was Friday. You so much touched my heart by your gift that I made up my mind to surprise you the following Monday. I decided that I was going to give you some beautiful, succulent apricots. These sweet apricots were only available in Pa Richard's garden."

"I know Pa Richard and I know his garden; the one behind his home;" said Alero.

"Good! I led three of my friends to the garden. The four of us climbed the wall into the garden and I was the only one who got caught by Pa Richard. The man first chained me to a tree for several hours. Thereafter, he thrashed me with a horsewhip. He whipped me so violently that I had bruises all over my body and it took two weeks for the sores to heal up."

"Oh my God!" exclaimed Alero, surprise written on her face.

"I was ashamed of myself. It was an ugly episode, which I didn't intend to share with anyone. I didn't want you in particular to know about it. I didn't want you to know that I had gone out to steal. What an embarrassment! What a shame! But I knew you would look for me. What explanation do I offer you when you see sores all over my body? Accident? What kind of accident? I felt it was better to go into hiding and I therefore relocated to my grandma's house. There, I nursed my wounds for two weeks. I returned one Sunday evening and my mother told me that you came many times the previous day looking for me. I was also desperate to see you. I couldn't sleep all through the night. I got to the school the following Monday only to learn that you had gone to Ghana. I almost ran mad."

Alero fixed her look on me for a long time. She stared at me as if she wanted to cry. Finally, she drew me to herself, scratched my head affectionately and whispered:

"That gorilla, Pa Richard, has no child. He didn't surprise me that he could behave so wickedly."

She stared at my face again, her eyebrows rose and fell enticingly and those eyes were now winking at me unconsciously as she said:

"I am so sorry about what happened to you." Alero then put her slender, pretty hands on my shoulders again. Her emotion now brought out her entrancing beauty and colour in a new dimension. For once, her beauty became dazzling. I had never seen such a Negro-goddess.

"You are very lovely", I told her.

We soon got to her home. There I left her to sort out her affairs while she agreed to see me again at 12.00 noon. Expecting 12.00 noon was like waiting for the outcome of a major surgical operation. Five minutes to the time of her arrival, I had stood by the window gazing. Alero came at the dot of 12.00 noon. She wore a pink gown with white stripes. It was superbly tailored. The gown was tight fitting at the middle and cut fairly low at the front showing the upper curve of Alero's lovely breasts. Her lips were fine and inviting, I had never seen Alero looking so beautiful.

She gave me her shy, sweet smile, that special smile I had missed all these years. Then her slim, wonderful body melted into my embrace. I caressed her dark, wavy hair and for the second time, I kissed her and for several minutes she gave me kiss for kiss. The quietness and calmness of a lonely home in a mid-day was dangerous to innocence and so I dared everything and Alero gave everything.

Alero left me at 2p.m.

CHAPTER THIRTY-THREE

I was to meet Alero again at 6p.m. I got to the Garden House and a message was already waiting for me at the gate to meet the Princess on Eyo Hill, inside this great estate, one of the few most beautiful and largest estates in Nigeria.

A royal guard took me through various paths that went through this land of beautiful shrubs, well-maintained lawn dotted with various tropical fruit trees that went on and on. This was the first time I was seeing the size and the extent of this beautiful estate. I must confess, I was overwhelmed.

I remembered the words of my mother: "The class problem is still there at the end of the day." The reality of that statement dawned on me so clearly now as I went through this sumptuous and rich estate.

"Will Alero's parents allow her to marry me? Will they accept the son of a commoner as their in-law? Am I really cutting my coat according to my size?" I asked myself these various questions. I could not answer any of them in the affirmative. For a brief period, I was confused and unhappy.

"Wouldn't all these be labours lost at the end of the day?" I asked myself again and again.

"But the girl loves me," I asserted. On this, I took some courage and followed my guard with new confidence. We soon started to climb the series of small hills that eventually landed us on the top of Eyo Hill. On this hill, we could see all parts of Toro.

Alero was sitting under a grape tree. She was alone. The guard brought out a bottle of champagne, filled her cup and also filled my cup and left. As we sipped our wine, we moved to the highest point on this beautiful hill. That warm, luxurious evening was laden with emotion. We were watching the blazing sun set over the rocky Gidigidi Hill in an explosion of colours. Gidigidi Hill was the highest elevation in the entire Toro Kingdom. It was about five kilometres from Toro. That evening sun-set on Gidigidi Hill was glamorous. I stared at Alero, the sensuous face and a full ripe body, she was the most beautiful lady I had ever seen. She was unusually quiet. I felt she was enjoying so much the beauty of the setting sun and perhaps carried away by the same for sometime. But when the silence became too long, I touched her gently.

"Alero, what are you thinking about?"

It was now I knew she was crying.

"Why are you crying? What have I done to you?"

"You've done nothing to me," she said, her words grew faint with emotion.

"What is the problem then?"

"Mayo! I don't want to leave you. I don't want to leave Nigeria, but I just must go back to Ghana."

"Alero, I too don't want to leave you," I spoke softly as I stared at the face of this most wonderful girl. She had the most beautiful skin, pale and flawless. She was damn pretty. I could watch her all day. I recalled now the day Alero became my bride at the age of seven, no other female since then had fascinated me like this famous Princess, whom all people called the EMERALD OF TORO.

The Cambridge School Certificate Examination was just three months away. I knew that the examination was so crucial to our lives. We must pass our examinations very well and so this was not the time for sentiment. It was a time to set emotion aside. I took Alero in my arms and fastened her possessively to my chest then spoke:

"I know how you feel. I know you love me but you have to go back to Ghana. Alero! I am going to give you one special gift."

Her face lit with quiet innocence, stared at me. That face now gave the hint of a smile.

"What gift are you going to give me?" she asked. Her lips pressed tightly together, trying to hold back her tears.

I am going to have Eight Distinctions in my forthcoming Cambridge School Certificate Examinations and I am dedicating all the Distinctions to you. I am going to work really hard, not because of myself or any personal glory but because of you. For if I must give a Princess a gift, it must be a princely gift. Now Alero, what are you going to give me?"

She suddenly brightened up, then stared at my face with a kind of calm wonder. Her beautiful face was still contorted with emotion, strangely that face looked more angelic now.

"Mayo! I have never thought about this," she said soothingly as she now stared at my face. Jesus! Alero's face was so captivating now "I don't know how many Distinctions I wish to give you or dedicate to you but I am going to give you a pleasant surprise. Just believe me!" Her eyebrows were elegantly raised and those eyes started to bewitch me again. I could see that Alero had now brightened up.

The following day, early in the morning, I set out on my long journey to Lagos. This time, it was Alero who accompanied me to the town square. At about 7a.m., a small bus picked me up and I waved to Alero and she waved to me. The parting was emotion-laden.

"Write to me immediately you get to Cape Coast."

"I will do," she replied. She was looking elsewhere, she was crying.

CHAPTER THIRTY-FOUR

The huge noise woke up the quiet, sleepy afternoon. The roaring of a thousand voices announced that something unusual was going on outside the gate. I rushed out of my house only to hear what seemed like the screams of a running mob. Now, I saw a mighty crowd surging towards me like a monstrous, unstoppable hurricane. I saw young men and young women coming like a deluge of locusts of vengeance, led by few men wearing white cassocks. A huge mahogany was in front of the crowd. Trees never walk, but alas, this one was walking.

"Why? How? What is happening?"

I shook myself trying to wake up from what I believed was a dream. But I realized with a thrill of terror that it was no dream. For some seconds, I stood staring at the on-coming avalanche. What am I to do? I restrained with utmost difficulty an impulse to run. But when I perceived that it was getting dangerously closer, I turned round quickly and did what seemed reasonable in the circumstance – I ran. But mother, who stood nearby, burst into a loud, prolonged laughter.

"Why are you running away? What is the problem?"
"Look!" I pointed to the crowd.
"They are members of Pentecostal Group on a crusade."
"And what of that moving tree in their front?"
"Tree?"
"Yes, that tree," I pointed to it.
"I see no tree."
On closer look now, the walking tree was a man, a giant, and what looked like branches were his raised hands. Honourable Weliweli, the representative of Toro District in the Western Nigerian House of Parliament was exactly like a tree on motion.

Seven and half feet tall, with a weight of 300 pounds, a Nigeria version of the biblical Goliath, had a queer grandeur. Those who used his weight to describe him called him: The huge hippopotamus. Those who used his height called him: The mahogany. Trees do not dance, but Mahogany was a great dancer.

Swinging his hips and contorting his body into all manners of shapes, one would almost swear that Mahogany had not a single bone in his flesh. His body wriggled ceaselessly like that of a snake being attacked by an army of dangerous ants. Holding the Holy Bible in his right hand, he looked morose and impatient, like a general leading an army on a crusade to take forcibly the holy land held illegitimately by the infidels. The huge excited crowd sang:
> *"Mo gbe Jesu mi de*
> *Mo gbe Jesu mi de*
> *Alagbara."*

Meaning:
"We bring unto you, Jesus
The warrior
The undefeated General."

The song aroused the entire community from a mid-day slumber and ignited an instantaneous fire that sent people stampeding unto the streets. Within minutes, there was a monstrous army surging forward, a huge armada of men and women on motion. By the time the crowd reached the small square in front of our house, the heavens and the earth had joined together, the physical and the spiritual hosts burst into a delirious ecstasy. Mahogany suddenly became a volcano and erupted:

"Mu ra ba! ba! ba!
Mu ra ba! ba! ba!
Ya! ya! ho! ho! Ho!
Ho! Ho! Ya! Ya! Ya!"

The other men in cassocks were switched on simultaneously as they too began to emit volcanic lava:

"O ma ca randa!
Ro ro ma ca randa!
Ri ma kapoli mamali kalika!"

"What's happening?" I asked
I stood there rigid and confused. "What are these babblings about? Is Babel Tower reincarnating itself? Has God decided to confuse human tongues once more?" Mahogany and one of the men in cassocks faced each other, shook their heads like two he-goats ready to go into a combat, their faces wild

and fearsome while fire and brimstone came out of their mouths. I knew they were not quarreling. But why are they behaving like two people about to go into a combat? Their words, violent and aggressive, yet I couldn't make any meaning from the hostile maze of nonsensical syllables coming out of their mouths.

The eyes of one of the remaining men in cassocks fixed on me with such heat that I found myself caught in a strange immobility. He also poured out frightening torrents of meaningless monosyllables that I began to fear whether he too was not a potential lunatic in the making. I turned to my mother:

" But you said these people are on a crusade. Why do they have to bring these magicians? What is their business?"

"Where are the magicians?" she asked.

"These men in cassocks and the giant – I mean all these making abracadabra."

"They are not magicians. They are men of God, speaking in strange tongues. They are under the fire of the Holy Ghost."

Just that moment, there was a deafening, earth-shaking: "Praise the Lord!", followed by a thunderous response of "Alleluyah!!" and a strange, mysterious, chilling silence suddenly descended on the crowd.

This was the incident that first introduced Honourable Weliweli to me, the Toro Representative in the Western Nigerian House of Parliament, a flamboyant politician, a man of the people, the

Mahogany of Toro District, an enigma and titanic figure in Christ's vineyard. The day was 31st December 1959. I was still very young.

It was now six years later. The profile of Honourable Weliweli had continued to grow. His fame and image loomed large everywhere. He had spent eight years in the Western Nigeria House of Parliament and was starting a re-election campaign that day. A formidable opponent from the Action Group (A.G) had, however, emerged. Chief Boye, the Action Group candidate was a dark horse. A terrific organizer and an efficient planner, his campaign seemed like a new broom, sweeping everything before him. Honourable Weliweli of the Nigerian National Democratic Party (NNDP) and his supporters went wild as Chief Boye appeared now to be shaking every place.

When two elephants clashed, the land was bound to quake. The quiet, serene atmosphere of Toro constituency, suddenly changed. Daily, there were reports of political clashes. Insecurity and anxiety began to grow.

After that historic dance of Queen Jennifer, the king and the queen took a three month leave on tour of the Caribbean Islands, the Island of Hawaii, Kenya and some other East African Countries. Prince Matete was now temporarily in charge of the kingdom. He had voluntarily conceded the throne to the present king (his younger brother), partly on health ground and partly because he wanted the ancient kingdom to be led by one of the most educated men of the nation.

But as Prince Matete woke up this morning and went through the dailies, he read about the various political clashes going on in his kingdom. He became suddenly alarmed. There were reports of political clashes between supporters of the NNDP and Action Group in Zia and in two other villages the previous day.

"This is most unacceptable." Prince Matete exclaimed.

That afternoon, he had a meeting with the two contestants: Honourable Weliweli and Chief Boye. The Garden House, Princes Matete's residence had temporarily become the official headquarter of the government and there in his luxurious Victorian Home, he had a meeting with the two party leaders.

"The polity is being unnecessarily heated. There are too many political clashes all over the place; and these have been making me unhappy. I have been hearing of threats and counter threats. Gentlemen, serving the people should not be a question of life and death. I want you to keep to the rules. I won't allow a situation that may degenerate into a breakdown of law and order. That will be most unacceptable. And I have invited both of you here so that you can operate according to the standard of democratic tenets and also put your supporters in check," said Prince Matete. For about an hour, he and Honourable Weliweli and Chief Boye went into a closed-door meeting.

CHAPTER THIRTY-FIVE

When Alero and I were parting in August, it was as if we were parting again for a long time. But time flew in a supersonic speed and we were soon back in Toro again.

I finished my Cambridge School Certificate Examination on 30th November and I left Lagos for Toro on 2nd December. Alero finished her own examination on 28th November, left Ghana on 30th November and arrived in Toro in the afternoon of 2nd December. She wore a maroon low-cut silk dress that clung to the curves of her beautiful body. Pretty, dark-haired, sexy-looking, Alero was dreadfully beautiful.

"As I put down my pen after writing my last paper, my anxiety to see you heightened. That night I couldn't sleep. I informed my aunt that I must leave Ghana the following morning."

"Why are you in a hurry? Can't you relax for about a week and have a good rest?"

"No, I am going to Nigeria to rest. I am not going to

rest in any other place", I told her.

"I never told her that I was hurrying to Toro because of love."

"Why didn't you tell her the truth?"

"If I told her, then I won't be here."

I looked at Alero. Her figure was sweet. She looked voluptuous and sexual. The tight sleeve dress she wore fitted her like a second skin. She was not aware how killing she was. I was so happy that she was back in Toro. I felt like a traveller in the Sahara, who having missed water for twenty-four hours, was now before a fresh spring of water and could go on drinking as much as he wanted.

The second week after Alero's arrival, we decided to visit her niece living in Zia, a small village about four kilometers away. It was not a day of blazing sun and we did the journey on foot through a lane linking Toro and the village. As we walked along the lane that wound its way unhurriedly amid the green silence of the beautiful rain forest, the fascination of the adventure grew. The splendour of an unspoiled, proud, virgin vegetation of Southern Nigeria, presented itself to us - wild, beautiful countryside caressed by the soft fragrance of early December air. The excitement was overwhelming. I had always loved to be with Alero, and we were so happy to be together again after very many years. It was as if those lovely days we spent together in the CMS School were back again.

As we walked down the narrow, lonely path, our minds

went on memory lane. We recalled the events of yester -years. It was a day of reminiscences when we talked about our childhood exploits.

We tried to relive those old days. We dramatized the sweet and the bitter of Toro CMS School. We were almost half way when Alero suddenly stopped, faced me, stared at me fixedly, hands in pockets, chest out, looking morose and bitter like someone who had lost all his earthly possessions in a terrible disaster.

"How are you Mr. George?" I exclaimed

"I never knew that I am an actress."

"You look precisely like Mr. George, the Hyena."

"You will be a fantastic candidate for Hollywood. Alero! It is my turn, now look at me!"

"Who are you going to mimic?"

"Just look at me!"

"Go on," she said sweetly, her burning eyes stared at me intensely. Alero's big eyeballs opened wider. It was as if those eyes were ready for the kill.

I looked left and right, surveyed the entire surroundings proudly as if I had just been appointed the General Overseer of the universe. I took hasty, haughty steps forward like someone in a hurry, stared arrogantly at the neighbourhood, an elegant, sophisticated man in the midst of barbarians, then swaggered like a general coming straight from a victorious battle.

"How are you Mr. Moore?" exclaimed Alero

"Good Heavens! I am a good actor too."

"Yes, you are. That was exactly how Mr. Moore behaved the day he fired our headmaster."

We mimicked Mr. Balogun. We made jest of the Assistant Headmaster. We played the game of hide and seek. We embraced each other numberless times. We teased and pursued each other on the flimsiest reason imaginable and did a hundred silly and childish things, all in the name of love. We were already in Zia when I realized that we had got to our destination. The time spent seemed like two minutes. Romantic love makes time to be so short.

We got to Zia only to be informed that Alero's niece was not at home. She had gone to the farm with her husband. And so we had to wait. The niece came back towards evening time.

The sun was till glowing in the western sky when we left Zia. But immediately it went down the western slope, it became dark. Our situation suddenly became desperate when blankets of clouds were now drifting about the sky.

"Mayo! It's going to rain."

"I perceive so. We need to hurry. Rain here is always accompanied by storm. The rain must not meet us under these huge trees. It can be dangerous." We doubled our steps. But the air gradually became cool. Flashes of lightning lit up the sky and loud peals of thunder harassed us ceaselessly from above.

"Oh my God! We are in trouble!" exclaimed Alero.

"There is no trouble, Baby! Take it cool. We will be all right."

We pushed on, walking and running as the narrow path permitted.

"Alero! Hurray! Look at those lights afar off! We are nearing the outskirts of Toro. We have made it. Our problem will soon be over."

As we moved further, lights from the various houses glittered now to our delight. We were already celebrating when suddenly we heard a noise from a nearby bush. We were highly terrified.

"They have come! They have come!" said a voice.
We stopped, looked at the direction of the voice and three strange figures appeared. They wore animal masks but from their features, I knew they were young men. Two of them carried shot clubs and the third, a shining dagger. I was in a quandary. To run away and abandon Alero to these strange men was most unthinkable. But I was frightened and dreadfully tensed up. Man will not die two times; I braced up for the challenge.

"You! You! You this fool, you son of a mere commoner, what business have you with a princess?" asked one of the men, now pointing his club at my face. "Can't you move with a lady of your class and stop playing the buffoon?" asked yet another. I recognized his voice immediately to be that of Coker; the boy Mr. Balogun always chose to dance with Alero in those days when we were in the primary school. I learnt that he was in one secondary school in Lagos. Alero had told me how he had been pestering her since her arrival in Toro to become his friend. The other voice was that of Fola, my friend in those days. I couldn't understand their intention.
"Stop!" One of them roared.
"Mister! Your life or the lady?" another bellowed.
"What do you mean?" I asked calmly.
"I am asking you to choose between this lady and

your life. Leave Alero and live; hold on to her and die."

"You mean I should leave Alero?"

"Precisely. And mind you, this is an order. And you have just five seconds to comply with the order."

"I am not leaving Alero, so please yourself."

"Young man! You are in trouble!" screamed the one talking to me.

"Serious trouble!" screamed the second, then roared; "Colonel!" beckoning to the third, the one with the dagger.

"Hack him down. Let him see that dagger in action."

That one opened the dagger quickly and was coming after me. He swore and cursed violently and he seemed like a man hell-bent on destroying half of the universe.

"Mayo! Mayo! Run! Run from this lunatic! Run for your life!" screamed Alero who was then trembling with fear.

I was the best in my karate class. I dashed forward in a flash, brought him down suddenly and the dagger fell off from his hand. I grabbed the dagger quickly. The other two seeing me now holding the dagger, ready to strike, ran for their lives. Coker was the one down, I pounced on him, held him by the neck.

"If ever I see you with Alero, you are a dead man. You understand?"

He answered me with a nod. I set him free and he rose up quickly and fled.

"Mayo! Mayo! So you can be this terrible!" exclaimed Alero.

"I can't hurt a fly; I am sure you know that."

Still puzzled, she stared at me in silent admiration.

A minute later, the rain started and it was very heavy. We were at the outskirts of Toro. I noticed that there was a small hut used by some palm-wine sellers nearby. We ran into it.

For hours, it continued to rain. We got to Toro late.

CHAPTER THIRTY-SIX

Each day, the election drew nearer. Contrary to the promise of Honourable Weliweli and Chief Boye, political clashes continued in many parts of Toro District. Two weeks after the meeting with Prince Matete, supporters of the NNDP and Action Group had a serious clash in Zia. A day after, another clash took place in Toro itself. When Chief Boye was rounding up his campaigns, he told his teeming supporters that he was going to have a landslide victory. But addressing his own supporters the following day, Honourable Weliweli boasted and vowed:

"Nobody can take this post from me, I am relinquishing it to no one. There is no vacant position for any Toro man in the Western Nigerian House of Parliament," he asserted forcefully.

"Look at me!" he said in another rally that day "I have many jokers in this pocket. I am yet to play any of them. But when the time comes, be ready for surprises."

The election day finally arrived. People trooped en-masse to vote. Alero and I could not vote. We didn't register and we had no voters' cards. And so that day, we took another trip to Zia and came back at 6p.m. By the time we arrived, Toro already wore an anxious look. Any moment, the result of the election would be announced. By 8p.m., the results were out. Chief Boye scored 38,300 votes and Honourable Weiweli scored 9,504 votes and lost his seat in the Western Nigerian House Parliament.

An all night party took place in Chief Boye's house to mark his victory. Chief Boye wore a huge, flowing agbada, the flaps of the huge gown now fluttering in the air. As he went round, thanking his guests, his eyes wore a joyous sparkle.

A dozen waiters in scarlets served the guests steaming pepper soup, wine, soft drink and guilder beer. There were also roast chickens and roast beef, depending on the choice of the guest.

Dayo, a friend of Chief Boye held him by the waist and exclaimed:

"Success has a sweet aroma. I can't express how delighted I am."

"Dayo, let me confess privately to you that I feel as if I have been appointed as the General Overseer of this universe. A friend has just phoned me. He said: 'defeating Mahogany of Toro is one of the 20th century's electoral wonders.' It seems just incredible to many people."

"Chief, I agree with the man who phoned you. Mahogany was one man to beat. The man boasted everywhere he went that he was unbeatable. In one rally, he told his audience that: 'a contest between an elephant and a rat is no contest. Chief Boye is just a rat.

The party that fields such a featherweight against me, a political heavyweight and a juggernaut, must be the greatest clown of this century. When a train collides with a motorcycle you don't need to be searching for the motorcycle because it will be crushed and ground beyond recognition. I am going to crush and grind Chief Boye. You will look for him, you won't find him'At another rally, he said, 'I have already won this election. I have told the people, and I have to say it again, that I have many jokers in this pocket.' Where are Honourable Weliweli's jokers now? Where does he keep them?"

"Don't mind the fool", said Chief Boye. "All through I was sure I would win. I commissioned a firm to find out the popularity rating of both contestants. The report of the survey showed clearly that I was going for a landslide victory. When the result was announced, I was not surprised."

"Chief, we told Honourable Weliweli that he's no longer relevant in the political equation of Toro District. But how did he react?"

"You are all small boys in politics. You small rats, what do you know? We've been in this game for quite a while," he said.

It was an ebullient, smiling Chief Boye that drove to Ibadan, the Capital of Western Nigeria on Sunday evening. He checked into a 5-Star Hotel, located on Mokola Hills in the centre of the city.
The House of Parliament opened the following

morning at 10a.m. By 9.30a.m., Chief Boye's car drove to a halt in the front of the house. Beaming with smiles, he came out of the vehicle in an infectious buoyancy. He was dressed in a flowing, beautiful, brocade agbada. About five dozen anti-riot policemen manned the front gates to the House. They all looked fierce and businesslike. A mountainous man like one of the sons of Anakim was the manager at the gate. He looked fearsome and hostile. As Chief Boye approached the gate, he flared an irritated glare at him.

"Can I help you, sir?"

"Yes, of course. I am Honourable Chief Boye, the newly elected Member of Parliament from Toro constituency".

"Chief, kindly give me a minute."

The man went through his register then stared at Chief Boye's face curiously.

"I have the name of Honourable Weliweli here as the candidate who won in that constituency. How did you come about your own victory?"

There was a puzzled look on Chief Boye's face. But he tried to control his emotion as he spoke now:

"Gentleman, I am the one who won in Toro Constituency. This is the certificate issued by the electoral officer," bringing out the certificate so that the officer could examine it.

"Please, save me that headache. I don't have time for that. I am not here for certificate verification. That is not my job. The few certificates I had examined early in the morning were all fake certificates. I am tired of checking fake certificates. Please, keep your own."

"What?" queried a bewildered Chief Boye whose composure suddenly disintegrated. Trembling in anger, he screamed:

"What madness is going on here? Gentleman! You must certainly have a superior officer with whom I can talk, show me his office."

"I am sorry sir, there is no other superior officer you can talk to. I am in charge here. And whatever I tell you is the final. Chief, there is no need to lose your temper because it will probably do you no good. Now I wish to advise you to listen, and please, listen to me carefully. I have an order from above not to allow in anyone whose name is not in this register. And since your name is not there, I am afraid you cannot go in."

As Chief Boye still stood rigid, baffled by the current drama, Honourable Weliweli alighted from his car and was now approaching. He and Chief Boye exchanged bewildered glances. Honourable Weliweli gave Chief Boye a long, burning look, his lips parted, giving out a derisive smile. The huge official who would not allow Chief Boye to go in, hurriedly stood to attention with all his officers. They all greeted Honourable Weliweli warmly. He also acknowledged their greetings. The gate was quickly opened for him and he entered into the House. This time, no one checked any register.

That morning, many Action Group members who claimed to have won in their constituencies were turned back at the gate. In a twinkling of an eye, the winners had lost their seats.

"Who is the author of this?" An aggrieved Chief Boye asked, puzzle on his face. Then, he bellowed:

"We are going to the court. No one can accept this. No one will accept this broad day executive robbery. No, we won't."

The man next to him laughed and laughed.

"Gentleman! Why are you laughing? Anything funny?" asked Chief Boye.

"I am laughing at you and your colleagues. Which court are you going?"

"We are proceeding to the High Court, and right now"

The man laughed again, then asked:

"Who controls the High Court?"

"Does anyone control the court?" asked Chief Boye.

"Chief, are you a new arrival in this universe? Don't you know your opponents control the court? And the court will keep on adjourning your cases till your mandates expire. Don't you know that? I will advise you not to act like fools. Think of another alternative but certainly going to court may not pay you."

CHAPTER THIRTY-SEVEN

Violence erupted few days later in most cities, towns and villages of Western Nigeria. Many towns were boiling. The aggrieved politicians mobilized their supporters and there were massive protest all over the region. Toro was on fire. Protesters arrived at Honourable Weliweli's house around 6p.m. They must have numbered about a thousand people. The Honourable had been hearing some street noises, then some wild shrills and gradually the voices became deep and heavy like the deep murmurs of a hundred herds. Suddenly, the voices graduated into a growing roar. He still did not suspect that all what he was hearing had anything to do with him until he noticed that the roar was drawing nearer. The house was already surrounded before he knew what was happening.

"Stealers of votes, come out! Thieves, come out!"

Honourable Weliweli heard those sentences distinctly. Next, were wild bellows. He ran towards one of the windows. Below was a large, angry crowd. He looked at the sea of heads below, his heart missed some beats. Charged, riotous, the crowd was on war path.

"I am in trouble, how do I handle this?" asked Hounourable Weliweli.

As soon as the mob saw him, a huge roar went up into the sky.

"Here is he! Here is the bastard! Come out," they yelled.

He knew trouble had come. He looked around, there was no escape route as the entire building was already surrounded.

"Don't waste our time by asking him to come out. We cannot afford that luxury," screamed a tall, slim man who seemed like the leader.

"You! Take that can," pointing to a young man. "Run to the next fuel station and bring some petrol. We are going to spray this building with fuel and set it ablaze. Run quickly, I give you just five minutes."

The young man sprang forward like a leopard.

Hounourable Weliweli knew that in about ten minutes, the man would be back and the house would be sprayed with petrol and set ablaze. He just must be out of the building before the petrol arrived.

"What do I do?" he asked. His mind was now reeling with various options but none seemed good enough to guarantee his safety. He stared at the crowd nervously.

"Appeal cannot pacify these people. Asking for mercy will be a waste of time since they had already made up their mind to kill me," he kept on muttering. He paced up and down restlessly, finally, he summoned up courage:

"I am going down to appeal to them. I will face them and tell them that I did not have hand in any electoral fraud."

"If you did not, why did you go to the Parliament to occupy the seat you did not win?" something asked him. He stood rigid, now momentarily paralyzed and confused.

"My sin is beyond pardon;" he mumbled. "My best bet is to escape at once. But how do I do it?" He looked down. If he jumped down from the window, he would land into the ready hands of the enemies below and there were over 500 people surrounding the walls. He remembered a secret route behind the building. He quickly rushed down, surveyed the route; there were about 50 people there waiting. He looked at his wristwatch; five minutes were already gone since the man who went for the petrol left. He was in a serious dilemma as he now stood staring into space.

Vera, his wife was wailing in one corner of the room. They both knew the end had come.
"I have warned you not to go into politics; now, see the result;" she screamed.
"That complaint cannot solve the present problem. Be calm, let us put our heads together and see what we can do." But his words only assisted Vera to grow more hysterical. He left her and dashed into the room, picked up his rifle and hurried down the staircase while dragging Vera along. He was determined now to confront the people face to face.
"Man will not die twice;" he asserted. He was bent on

killing at least five to ten people before he submitted to the angry mob. He got to the ground floor and fired several shots through one of the closed windows to scare off the crowd outside. On hearing the sound of his gun, most of the people took to their heels. But the die-hard stood their ground. Some were smashing his windows but they could not get in all the same because the windows had iron bars.

"You bastard! There is no escape route for you. We are going to slaughter you like a ram and use your blood to appease the angry soil of Toro," bellowed the leader.

Honourable Weliweli opened his door suddenly and opened fire. A volley hit the leader on the leg and he fell. He shot two others on the legs and they also fell. Their colleagues seeing their falling comrades knew that the Honourable meant business, they took to their heels. The Honourable took his wife who was shaking behind the door and dashed out of the building. As they got into the open air, he fired several shots into several directions and people who stood by, ran for their lives. It was now time to move. He held on to Vera and started to run. They had run almost 50 yards from the house and an adjourning bush was only a few yards away and the Honourable was already rejoicing that they had surmounted the most critical obstacles when Vera screamed loudly and suddenly tore herself loose from her husband.

"My certificates! My certificates! I placed them on the bed. I must pick them;" she screamed.

"No! No! You cannot go back. Are you crazy?" The Honourable rushed forward quickly, pulled her back but Vera wriggled out of his hold as if possessed by a strange demon and flew towards the house.

"Don't go! Don't go!" The Honourable screamed loudly. But strangely Vera ignored all his warnings. Honourable Weliweli stood on the same spot, helpless. Vera disappeared into the house. For about 50 seconds, she spent inside the house, the Honourable stood there shivering. She was out at last. But that moment, certain hoodlums swarmed out of a nearby building with double-barreled guns. They opened fire on Vera and Honourable Weliweli watched helplessly as Vera went down in a hail of fire.

The men fired several shots at Honourable Weliweli and missed. He too returned the fire and gunned down two men, then took to his heels while hails of bullets were trailing him as he ran. Bullets were whizzing from all directions; it was a miracle that he was not hit. He dashed into the bush and disappeared into the bowel of the dark, evergreen forest before him.

CHAPTER THIRTY-EIGHT

Prince Matete had been in Lagos for the past few days for a medical check-up. The doctor said his blood pressure was high and he had to remain in bed for proper observation. He was on his sick bed when news reached him that Toro was burning and that Honourable Weliweli had shot and killed some people. He phoned the Commissioner of Police at the Provincial Headquarters and the same dispatched quickly a strong contingent of his men to Toro.

The anti-riot police-men raced to Toro. But before they got there, Toro people had been wrongly informed that Honourable Weliweli was sending a contingent of police to Toro to fish out people opposed to him and deal with them. The town crier quickly rallied the people for a revolt "Toro People! Rise up for your defence! Defend your children and property!" he announced.

The people rose up. Some men carried double barreled guns. Hunters carried dane guns. Young men carried clubs and cutlasses. They met the police contingent at the outskirts of Toro. The road to Toro was already blocked by the people before the police arrived.

"You won't enter Toro. You, enemies of the people - turn back! We don't need you, just turn back and go."
But the head of the police had an order to restore peace. He was not ready to condone any nonsense. Neither was he prepared to succumb to any intimidation. He directed his men to break up the barricade and Toro people opened fire. The police returned fire. And for about twenty minutes both sides were engaged in a fierce gun battle. By the time the battle was over, forty-nine indigenes of Toro lay down dead and over two hundred people were wounded. Five policemen were killed and several injured. It was a black day in Toro.

Few other towns also erupted simultaneously. By the evening, the policemen were withdrawn from Toro to attend to a more serious problem elsewhere. By this time, the story had become clearer. People knew now that it was Prince Matete who invited the killer squad into town and most people rose up in anger against Matete's family in a war of revenge. But Prince Matete had sent the police to protect Toro people. But the enemies had twisted the story round. And Matete's family was in trouble.

The Oro people were members of a secret cult. The

members were not known by anyone. They operated in absolute secrecy and mostly in the night. But one of the most influential members of Oro group lost his wife and five sons that evening. They were killed by the police. The man now, an angry lion, roused up all Oro members for battle.

"I am not going to rest until all the members of Matete's family have been killed and it just must be this night," he vowed. Toro was burning.

It was a friend who alerted me that the lives of the members of the Matete's family were in danger. "They are going to be killed tonight. That decision had been taken already. If there is anyway you can alert them, do so quickly."

I rushed out of my house. I needed to tell Alero to run into hiding. As I ran down the road, I could hear the huge roaring of a surging, angry mob afar off. I ran through some hidden, secret paths, my heart panting anxiously as I ran.

"Where is Alero? Is she safe?" These were the questions on my lips as I ran down the street. I was in for greater shock when I got to Matete's house. The imposing gate had been pulled down. The beautiful doors to the house and fanciful windows had been badly smashed. I learnt that the security men were overpowered and the angry mob entered into the compound and carried out a terrible destruction.

"What of the wife and the children?" I queried. "They all fled in different directions, I can't say I know the whereabout of any of them," said an eyewitness.

I stood rigid, dazed, now paralyzed with anxiety. Later, I made frantic efforts to look for Alero. I checked a few places where I felt she could be hiding. She was not there. I returned home few hours later, tired and frustrated. I went into my room and started to pray to God to protect Alero wherever she might be. I had prayed for two hours when about 9p.m. there was a knock on my door.

"Who is it?"

"It's me." It was my mother's voice. I hurried to open the door, my heart was in my mouth as I stared at mom's face. She looked so worried.

"I don't want to give you this information but on further reflection, I feel it will be most unfair if I keep it from you," she said. I stared at her face expectantly but she remained hesitant now as if the information she was about to give was too heavy for the mouth to pronounce. I knew something terrible had happened. I suspected that Alero had been captured and perhaps murdered.

"Mother, please tell me! Has the mob killed Alero?"

"No one has killed Alero but a friend had just informed me that Alero's hideout had been discovered and she had been abducted by the members of the terrible Oro Fraternity. I was told that she had been taken to their sacred grove."

"Why their grove? Why should they take her to the grove?"

"The woman said they intend to sacrifice her to their god. I am told that they are going to kill her today at 12 midnight."

"What! Oro people will kill Alero at 12 midnight?

Human sacrifice in 20th century Nigeria! Is that possible?" I asked. The whole thing sounded so strange and so awful.

But I recalled that moment that a lot of strange things had happened since the last twenty four hours that I would be a fool if I thought that certain things were beyond the evil people of Toro who had now gone crazy. Most of what had happened in the last 24 hours were stranger than fiction. I could not believe that people could pour petrol on other human beings and set them ablaze, and this had happened. I could not believe that Toro people could be so mad as to be burning the most beautiful buildings in their town and this had happened. I knew the abduction of Alero must be a fact.

"Alero to be sacrificed to an idol, that is not acceptable," I suddenly screamed like a mad man.

My mother held me tight and sealed up my lips with her hands.

"My son, there is nothing anybody can do now. Law and order have broken down. Everybody is doing what he likes. Evil people are now on the rampage. Who can stop them? I know you love Alero so dearly. But what can we do? Please take heart and bear everything like a man."

"How can mom expect me to accept the abduction of Alero and her possible slaughter like a ram to a god? How? How does she expect me to bear such like a man?"

Since she gave me that terrible information, mother was deeply worried. She didn't know what I was going to do. She could not guess what my next line of action would be. She was on red alert, watching carefully my next moves.

My father was away in the farm. For the past two weeks, he had been busy harvesting and drying his cocoa beans. October to December was cocoa season in Toro. My father had two double-barreled guns. I was aware that he had taken one to the farm. But before going in search of the second, I needed to calm down my mother and also convince her that I had accepted everything she told me; and also let her know that I had laid the whole matter at the court of Almighty God and had accepted the situation as a fate or destiny over which I could not exercise any control.

I came out of the room and saw my mother where she stood in the corridor – a terribly disturbed, fearful and anxious woman.

"Mother! It is time for you to go to bed. I have accepted all what you told me and I am taking the matter as a man. There is no tragedy that befalls any man that has not happened to someone else before. Mother, I want to retire to bed. Please go and sleep."

I cannot describe the spasm of relief I saw on my mother's face.

"Mayo! You are a wonderful boy. You are the son of your father. You are a great child. May God continue to bless you. I am really proud of you. Good night, my son."

I entered my room and locked the door. Within five minutes, I was snoring. I got up quietly twenty minutes later and opened the door. I made sure the door did not make the slightest sound. I tiptoed to the door leading to the room of my mother. She was already asleep. She was snoring.

"Good! It is time to move." I told myself.

I walked quickly into my father's room, opened the door and switched on the torchlight in my hand. There, on the wall, was the double-barreled gun. It took me only a few minutes to locate the cartridges. I smiled to myself and said:

"These are enough." I tucked them into a bag, put on a large voluminous agbada in which I could hide the gun and sneaked quickly out of the main door. In the next minutes, I was walking down one of the streets of Toro.

CHAPTER THIRTY-NINE

The decision as to what to do took me a few seconds. And what was it? I was going to storm that sacred grove (Igbo-Oro) which nobody must venture into except the members of Oro Fraternity. Of course, this was a death warrant. Like a man carrying a suicide bomb, I knew I was going there to die. But death did not scare me. It didn't frighten me for a second. Whatever would kill Alero must kill me. Love for Alero was crying in my flesh, singing strange songs. A demonic rage controlled my passion and death had no meaning to me.

"I will die with Alero. I will die like a man. But before I die, I am going to leave an indelible mark, something that will serve as a memorial for the future generations," I asserted forcefully.
I first heard about Oro grove six years ago. My father and I were returning from the farm when I saw a narrow but a fascinating footpath.
"Where does this lead to?" I queried.
"It leads to Oro grove."

"And which place is that?"

"It is a sacred forest where members of the Oro Fraternity have their shrine."

"What is Oro Fraternity?"

"Oh! Terrible people. The fraternity does a lot of heinous things including human sacrifice."

"Human what?" I almost jumped up.

"They kill people for rituals."

"Even in 20th century Nigeria?"

"Yes, in 20th century Nigeria. When you hear that certain people are missing and they cannot be found, such victims are in most cases kidnapped by Oro people."

"But the British governed this land for about 100 years. They left only a few years ago. They were no-nonsense people. You mean Oro people operated under their nose?"

"They did, my boy. Oro Fraternity is a secret society. The Oro people operated secretly and they had a strong and superb network that could not be broken into very easily. Whenever they abducted or kidnapped any one, they normally left no trace behind. Even if anyone calls on the police, the police would not be of help. They are terribly demonic people. They are also magicians and enchanters – people who would curse a tree and the tree would dry up and shed its leaves immediately. Boy! Let us leave them alone; the less we talk about them, the better."

I stared at my father's face, speechless with shock. But I still had some more questions to ask.

"The Oro Grove – their grove, have you ever been there?" I asked my father.

"I have never been there. What would I have gone there to do? No one goes there except a member, I mean the initiated. If anyone goes there by mistake, he is a dead man. It is not a place for anyone to go; it is a terribly frightening forest. It is a common belief among Toro people that the dead and the living mix freely in this grove we are talking about."

"Dead and the living mixing freely?"

"Yes! I am told that in the grove, demons and principalities hold open markets regularly and exchange goods. There, witches and wizards hold their seminars and workshops in the deep of the night when the earth is in deep slumber."

"The Oro people who go there, what do they go there to do?"

"They go there to do sacrifice at the shrine of Alaworo, one of the founding fathers of Toro. I am told they also go there to meet their ancestors who died in some distant past to ask them for wisdom for solving any intricate problem they may be facing. They normally go there in the dead of the night."

"Why?" I queried.

"The dead are not generally seen during the day time."

All the above I recalled now as I walked down the street that night. The time was 10.50p.m. It was dark everywhere. The streets were all empty and I met nobody as I went. It was exactly 11.10p.m. when I got to the outskirts of Toro. The tropical vegetation before me looked dreadfully dark and terrifying. And through it went a narrow footpath. I was to walk through the path. Everything before me was as dark as Erebus, and as I began to walk down the path, I was afraid for the first time. I switched on the torchlight briefly, saw the next twenty to thirty metres and quickly switched it off again. This was the technique I used till I got to the junction where a narrower footpath went to the left – the frightening path to the dreadful Oro grove.

At the entrance to the path, there were several "peregun" trees on both left and right sides. I put off my huge agbada, rolled it into a small funnel and threw it away. I didn't need it any more. I loaded my gun. The bag containing the cartridges, I fastened to my back. The gun now on my left shoulder and the torchlight on the right, I was ready to start climbing the range of hills that led to this strange and mysterious grove.

The bush around me was the thick, evergreen selvas of the Amazon type. Huge, tall trees going up into considerable heights. Everywhere was dark and gloomy. As I moved deeper and deeper into the dreadful and growing silence of the enormous darkness before me, the confidence that had sustained me up to this moment appeared to be draining off little by little. I climbed the first hill and descended a slope, I climbed the second and descended another slope. As I started to climb the third, I could see ahead of me about two to three hundred lighted lamps. Remember, I was in darkness.

"I had gotten to my destination at last," I mumbled.

I had long put off the torchlight.

Now, I crawled silently in the dark towards the various lights. When I was about 50 metres to them, somebody coughed from where the lights were and a female voice spoke up:

"Someone is approaching," said the voice.

"Someone?" queried another voice

"Yes! His smell reached me ten minutes ago. He is a man." Then came a sound like the hooting of a thousand owls.

"Hiyeh! Hiyeh!! Hiyeh!!!"

"The man is drawing nearer. He is now dangerously close," said the voice. I did not see the person speaking. I stayed glued to that spot, fear on my face.

One by one, the lights before me started to go out. The last one went out and the entire place became frighteningly dark. But the same voice parted the darkness.

"Young man! Where are you going? Why do you disturb our meeting? Who are you?" the voice spoke from the thick, impenetrable darkness before me, I was afraid. "Should I turn back and run?" I asked myself.

I paused a little and I just found myself saying:

"I am a Prince." I did not know why I called myself a Prince.

"Prince?"

"Yes."

"Oh, no wonder! It is only a Prince that can do what you did to us. We would have roasted you for this offence but we have a vow not to touch a Prince. We are witches and wizards of Africa, South of the Sahara, holding an important conference. But why do you have to go out at this time? This is a wrong time. But all the same, put on your light and go. The road is already cleared for you. Proceed."

I stood up shivering. I put on my light. Just that moment, I saw about 300 birds flying off from the pitch earlier on occupied by the various lights. I felt a rising panic as I moved on. The pitch scared the hell out of me and I felt I was going to faint. I moved on. Soon I was on the top of the hill where the voice seemed to be coming from, but I saw no one. I walked for about 50 metres over what looked like a plain, and still there was no evidence of any human being in sight.

"Who then was talking to me? Where was she hiding?" Another slope immediately lay before me and I hastened towards it. My heart was beating fiercely and I felt as if one invisible hand was about to hold me. I got to the valley below and as I started climbing a new hill, I remembered now that I would have to climb seven hills before I got to my destination.

I was on top of the fifth hill when all the surrounding trees began to moan. The wind was talking above my head. To the right, I heard the noise of what seemed like a huge open market in session. I heard the voices of many hawkers. I heard one very distinctly:
"All dwellers on earth and in space!

Come and buy.
All who have recently departed from the earth.
This is where to purchase your goods.
You just must buy my items.
Because you will need them on your way."
I stood there frozen. I could feel some hands on me but I saw no one. Some people were pushing me.
"Give way!" a voice told me.
"Do not collide with me. Don't you have eyes?" asked another voice. But strangely I saw no one.
"My God! You are stepping on my items," screamed yet another voice. I moved forward quickly and soon it appeared that I had left the market behind. The moon had come out large, and I saw by my right what looked like many shadows of human beings. Alas! The shadows were moving and one of them suddenly stopped to talk to me:
"We are the ones that have recently left the earth for the land of the dead. Don't look at us! Don't stare at us! Hasten your steps! Leave us quickly!"

I ran quickly down the slope. Before me was a small brook. Suddenly, it appeared as if I saw some strange beings drinking water from the brook. They were over twenty of them. They looked like miniatures of human beings: short little creatures. I stood transfixed to that spot. The mischievous creatures also stood looking at me. They started to back away while looking fixedly at me. The brook started to wail like a bereaved woman. Its doleful cry sounded like hundred voices of people in agony. My hair suddenly rose up. I was afraid. I turned round quickly and wanted to run back but alas, those strange mischievous creatures were there standing on the path I had left only few seconds ago, all now smiling at mc and coming closer and closer. I turned round again and ran forward now dizzy with fear. I jumped over the brook, ran desperately to escape the mysterious beings. It did not appear as if they were pursuing me because I did not hear their footsteps. Not long, I saw a narrow tunnel before me; then I stooped.

"Should I enter it? What is inside?" Alas, those strange beings were dangerously close and I ran into the tunnel. Having run for about 50 metres inside the tunnel, and those mysterious beings seemed not to be following me any longer; the end of the tunnel came into view. I moved ahead quickly and began to climb another range of hills. By the time I got to the top of the last one, which was the seventh, I saw ahead of me a circular house and several flames of light. Without being told, I knew I had gotten to my destination at last.

CHAPTER FORTY

Before me was the home of Death, the den of the terrible, the dreadful enclave of the Oro people, a place never to be visited by the uninitiated, the home of horror, the deadliest zone.

I had switched off my torchlight and I crawled noiselessly towards the dreadful home. About fifty metres to the building, I stopped. "Fresh plans for fresh contingencies; it is time to plan my next line of action," I said to myself.

Just that moment, I saw Alero's gown hung on a stick outside the circular building before me. This was the same gown she wore when I was with her in the afternoon. A huge man was coming out of the building carrying a big pot, full of blood.

"My God! That is Alero's blood," I moaned. They had killed her already. I have arrived too late. I had the intention of saving Alero if she was still alive. But the terrible deed had been done." I broke down shivering in agony. I wanted to scream aloud. I wanted to wail like a bereaved mother who had lost her only son. I wanted to cry, till my head exploded. But a terrible rage suddenly seized me.

"This is no time for wailing. Boy! It is time for action. Alero must not die just for fun; you must avenge her death," something told me. Just that moment, I felt strangely energized and I became a furious hurricane, a huge tornado and a dangerous demon. I took my gun and ran forward quickly. There was no reason to hide anymore. I came to give battle, and the battle I was ready to fight now. The man saw me rushing forward rather too late. I took a good aim at him.

Takoh! Takoh!!" I shot at him.

"Yeh! Yeh!!" The heavy man screamed. He staggered as if he would fall down, but he suddenly stood rigid, and then roared:

"I neutralize the power of those bullets
I render them of no effect
When a duck eats a diet of stones.
It never excretes stones but water."

He then opened his mouth wide and coughed out a huge volume of water.

"Those are your bullets," he told me.

If that were meant to frighten me, he was mistaken. I had no patience for such theatrical show.

I took another good aim at him and shot again. But this time he laughed hysterically like a mentally deranged, and then opened his mouth wide, let out a huge cough again and vomited all the bullets and threw them at me.

"Have your bullets. I have coughed out bullets this time so that you can know that they are your own, examine them. I want you to be sure that they are really your own." He now stared at my face and asked:

"Anything more?"
I looked at the bullets; they were those I used to load the gun. For the first time, I was afraid.
"Have you finished or do you still have some more dramas to perform?" he asked me. I stood shivering.
"You are in serious trouble, my boy! No one ever fights me and lives. Have you not heard that every wound inflicted on an Ose tree only makes it grow fatter and more robust? I am an Ose tree; any wound inflicted on me only makes me stronger and more vibrant."
He shrugged proudly, stared at my face and barked:
"I am Kulibali, The terrible.
The father of all magicians.
The earth's most deadly being.
The man no one ever prays to meet.
The thunderbolt that electrocutes.
The hurricane that neither man nor elements can withstand.
The volcano that erupts and everyone runs for cover.
The frightening demon that carries death in his pockets
I am an invulnerable force of nature.
The invincible man."

The man poured on himself a frightening torrent of appellations and I began to shake. He smiled grimly once more and shook his head, then announced:

"Your bullets are just like the bites of sand flies. They can never have any effect on me. Steel, swords, cutlasses do not have any effect on me. Never! You are just wasting your time shooting at me."

I was still trembling with fear but I never could explain how another demonic rage seized me again and I screamed:

"If bullets, steel and swords cannot penetrate your skin, then have this!"

I dashed forward quickly and threw at him a deadly uppercut.

"Hold it! Stop there! Let that hand hang in the air" he roared.

And strangely, my left hand suddenly hung in the air; neither could I move it further nor bring it down.

Then the man said:

"What you have done is a sacrilege

It is a rule; no one must ever raise his hand to fight me.

No one ever sees a tree with prickles and give it a kick

No one ever quarrels with a bunch of palm fruits and gives it a punch.

When a young man sees a cobra, he must first stop for fear.

When an antelope comes face to face with a lion, fear must grip him.

No one rushes to embrace a burning bush

A bunch of cowage is not a flower a young man must rush forward to embrace.

No!"

He stared at me and sent out a dry, angry laugh.

"Give me that gun," he ordered.

A terrible spell fell on me as I handed over the gun to him. I watched him now in silent amazement.

"Boy! I tell you, you are in deep trouble."

I surveyed the face of the terrible monster before me with lethargic horror. My body began to tremble uncontrollably. The monster gave me a dreadful stare and said:

"You are here because of the lady in our shrine. It is nice you are here. You have just come in time to save us from a small predicament. We would have sacrificed the lady to our god before you came, but our god would not accept a member of one gender. It insisted on having male and female at the same time. Now that you are here, nothing is delaying us anymore. The sacrifice can now go on."

As he spoke, a mysterious chilling air suddenly filled my surrounding. I stared at him; I knew I was in the soup. I had done what I should not do. I had walked into a den of the lions with my eyes wide open. I knew I was going to die. There was no escape route for me. I surveyed the gloomy environment whose mournful eyes now stared at me and I realized with thrill of terror that at last, I had reached my graveyard. He waved his charmed hand before me and said:

"Remain rooted to that spot. The door frame never shifts."

I suddenly became a lifeless tree. I stood there rigid as his enchantment hung on me like a terrible cloud. Now completely hypnotized, I watched him entering into the circular building before me. What he was going there to do, I did not know. But I stood glued to that spot, speechless and confused.

Suddenly, I regained my consciousness. I could not explain how.
"Why am I here?" I asked myself. Just that moment, I remembered my mission.

"Mayo!" I mumbled. "Remember! You have not come here to live; you have come here to die. Why are you now afraid of death? What is death after all? Your mission is to come here and lay down your life willingly and die with Alero. But that is not all; you must not die without leaving a mark. You must leave a memorial behind that will serve as a warning to all generations. You are not here to die just like any ordinary person. You are a special being, a man who must be celebrated, a giant who must die like a hero. When an elephant dies, it doesn't go down alone; trees and shrubs must go down with him!"

Just that moment, I remembered the small bottle of acid I had in my pocket. I intended to drink it if I got caught or in case I was being tortured. The acid would kill within two minutes. It was a liquid. I suddenly recovered my confidence.

The man was out of the circular building; now ready for the kill. He looked terrible. He held a huge chain in his left hand and my gun in the right.
"You are in trouble, my boy," he growled once more. He swore and cursed as he approached me. In a flash,

I brought out the small bottle containing the acid and splashed the content on his broad, terrifying face. The monster let out a dreadful scream:

"Yeh! Yeh!! Yeh!!! He has killed me! I am dead!" He howled as he fell down flat and started to roll on the ground. The more he tried to rub off the acid from his face, the more he spread it and the greater the pain. I picked up my gun quickly from the ground and as I was trying to reload it, two other men, with dismay on their faces, rushed out of the circular building; now ready to fight. They looked terrible.

"Where were they hiding before now?"

I had discovered that their power was in their spoken words. With the words, they could hypnotize and do many, dangerous things. I was not going to allow these ones to speak. I did not give them a chance when I dashed forward like a flash of lightning and hit the first one on the chest with the mouth of my double-barreled gun. He fell down screaming in pain. I flew in the air, gave the second a deadly hit on the cheek with my right ankle.

He first staggered like a drunk. I rushed forward again; gave him another hit, and he fell down flat. The leader, the huge monster could no longer see.

"My eyes! My eyes!" he cried in agony. The second man was bleeding from the mouth. Perhaps two or three of his chest bones were already broken and he was no longer in a position to offer any resistance. The third was still in a daze, but he could recover. I took the chain to fasten him securely to a nearby tree

I reloaded my gun and was now ready to enter the circular building.

Taking one cautious step after the other, I entered the dreadful building. Inside the building, I saw some native lamps (*ogunso*) positioned at strategic points. The floor on which I walked and the walls were polished with red sand. The smoothness of the surface was breathtaking. Watching carefully for any movement and looking right and left, I was on red alert. I went in, one step after the other, deeper and deeper into the bowel of this mysterious building. Suddenly, I heard a voice behind me.
"Stop there! Don't move further!"

I turned round with lightning speed and before me was a short man, a chimpanzee-looking creature. Smoke was coming out of his nostrils, but he was not smoking. He had no cigarette in his hand. "Where comes the smoke?" I did not know. I wanted to rush forward quickly and attack him but the demon suddenly roared:
"Let the ground you stand upon turn into a glue
Let it hold you firm and securely
Remain rooted
Remain standing
The door frame never shifts."

I found myself caught in a strange immobility again. I stood on the same spot, I could neither move nor talk. Strange enchantment caught me in its trap. The short man gave me a terrible stare and said:

"I watched you fighting those people. I can confirm that you are a very great fighter. But you still have one more battle to fight, my boy! You have won all your previous fights. But I can tell you the result of the one you are about to begin. You are not only going to lose it, you are going to end up in my pepper soup pot. Look at it," (pointing to a huge pot by the left) from which heat was coming out with ferocious force. The man gallivanted and went to the pot, brought out the boiled hand of a man and gave it a bite. Pointing to the pot again, he said:

"Boy! That is your final destination. Your own parts will soon replace the one I have just eaten. That is as sure as death. You have escaped from the frying pan but you have now landed in the fire. You have fallen from the tree-top and have now landed in the deep of a well. You have decided to collide with lightning. You have chosen on your own accord to dance with the tiger. And you are ending in no other place other than its belly."

He stared at me fixedly. He seemed both serene and insane at the same time. He then let out a frightening roar of laughter and said:
"Boy! I welcome you to OUR HOUSE. I am 70 years old and I have fed on no other diet since I was born other than human flesh. Look at the shrine (pointing to the left), it had "chopped" more than 50,000 people since Alaworo entered the ground on that very spot two thousand years ago. The spirit of Alaworo neither takes water nor wine; it drinks only human blood."

"Bobo!" he screamed suddenly.

"May the gods show kindness to your Majesty!" roared a tall, huge man who suddenly materialized from nowhere.

"Sharpen your knife and get it ready for action. My pepper-soup will taste good tonight. We are having the kidneys and livers of this young man and those of that young lady for dinner. Prepare the woods where their remaining flesh shall be roasted. We are already having the food that can last us for weeks. But before you go, you will have to tie this young man to the second stone where we put the lady."

The old man suddenly moved forward and touched my chest with an amulet.

"Give me that gun," he ordered, and I gave my gun to him without a protest. A sort of confusion hung over me and I could no longer think properly.

"Now, move!" he commanded me. My legs just obeyed automatically and I began to move.

The huge man held my hand and we walked for about ten metres; he then opened a door to the left, and there, looking tired and weak, was Alero in panties and one loose top, firmly but roughly tied to a huge stone. In a minute the man tied me to the second huge stone. I was already firmly tied to the stone, now completely helpless, when I began to regain my consciousness.

I stared at Alero and Alero stared at me, tears raining down her face. A look of shock and surprise lit her innocent, swollen face as she queried:

"Where did they capture you in your own case? And what is your offence?"

"It is a long story. But since we have only a few minutes to live, I cannot tell you now; may be I will tell you in heaven. I'll give you the detail when we get to the other world."

"I knew you would look for me," she spoke in low tones.

"What else do you expect me to do, - to be taking a siesta when I heard that you had been captured?"

"In trying to save me, you have also now become a casualty. Oh, my God!" She looked terrible as she cried. She kept on glancing at me with a mixture of compassion and sorrow.

"Alero! That is enough. Even if we are going to die, let us die like giants, let us die like heroes and heroines. And we may not die afterall."

"How?"

"I don't know."

We were still talking when the cannibal, the old chimpanzee-looking man appeared and I felt a sudden shiver. He carried my gun in his right hand. The ugly, monstrous creature opened his mouth and roared:

"We normally kill a tortoise with its own sword. I am going to kill you with your own gun!"

We stared at him, horror on our faces. But just that moment, the other man appeared.

"I have sharpened the knife and it is ready." It was a

long shining knife. I stared at it, shivering with anxiety
"Do I?" he asked, staring at the old man's face.
"No! I want to have the pleasure of killing these ones myself. Go back and prepare the roasting platform."

"So I should not bother myself?"
"No. You don't need to. I am going to perform some little rituals, then shoot them, thereafter I will call on you to drag their bodies to the shrine over there and slice their throats. Alaworo will have fresh blood to drink this morning."

The big man left and immediately the monster touched our faces with one amulet, he then began a long, dreadful conjuration:
"Alaworo! These are your preys.
They are what we bring to you this year.
Let this year be a happy year.
As you drink the blood of these ones.
Bless the land; bless the people.
May the blood of these ones sweep away pestilence and all epidermics from Toro."

He went on and on. Alero stared at my face and just that moment, she saw the neck-chain that I wore.
"Touch the chain on your neck and pray with it," she whispered.
"What do you mean?" I queried.
"That chain on your neck was given to me by a Reverend Sister; a holy woman. Just touch it and pray with it."
"And if I do that, what happens?"
"Just do what I ask you to do."

I was ready to do the last wish of Alero. After all, I had come there to die with her. I touched the chain with my chin and asked God to save us if He can.

The monster had finished his ritual and he took my double-barrelled gun and aimed it directly at my head. He was standing about six or seven feet from me. I closed my eyes; tense and nervous; expecting his shot. I did not wait for too long. The gun boomed. I heard the loud sound. I opened my eyes suddenly. The gunshot hit the rope very close to my head and part of the rope suddenly gave way. As I tried to move my body, I just saw myself in a dangling position and my two hands were free. There, few inches to me was a stone; about the size of a beer bottle. I grabbed it quickly and flung it onto the monster before me. It landed on his forehead and the monster fell down flat. Everything happened in the twinkling of an eye. I could scarcely believe it.

I saw the monster now foaming from the mouth. But the rope still held my legs and my waist tightly to the stone as I began to make desperate effort to extricate myself. If the huge man with the shining knife came on the scene, then our hope would be sealed forever. I struggled desperately to get out of the rope. The two minutes I was struggling seemed like a long stretch of eternity. I was out at last. I grabbed my gun quickly, just that moment, the huge man with the shining knife, appeared.

"What is happening?" he asked as he saw me standing, now shocked and unbelieving.

I aimed the gun at him and before I could shoot, he ran quickly and dashed into a nearby bush. I shot at the direction but I could hear his footsteps as he ran desperately down an adjacent slope.

I quickly loaded the gun again and got myself ready for another attack. I hurried to Alero, brought out my German knife from my pocket and in a minute, I set her free.

The monster was still down foaming in his mouth. As we ran out of the building, I brought a firelighter from my pocket and set the building and the shrine on fire. The fire immediately became an enormous conflagration.

"Now, let us go. One of the men has escaped;" I told Alero and then gave her her gown that was hung on a pole outside.

"The man must have run to the town to bring some more members. Which means - we must get out of here quickly. We must get out of the tunnel before our enemies come with their reinforcement. They will soon come. They will come within the next thirty minutes."

I held Alero's hand and started to run back through the same route I took only about an hour ago. Within five minutes, we got to the tunnel. I was momentarily paralyzed with fear.

Now I remembered the brook and the strange beings that were smiling at me. "Suppose they seal up our path, what do we do?" As we ran inside the tunnel with me in front, I hesitated to tell Alero anything about these strange beings that confronted me about an hour ago. A great relief came upon me when we got to the end of the tunnel and I looked towards the brook, there was nobody there. We jumped over the small river and by the time we were descending the last hill, I knew the battle was half won.

"Can we make it to the outskirts of the town before our enemies surface?"

This was the question that came to my mind as we ran towards the junction where a bigger path led to the town.

We were now descending a slope with a steep gradient and Alero had become very tired. Appeals to her to put in the last effort so as to make the junction did not achieve much result. She had not eaten anything in the last 18 hours. She had struggled so hard with her abductors; till no strength remained in her. She needed rest so much. She also needed water to drink, neither could I provide. Almost fainting, I urged her on. Suddenly, we heard some voices. We stopped. We heard the sounds of some approaching steps from the direction of the town. I held Alero's hand and quickly dashed into a nearby bush. We hid behind one huge tree and remained motionless.

The enemy's reinforcement had come. It consisted of eleven men; armed with dane guns and double barreled guns. They carried touches made from waste oil palm-products (*sugudu*). Some had amulets tied round their necks and palms. Others wore small jumpers covered with all sorts of charms and talismans. Anger, surprise, venom were on their faces. Hurrying towards the shrine like people desperate to put out a dangerous fire, these terrible bulls charged forward, bent on nothing short of war.

"Who could have done this? Who could have done it?" asked the man who led them.

"Since time immemorial, we have not had this type of experience. No. No. No. Never! A strange man in Oro shrine? And has killed the Chief Priest and three other priests? This is sacrilege. This is an abomination. All the gods and goddesses of Toro, what offence have we committed? Alaworo, the great magician, what have we done to annoy you? Our ancestors in heaven, why should you allow this kind of tragedy to befall us? Why? The great Oduduwa, our great, grandfather in heaven, are you sleeping? If you are sleeping, wake up!" The man went on and on.

"Whosoever did this cannot go unpunished," said the man at the rear.

"Gentlemen!" One of the men shouted suddenly. "Enough of all this display of emotion. It serves no useful purpose. After passing through the tunnel, we need to distribute ourselves. The man is still within the shrine. He cannot easily escape. It is about thirty minutes ago; he stormed the place. I imagine that he must have released the lady and they will be hiding somewhere around the shrine. We know all the nooks and crannies. They cannot escape. They are in trouble."

In a few minutes, they disappeared into the hills. We came out of our hiding place and started to run towards the town.

"Is there yet another group on the way?" We did not

know and because we did not, we had to do the journey mostly in the dark falling down in several places and quickly rising up again. Thank God, we met nobody all through. As we entered the first street and could see before us in that early hour of the morning, the troubled Toro in deep slumber, while an eerie silence reigned everywhere, my heart that had been beating so fiercely calmed down.

But we were in for a fresh dilemma. I suddenly realized that I could not go home. Neither could Alero. That man who escaped from Oro grove must have seen me. If so, he would have briefed our enemies that I did what I did. And so, the enemies must be looking for me. Even if he did not recognize me, any fool would have guessed that only a close relative or a boyfriend of Alero, could have gone to Oro grove to set her free. No other person could have shown such audacity. No man who was not emotionally committed to her could have made such desperate moves and put his life on the line. Whichever way, I knew there was no way my name would not come up for mention. I had certainly become a target. I had stirred the hornet's net. I was in trouble.

"Where do we go? Where in Toro can we successfully hide and escape the hands of these formidable enemies who are now after our throats? Where?"

CHAPTER FORTY-ONE

As we stopped in the first street on the outskirts of Toro and hid behind some acacia trees, completely baffled and destitute of any idea as to what to do or where to turn, Alero stared at my face.

"We must take one decision before those people gone to the grove invade the town and start to look for us. Where do we go?" she asked me. Then something suddenly occurred to me.

"Can't we try the Vicar's house? I mean Pastor Francis's place."

"Are you sure his vicarage will be safe?"

"I can't think of any safer place," I replied

"Let us go quickly then. Our enemies, after failing to locate us in their shrine, will soon storm the town."

Pastor Francis lived in a storey building inside the CMS compound. The place was within easy walking distance. The time was 2:15a.m. Toro was in deep slumber. Everywhere was dark and quiet. A grave-like, terrifying solemnity had descended on the earth again. Even the streets where burning, arson and

313

looting raged on a few hours ago and where terrible beasts unleashed reign of terror, had cooled down. All had finally succumbed to the inevitable demand of nature, and in that oasis of silence, all were now sleeping, the long, deep sleep of their creator.

We got to the frontage of the Vicar's house and we stopped. Then, I advanced towards the silent house and knocked the door.
"Who is it?" a voice queried.
"It's Joseph. I want to see the Vicar. I need help." I did not mention my real name.

There was about a minute silence, thereafter, some muttering followed, and then I heard steps walking towards the door. The bolts were drawn and the Vicar with a lantern in his hand appeared.
"Yes! Can I help you?" he asked.
As he saw me, I could see alarm on his face, a young man with a double barreled gun in the middle of the night.
"Man of God! Be calm, I am not a dangerous person. We are here because we need help."

I explained quickly everything that had happened. As I related my story, the fear on his face returned, and seemed to be growing bigger as the narration progressed. But he could not deny us help; seeing we were in grave danger. He took a long, deep sigh and asked us to come in. Then, he opened a door to a room by the left which turned out to be his library and asked us to sit down.

For a brief moment, he disappeared into a long, dark

passage, leaving us with the lantern. When he reappeared again, his wife was with him.

"Princess Alero! Good heavens!" screamed the wife as she saw Alero. "My God! Who did this to the Princess? This is outrageous. This is unbelievable."

Pastor Francis stared at Alero.

"Your Royal Highness! Please, pardon me. I did not recognize Your Highness. I am so sorry."

"I understand."

"I don't want anyone to know the identities of our guests most particularly our servants in the boys' quarters. Let's do things with caution," whispered the pastor to his wife.

Hannah, the Pastor's wife took Alero and disappeared into the darkness before us. When they came back, Alero was already beautifully dressed, now looking radiant and delightful again. The Vicar and his wife sat behind a table before us and the Vicar started to talk in a voice hardly louder than a whisper.

"I am told all roads leading to this town had been barred. Men are positioned in each of the roads to arrest and burn all known supporters of Honourable Weliweli and the members of the family of His Royal Highness – Prince Matete. And if anybody should alert the enemies that I harbour any suspicious person here in the vicarage, I am sure the hoodlums will storm this place and probably burn down this building. We must exercise every caution. Spies are everywhere. I have two male servants sleeping in the boys' quarter, if they know that any of you is here, they may give out the information to the enemies. But if everyone does his or her part of the job diligently, I believe everything should be all right. The immediate problem will be how to get both of you out of Toro to a safer place. We will try to fix something somehow."

I told the Vicar that with my attack on Oro people, they would desperately be looking for me. "I need to get information quickly to my mother so that she could go into hiding. Her life is also in danger."
"I will send a reliable person to her immediately;" the vicar replied.

Food was later set before us. Alero had not eaten for the past 18 hours. As we ate the food, the Vicar and his wife disappeared again into one section of the building. When they came back about twenty minutes later, the wife took Alero away while the Vicar also took me to a room where I would rest. I must have slept for about three hours or so when some loud knocks on the main door woke me up. I stampeded out of my bed.
"Who is knocking? Have our enemies been alerted that we are in the vicarage?"

Nervous and agitated, I hurriedly dressed up. I stood there gripped by great impatience and anxiety. But the visitor that morning turned out to be the sexton. He wanted to find out whether he should ring the bell that summoned the early morning worshipers.
"Don't," the Vicar told him. "The time is not right for that. Aren't you aware of the problem going on in the town. Who will come?"
"Pastor, you are right. They are not likely to come.

Apart from the political upheaval, many members of Oro Fraternity are all over the streets. They are searching from house to house."

"Why?"

"They said they are looking for Princess Alero and one young man."

"What offence have both the Princess and the young man committed?"

"Their offence is a grievous one."

"What is it?"

"They were alleged to have gone to Oro grove."

"And what is the offence in that?"

That question suddenly turned the sexton into a roaring hyena.

"An uninitiated person – to go to Oro Grove! No, certainly not. It is a forbidden act. For a woman to go there, see all the secrets and escape, is the greatest sacrilege. It is the highest desecration of what Oro people hold sacred. The Oro people are all over the town; looking like injured lions. They say they will check every house; I am sure, they will soon show up here."

"In my vicarage? Never. They dare not."

"Pastor, they will come. They vow not to rest until they have apprehended Princess Alero and the young man in question. They believe the two are in Toro. They cannot escape. The Oro people say that the two young people had known what they should not know. They had seen what they should not see. They had unmasked the masquerade. Their offence is beyond pardon. They just have to die. That is their verdict."

"I won't allow them to come into my compound; this is God's place. This is a holy sanctuary. I will not allow a single idolater here."

317

"Pastor! Please, don't dare them. They are terrible people. When they come, just take Hannah and run!. Let them search where they want to search. Don't play with death."

When the sexton had gone, I sat on my bed, nervous and confused. I could see that we were in real danger. To get out of Toro would be near impossible. Again, if the enemies chose to come in large number and surround the vicarage, the Vicar would have no choice than to surrender us. And since they could come at any time, I could see that our present haven was not a safe sanctuary after all. We must leave the place almost at once. Where do we go?" To that question, I had no answer.

Just that moment, the door to my room opened and the Vicar came in.

"The Oro people are desperately looking for you and Princess Alero. It is really urgent that we must get you out of here. I have some guests with me – Rev and Mrs. Longe. They ought to have left yesterday but for this crisis. They want to leave this morning and I have discussed with them; and both are agreeable to my proposal."

"And what is it, sir?" I asked.

"Rev Longe will leave his wife behind. Princess Alero will be carefully made up as Rev Longe's wife and they will leave here at 6.a.m. They will leave in that Volkswagen car (pointing to it). I will drive my own car, it will be in the front and Rev Longe's car will follow. After I must have taken them through the men making trouble on the outskirts of the town, and when I am sure they are in a safe place, I will leave them to continue with their journey."

"Do you think that will work, sir?"

"Yes, it will. I have prayed about it. We are sure God will provide a safe passage."

"What happens to Mrs. Longe?"

"She has agreed to spend a few more days with us and later on join her husband. From what we have gathered so far, it will be hazardous to hide you here, I have made an arrangement to take you to a small farmhouse about half a kilometer from here. There I have a small hut. You will hide in the roof of the hut. You are not to come out of the place except you hear some agreed signals. Food and other necessaries will be brought to you there."

By 5.30a.m., Alero had been beautifully camouflaged in a woman's dress. The face was made up. She was dressed in a "buba" and "iro" with a heavy headgear to match. Everything looked all right to me. The Vicar faced me and said:

"It is time for you to depart for the hut. The people will soon be waking up. We must not take chances."

I stared at Alero's face. She also stared at me. Her burning eyes gazing at me spoke hundred times more than words. I was tensed and nervous because the stake ahead was too heavy. The chances were fifty fifty. She could be discovered. And if that happened, it was automatic death. As she was going, our parting might as well be forever. She might probably be going to her graveyard. I stared at her intensely, now silent sympathy flashing between us. She was about to cry. I also was trying everything possible to force back the tears that had already welled up in my eyes.

It was 5.40.a.m. and it was time for me to leave
"Well, good luck!" I told Alero.

"Goodbye," she replied. Her eyes were moist with tears. I tried not to look at her face since I too was crying internally.

I felt highly dejected and extremely miserable that I would not be around to see Alero depart. There was no time for such luxury now. The Vicar wanted to make sure that only a limited number of people knew that I was in the house. He wanted me out before people began to wake up.

Our journey was through a highly wooded forest. The trees whose branches were above us, provided a thick canopy with their evergreen leaves. It was a virgin vegetation that no one had touched since pre-historic time. We walked for about 500 metres, then we entered into an open space and before us was a cassava plantation. And about another 500 metres was a small hut on the top of a small hill. It was a mud hut with a room where one could rest. The remaining space contained the kitchen and other facilities. We entered. I climbed into the roof and got a space where I could sit and rest my back. I sat down dejected, sunk in the depth of despair.
"Don't forget all the warnings."
"I won't forget, sir," I replied.

"Other people come to this hut. Please don't come

down except you hear the agreed signals. You never can know - the next visitor to the hut may be an enemy. I mean somebody who must never see you. You are warned."

"I won't come out," I assured him.

"Good."

When the Vicar had gone, I looked around. I saw here and there cassava plants and few palm trees that were now to be my companions. For how long? I could not tell. Now I had become a prisoner. I was no longer in charge of my own destiny.

Far in the eastern sky, the daylight seemed to be approaching. I remembered Alero and I felt very sad that I could not see her off in this latest perilous adventure into the unknown. My heart beat furiously once more. I tried all I could to calm it down but I couldn't.

I had only spent about ten minutes in this new prison when I heard the sound of the Volkwagen car.

"Rev. Longe and Alero have taken off. The hour has come," I mumbled. About four minutes after take off, my chest suddenly plunged into a cauldron of racing pulses, my mind ran through a long list of possibilities.

"What if the hoodlums ask them to come out of the car for thorough checking? What if they are able to see through the camouflage? What if they discover Alero?"

Several of these ifs came surging into my mind now; and the foolishness of the entire arrangement appeared so clearly to me. I was frantic with anxiety.

But that anxiety suddenly turned into an alarm as I heard a huge roar from the western gate of Toro. And I remembered now that that was the gate Rev. Longe's car must pass through before going out of the town. I panicked. Then I heard another huge noise again.

"Whose noise is that?" I queried as a chill ran through me. I sat rigid now trying to listen with all my might. Then, came once more the noise of a massive, swirling crowd. I could hear now a continuous, thunderous roar of:

"Awo! Awo!! Awo!!! Awo!!!!" And that was the slogan the hoodlums always shouted whenever they made a catch. "My God! Have they caught Alero?" I asked, panic on my face

For minutes, I lay in great impatience and anxiety.

"Hurray! Hurray!!" came another growing roar.

"The people are celebrating! They have surely made a catch. The cat has been let out of the bag. My God! They have caught Alero. I am in trouble. I must descend and go out of this hut and stay in a location where I can know precisely what is going on." "But you have been told never to come out of this hut except you hear the agreed signals; haven't you?" something asked me.

"That rule has no meaning now. If Alero is already captured, why am I here? Why should I be hiding here? What is my business in this place?"

"But you are not sure whether Alero had been caught or not. It is true that you are hearing a huge roar but the roar can be for another reason." I consoled myself.

"What other reason can be responsible for the huge noise I am hearing? Whichever the cause I deserve to know. Man will not die two times. I am going down to find out." Then I remembered the warning again. The words came now as if they were being repeated to my hearing.

"There are some hunters who come to this area to hunt for game. They can come anytime. They must not know that you are here. You never can guess which of them is a member of the Oro Fraternity. Under no circumstance must you attempt to come out except I ask you to do so. You are only to answer to calls from me and I will always precede my call by the sentence: Peace be unto you." With all these strong warnings, should I still come out? My mind said 'no' "But how do I know what is happening to Alero at the outskirts of the town?" I queried. There was yet another huge noise. My fingers were trembling. My anxiety had now become unbearable.

"Whatever happens - good or bad, the information will reach you latest by 8.a.m. Try to cool down, my friend!" I encouraged myself. Soon it was 7.a.m. The bright lovely sun appeared in the eastern sky. But the brightness did not warm my heart in anyway. Now I started to count the time by seconds and minutes. Around 7.30.a.m., it appeared I heard the sounds of approaching steps.

The long awaited news has come at last. I stood suddenly still. That moment, I heard the booming of a gun. I shook as a shudder ran through me. The sound was so close. The man shooting must have aimed at me directly. "Have I been discovered? Has someone let out the secret that I am hiding inside the hut?"

I moved to one corner of that roof. Then, I saw a hunter holding an eagle. About two minutes later, he disappeared through the footpath towards the Vicar's compound.

Gradually, 8.a.m. came, I neither saw the Vicar nor his son. Then came 9.a.m., then 10.a.m., then 11.a.m., I tried to look out; no one was in sight. By now I knew the unexpected had happened.

"If the arrangement had worked according to the plan, the Vicar or his son should have been here. That is too sure. The enemies have captured Alero. The Vicar has been held by the hoodlums for collaborating with the so-called enemies of the people of Toro. All these need no debate anymore. They are simply the facts," I mumbled.

"What do I do?" I asked myself. Something suggested to me to come out of the hut, crawl through the bush towards the Vicar's house and from a safe distance, assess what is going on. If indeed there was trouble and Alero had been killed, it would be foolish and most unnecessary to remain in my hideout. "Why am I living if Alero has been killed?" I asked myself. My heart suddenly became strong as an iron bar again.

"I am going to die also at the outskirts of Toro. But at

least, ten people will go down with me."

I loaded my gun. "Son of Williams! It is time again for action. The bell is summoning me to the battle; and to the war front, I go!"

I was trying to descend from the roof when suddenly I heard the sounds of some approaching steps and then stood still.

"Peace be unto you," said a voice from below. "You can come out now," the voice advised.

I came down hurriedly and before me were the Vicar and his son.

"We are happy to inform you that Alero had gone. The plan worked beautifully because it had the blessing of God. My car was in the front of the one that carried Alero and Rev. Longe. I only left them when I became sure that they had gone beyond all the trouble spots. Alero must have gone beyond Ibadan by now. She will definitely make Lagos by 12.noon."

It is not easy to describe the spasm of relief, which swept over me. Just few seconds ago, I had thought everything was lost but now it was exactly the opposite. I was so happy. Bread, tea, milk, fried egg and butter were set before me and I ate my breakfast voraciously.

CHAPTER FORTY-TWO

The Vicar and his son left me about eleven hours ago. I looked at my wristwatch; it was 10p.m., darkness stared at me from every direction. The Vicar and his son had not shown up again and I doubted if any of them would show up that night. I was hungry. But I had strict instruction not to venture out of my present prison. I did not know whether this was where I would spend the night. Having gone to Oro Grove in the dead of the night, I did not have any fear to spend the night where I was. "But how long will I keep in the present prison?" I had no precise idea and that gave me a lot of worry.

"Peace be unto you!" a voice suddenly intruded into the darkness from below. I hurried down to meet the Vicar. I did not know why he had chosen to come without a lamp but he came with news that was not cheering.

"The general situation in the town has worsened," he said. "My vicarage is already under secret surveillance and this is the reason why I choose this time to come and without a lamp. The fact that neither you nor the princess has been found by the Oro people has turned them into ferocious animals. They are all over the streets searching from house to house. They have strong suspicion that both of you are being hidden somewhere in the town and they have made a vow not to rest until they fish you out and kill you. I am told that their priests made a vow neither to eat nor drink until you and the Princess are sacrificed at the shrine of Alaworo, their god. The evil people are on the rampage and we have really serious problem in our hands.

The sexton has alerted me that there is a strong suspicion in the town that I may be hiding both of you in the vicarage. He told me that there is a secret plan to surround the vicarage suddenly at about 8.a.m. tomorrow morning. It is now desperate that I should get you out of Toro early tomorrow, if possible at dawn."

"I can go through the bush. By the time I walk three days in the bush, I should have gone beyond Toro and its surrounding villages where people can identify me."

"That proposal is not all right," he told me. "I am told the people are already in possession of your photographs and the same must have been sent to rioting youths in other towns and villages. Toro is not the only place rioting. I hope you know that?"

"Yes, I know."

"We need to exercise a lot of caution. We need to be very careful in taking any step. But I have finalized one arrangement which I am sure is good enough."

I stared curiously at the Vicar's face, now anxious to know what he had arranged.

"A trailer carrying bags of cocoa to Lagos will leave Toro early tomorrow morning and the driver has agreed to hide you in one of the cocoa bags. The man is an Ibo chap; he is a highly reliable person."

"If the rioting youths at the outskirts of the town insist on searching the bags, I will be completely helpless. I will be totally at their mercy. The arrangement does not seem good enough to me, sir, I am so afraid."

"You don't need to worry. The situation is not as bad as that. Two trailers left Toro yesterday; they were not searched. One had also gone today. My informant told me that they only asked the driver to remove the covering tarpaulins in order to check what was inside and nobody touched any of the bags. You will be inside one of the bags. The arrangement is good enough. In any case, we will support it with prayer and it will work."

I had to agree to the arrangement very reluctantly even though I was not completely satisfied with it.

I spent the night in the vicar's house, but all through the hours between 11p.m. and 5a.m., I rolled on the bed most of the time. I could not sleep.

"What if the Oro people decided to storm the vicarage in the night?" It was in my best interest to be on my guard. Like a pastor who is praying for a lunatic and who certainly must not close his eyes while praying, I was on red alert. I looked at the arrangement, each time I saw so many loopholes in it, but I had to go. My present haven was no longer safe. I had to take the only plan available and make use of it.

As I waited anxiously for the morning, my nerves were tense. Yes, 5a.m. came at last and the Vicar knocked at my door. I hurried out of the room, and in the next moment, we were outside the CMS compound. It was still very dark. The air was cold and dry. Soon we got to the store and there was the long vehicle that was carrying hundreds of bags of cocoa to Lagos. Mr. Okoro, the driver, took me to a private room while his men were busy carrying the remaining bags of cocoa from the store to the trailer. Exactly 5.30a.m., he came to summon me. I walked briskly out of the room. He mounted the huge lorry and beckoned me to follow. And there in the extreme right corner of the lorry was a huge empty bag.
"That is the one meant for you. Go inside it," he said.
I entered into the bag.
"Please kneel down."

I knelt down and cocoa beans were poured into the remaining space reaching up into my neck. A small opening through which I could take in fresh air was provided and after that the bag was closed at the top. It was really hot and uncomfortable but the arrangement was to quickly take me out of the bag after leaving Toro and its surrounding towns. A tarpaulin was soon spread over the bags. Two minutes later, I heard the driver locking the door and the engine roared into life. With a sudden jerk, the huge lorry surged forward and started to move. I could not bid farewell to the Vicar. Now, we were on our way.

A huge apprehension laid on me and my pulses ran out of control. Life and death were now beckoning to me. I could not touch Alero's chain on my neck but I assumed I was holding it. I heard myself saying, "God, I am in your hands. Please be merciful unto me."

About four or five minutes after our take off, the trailer jerked once more and came to a complete stop. I knew we had reached the dreaded spot – the notorious outskirts of Toro in which many people had been roasted alive in the last few days. I could hear the footsteps of about a hundred people. Next, were the riotous and aggressive voices of many, then the shrill and raucous polyglot of languages. I stayed there, rigid. I wanted to dissolve into the thin air but I could not.

"Boys! Remove the tarpaulin. Get inside the vehicle and feel the bags one by one. We got an intelligence information that some people are being smuggled out in cocoa bags;" screamed a loud, intimidating voice.

The back door of the vehicle was flung open and many men catapulted in.

"The game is up. I have finally boxed myself into a corner;" I mumbled. I suddenly plunged into a cauldron of racing pulses. One of the big men that came into the vehicle and who I guessed had spent the last three days reeking of drink soaked in marijuana, growled:

"Check all the bags! I say all; don't leave anyone out." This terrible monster stood on a cocoa bag, his frightened men saw the warning in his eyes; stumbled into each other as they stampeded into action. They were now going from one bag to another. The generalissimo stood there erect; his eye balls emitting fire. My bag was at the back row, next to the driver. I knew there was no escape route for me. That I was going to be discovered was now certain and horrifying. I had prayed to God but God had chosen not to be merciful and I did not know the reason why.

"Jesus! Jesus!! Jesus!!!" I mumbled again and again. Despite my repeated calls on Jesus, the men were getting closer and closer and I became more and more apprehensive with fear. Just that moment, Psalms 91 came into my mind:

"He that dwells in the secret place of the Most High
Shall abide under the shadow of the Almighty God
I will say of the Lord, He is my refuge and my fortress.
My God in Him will I trust…"

Even with the recitation of the above, the men were getting closer still. There was only one bag between me and the bag being searched. I had entertained faith that God would intervene. For reasons best known to Him, He chose not to this time.

Then, one of the men moved to the bag next to mine. I became terribly tense. My body was sweating profusely in the cold, bitter January morning air.

"Will something happen? Will luck intervene on my behalf? Will God who everyone says is merciful show mercy this time and prevent this man from coming to my bag?"

No. He didn't.

"It is finished!," I mumbled as the man finally moved

to my bag. I was engulfed by a kaleidoscope of emotions. Words could no longer describe what was happening to me. As the man started to feel the bag, I went into a fit. He touched where my right hand was; it must have occurred to him that that section was different from cocoa beans. He felt my hand again.

"Is this really cocoa or what is it?" His facial expression changed. Just as he was about to shout, a scream, loud and overpoweringly loud, came from below.

"Caleb! Caleb!!!"

"Yes, sir!" answered the man searching my bag.

"Come down quickly. I am told your son has fallen into a well" "My son! My son!! Oh my God!" screamed Caleb as he stampeded out of the vehicle.

"Will he report his suspicion to his men? Will people come in with a knife and open my bag?"

Several of such questions pestered me now. I knew the game was off. I was shaking while a strange situation below was determining my fate. There were many voices and much shouting and I didn't know precisely what was going on. This period of tension lasted about two minutes but it seemed like a century. Finally, I heard the driver closing the door and another roaring of the engine conveyed the good news to me that the vehicle had been passed and was now on its way. A minute drive after that, I knew we had scaled over the first and most critical hurdle and my heart began to warm up for joy.

About ten minutes after that and in the heart of the bush, the vehicle came to a stop. The covering tarpaulin was removed and somebody climbed in and I soon discovered that the top of my bag was being opened. A minute after, I came out of captivity and breathed fresh air again.

"Hurray! Freedom at last!"

From that spot to Lagos, we had a smooth ride. I was so excited. I got to Lagos around 5.p.m. and No 805 Coker Street, Mushin, where Alero told me she would be staying, was my first point of call. I pressed the call bell and a middle-aged woman with a fine face peeped through the window.

"Yes, can I help you?"

I would like to see Alero."

Who are you and from where?"

"I am Mayo from Toro."

"Mayo! The one who has not allowed the Princess to eat for the past 24 hours? Just come right in," said she. She then embraced me.

"Alero!" she shouted.

"Yes ma!"

"Your Mayo is here. No more anxiety again about his safety."

CHAPTER FORTY-THREE

I was expecting Alero to rush forward, embrace me and kiss me.

"Are my soul and spirit not longing for her since we parted? Is my body not thirsty for the caresses of her tender, pretty hands? What other time can be lovelier than now to celebrate our escape?"

Now that our lives had seen a new dawn, and our destinies had taken a new colour of sweetness, I wanted to hold Alero, hold her tight to my chest and listen again to the soft rhythms of the breathing of our hearts. But as Alero set her eyes upon me, she stood up quickly and dashed into the room and closed her door. I stood there, shocked.

"What is happening?" I asked her niece.

"Alero! Won't you welcome Mayo? But you have been dying to see him. What's the matter? Why do you run into the room?" her niece queried.

Just that moment, we heard a huge scream from the direction of the room. Her niece, shock on her face, hurried to her. I stood glued to that spot, confused. I didn't understand that evening drama, as it grew complex by seconds.

Alero suddenly opened the door, tears now on her face, she hurried towards me. She did not get to me when she stopped and exploded.

"But why must you do what you did? Why must you put your life on the line? Why must you expose yourself to such great risk and grave danger? Why must you go to Oro Grove?

For God's sake, why?"

"Have you forgotten the Lord's teaching?" I asked her.

"And what's that teaching?" she asked.

"That a man must be prepared to lay down his life because of his friend."

Alero stared at my face unbelievingly and then exclaimed:

"Oh Mayo!

The only one that remained with me when mother and all others deserted me.

The only partner in a storm.

The soul mate in time of desolation.

My missing link.

The joint owner of my destiny.

The man who demonstrated to me what true love is all about.

There is no way I can repay you for all you did for me."

Her words rang out with pure sincerity.

"You don't need to repay me for anything. I only did what I was supposed to do," I told her.

But she still stared at my face, as if there was something strange or spectacular about me. She shook her head and spoke up again, this time in a language full of emotion.

"You spurned death.

You demystified terror.

You assaulted and raped the dreadful Oro Grove.

You walked boldly into the den of the terrible.

Where even angels fear to tread.

You dared the demons and principalities.

You made a public show of them all.

You derobed the Oro people and Oro shrine of their ancient toga of terror.

You did what no other man had ever done.

You are a pride to the generations of the brave."

"Alero! I feel highly flattered." I replied.

Her niece, smiling, slipped out of the room. My arms were now open, waiting for her. She walked towards me. Nervous tears still shimmered in her shadowy eyes. Starring at me with those lovely, mesmeric eyes, she was certainly not aware how alluring she looked.

Alero embraced me. She closed her eyes in pleasure as I now stroked her hair. I have always admired Alero. I have always been in love with her fine, feminine and pretty shape. The touch of her lush, fresh body was intoxicating as her soft, bewitching eyes were simultaneously communicating and singing all sorts of amorous tones. For minutes, we were left there panting in sweet tranquility.

"It's most wonderful having you in my life," I told her.

"Oh my dear Mayo! How I love you!"

Alero and her niece arranged a room for me where I spent the night, I was scheduled to leave them the following morning for my friend's house. But it was the voice of Major Chukwumah Kaduna Nzeogwu that woke me and all Nigerians the following morning 16th January, 1966.

"In the name of the Revolutionary Council of the Nigerian Armed Forces, I declare martial law all over the provinces of Nigeria. The constitution is suspended and the legal government and elected assembly are hereby dissolved. All political, cultural, tribal and trade union activities together with all their demonstrations and all unauthorized gatherings, excluding religious worships are banned until further notice."

There were jubilations all over Lagos and Nigeria's major cities. Sir Abubakar Tafawa Balewa, the Prime Minister of Nigeria and Sir Ahmadu Bello, the Premier of Northern Nigeria, Chief S.L Akintola, the Premier of Western Nigeria, and Chief Festus Okotie-eboh, the Federal Minister of Finance and a number of top military officers were killed in the military coup. But by 10.a.m. that morning, Major Chukwumah Nzeogwu and his rebellious troops had been overpowered by the troops loyal to the Federal Government of Nigeria. And it was General J.T.U Aguyi Ironsi, the Head of the Army, that eventually took over power as the new Head of State.

CHAPTER FORTY-FOUR

During my temporary stay in Lagos, I lived with Fidelis, a friend who was working in the Works Department in the city. Fidelis was a year ahead of me at Igbobi College. His one room apartment at 302 Lawanson Street, Surulere, became my new home.

My stay in Lagos turned out to be the most exciting period of my life. It was fun from morning till evening. Lagos City offered a huge variety of entertainments. There was no dull moment. I had been in Lagos for four months now. The result of my University of Cambridge School Certificate Examination was expected that month. Alero and I continued to see each other at least three times in a week. Each new day brought us a new colour of sweetness. My life became one long stretch of unending, romantic bliss. We had visited together virtually all the important places in the city and its suburbs but that morning we were going to Lagos Bar Beach.

The bus dropped us at Marina. Left and right, short

succulent coconut trees were talking in whispers. The leaves on the various trees were murmuring. Hibiscus, cana lilies, roses in riot of colours were smiling at us. The pear trees moaned. The grasses on the beautiful green lawns were hissing. Across the road was the Apapa Wharf. Twenty ships stood in the harbour. The water of the lovely harbour stared at us with inquisitive eyes. Then it began to smile. It was a strange, weird smile. Its ripples beckoned us to draw nearer. But the time was not there to enjoy the delightful, strange scenery.

There were many beautiful buildings all around but one stood erect, huge and tall like Goliath of Gath. "That is the State House," I pointed it to Alero "That was the House used by Sir Fredrick Lord Lugard, the first British Governor-General of Nigeria. It was also the official residence of all the succeeding British rulers. It became the official residence of Sir Abubakar Tafawa Balewa, Nigeria's first Prime Minister until he was removed from office four months ago in a military coup. The present occupant is General J.T.U. Aguyi Ironsi, the Military Ruler of Nigeria."

"It is a beautiful building," said Alero "Everywhere the white man goes, he creates another Europe. It will be marvelous if this kind of glamorous environment can be replicated in a thousand places in the country." "That will be wonderful. Alero! We need to hurry. We have two kilometers to walk. The sun will soon assert its tyrannical rule over Lagos. Let's hasten."

Having walked for about ten minutes, we got to the

bridge that linked Lagos Island with Victoria Island. "This city is on water," Alero observed "Nature has just created another Venice in Africa."

Before us that morning was Victoria Island. As far as we could see, was a beautiful rolling plain. The superb greenness of the lawns in the front of the warm, luxurious buildings, was a great delight. The air here smelt fresher. For minutes, we walked through the quiet, green neighbourhood. Everywhere was like a field of rainbows.
"These are homes of Nigerian millionaires and the Europeans that live in the city," I told Alero.

'It's a lovely place. I am wondering why my daddy has not considered it fit to acquire an estate here. This is another veritable Garden of Eden, the original garden couldn't have been more idyllic."

Ten minutes later, we were at the beach. Even that early morning, there were many holiday makers there. The water of the Atlantic Ocean tossed up and down restlessly. We hired a space inside one of the tents. We put down our bags and changed into our swimming suits. The next minute, we were right inside the warm, beautiful water of Lagos Bar Beach. I couldn't get more than a few feet from the shore. But Alero was swimming like an excited, lovely whale, piercing through the waves with effortless ease. We had been swimming for about thirty minutes, and a strong wave was rolling to the coast, angry and furious. Alero dashed into it.
"If you are not a professional swimmer, do not dash

into an angry wave," the experts who stood by warned. Alero heard but she had no time for such talk. She disappeared into the water and went away with the wave.

Two minutes, three minutes, four minutes, I didn't see Alero again and I panicked. A moment later when she did not surface, I became terribly frightful.

"Has she drowned? Where is she?" I queried

"Alero! Alero!!," I shouted and few other people joined me to shout her name.

"Rush for the rescuers," somebody advised me.

"But we were warned not to dash into an angry wave. Why did she do it? Jesus! Why did she do it?" a concerned sympathizer screamed. But just that moment, I saw what looked like a human being in the crest of a new angry wave, rolling furiously back to the beach. It was Alero riding and smiling. She was in charge.

"It is she! It is she!!" I shouted. As the wave landed her, another started immediately and Alero dashed forward again and was about to enter into it but I moved in quickly and snatched her.

"You are not going back."

"What is the problem?" she asked me

"We were highly terrified. We thought you had drowned. I was about to call in the rescuers when you suddenly appeared."

"Rescuers?"

"Yes, my dear."

"You must be joking. Those ones standing over there, whom you call rescuers, are mere amateurs. I am a professional. What do they know? I won all the medals as the best swimmer in my college. Water is my second home. It is another world for me. I have a diving licence." she exclaimed.

"Even if you are a whale, you have had enough," I told her firmly.

As she came out of the water, rolling her buttocks, while her fine, innocent hips winked amorously. I looked at Alero, my senses were momentarily paralysed by her terrific shape. Looking at her was very arousing. Alero was beautiful. Her eyes were soft and cool. As we stood in that beach, in the warm, luscious air, honey on her lips and a smile on her face, and above her, a sensuous, morning sky, Jesus! Alero was attractive. I couldn't take my eyes off her face and her legs. They were so fine.

Suddenly, she became conscious that I was looking at her and she asked me:

"What are you looking at?"

"A beautiful, black lady," I replied.

"Is that all what you see?"

"The sweetest woman among the female species."

"Anything else?"

"My Ebony Eyes whose face will forever dazzle and intrigue men of this generation."

"Anything else?"

"The only woman of my dream."

"Is that all?"

"The lady whose delicious aroma makes me crazy."

"Is that all?"

"The other component of my chemistry, without

which I am not complete."

"Man O man! You men always make a woman look bigger than she really is but we women love it that way. What next? Now that we are no longer swimming, what do we do?"

"Let's go for a walk."

The rays of the sun were becoming brighter but the heat was still bearable. We had a forty minute walk along the beach. On our way back, we bought some meat pies and soft drinks from one of the restaurants and settled down in our tent. After we had finished eating, we lay on our chests, staring at the lovely, blue sea. I surveyed the beautiful shape of Alero. I dreamt about the future when she would be my wife, and I her husband, when we would live in an ecstasy such as we had never known before. I did not know how long my mind wandered away.

"Mayo! You are quiet, what are you thinking about?"

"I am thinking about you."

"About me?"

"Yes, of course."

"How?"

"I am thinking about the time we will get married and become husband and wife."

I stared at Alero's face. Her hair floated around her shoulders. She was a hell of a beauty. She also stared at me and then queried:

"How many times shall we get married? Have you forgotten that we got married at the age of seven?"

"How can I forget? But that one was only witnessed by few people and was done without the consent of our parents. It was also done in the secret."

"You want an open one, isn't it?"

"Yes, I want one the entire world will witness so that no one will accuse me of stealing my wife."

"Okay, you have won. Mayo, can you still remember the first thing you did to me the day I became your bride?"

"I remember."

"You remember that I annoyed you and you lost your temper and gave me a slap on the face?"

"Why must you plague me with the reminders of my childhood folly now?"

"I need to because as your wife, I am still going to annoy you a million times. Will you hit me again?"

"What type of question is that? Why must I hit you? Am I a gorilla?"

"When you hit me, you weren't a gorilla."

"That is true, but we were innocent children that could not distinguish right from wrong."

"You want to tell me that you have changed and have matured over time?"

"Precisely."

"You know I have a hot temper and I can behave funny occasionally."

"Yes, I know that."

"You mean your patience would not snap again in any of such occasions?"

"I promise to love you and forever cherish you. The English people have a saying – England with all thy faults, I love thee still;. I want to say also that Alero with all your faults, I will always love you."

"You are sure you won't beat me even when I lose my temper and behave terribly?"

"I won't beat you. Why should I beat the one I love? Why should I beat a Princess?"

"You are a man, you mean all through you won't want to show me your superior male virility?"

"Why should I do such a thing?"

"Mayo, why can't you be honest? I appreciate your points but I have gone to all this length because I know my temper. I know I can be violent in my anger. But I am doing all what I can to change because of you. I know there will be occasions when your patience may snap. Even if you beat me, I am still going to love you. I am not going to leave you. As I look at the future I can see that I will give you a hell of trouble. But never mind, I am also going to give you a hell of love."

Alero now smiled as she gazed at me in quiet admiration. Good God! She had a lovely smile. Her sparkling eyes started to torture me with their tenderness again. The rays of her charming eyes wounded me with their delectable magnets. She stood up and I also stood up quickly, I wanted to take her, hold her, kiss her and taste the honey on her lips. Every minute Alero looked different and more attractive. But Alero wriggled out of my hold and ran. I ran after her. I wanted her, I wanted her badly. Every fibre of my soul and every cell of my body wanted her. I pursued her until I grabbed her. She stared at me.

"Did anyone ever tell you that you are so fine and irresistible when you look like this?"

"How do I look?" she asked me.

"I am not sure I can describe precisely how you look. You are pretty, hot and tempting. I am going to love you. I am going to taste the sweet nectar of your beautiful lips," I told her.

She looked at me, her angelic smile sent passion through my cells. Her eye balls rolled – those eye balls were now talking to me in an unusual romantic language, saying things in codes which only two of us could decode. Her eyes became dazzling as they were singing strange mysterious songs. Alero was an amazing girl.

As I held her possessively to my chest, I could feel the wonderful future we were going to have. That future rolled its various captions before my eyes – all glowing pictures about the lives of wonder and exploits that lay ahead. As we kissed again and again, I stopped suddenly to look at the face of Alero again. I wanted to find out and make sure that the woman in my embrace was my own Alero. Yes, she was. I stared inquisitively at her. No other lady I knew was as glamorous and elegant. I held her so tight. I wouldn't let her go.

"You are that very woman I have been looking for. I love you," I whispered in a way that not even the inquisitive water of the Atlantic Ocean tossing up and down before us could hear my words.
"Mayo! I love you too."

For long, we talked in whispers. What really were we talking about? I cannot remember precisely now. We spoke amusing words. We talked of love. We talked and talked but our ears were not tired. They were not weary of hearing the same thing said over and over again because they were capsuled in love and love never bores. Love is like a good wine which grows sweeter with age.

As I fastened Alero to my chest and the tips of her firm, erect nipples of her sumptuous breasts wounded my chest with their sweet, delicious touches, our whisper became deeper. Alero's smile became fainter on her face. She stared at me now with frightening tenderness and longing that my body started to ache. I kissed her and she kissed me back with a ferocity that made my body break out in a sweat. Alero's body knitted to me gave me such delicious pleasure the kind I never knew existed. She put her arms round me to draw me closer still. We were going to enter into each other and for ever became one inseparable whole.

We did not leave the beach until 4p.m.

CHAPTER FORTY-FIVE

We got to my apartment at 5p.m. Fidelis was already waiting anxiously for me. He had received a telephone call from Igbobi College that the result of our Cambridge School Certificate Examination was out.

Alero and I raced to the place. The Principal sat behind a huge mahogany table, he raised up his head as we entered his office. He had refused to close that evening because he knew many students would keep on coming. I wore an anxious look, but a broad smile from his face immediately assured me that all was well. The result sheet lay before him. He glanced through it inquiringly.

"Mayo Williams! You scored distinctions in all your eight papers and by this feat qualified for an automatic scholarship from the Federal Government of Nigeria. The government will sponsor you in any university of your choice. Congratulations!" he shook my hand.

Alero lifted me up. I never knew that she could carry me. She was so happy.

"Mayo! You said you were going to give me a gift and you fulfilled your promise I am so proud of you," she exclaimed as she embraced me.

"But you are the author of my success," I told her.

"How?"

"You are the prize I am doing everything possible to win. When a commoner wants to marry a Princess, he must do something spectacular. I have just started."

The following day Alero's aunt phoned from Accra. She also had six distinctions and two credits. She topped her class. She had already applied to the University of Lagos to do LLB Hons in International Law. It was a week of celebration.

I had earlier on applied to George Bowen University in Washington D.C, USA to read Political Science. I sent my result to the university by telegram the following morning and that very day I got an offer of admission. The offer said that I could start in the Summer Session, that is, the last week in May, if I so wished.

I took my result and my admission letter to the Federal Ministry of Education, Lagos the following day. Three days later, the Ministry phoned me that my fees had been paid to my university. "Report today for your traveling documents," the official told me. It was now I realized that I never told the official that I had the intention of going in September instead of May.

"Your fee has been paid and the university is reserving a place for you right away. Why must you delay your going till September? How? What for?"

the officer asked me. I stammered few unconvincing reasons. The man stared at my face unbelievingly.

"My friend! Why can't you behave like a man? Many young men are looking for this kind of rare opportunity. The ministry is not changing anything, go for your study," he told me.

I left the ministry, confused and unhappy. I never imagined that I would be leaving Nigeria so soon; but I discovered painfully now that I had less than three weeks to leave. I had unknowingly boxed myself into a corner. "Why am I so foolish?" I queried.

"But how can I leave Alero? And why should I leave her now that we are in a deep romantic bliss?" I asked myself. I never imagined any separation so soon from Alero but it was coming, so unpalatable and yet so sure.

Fidelis left that afternoon for Benin City. He was on four week vacation. He promised to come back before the date of my departure. He, however, left sufficient food items at home so I didn't lack anything. I sent a message intimating my parents about the new development, Mom sent a message back that she would be coming to see me off and daddy sent money to me to buy all the necessary materials I would need for my journey.

The following week, Alero and I were so busy. I went to the American Embassy for my visa. We also went to Balogun Central Market daily to buy one item or the other. I couldn't believe it, the days were running now with lightning speed, and soon, I had four days left.

One of the days, we went to Casino Cinema. "Paradise is Hot", the latest film we loved to watch, would go on the screen at 10p.m. I had watched it in the company of Fidelis. It was action-packed and entertaining. We got to Casino Cinema only to meet a huge crowd. It took sometime before we could purchase our tickets. As we sat down and the film was about to start, there was a sudden stir. Then the announcement:

"There is a phone call that a bomb has been planted somewhere in this Cinema House and the bomb is scheduled to go off in the next few minutes. We don't know how true this information is. But since we cannot toy with the precious lives of you people, will you please vacate this cinema hall immediately? We will reschedule the film for another day." Everybody stood up at the same time. A great mass of people rushed forward. A monstrous army soon invaded the way out. The panic soon became a pandemonium. Alero stood up in fright.

"Please calm down," I told her. "The telephone call might have been made by a frustrated guy who could not obtain a ticket to watch the film."

It was a lot of job holding Alero not to join in the general stampede. Many of the people were wounded trying to get out at the same time. We got the information later that it was a false alarm.

As we walked towards the bus stop that night, I was very unhappy. I was looking for something which Alero and I could share before my departure and I felt a 3-hour film would be good enough. Now, the whole thing had been ruined.

We got to the bus stop only to meet another obstacle. For ten minutes, no bus showed up. We later learnt that the staff of the Lagos Municipal Transport and the City Taxi Service had gone on strike only half an hour before.

"There was no formal warning. These people must be stupid," I spoke in anger.

"Mayo! What do we do now?" Alero asked me.

"I don't know. But let us stroll down the street, in the process we may know what to do."

As we walked down Yaba Road that evening, there was just one alternative before us – walk our way home. But the distance was the problem. Alero would have to walk nine kilometres, and in that hour of the day, it was not something advisable for a young lady to do. My own house was just four kilometres away.

"Let's go to my house", I told her.

"I didn't tell my niece that I won't be home for the night and she may take offence."

"You will explain to her."

"That explanation may not do."

"But what other choice do we have now?" I asked her. For minutes, we reasoned together, in the end, she agreed to go with me.

The journey to my home turned out to be more exciting than we had anticipated. It was around 11p.m. and Lagos seemed to be just awaking. Lagos is the most lively city on earth. All the streets were busy talking. All the street corners were singing. In all the junctions, were orchestras and people dancing.

Lagos never sleeps, never rests nor enjoys any dull moment.

The moon was full. The air tasted nice. The various street lights smiled deliciously above our heads. I looked at Alero, her statistics came out in the jeans and blouse she wore that night. Straight legs, slim, pretty body, sumptuous hips, firm and pointed breasts. World's prettiest women are moulded in figure 8, Alero came out in enticing figure 8 that night. It was hard to believe how beautiful she was. I stared at her with frightening intensity and asked myself:

"Should I leave this one in the midst of Lagos wolves? Is it proper to leave Alero in Nigeria and go to America when what I want in America can be obtained locally? Can Alero withstand for long the huge number of men who will be pestering her to be their friends?" A catena of questions bombarded my thoughts for answers. I didn't know how long my mind wandered away. But Alero suddenly touched me.

"Why are you quiet? Won't you talk to me again?"

"I am sorry, I was thinking about something."

"What about?"

"I was thinking about you."

"Me? Why? How?"

"I don't feel I love to go to America. I prefer schooling in Nigeria where I can see you when I love to."

"But don't forget that an external exposure can also be an advantage."

"That is true."

"You are only going for four years. What is in four years? In a twinkling of an eye, four years will be completed and you will be back."

"Do you sincerely want me to go?" I asked her.

"Even if I don't want you to, the government has already paid your fees, any excuse not to go now will make you look irresponsible or don't you feel so?"

"That is true."

"Alero! I am so much afraid."

"Afraid of what?"

"Afraid of what may happen to you."

"And what about it?"

"Men are always flocking around you. They are always competing for your attention. Day before yesterday, it was a young bank director who trailed you with his car because he was bent on knowing your home. Yesterday, it was a colonel of the Nigerian Army who threatened to kidnap you if you refuse to be his friend."

"That one was a clown. He was just trying to be funny," cut in Alero.

"Assuming he is not."

"Then he will be risking a life behind the bars. I am sure he won't dare that. I am used to all such male harassment. I surely had more of it in Accra. To me it is a non-issue at all."

"You say it is a non-issue?"

"Yes, it is a non-issue because I can ask a driver and a car to be sent down to me immediately. If I don't take a street stroll, no one can hustle around me. I have so far enjoyed my freedom as an ordinary person but if that is causing you some anxiety, I may decide with effect from this moment to live as a Princess."

Then Alero stared at my face, a narrow, mechanical smile lit her lips, then she said:

"Mayo, you have looked at this matter purely from your own selfish angle but don't you feel that I too have some anxiety?"

"Anxiety about what?" I asked her.

"Anxiety about you."

"How?"

"What I see daily on television shows that Washington D.C, where you are going, is the home of America's most glamorous women. No Nigerian who had ever gone to America to study, had come back without an American woman by his side. Don't you feel that should cause me some anxiety too?"

"You feel I can get there and pick an American girl as my wife?"

"I don't know. It is you who can say."

"Why can't you know? You mean you don't trust me?"

"Why can't I trust you? But trust seems not to be the issue here. Those who went to America and came back with American girls promised their Nigerian girls that they would remain faithful and apparently they meant what they said. But circumstances along the line, and perhaps beyond their control, made them renege on their vows. How am I sure that the same thing cannot happen to you?"

"But you know that kind of scenario is impossible in my own case. I am a different person and our love is so different."

I held Alero's hand and stared at her face.

"I want to assure you that whatever happens in America, I will remain faithful to you. Take my words as my vow."

"I think I am happy to hear that." said Alero.

We had now got to Lawanson, the most popular bus terminus in Surulere District of Lagos City. It was 11.30p.m. All the shops were open and the restaurants were very much alive. The food vendors who did business by the roadside were there with their teeming customers. The woman who sold fried bean cakes sat behind their hot ovens. Those who sold fried pork and mutton winked at us from their various corners. But we did not wait. About twenty minutes after this, we were in my apartment.

I led the way, opened the door for Alero to go in.

"It's a most beautiful evening walk. I am so happy that the buses and the taxis are on strike after all", said Alero. She now went into the room, put off her dress. She came out wearing one of my shirts. Even in such informal dress, Alero was incredibly beautiful.

She stared at me and smiled. She smiled like this whenever she was up for a mischief. I did not know what she was up to that night. The entire room was full of her warmth. But she just walked past me and went into the kitchen, boiled some water and prepared two cups of tea. As we sat facing each other, talking over our tea, Alero stared at me curiously.

"What is the matter?" I asked her.

"You this guy, you stole my heart when I was an innocent child and you have been keeping it ever since. How cruel you are!"

"But you never tell me that you want your heart returned to you."

"How can I tell you that, when you have bewitched

me and I cannot think of anything besides you, and when I am never happy outside your orbit? For reasons I cannot explain, my soul is always craving for you. Even when I was in Ghana, my heart was not there, you kept it with you here in Lagos."

"But don't you feel that I should be the one to accuse you of stealing my heart?"

"How?" queried Alero.

"You fascinate me with your beauty. You hypnotize me with your smile. You intrigue me with your lovely shape. You dazzle me with your wonderful eyeballs. You charm me with your exotic, amorous body. Mere looking at you, stirs up my passion. You have caused me perennial obsession not just for a few days or years but right from the age of seven when I set my eyes on you. You were the one who taught me the ABC of love when I was yet tender and innocent. You showed me what true love was all about. You tormented me with your elegance. You enthralled me by your attractive dresses. You made me dream and fantasize day and night because I love to possess you. You shot my vision high, higher than the peak of Mt. Everest, the day you accepted to be my bride at the age of seven, you a princess, and I a poor boy from a poor home and a son of Mr. Nobody. You told me that my birth and low estate were no barrier to your love. You gave me a new dream and a new vision. You threw me into a wild world of imagination. You gave me the stimulus and the road-map that I could conquer the world if only I could have the will. You told me that whatever I ask the world and can sincerely and diligently pursue, the world is bound to give me.

But shortly after you raised up my passion, and hope, you disappeared to Ghana without notice, and for years gave me sleepless nights. You kept me awake to count the stars at night when I was supposed to be sleeping. Remember, I was just thirteen when you took away my joy with you to Ghana and for six years I walked like a body without a soul."

Alero stood there rigid, looking at my eyes. My words held her captive. But she knew they were the truth, finally she spoke:
"Mayo! You said I gave you sleepless nights?"
"Yes, you did."

Then she looked at me and smiled. It was one of her usual, infectious smiles.
"The whole journey is just beginning," she told me.
"I am still going to give you more sleepless nights because I have made up my mind not to leave your life for a moment. Even when we are not physically together, my spirit will always be with your spirit. I am still going to give you more torments, but they will be sweet torments this time. I am still going to wound your heart, but this time with love melodies. I am still going to enthral you but this time with my loyalty and commitment to our friendship and love."

Then she stopped talking. She shook her elegant body alluringly and my body came alive. Goodness! Alero had a beautiful shape. Her body had always fascinated me. She rolled her buttocks, shaking every movable flesh, her busts thrust up invitingly as she walked towards me. I had always warned her not to shake her body that way, it drove me crazy. I opened wide my arms and her pretty, magnificent frame melted into my embrace. Then Alero whispered to my ears in a voice that the walls, the furniture and the utensils of that house could not hear, no matter how they tried.

"I am going to love you with passion. I am going to give you eternal delight."

"I also promise you that I will prove worthy of your love."

I kissed Alero, then left her lips a little while, I, stared at her face. Her nice, astonishing eyes cast a spell on me. Alero was too romantic for comfort. I just loved her. I loved her seductive and beautiful eyes. She had the sexiest eyes I had ever seen. She looked so pretty, much prettier than Alero I knew. She kissed me with passion, then suddenly drew away her lips when the flame of that kiss was spreading fast into other parts of my body, then whispered softly in my ear:

"I am going to overfeed you with love portion. I am going to satiate your thirst with love obsession. I am going to show you what real love is all about."

My body ignited fire. My strong arms were all around her. I stared at Alero, she had suddenly become a different woman, her features were more exquisite, her eyes more luminous and her beauty more dazzling. My lips were on her, fierce and hungry. I was going to devour her. My tongue went deep into her mouth, exploring all directions. For long, it went in a wild foray, searching for the secrets of its hidden pleasure. As I massaged the smooth, chocolate skin of Alero's back, I felt deep inside me the sweetness and honey of that glossy, luxurious skin. My God! Alero was impossibly delicious.

As I held her tight to my chest, I felt very jealous of an imaginary man who might wish to steal Alero from me. And I knew for sure that there were thousands of men who wished to do just that. I knew Alero loved me and I knew she would do everything within her power to be loyal to me. But my male instincts warned me to be vigilant. Various questions were now pestering me for answers:

"Is Alero up to the task ahead? When you are no longer in Nigeria, can she withstand the pressure from the deluge of men who will be asking for her friendship? Can she successfully outplay the Nigerian young men – those terrible schemers - cunning and masterful in their techniques?"

I could not answer all these questions in the affirmative. I recalled now that Eve loved Adam so well and yet Satan crept in adroitly and deceived her. Only a fool would underestimate what Lagos young men could do and I was not a fool. I knew some young Lagosians are terribly brilliant. Some are impossibly cunning. Some could outwit Satan himself in a game of chess. Heavens might fall but they would get whatever they wanted. I looked at Alero – my only prayer was that she would not have an encounter with such "Ivan The Terrible" or those terrible desperados that operate in Nigerian main cities.

Since I could neither exercise any control over where

Alero would go nor whom she would meet when I was no longer in Nigeria, and since Alero's beauty would keep on inviting men to her as the honey invites the flies or the lovely, highly attractive Italian plains kept on inviting the eighteenth century's adventurers, I concluded that there was no way men would not be hovering around Alero. I therefore made up my mind to take Alero that night through a rigorous sex exercise she would never forget.

I resolved privately that I would not be gentle with her in bed that night. I was going to throw open all my arsenals and do the exercise as if mercy was alien to my nature. I would be unkind and rough. I would treat her as if I were dealing with a young, proud, rude but beautiful lady who had insulted me but circumstances had strangely landed on my laps and I decided to punish. I would screw her, screw her hard as if I were on a war of revenge. I would be ruthless, showing her no mercy and no compassion.

"But why will you do such a thing to her? Why will you treat so wildly a lady who loves you so much? What is her offence?" I asked myself. But another part of me quickly responded:

"You must do so because if by accident Alero falls into the hand of a sex desperado, he will treat her to a violent, sex orgy and he may use that technique to steal her heart." I suddenly grew afraid, "I am not going to allow that," I told myself.

That moment, I recalled the story of Victoria and Professor Thomas. Victoria was a young college graduate and Professor Thomas was a Professor of

English in one of the Nigerian Universities. Both were in love and were planning to get married.

"Nice, lovely, humane gentleman. Brilliant and industrious, every week he composes a poem admiring my beauty. He makes me look more beautiful than I am really. He so much loves me", Victoria told her friend.

Then, something happened. Victoria travelled to Jos to see her grandmother and was returning to Lagos, her base. Her bus was attacked by night marauders at a point about 400 km to Lagos. It was 11p.m. The marauders killed three of the passengers. But a young man, Felix, a sturdy, well built garage manager held Victoria's hand and they escaped into the womb of a nearby grassland. Two marauders hotly pursued them, shooting sporadically but they ran for their lives. They ran and ran into an unknown wilderness through a long narrow footpath until the marauders gave up. They went on and on through the footpath until they got to a group of huts. But the huts were all empty, the dwellers had gone to a nearby town to spend the week-end. The moon was full and they could see things clearly. They decided to spend the night in the hut and seek for help the following morning. But Felix was a terrible person for a young lady to be alone with. He was a lover of beauty but he was also a sex pirate. The moment he spotted Victoria in the bus, he was just imagining how good such pretty lady would be in bed. Alone with this kind of man, in the interior of a wilderness, Victoria was in trouble. She did all what she could to resist Felix but Felix was a master in this game. He was handsome, well-built, full of muscles and had attractive physical features but he was a wild man. He physically subdued Victoria and treated her to a wild sexual orgy, the kind Victoria never imagined existed. A sex pirate, Felix was a tireless machine in bed and for four hours, drove Victoria through a marathon heat of erotic pleasure. She reached her orgasm over and over again but Felix drove her on still like a vehicle that had no brake. The experience was too much for her. It was a different Victoria that left the hut the following morning. Two weeks later, Victoria escaped from home on her wedding day and ran away with Felix.

I knew that there could always be a Felix in the life of any woman. If such Felix emerged, my duty was to ensure that he could not take Alero away. I made up my mind to surpass the performance of any imaginary Felix that night. I was going to beat the best record of any sex pirate. I resolved to take Alero through an experience no other man could venture to take her. I was going to take her to the maximum limit. Yes, I was going to take her through some hours of hot, terribly intense and violent erotic pleasure. That to me was the only guarantee I had to prevent any man from stealing Alero when I would be away. I had a real task in my hand.

Funny enough, Alero did not know that a terrible battle was raging on in my mind. She could not guess that in the mind of this attractive boy-friend of hers, a conspiracy was on. I stared at her face, it was so lovely and innocent. As I massaged her soft, luscious skin, I looked at her face again. Her eyes were burning with wild anticipation. She was the loveliest female I had ever seen, "Honey! Have I told you how beautiful you look tonight?" I asked, whispering the same in her ear.

"Darling, you are yet to tell me. Tell me now by your words. Tell me through the melody of your sweet touches. Tell me by your kisses. Tell me …". I did not allow her to finish the last "tell me" when I grabbed her and started to kiss her.

For minutes, we spoke little but contented ourselves with kissing each other. Kiss after kiss soon raised our desire to a firestorm. But I never left her mouth. I kissed her again and again with a ferocity that suddenly made her body start to ache.

Then I kicked the door to my room open and I drew Alero along. But as we went, I never left her mouth for a moment. She was one hell of a woman and damn pretty too. We kissed each other with a kind of wild desperation. I surveyed the curves of Alero's pretty body. If she had been seductive before, she was now irresistible. Now, I wanted her. I wanted her badly. I couldn't remember ever wanting a woman so desperately. As I pulled down her knickers, I could feel the gyrations of her warm, tempting hips. Our kisses became violent and her buttocks began to quiver in hot anticipation. My male organ stood up, strong, thick and powerful. Alero parted her legs for me to find the warm mouth that was waiting eagerly below. In a moment, we were making violent love. Every cell of mine was burning with sensation as I tasted the delicious interior of Alero. "Goodness! You are so sweet," I murmured. For several minutes, her roundish, succulent, buttocks palpitated like two mighty breasts. As she held me tightly to herself, and her nice succulent hips and mine engaged in hot pounding rhythms, a frisson of pleasure ran through our loins. "Honey! You have a beautiful body," I whispered

As I pounded her, she went wild. She moaned: "Oh please, please, I beg. I am not sure I can take much more". She quivered and gasped. The blood was racing through my body and I could not slow down. Rather I pounded her more fiercely. Her hips now thrusting hungrily against mine, our love-making became hot - really hot. She groaned loudly as the sensation spread. Kissing her again and again, I sent erotic fire into her cells. The thrilling became unbearable as she suddenly screamed out: "Mayo! Mayo! I can't take more, please,… please". But the scream excited me to pound her the more fiercely until her body exploded and shook feverishly as if it would dissolve under the hot unbearable sensation. And almost that moment, I reached my orgasm, and the room went into abrupt silence.

About ten minutes later, my passion to have her again began to mount up. Alero had an amazing body. She was the epitome of the young African womanhood. Now, completely naked before me, the body was impossibly lovely. Her attractive figure was beckoning to me again, inviting me into another fresh excursion into the sweet delight of the flesh. I stared at Alero, she looked like a rose. Her figure had it all: beautiful legs, pretty hips, attractive flat belly, ripe, pointed breasts, sweet innocent face, thick and lustrous hair, thrilling, lovely body frame and glistening, flawless complexion. She was all honey and sweetness.

I started to massage Alero's slender, delicate arms again. My God! What a lovely skin she had! "Honey! Your skin is like a polished ivory, so cool, so smooth and so beautiful. You are the loveliest woman I have ever seen," I whispered. As I continued my massage so also I whispered more and more love words into her ears, each phrase more erotic than the last. My impatient fingers caressed her rich, magnificent breasts. Then I moved further. I stroked her nipples with my thumbs over and over and her body suddenly came alive. The nipples responded and swelled up. Within minutes, they became erect. I could observe now that Alero's passion was building up again.

It was a warm airy night. A sweet tasting moonlight splashed its rays through the windows. I looked at the moon, then looked at Alero. Her eyes were soft and tender like the moonlight. The tautening of her sensitive nipples made Alero so incredibly pretty. She gave me a sensuous look and a desire to have her again flashed though my loins. My caresses were thrilling her as her body began to ache
"You are so lovely," I murmured.

A fiery passion was burning in her eyes. Her pelvis which appeared to be singing mysterious songs now went into endless shivering. Now, she wanted me, she wanted me badly. Her need became so over-powering as she hugged me and turned her face up for my kiss. As we came together in a rush of desire, she kissed me again and again. I kissed her back with a passion that nearly doubled her own. I kissed her hungrily. I kissed her until her body started to ache. It ached so violently but I didn't leave her mouth. I deepened my kiss. I kissed her long until she started to moan. I fastened her sweet body possessively to myself. But the closer we were, the more I felt I could never have enough of her. Alero's body was too delicious.

Quivering under my thrilling sensation, I entered into her. Her inside was sweet, soft and warm. Her body shuddered with pure pleasure. As I pounded her, my mouth was on her, hot, hard and impatient. She responded sending hot salvo of pleasure into my loins.

"Good God! You are so beautiful!" I whispered. As I pounded Alero, her buttocks kept on shuddering as if she could no longer exercise any control over them. Now, I remembered my mission to take Alero to a level where no man could venture to take her. A demonic spirit took control over me, my passion went into a high gear, my male organ suddenly received an unusual energy. It now became a ferocious power-machine, a really hot dynamo. I couldn't understand neither could I explain where the energy was coming from. I pounded Alero so fast. I pounded her with such baffling rapidity and terrific speed and passion as I suddenly turned into a terrible sex machine. The response from her was violent. Alero's hips suddenly picked up speed. The pelvis gyrated so fast, and with so much lust, showing to me that she could match my speed and passion. For several minutes, she gave me fire for fire. The exchange became too hot that the bed screamed out in agony. But the more I humped her, the more frantic my fervour, the more she too longed for more. Alero reached her orgasm so quickly in our first encounter but this time she seemed like an insatiable vault. The fiercer my thrusts, the hungrier she became. It was as if she had resolved never to succumb to my fire power no matter how fierce it could be. Thrusting hungrily against mine, I almost could not keep up meeting her thrust. She moaned and moaned and moaned. I knew she could not endure for long the heat and pulsing waves of pleasure I was pumping into her quivering frame. Her hips hungered with voracious appetite as I drove faster and faster, deeper and deeper with long frenzied thrusts into the very heart of her interior.

"Alero, you are too delicious for comfort," I whispered.

She responded wildly, her eagerness and urgency to have more of me suddenly expanded. The hot friction generated as I slid in and out of her in terribly rapid succession, threw her voluptuous buttocks into an endless shivering. As I thrust deeper and harder, a sensation more intense than the previous orgasm she had experienced washed over her in waves until she suddenly went wild with excitement. The sensation became overpowering and she moaned loudly:

"Mayo! Mayo! It is too hot. I can't bear it any more, please!" she bellowed. Rather than slow down the tempo, I pounded Alero more fiercely. Then she screamed.

That scream excited me the more. I pounded her

more hungrily. The delight and emotional excitement sent Alero's intense burning passion to the climax and her body convulsed and convulsed while her clitoris erupted releasing hot, sweet, watery lava, giving me the happy news that Alero had surrendered to my superior fire power at last. Just that moment Alero screamed out loudly. She screamed again and again as her sexy amorous frame shook deliriously while her hands gripped me like two giant magnets, then she screamed and screamed and screamed in an uncontrollable voluminous noise of joy. And just few seconds after, my body exploded and got its calm at last.

Few minutes after this, we fell asleep. I woke up around 4a.m. I looked at Alero, she was fast asleep. It was a warm, delightful night. Both of us had slept completely naked for hours.
I stared at Alero, her hair arranged in romantic coils and clusters hours ago was now a huge disorderly bush. Her succulent, delightful, troublesome breasts seemed like two huge ripe fruits. Rosy and provocative, they were secretly smiling at me again. Her pointed, tautening nipples were winking at me amorously. Alero's eyes were closed but her thick eyelashes refused to go into slumber. They stood up, their seductive looks seemed to be inviting me into another fresh exploration into the wonder of Alero's body.

Alero slept backing me, with her sensuous protruding buttocks sitting inside the hollow of my loins. I didn't know whether she did this innocently or intentionally. Whatever it was, this kind of body positioning could not but provoke trouble and this time it did. As her smooth, soft, baby-like skin of her back massaged the plateau of my chest and her delicious, sumptuous hips warmed the deep hollow of my loins, my male root started to rise up again. How insatiable is a man male-root? Why is it perpetually hungry and seeking for what to devour? With two explosive sexual encounters, I suspected that Alero should be tired. There was no reason to trouble her further. That, in my view, would be going too far. I made up my mind not to wake her up. But a searing sensation went through my loins.

I stared at Alero. This morning she looked like the rainbow. Her body appeared to be sending out romantic rays. Her eyes were like a mirror in the sun though they closed in sleep yet the eyelashes kept on sending out amorous flashes. I looked at Alero's nice, glamorous body now completely naked before me. Jesus! The body was a killer. A burning sensation washed over me in waves. Alcro was incredibly beautiful.

Various questions now sprang from my mind as I looked at Alero again and again:

"Why does she have such a bewitching shape? What was nature thinking about when it created her in a shape that is extremely sexy and tormentingly attractive? Why is she made so lovely like a beautiful rose and charming like the lily at dawn? Why is her face so cool like the moonlight? Why does her figure fill the heart with perennial longing like the imaginary El-Doraldo? Why does her body taste like the sweet wine, the more you take the more you want to have? Why is her presence so warm and so enchanting like the Hawaiian sunrise?"

I did not like to touch Alero again. The two sexual encounters we had were enough. She deserved a good rest. But I found it rather strange that as I stared at Alero, I was gradually growing delirious with passion. The delicious, magnificent body before me had started to intoxicate my nerves. Looking at Alero in a nude form seemed like sipping a strong, aromatic wine. As my eyes surveyed her pretty statistics, I was getting more and more drunk. Alero's rosy breasts were talking to me. They were beckoning me to come. I resolved never to go near them. But my right hand surprisingly responded to their call. My fingers landed secretly on one of Alero's breasts. As if fearful to start exploring the wonder of that fascinating mystery, they stayed on the breasts for some time. When they finally gathered enough courage, they went slowly to the nipple. I couldn't believe it, my fingers were again caressing Alero's nipples feverishly. Later my entire body moved towards Alero as I started to suck her left nipple. Her nipples were nice and succulent. I rolled the right one between my fingers while I sucked the nectar of the left. My hot, wet mouth was full as her breasts responded and ached with need. Alero gradually woke up from her sleep.

The nipple in my mouth was swelling up little by little, the one being massaged by my fingers was also growing bigger. Simultaneously they became ready and erect.

Alero felt a rising thrill as she turned her face towards me. My mouth left her nipple, moved up progressively, searching desperately for Alero's mouth which was also impatiently searching for mine. The two soon found each other in a warm, delicious kiss. We kissed again and again. The kisses soon became long as we refused to leave each other's mouth. But the kisses triggered off fresh new passions in our loins. As I kissed Alero's soft, sweet lips again and again, she guided back my fingers with her right hand towards the nipple I was earlier on caressing. As I massaged the nipple, our kisses became wild once more.

My right hand now between her legs, I fingered the bud of her clitoris. And under few minutes of intense pleasure − massage, the clitoris gradually became wet and large. Alero's sumptuous hips began to ache and her pelvis started to moan in a growing frenzy of desire. "Oh please! please!," she moaned in desperation and need. I entered into her. My manhood fired her thighs and buttocks into a shuddering start. Her thighs ached as she moved her hips in erotic dance to meet the demand of my pounding manhood. My manhood and her buttocks soon found themselves in a terrific rhythm as her soft, fleshy hips writhed under me in a delicious ecstasy. The heat of the pleasure generated by the friction of our bodies became too hot that Alero and I became crazy at this same time. She was hot, smooth and good in bed.

There was too much of her to enjoy. My manhood

went on foraging into her delicious interior like a miner panning for gold and each second and each minute took me into a new plateau of pleasure. As my manhood rowed downward for the secret embedded in Alero's delectable interior, each minute exposed me to a new tasty, terribly delicious honey of her dark, rich, virgin land, crying now to be explored. As I drove into her harder and harder, my cork stroking her where she so desperately needed to be touched, her hips convulsed violently and involuntarily until both of us were panting for sexual play. The tempo increased, it became hot until Alero shuddered and shuddered and shuddered until she finally cried out:

"Mayo! Mayo! I want it that way. Just keep on doing what you are doing to me." Two minutes later, she cried out again:

"Please! Please! Don't stop," she cried in desperation grinding harder and harder her erect clitoris against the top of my wild, enthusiastic manhood, Alero went wild as if she was being touched by a high voltage wire. Grinding the clitoris still fiercer and fiercer, she gasped and gasped as if she could no longer find her breath. Wrapping her legs around me, my manhood and her clitoris rubbed each other ceaselessly, went over each other, over and over again in an erotic massage that had no end. Our motion became faster and faster until Alero's body jerked with spasm after spasm, until she screamed out:

"Mayo! Mayo! Hold it! Hold it! she begged, she pleaded and begged out loud. But it was impossible for me to stop neither could I lessen the tempo now. My cells were already electrified by the waves of pleasure generated by Alero's romantic body.

"Oh Mayo! I am going crazy", she moaned, I screwed her harder and harder until her body shuddered and shuddered violently and she cried out once more: "No! No! No!"

But my manhood massaged her clitoris more and more, fiercer and fiercer, and she screamed out loud: "Please! Please!" she pleaded. But my hard, hot cork, strong and erect, continued to pleasure-massage her clitoris, going over it, over and over, and over, and this for several minutes, until she reached her orgasm again and again and again until we lost count. A minute after I finally left her, she was asleep.

I woke up around 7.30a.m. I rolled over hoping to feel Alero's warm body, but the other side of the bed was empty. Alero was no longer there. I quickly stood up, rushed into the sitting room, she was not there either. "Has she gone? Why couldn't she tell me that she was leaving? Why should she leave without any departing word?" I didn't understand. I went to the main door, surprisingly, everything was intact. No one had opened the door which meant that Alero was still inside the apartment.

"But where is she?"

"Alero! Alero!!" I bellowed. There was no reply. I rushed to the toilet, she was not there. I looked into the kitchen, there I found her in one corner, crying

"What is the matter?" I asked her.

She did not answer, only her scream grew louder. I knelt down before her. I had never seen Alero crying like this except when we fought at the age of seven. I stared at her, her face frightened me.

"What is the matter? Kindly tell me." As I now tried

374

to hold her, she screamed wildly:

"Don't touch me."

I stared at Alero, confused. "What am I to do?" The more I pleaded with her, the angrier she became. For over twenty minutes, she sobbed uncontrollably and all efforts to pacify her failed. I did not know how to handle this kind of situation. I was in trouble.

"Alero! But you know how much I love you, why are you doing this to me? Why?" Drops of tear were raining down my eyes as I was now crying like a small babe.

"For God's sake, what have I done? Please tell me," I pleaded.

She stared at my face. She could not withstand seeing me in tears at the age of seven. Seeing me crying again, she must have been touched to her marrow. She gradually stood up, lifted me up, and went into my arms. We remained there in stony silence, fastened tightly to each other for several minutes. I can't remember now how long we remained in that position.

Gradually, Alero lifted up her tear-stained face towards mine and queried:

"Why did you do that to me? So you don't love me after all. For if you love me, you wouldn't hear my moans and ignore them. I screamed and I told you that I could no longer contain the heat of your love-making. It was too much for me. But you have no heart. You have no feeling. You showed neither emotion nor sympathy. You dealt with me like a sea pirate would deal with a prostitute. You were so wild, you were no longer the Mayo that I knew. You were like a sex-addict on the loose. You handled me as if you had decided to punish me for an undisclosed offence. What did I do to you to merit such treatment? What was my offence? I want to know."

I wanted to talk.

"Please, hold it. I am not done yet. All through my life, I have been loyal to you. When my parents were opposed to our friendship, and they said as a princess, traditions did not permit me to marry below my class, I stood by you. Didn't I? I gave you total commitment. With storms from all directions, I never deserted you. I stood my ground. I didn't fail you, not even once.

I handed over my body to you, believing that you would cherish it and handle it like a gem but you handled me like a football that all men kicked about. To you, I was no longer a table marked "reserved", I am just an ordinary woman, perhaps a whore who can be debased and treated wildly. You forgot the honour and dignity due to my person."

"Alero! That is enough," I told her firmly.

"You are not being fair to me. I did not do what I did to spite you. I felt I was doing what I did to please you. How does it now become an offence?"

"You said you were doing that to please me?"

"Yes, that was my intention."

"Is that the reason why you handled me like an hyena would handle an antelope? I put it to you that you are not speaking the truth."

"Alero, I have promised that I will never lie to you. Why should I? To achieve what? Come on, let us reason together on this issue. If love between a young man and a young lady is passionate and hot, it stands to reason that love-making between such a man and a woman will be hot, fierce, and perhaps wild. If the man is wild, it is surely not because he is cruel and unfeeling, too far from it. The body is only conveying what is in the heart. If the love is hot, the love-making is bound to be hot. It cannot be anything less."

Alero kept quiet for a long time. Finally, she spoke: "I misunderstood the situation. I got it all wrong. Let us forget about it. I am deeply sorry."

She wrapped her tender, lovely arms round me and started to kiss me.

"Mayo! I love you and I will ever love you."

"Alero! I love you too. You are the only woman in this world who excites me."

Alero looked curiously at my face.

"My dear, I have promised never to tell you, but I feel I need to confess the truth to you."

"About what?"

Then Alero smiled shyly and said:

"Though you handled me wildly, I did not hate the way you made love to me. To tell you the truth, I really loved it. But you must promise me one thing."

"And what is that?"

"That you will never do the same to any other woman."

"But you know I cannot. You feel I may not be loyal to you?"

"No, that is not the issue. There is no man who is above temptation. If you do what you did to me to another woman, then our relationship will be in danger. Such a woman would be desperate to have you. She will never leave you. She will love to possess you by whatever means at her disposal. And this is the danger I see that is making me unhappy. To confess to you, the way you make love gives me a lot of anxiety. It is too hot and too delicious for comfort. Any woman who has you will love to suck you dry. No child would taste honey and will not ask for more. Any woman who tastes you will refuse to release you. To tell you the truth, that is the reason why I am crying."

"Alero! I vow never to have any sexual dealing with any other woman."

"Are you sure, Mayo?"

"I am sure."

"You are sure you won't give what belongs to me to another woman?"

"I won't, I assure you."

"Mayo! I am not done yet." I stared at Alero's face expectantly.

"All through my stay in Ghana, was this what you were doing? Was this what you indulged in, sleeping and making love to girls? Making women scream?"

"God is my witness, I didn't have any affair with any girl."

"Mayo! How come? How did you become so perfect? Where did you attend sex workshops? Who are your trainers?"

"I don't know of any workshops, neither did I attend any training. One thing I want to assure you of is, I have not been cheating on you. Believe me sincerely."

"But you haven't answered my question. How and where did you learn all what you did to me? You couldn't have got all those techniques out of the blue. How did you come across them? How did you come across those styles that can run a woman crazy? Who taught you? Who taught you the techniques of how to make a woman scream?"

"I didn't learn them from anyone."

"I cannot believe you. I cannot believe that you were

never an apprentice to somebody. If you were not – how did you gather the skills? How did you master such terribly hot techniques? How?"

"But you are the one who gave me all the techniques."

"How? queried Alero.

"Your beauty intoxicates my nerves, it makes my cells drunk with raw energy. I discover strangely that I cannot have enough of you. The more I have you, the more I want to have. Your alluring shape overcharges my system. It gives me an unusual vigour, an unusual power, and an unusual obsession. You are like a sweet wine that one tastes and one cannot just stop. And inside, you are vast and mysterious."

CHAPTER FORTY-SIX

I left Nigeria for the United States of America the third day. My mother, Fidelis and Alero saw me off at the Lagos Airport. Parting with Alero gave me terrible emotion. At the airport, we clung to each other and wept and wept as if we were little, innocent children.

"I don't like to leave you," I told Alero "I want to be in Nigeria because of you. I want to be where you are. But it is you who said you don't mind if I go."

"Mayo! You should go. Take heart. This is a God-sent opportunity and I don't want you to miss it. Four years will pass just like that. In the twinkling of an eye, you will be around again. When I went to Ghana, I knew the way you felt, but here I am again. This is how I look at it."

It was our agreement that I should spend four years in the USA, obtain my Bsc degree, come back home to marry Alero and return to USA for my Msc and Ph.D degrees. Leaving Alero for four years seemed like going to the moon for four centuries.

My plane took off from Murtala Mohammed

Airport, Lagos at 10.p.m. that Thursday and we landed at JFK Airport at 6.a.m. American time. I had a brief stay in New York City with Olumide, my friend who came to pick me at the John F. Kennedy Airport.

A week later, I left New York City for Washington D.C. I arrived at Washington D.C late on Sunday. I walked down the 10th Street and found a hotel and checked into it. I reported at the University the following morning. It was a fascinating environment. G.B. was a unique blend of old and new architecture and I so much loved its beautiful landscape.

The week for orientation for new students had come to an end. It was the beginning of my third week in George Bowen University (GB). That afternoon, I had gone to the School of Business and Public Management to attend a lecture on one of my electives. As I came out of the lecture room, I couldn't remember now what attracted me to the Garden of Rose. At its eastern end and close to a cluster of flowers sat a lady. I knew I had seen the face before. I looked at her again. Yes, I could recall that she was one of the two ladies I saw sorting the mail two weeks ago when I went to the University Post Office to post a letter to Alero. She was the brighter of the two and her hair seemed too huge for a natural one. This evening, she sat down relaxing, or what exactly was she doing? She had a fat book by her side but she was not reading it. What attracted me to her was the T-shirt with the map of Nigeria on it. "Is she an Afro-American who had recently discovered her root? Could it be that her ancestors came from Nigeria?" I was curious. It was this curiosity that led me to her.

"Hello, my name is Mayo Williams."
"Hi," she replied. "I am Irene Roberts," she shook my hand warmly.
"A Nigerian?" I deliberately asked that question to tease her because of the Nigerian map on her T-shirt. But I was surprised when she replied:
"Yes, I am a Nigerian. I know you must be a Nigerian too judging from the way you speak." That she was a Nigerian, I couldn't take seriously to start with because her intonation and accent were American.
"I have heard your name before though I can't immediately place it now. How long have you been in the USA?" asked Irene
"Just a fortnight;" I replied.
"A student?"
"Yes;" I replied
"Your Course?"
"Political Science."
"I am a second-year student of Law;" she said smiling.
Knowing that she was a Nigerian, and feeling more confident now, I asked:
"Irene, do you mind if I ask you to tell me more about yourself?"

"Of course not. I have been in the USA since I was 13. I had my secondary school education here. My father, Barrister Ayo Roberts is one of the legal luminaries in Lagos. He was awarded the prestigious Queen's

Counsel (QC) by Her Royal Majesty, Queen Elizabeth II of Great Britain some few years back. He has a flourishing practice. He wants me to have an American education because he had one himself. My grandfather – the Great Daniel Roberts, was a Sierra Leonean who migrated from Freetown to Lagos in the 1880s. He too was a lawyer."

"So yours is a family of barristers?"

"If you say so, I will agree with you."

After I had given a brief introduction of myself, I spent the next thirty minutes with Irene and discovered that she lived in one of the apartments in New Haven. She did 20 hours in a week in the University Post Office just to while away the time as she was well off financially. Her father, according to her, wanted her to marry a Nigerian for obvious reasons. "But I have not thought so much about that," she said. She was of medium height, good build and with bright and good facial appearance. She was, however, hot-tempered, that attribute, I knew later. Irene and I became friends.

I received a letter from Alero six weeks after I arrived in the USA and I felt so excited.

Coker Street,
Mushin, Lagos.
28th June, 1966.

My dear Mayo,
I got your letter. I am so happy that you have settled down. Your description of Manhattan in New York City and the

Central District of Washington D.C excites me. I feel so delighted that you are already enjoying your new place.

You will not believe it, I have just arrived from Toro. My father had repaired his house and the building now wears a new look – more beautiful than the one you knew. Toro is fast recovering from the damage inflicted on it by the vandals. At least ten members of the Oro Fraternity are in the police net. Very many other members had escaped into the Republic of Chad immediately the Military Government took over the affairs of Nigeria. The new government is requesting for their extradition.

Peace is already reigning in every part of Western Nigeria. All the illegal road blocks had been removed. All the people who became emergency Emperors during the period of chaos in the region, are now resting calmly in various police cells awaiting trials. The Age of Terror has ended and the region breathes a new air of peace again.
The king and Queen Jennifer are back from their long tour of the East Indies, Island of Hawaii and the Caribbeans. Both of them personally led a detachment of the Nigerian Army into the notorious Oro Grove. Work is going on day and night now in the place. The king is turning the place into a museum and a centre of tourist attraction. And the new Government of Western Nigeria has approved that a two lane road linking Toro and the Grove be constructed and work has started.

Daddy insists that I should leave Coker Street, my present place of abode, and move to a suite in a hotel in Victoria Island... "A princess must live like a princess," he said. As a result of the unhappy incident that befell me in Toro when I was kidnapped, he has instructed that three guards must always accompany me wherever I go. That order I have so far resisted. I am enjoying my freedom. I want to live my normal life. I don't want to live under anybody's surveillance anymore. I now have a car and a driver. That arrangement is all right. It is the question of guards, I seriously object to.

"I cannot accept a repeat performance of what happened in Toro," said daddy. I don't know how long, I can resist him. The three guards have not arrived yet and I pray they will never arrive. I don't need them.

I am enjoying my stay here at Mushin. I don't like leaving my niece. She has been so nice to me. But I have to move in accordance with daddy's directive. Immediately I move into a hotel suite, I will let you know.

I almost forgot the greatest news of all – I got a letter of admission to the University of Lagos the week you left Nigeria. My course – LL.B Hons International Law will commence this coming September. I may probably leave the hotel for the University residence, if the residence is good enough.

Mayo temi nikan (meaning: Mayo that belongs to me alone), I count the stars every night because every minute, every second, I feel like seeing you. You've struck me with your arrow of love, and the love poison in that arrow, cannot make me rest. Mayo! I love you. I will always love you. And believe me sincerely I will ever remain your bride.

Sincerely yours,
Alero.

I replied Alero's letter that same day. As I got to the Post Office to post the letter, I ran into Irene again. She was closing for the day and she came straight for me.

"Hello Mayo," she smiled at me infectiously.

"Hello. Nice to see you again."

"You are looking so bright, a good indication that you have settled down and you are already enjoying GB."

"You are right."

"Where do you go from here?" she asked me.

"I am going to the main Library. I want to check one journal which Professor Stone recommended during his lecture this morning. You've heard about Professor Stone, haven't you?"

"No, who is he?"

"Professor Stone is a scholar of American Political History, and a very brilliant one at that. He has been an adviser to several American Presidents right from David Eisenhower, J.F. Kennedy and the current President Lyndon Johnson. He is a well-known, respected authority in his field."

"Then he is one professor I would love to know. I must confess to you that I almost don't know what goes on in any other faculty except my own. Faculty of Law, my faculty is a large school with ten different departments and GB Law faculty is noted worldwide as a school where the best lawyers are trained. That was why I opted to come here two years ago to study law. Perhaps I would have gone to Harvard or Yale. The Law faculty here has a galaxy of brilliant scholars. I say this not because I am here, I say it with all sense of responsibility." Then Irene stared at my face again, her finely moulded lips coined in a mechanical smile, as she asked me:

"Any news from Nigeria?"

"Nothing so far, there may be some before the month runs out."

"Mayo! You are looking unusually bright. Your mood is buoyant and your face radiant like that of a young man who has one secret reason to be happy but who is not willing to share the same with anyone. And if you may ask me, I can guess why you are so bright."

"And why am I bright, if I may ask?"

"You've just received a message from your fiancée."

"You never told me that you are a seer."

"We women understand you men a lot. If I look at the face of a man for a second, I can guess two or three things happening to him that moment."

"You never told me that you are a student of psychology?"

"You cannot do Law without a good knowledge of psychology, if not, you will be a poor attorney."

Then Irene stared curiously at my face again. She was an intelligent lady and someone who will make a good lawyer. Her eyes traced me with some interest.

"Mayo! I haven't forgotten. You promised to call on me when we met last, I am yet to enjoy the honour of the executive visit of a Nigerian Federal Government scholar, that learned representative of the most prestigious black nation on earth."

"Irene! I know you are skilled in psychology but you haven't told me that your are also skilled in flattery."

"No, I am not flattering you in anyway. I am only telling you a point of fact."

A narrow smile lit my face as I stared at her.

"Irene, on a more serious note, I was just about to ask you whether you would be free on Saturday. Are you likely to be free between 5p.m. and 6p.m.?"

"Yes, of course."

"I will see you then."

I quickly posted Alero's letter. But I could see that Irene was still waiting for me. Irene and I strolled down the street towards the faculties. We talked as we went. I stared at Irene, I surveyed her more inquisitively now. She had almost the same height as Alero. She had a huge hair. She had nice, big, pointed breasts. She also had good straight legs. Her back view was beautiful. Her face was fine. She had artificial nails, though quite fine. Her eyes lashes appeared like made-up ones, they seemed like those used by artistes in their movies. She was dark in complexion. She was a fine lady by all standards. But she could not compare with Alero. Alero belonged to a special breed of women. She was the finest among the finest women I have ever seen so far, the most classy among women of class. She was a natural-born princess, and never less than a princess. While Irene was fine, Alero was bewitching. While Irene was good-looking, Alero was charming and magnetic. While Irene looked like a beautiful palm leave, Alero was like the palm frond, the only leave that stands upright among the leaves of the palm because it is the newest, the finest, the most colourful and the one that has no rival. Alero was like a new moon-glamorous, yet cool and innocent. She wore an indescribable aura as a clothe. This comparison I was making silently as we discussed that evening. Comparing Irene with Alero might not be fair because Irene was also beautiful in her own right. She is an extrovert. She is an articulate, bright and ebullient lady. She has very many qualities apart from her bodily charms.

The buildings of the faculties were now so near and we have got to the junction where Irene and I would have to take different routes. I shook Irene's hand, it was soft and lovely. I stared at her face admiringly. "Irene this is where I have to leave you. I found your company so beautiful. Are you going to your hostel?"
"No, I am going to the faculty. We are treating Dred Scott's Case tonight."
"And who is Dred Scott?"

"Sorry, I speak to you as if I were talking to a colleague in the Law faculty. Dred Scott was an electronic engineer in a Broadcasting Company in Chicago. He was the Chief Engineer and the Head of the Technical Department. The two transmitters used by the company he worked for, got burnt and the company sacked him for negligence of duty and incompetence. Dred Scott sued his employer alleging that he had not been given a fair hearing. My class is divided into two groups – one group is holding brief for Dred Scott's employer and the other for Mr. Dred Scott. Professor Garwin, the Head of one of the Law Departments is the Presiding Judge. I am leading the team of lawyers that is holding brief for Mr. Dred Scott. This evening promises to witness one of the most elegant battles ever held in the Law faculty. My group has prepared very hard for this case. I am sure we are going to carry the day. It's going to be exciting." Irene spoke with passion. Then she stared at my face and asked: "Mayo! Will you like to come?"

"I would have loved to but I have two assignments which I must submit tomorrow morning. If I can finish early, I will join you, may be at the tail end. You have stimulated my appetite by the way you talked."
"You need to be there, it is going to be beautiful. It will be exciting. This is the kind of dry rehearsal we do from time to time. The faculty does it to prepare us for real court situation."
When you have something of this nature next time, just let me know. I will love to watch it."

I could not join Irene in the court that night. But the two law students in my hall talked so much about that evening's legal battle over our breakfast the following morning.
"Irene was impossible," said Barry Hilton, a 300 level law student.
"She will make a first class lawyer. I enjoyed her argument best when the judge asked the two leading lawyers to address the court on the point of law. Irene stood like Cicero before the Roman Senate. Words rolled out of her mouth like they rolled out from Demosthenes, the legendary Greek Orator.

Her expressions were elegant and her presentation was flamboyant. Soft spoken, suave, persuasive, she was able to catch the sympathy of the judge in her first few sentences and hold it to the end. Her legal citations from America, Canada, Britain and India were beautiful. She radiated youthful vigour, ease and confidence. The Judge for minutes sat mesmerized. Professor Garvin must have felt so proud that this one was one of his own products. I felt so proud too. "I love Irene," said Amos Goldman, another law student.

I was happy for Irene. Even before our scheduled meeting that Saturday, I had become very anxious to see Irene, the Nigerian-born law student whose fame had started to travel.

I knocked Irene's door. As the door opened, she rushed forward to embrace me as a smile of shy sweetness lit her face.

"I couldn't make it to your Dred Scott's case but your name is all over the campus. Everyone has been commending your brilliant performance. I am so happy for you."
"Mayo! I feel highly humbled by the various comments and commendations. The one that makes me feel so wonderful was the commendation of Professor Garvin. He embraced me and told me:
"You are simply marvelous."

I stared admiringly at Irene, then hugged her.
"It's a job well done."

There was warmth in her look. She then took me round her room. The furnishing was tasteful. The rug was imported from Britain, the chairs and the table from Italy. At one corner was a beautiful portable television. There were two pictures pasted tastefully to the wall.

That of Barrister Roberts Q.C and another, Mrs. Roberts, both parents of Irene. On the table was a smaller picture of a young handsome man.

"That is Lere Adams, a medical student at Howard University, my fiancé," said Irene.

Then Irene took me to her small beautiful kitchen
"Mayo! What do I cook for you?"
"Do you have to go into such trouble?"
"Just tell me your best Nigerian food, I have all Nigerian food materials here and it will be ready in twenty minutes."
"Irene, you don't need to go to that length. Let's just sit down and talk over a bottle of wine. There are too many issues about Nigeria to discuss."
"No. Do you like ikokore?"
"Yes, of course."
"I am going to prepare kokore for you. Just go and sit down. Switch on the TV to a channel of your choice. I will soon join you."

Twenty minutes later, hot, delicious kokore prepared with fresh fish, green vegetable, shrimps and liver was on the table. Irene was a fantastic cook. It was the most delicious food I had ever eaten since I arrived in the USA.

As we ate, I gazed secretly at the face of Irene but one time our eyes collided because she too was trying to steal a look at my face at the same time.

"A rigorous, confident, intelligent law student, a fantastic lawyer-in-the-making, a superb cook, Irene you possess many sterling qualities that make me feel really jealous of Lere Adams, your fiancé."

"Thank you for the compliment," said Irene who smiled at me infectiously.

While I later had brandy, Irene only took coffee. We discussed up to 10.p.m. on the volatile political situation in Nigeria and the adventure of the Nigerian military boys into politics. I found Irene's company a most rewarding, intellectual exercise.

CHAPTER FORTY-SEVEN

I was spending my seventh month in George Bowen University. That week, I got a letter from Alero. She had resumed at the University of Lagos and had registered for her Law Degree.

"The students, the teachers and the new place are so exciting. The University has a wonderful location. With an attractive lagoon at the background, a lovely rolling plain in the front, with graceful shrubs and flowers greeting the eyes at every turn, the entire landscape looks like a wonderful garden. I love it so much," she wrote.

As I finished reading the letter and looked at the various lovely pictures Alero took by the lagoon side behind her university faculties, my obsession to see her again grew so strong.

"Take heart," I told myself "In about three years, you will see her again."

The World Conference of historians started that very week at the Conference Centre of GB. A galaxy of the world's brightest historians assembled at Washington D.C. Professor Stone was delivering a paper at the conference. He was a superb teacher with a great sense of humour, his language – warm and elegant and his diction - beautiful. He radiated charm and buoyancy that made being around him a great pleasure.

All the other lecturers read from their lecture notes. But Professor Stone, never brought any lecture note to the class. He would talk for two hours non-stop, quoting dates and statistics with effortless ease. He was simply brilliant.

But on this particular occasion, when he was not going to speak to university students, but to eminent and renowned scholars of history, he prepared a note. By the time he finished his breakfast that morning, he had just six minutes to get to the Conference Centre. He was delivering his paper at 8.30a.m., and his was the opening lecture for that day. The lecture note was already in his car. He hurried out of the house and entered into the car but the car refused to start.

"Angela! You will have to drop me at the Conference Centre, I don't know what is wrong with this car. I have only five minutes left."

Professor Stone wearing an anxious look, rushed out of his car and ran into the house to hasten his wife. Angela quickly took the key of her own car and they were soon on their way. As the car was about to park in the front of the Conference Centre, the booming voice of the chairman for the day came over the air.

"We had a highly stimulating session yesterday. This morning, we are starting off with an exciting topic: History and Society. Ladies and gentlemen, may I invite Professor R.D. Stone of George Bowen University to deliver his paper."

Professor Stone rushed out of the car. It was that moment he discovered that he did not take his lecture note out of his own car.

"Angela! The paper I am scheduled to read here is in my car. I left it on the passenger's seat. Turn round quickly and kindly assist me to bring it."

In the meantime, Professor Stone hastened into the hall. He walked into a tumultuous and deafening applause. As he proceeded towards the podium, the applause grew louder. He got to the podium at last, stared at the faces of his colleagues and thereafter began to speak. He delivered a two-hour lecture non-stop without a note. His language was superb, high-flowing and vigorous and his reasoning terrific. He raised three new historical theories which became the central issues of discussion for the next few days. His lecture note which his wife went for, never reached him. It was nice, it didn't. The brilliance of Professor Stone stunned his colleagues, his reputation soared sky high.

As Professor Stone entered our lecture room a week later, we all stood up to give this great scholar a resounding ovation.

"Ladies and gentlemen, it is a privilege and honour to have before us this morning, the world's best political and social historian, the one and only Professor R.D. Stone." said the class representative. A huge applause went on and on. The Professor was caught unawares. Nobody warned him that we would do what we did. For about five minutes, he stood there in the aura of various praises and eulogies from the students.

"You are a great source of inspiration to the younger generation. We love and cherish you Professor Stone," said Mariam, one of the female members of our class. I have never seen a man so humble in success. He thanked us for the honour done him and thereafter, started his lecture.

The academic year was almost finishing when Irene phoned me one morning that she would be celebrating her birthday the following Saturday and requested that I should be there.
"It's going to be a small party and I have only invited those of you who are close friends," she said.
I was at Irene's apartment that Saturday and it was a small party. Only six people were there: Mary James, the daughter of an American Senator from California and Anna Christian, a daughter of popular American Lawyer – both ladies were from the Law Faculty of the university.

Then two young men whom Irene introduced to me as her friends: Lere Adams, a Nigerian Medical Student from Howard University, Washington D.C. and Joseph Nwachukwu, another Nigerian studying

History and Archeology in the same university. From all what transpired at the party, I could see that Irene and Adams were really in love. The two were always together and very intimate.

"Board Member," the famous record of the Nigerian Juju Legend, Ebenezer Obey, provided the beats we danced to that evening. Irene went into the arms of Lere Adams, the pair was a beauty to watch. James Brown's famous song – I FEEL ALL RIGHT, soon ignited the air, and we all danced like men and women on the fringe of lunacy. There was plenty of wine and food. We really enjoyed ourselves.

I returned late from Irene's party. I could no longer go to the library that evening and therefore decided to read in the room few articles on Nationalism in Modern Africa written by Professor W.J Ken Post, a Professor of Political Science, University of Birmingham in Great Britain. Professor Post had been one of the few scholars who had shown great interest in African affairs and whose work had been one of the most analytical I had read so far. I read his articles and few other works far into the night because I would be facing a major examination the following Monday. The examination came and went. Two weeks later, the results were out, and I had distinctions in all my courses and also won Woodrow Wilson Prize for being the best 100 level student of Political Science. It was a good start.

That evening, Irene visited me around 7p.m. She looked particularly radiant in her pink gown. Her attractive shape came out, and the various curves made her look pretty. She only spent about three minutes. As I escorted her out of my apartment and we walked down the corridor, Irene stopped.

"Do you know why I have to call on you this evening?" she asked.

"Irene, you are yet to tell me."

She stared at my face and smiled broadly.

"I like to congratulate you on your recent brilliant performance. Since this university started 107 years ago, yours had been the best performance so far at 100 level. You have set a record and your name has entered the honours list. I saw it in the university bulletin. Coming from Nigeria, you make me feel so proud. And being a black man, I feel prouder. You have been a very worthy ambassador of our race. I like to congratulate you once more." She suddenly drew me closer and pecked me on the cheek. She waved to me as she hurried down the corridor, leaving me standing there, while surveying her pretty figure as she went.

I felt proud. I wished Alero were with me that night. I had always loved to win all academic laurels because of Alero. It was nice, I started well again in this new environment.

CHAPTER FORTY-EIGHT

I rene and I only saw each other occasionally in my second year. But I got to my room one day and met her note.

"Mayo! You must try to see me today unfailingly."

"What is the matter?" I queried. I couldn't guess any possible reason for her asking me to see her. I was curious. I was with Irene at 6.p.m. that day.

She was looking very sad. Her buoyancy and ebullience were gone.

"What is wrong with you? Are you sick?"

"Mayo! I don't know how to answer your questions. I am expected to be at the National Cancer Centre at Baltimore tomorrow. I had been there once when I saw something that appeared like a lump in my right breast. The experts there did series of tests and I am asked to come for the final result tomorrow. If they diagnose cancer. I will be shattered. I need somebody to accompany me to the place and stand by me. Lere Adams would have done just that for me but he is gone to Nigeria. His father is seriously sick and he had gone to bring him down for treatment. Mayo! Will you accompany me?"

The day was Thursday. I had just two lectures the following day. I could skip them because of Irene. I was ready to do anything within my power to make Irene happy.

"You haven't answered my question: Will you go with me?" she looked at my face pleadingly.

"Yes, I will go."

"That is very kind of you."

I took Irene in my arms.

"Baby! I want you to look bright. All is going to be well," I told her. "When do we start off tomorrow?"

"We shall leave here at 7 a.m."

"I will be with you five minutes before the scheduled time."

We left Washington D.C. in the morning by train. It was a chilly day. The weather was really bad. It was cold the previous day but no one could guess that the change for the worse could be so sudden. We got to Baltimore National Cancer Centre at 9.30.a.m. We had to wait for another thirty minutes because Irene's appointment was for 10.a.m. The remaining thirty minutes seemed like eternity.

I needed to prepare Irene psychologically for the worst, and I started to speak to her:

"The worst is surgery, and even if the report says that, that is just a small issue because the people here are experts in their fields. They would do the best job."

"I don't want anyone to cut my breast," Irene cut in. The worry on her face returned in its full strength.

"I understand that they don't need to cut the breast

all the time, depending on the nature of the lump."

"The breasts are the greatest assets of a woman. They are what give her sweet, feminine nature. Why should I lose mine?"

"You aren't going to lose yours. Be calm. There is no cause for alarm. And really there is no cause to get unnecessarily agitated."

I looked at Irene again, she had beautiful pointed breasts. They looked rosy and made her look so sexy. They gave her such pretty figure. I could see the reason for her worry that morning.

The clock ticked in seconds, 10a.m. was gradually approaching and our anxiety was growing. It was 10a.m. at last. "The moment has come," I mumbled.

My heart was beating very fast. Irene wore an anxious look. An elderly woman in her late 40s came out of a room, looked curiously into the faces of the people sitting and then queried:

"Is Miss Irene Roberts here?"

"Yes, I am here." Irene stood up. The woman beckoned her to come. I also stood up, walked to her quickly

"I am Irene's friend, can I join her?"

"Yes, if you like."

We entered into a smaller beautiful office. The woman asked us to sit down, then entered the next office, apparently to inform her boss that Irene brought a friend along. The door opened again and the woman asked us to go in. The doctor sat behind a beautiful metal table and beamed out a smile as we entered his office.

"Miss Roberts! What seemed like a lump was not a lump and it is not cancerous. By now what you saw must have gone or is it still there?"

"Not at all, Doctor."

"Let me examine you again just for few minutes."

Irene and the doctor went into the examination room. Five minutes later, she was back smiling.

"Miss Roberts, there is no cause for alarm, Good morning."

Irene and I embraced each other. As we left the doctor's office, our joy knew no bounds. I was so happy for her. Her buoyancy and brightness were back. Irene's face became very attractive again.

"I told you that all will be well."

"Yes, you said so but it was so difficult for me to believe you."

I never knew that the entire exercise could be so short. In the next one and half hours, we would be in Washington D.C. again and this made me feel excited. We got to the reception, all the people stood as they listened attentively to the weather report:

"This part of the USA is having its worst weather in 40 years. Everyone is advised to stay indoor for the remaining part of the day as the weather situation will progressively grow worse in the next twenty-four hours."

I was shocked. It was very cold when we left Washington D.C. But I expected the situation to improve as the day progressed. We planned to return to our university by the next train, but we realized now to our dismay that going back immediately was no longer possible.

I was so unhappy but I didn't want Irene to notice the change in my mood.

"What do we do?" I asked her.

"I am sorry Mayo, we may not be able to leave Baltimore today. We have to look for a hotel."

Getting out of the hospital itself was now a big problem. A good Samaritan offered to drop us in a nearby hotel. Driving was extremely difficult. The visibility was poor and the road was full of ice and very slippery. One and half hours ago, the visibility was fairly all right. Now, it was a hell of trouble getting us to the hotel. Hotel EL Doraldo was one of the finest in Baltimore. It had nice facilities.

Irene booked a room and I booked the one next to her. Later, I joined Irene in her room. Joyful and hilarious, Irene seemed as if she had won a million dollars in a popular lottery. Now the gleam had returned to her face. She had become her natural, ebullient self.

For hours, we were in that room watching various exciting programmes on television. We also spoke about students' politics at George Bowen University and the candidates who were likely to contest for the post of Students' President. As Irene spoke to me, so also was I becoming more and more fascinated by her. She was a good talker. She was pretty too. Her eyes winked at me amorously whenever she spoke. I didn't know how to tell her, those eye balls and the way she rolled them, were gradually making me uncomfortable.

Her relentless stare started to generate romantic heat in my cells. Irene was unusually charming that morning. As I looked at her, the blood was racing through my body.

I had visited Irene in her room at the university hostel. I had even spent three hours with her before, but the situation was so different from this one. In the university hostel, her colleagues kept on coming in and going out, but here, we were alone. A young man and a pretty young lady, alone in a hotel room and this for hours, the atmosphere was not what I ever bargained for. It was too tempting for comfort. Irene's beautiful figure had a potent effect on me and my cells were growing hotter with the passage of each minute. I was feeling very uneasy as her nearness started to intoxicate my nerves. As I touched her hand, I was aware of that delicious current running right through me.

"I am not a stone, neither am I an angel. I am susceptible to the charms of a pretty woman. What am I to do?" I secretly asked myself.

I stared at Irene's lovely lips. I felt a driving need to get closer to her, take her in my arms and kiss her. Tension was growing inside me but I strongly made up my mind to exercise every control over my feeling. I wouldn't love to put myself in a situation in which Irene could accuse me of taking undue advantage because we were together. I stared at Irene, the girl in the pink blouse before me was beautiful. I needed now to switch my mind from Irene's sweetness and look for something else to engage my attention. Fortunately, I found one.

"Irene! Assuming the doctor's report was not favourable," I asked her.

Irene stared curiously at my face.

"And they have to cut off one of your breasts."

"I would have been shattered. You would have had a lot of problem in your hands. All through the journey, I was praying silently not to become a problem to this young man who had volunteered to accompany me."

"What would you have done?"

"Mayo! I don't know. But you would have had a lot of problem handling me. Let's thank God for everything."

It was a mistake on my part to ask that question from Irene. The problem I wanted to escape from came in a stronger form. Irene was a beautiful talker. And the way she rolled her eye balls when she talked, fascinated me intensely. Her eyes winked enticingly, making her so lovely. She was surely not aware of how sexy she was when she talked. Talking made her figure so intoxicating. As I listened to her, my system was growing hotter and hotter. It was as if I was having an anarchy inside me.

"You have admirable eyes," I told her.

"Mayo, many men always talk about my eyes. I wonder what they see there."

"They are very beautiful. Whenever you speak, your eyes seem as if they are talking too, making them so adorable. Your diction is very good and your pronunciation superb."

"Thank you for the compliment."

"Irene though the weather had disorganized today's plan and had spoilt our fun, but we must celebrate. Giving you a clean bill by the National Cancer Center, is enough for celebration, don't you feel so?"

"What do we do?" she asked me.

"I had phoned the restaurant for a special lunch. We are going there on my bill. I must give you a special treat."

"Mayo! How? Why must you do such a thing? You want to incur unnecessary expenses because of me – why?"

"Irene, I won't welcome all those questions. In this kind of situation, I am not a democrat. I am not asking for your views or ideas, I am only communicating to you what I have decided already. I know you had spent very many years in America and had imbibed the western culture of consultation, debate and agreement, but be an African girl this time. I am taking you to the restaurant. Get ready for 1.30p.m. Is that okay?"

"Okay," she replied.

At exactly 1.30p.m., we came down to the first floor. We walked hand in hand to the restaurant which was just about a stone throw. We took our seats in one extreme corner where we could have some privacy. A waiter soon came to attend to us. He took our order. Ten minutes later our food was ready. We had noodles, shrimp rolls, pork and perking duck. The food was wonderful.

After leaving the restaurant, we bought two bottles

of West Indian rum and two bottles of French wine to keep us warm throughout the day. As we watched the television programmes and sipped our wine, my passion started to rise up. I hungered for Irene now with a ferocity that went beyond the ordinary.

I have had many temptations, but finding myself locked-up with a pretty lady in a hotel room was one I had never experienced before now and I had no previous knowledge to fall upon. Irene's nipples pushing against her brassiere started to torment me. The heat was becoming too much for me.

I looked at her lips, I began to wonder how sweet they would be. I felt a driving need to get closer to her but I didn't know whether I would be stepping beyond my bounds. I stared at her face for an unspoken invitation, there was none. What I read from her face was ambiguous. The message was not clear. But my loins ached inside me. Irene's plump and pretty body continued to send continuous salvo of searing sensation into my system and that system was burning and I was growing more and more uncomfortable. I felt like seizing Irene and kissing her with the fiery passion that was gnawing through my system.

The day passed slowly and anxiously. Soon it was dinner time, and we went down to the restaurant. We spent considerable time over our dinner. We had long heated discussion on the GB student politics. Irene was highly articulate and brilliant. But as I gazed at her attractive face that night, my nerves were rioting. My breathing became erratic.

"You look so pretty tonight Irene. I love your alluring eyes."

"Mayo! You have a good look too. You've been one of the most romantic guys I have ever seen."

As we left the dinner hall and were going to our rooms, I took Irene's left hand in mine. It was warm and lovely. I wanted her now so badly. My body was aching with the need to be one with her. Her closeness to me had shattered all my control. As we started to climb the staircase that led to our rooms, I held Irene by the waist, the contact was electric. She was simply irresistible. My heart was beating fiercely now and I became very nervous. Finally we got to Irene's door. I had planned and rehearsed internally within me what I would say at this point. And here is it:

"Irene! Your presence and pretty figure have given me the most intoxicating feeling that I have ever had in my life. How much I love you!" After saying that, I was going to embrace Irene and kiss her. We were now at Irene's door but strangely courage failed me at this critical moment.
"What if she refuses to kiss me? What if she resists my embrace? What if she takes offence? What if …?"

My mind came up with several ifs. My body and system were anxious and willing but my hands became temporarily paralyzed with fear. My heart was thudding inside me. I only stared at Irene's face. She stared at mine appealingly, then said:
"Goodnight Mayo. I hope the weather will be fairer tomorrow."

Then she opened her door, entered her room and the door closed after her. The sound of her high-heeled shoes echoed as she went. I heard her drawing the bolts. I remained frozen to that spot for almost a minute. I was so highly dejected. I couldn't believe it that I was such a coward.

I finally left Irene's door. I walked towards my door. My legs were weak as the spirit appeared to have left my body. I opened my door and went in.

I switched on the television set. I tried several channels, all the programmes were lousy. They didn't interest me. I lay on my bed, I couldn't sleep. I was restless. My mind was not in that room, it was with Irene. For long, I lay on top of my bed, but was too far agitated to sleep. I therefore switched off the light, yet sleep did not come. So I sat and stared into the darkness for a long time. My need to taste Irene was too overpowering. I couldn't guess how long I remained in that restless position, but sleep eventually came to snatch me from this terrible, self-imposed torture.

Surprisingly, I slept soundly and I woke up around 7.30.a.m. I stood up, switched on the television, it was the weather report that was on again. The weather had gone worse than that of the previous day which was Friday. From every indication we might not be able to get out of our present prison in the next 24 hours. The events of yesterday flashed back into my memory and I resolved that whatever happened, today must be different.

I quickly had a warm shower, dressed up and by 8a.m., I was ready to see Irene in her room.
I knocked her door; there was no reply.

"Are you still sleeping?" But that moment, the bolts were drawn and the door opened. Irene came from the bathroom, the foams were still on her body. She wrapped herself in a big towel but her back and the upper parts of her chest were bare. The upper ridges of her breasts were fine and inviting. The legs were beautiful and the part of the thighs that I could see was extremely sexy.

"Mayo! I rushed out of the bathroom to open the door for you. As you can see, I haven't finished bathing yet. Please sit down. I will soon join you."

Irene hurried back to the showers. I had seen her soft, ripe body, then came my fit again. An intense burning passion was cascading through my system. The heat was gradually becoming unbearable.

My brain was doing all kinds of mathematics and balancing various difficult equations. As Irene finally came out of the bathroom, wrapped only in a towel, a desire flared through me. Now or never. I couldn't just explain how I found myself on my feet. I rushed forward, held Irene and embraced her. I was ready to go to jail for rape; but I was not going to spare Irene this time. The sensuous face and lovely body were too much for me. My embrace was wild and warm. I crushed her to my chest and kissed her with passion. Irene kissed me back hungrily. She had been expecting this for the past twenty hours and her desire had built up into a voluminous, insatiable greed. Her arms wrapped tightly around me. She would neither allow me to go nor move. She kissed me with a wild passion that had built up for many hours. She kissed me with such violence that our bodies began to ache. For about four minutes, she was in charge as her exploring tongue spread fire into all parts of my mouth. We kissed and kissed and kissed until our shivering bodies collapsed on her bed. Her towel fell off her body and her two roundish, rosy breasts came out of captivity. Her pretty, full ripe body was now naked before me. Like a rum-induced nightmare, I suddenly went crazy. I kissed her hard, even in the heat, Irene tried to stare at my face and queried:

"Why are you just kissing me now? We've been here for over twenty hours. Why didn't you kiss me yesterday? Why did you ignore me for so long. Don't you like me?"

"Who is that man who will not like an angel like you? Irene, you are lovely. I'd wanted to embrace and kiss you right from the moment we entered this hotel room but you won't believe it, my courage failed me."

"Why?"

"Because I couldn't guess how you would react– assuming you take offence."

"What has given you the courage now?"

"Because my torture had reached its peak and has become unbearable. I could no longer endure it."

My fingers caressed the moist nipples of her abundant breasts. Irene wrapped her arms tightly round me as her kiss became deeper and my caresses grew more intense. She kissed me with a kind of wild desperation while her attractive body frame quivered feverishly in anticipation.

"Mayo! You have punished me for too long, leave all the preliminaries and make love to me."

She could not stand the torment of waiting anymore. Her eyes were soaked in desire. She was impossibly romantic. I could see the fiery passion burning in her eyes. The intensity and vibrancy of her passion seemed as if they would consume everything in sight.

As my burning flesh entered into hers, she went wild. Her hands tightened on my back, bringing me closer and closer, wanting me more and more inside her, wanting my male root to go into the very core of her need. For the first few minutes, she was in charge as her rich, fleshy hips moved against me in wild abandon, drawing me deeper and deeper into the very depth of her woman-hood. She wrapped her legs around my hips. I dug deeper and deeper into her rich, delicious interior. My movement was fast, intense and relentless. Within a minute, she went wild as she was now lost in a sea of sensation. Her motion became faster and faster as her two hands gripped me like a huge, cruel trap. Her kissing became so hot that I felt my tongue would dissolve into her burning mouth. Her system had become terribly overcharged and I remembered now that the only thing that could quickly calm her down was to screw her hard, really hard. I was a master of the game. I knew tremendous amount about how to make a woman scream. But I wanted Irene to first empty all the weapons in her arsenal before I started my own romance game. Suddenly, I took over from her. I screwed her hard, then harder, and harder still. She had been moving her hips so fast against my cork, but I now took over in a tempo she could not match. I moved in and out of her in an amazingly terrible speed the kind she had never experienced before. My speed threw her system into turmoil, the pleasure of the sweet friction became terribly intense as I pounded her savagely, sending erotic sensation into all her systems. Within two minutes, I gave her more than what she could take and she cried out in a delirium of passion. I was so pleased at the sound of her scream. I now went into her in three minutes of another rapid screwing. Her pelvis danced violently below me in a fiendish contortion. I pumped her so fast and so fierce and so hard, the sensation became too much that she could no longer stand the almost unbearable pleasure and she screamed. Rather than lessen the tempo, I increased the heat. She screamed and screamed and screamed and screamed. Her hot pretty, plump frame shook and shook and shook and shook and continued shaking violently until it got its calm at last.

For several minutes, Irene clung to me and we seemed like inseparable siamese twins. Then she whispered to my left hear in a soft distant voice:

"Your love-making is too hot, just too hot. Mayo, you are not only super in academics, you are also marvelous in bed."

I stared at her face, then smiled. "This one has only seen the tributary and is screaming, what will she do when we get to the main river?"

My system was just waking up. I had not seen a woman for one year or more now. I loved Irene's love-making. She was a terrific and vigorous partner in bed. She had whetted my appetite and I was now very hungry to taste her again. But I made up my mind not to rush her. I wanted to be systematic in my approach. I didn't want to give her a sensory overload. First, I gently stroked her nipples with my thumbs over and over. She groaned as the sensation spread. As my erection hit her clitoris, her body convulsed and convulsed and convulsed without stopping. Suddenly, I took her again.. The first exercise was a child's play. It was done according to Irene's dictate. This time, I was in charge. I stimulated all her sensory organs at the same time and Irene went wild right from the first minute. I caressed her moist, erect nipples, kissed her again and again, screwed her hard while whispering love words into her ear - all at the same time. Irene's body instantly became intoxicated as pulsing waves of intense pleasure cascaded through her. As her body yielded to my erotic mastery, I drove Irene crazy as I took her deeper and deeper into a sexual daze.

When we finally finished, we remained in each other's embrace for very many minutes.
"You have given me too amazing an experience. It was as though I had never known a man before. Mayo, you are enfant terrible."
For minutes, Irene stared at me curiously.
"Irene! Never before had I too been overcome with such physical desire as what swept over me when we were together yesterday. You have amazing eyes and a beautiful body."

We were almost late for breakfast. We got to the restaurant at 9.50a.m. We had toasted bread, sausage and tea. We bought several bottles of wine and retired to Irene's room.

I checked out of my room that morning now that Irene and I were already united in love. The weather remained bad, but neither Irene nor I thought about the weather now. We were so much enjoying our present bliss.

We had no time for lunch that afternoon. We were in bed throughout the day. We made love over and over again. The more we made love to each other, the more we itched for more. Our bodies appeared now to have developed insatiable lusts for each other, the more they came together, the more they itched to remain with each other. And so, the more I forayed into Irene's sweet, exciting body, the more I found it so fascinating. We would have loved to be there for eternity but the weather conspired and brightened suddenly on Sunday evening. On Monday morning, as early as 6 a.m., we checked out of the hotel to take the next train to Washington D.C.

Irene whispered into my ear as we were about to part in the front of the Academic Office to go to our different hostels.

"It is my most delicious outing. Thank you, Mayo!"

CHAPTER FORTY-NINE

We arrived at the campus on Monday morning around 9.a.m. I was going to attend a lecture at 10a.m. The series of lecture on "Liberty" which commenced the previous week was to be rounded up that week. I went to Amos Sanders, a colleague, just to glance through what they did on Friday when I was away.

"We had a marathon lecture of three hours on Friday," he reported, then he threw a bombshell: "Professor Wallace will give us a test this morning."
"Test?"
"Yes, a test."

I stood, frozen to the spot.
"What is the problem?" he asked me
"I was not around on Friday. I traveled out of the city. The bad weather caught up with me and detained me in Baltimore. I have not prepared for any test."
"You can glance through my note, if it can be of help. I hope you can make some sense out of it."

It was a highly voluminous note. The more I read it,

the more confused I became. After about fifteen minutes, I gave Amos his note and I prepared for the Armageddon ahead. One could not gain from both ends. I spent the week-end enjoying love-making, it was now time to pay the price. I never played with my academic work. But I recalled now that the weather was fair enough on Sunday but Irene and I opted to use the extra hours to see more of ourselves. It was my most delicious outing since I arrived in the U.S.A.

The test was an unusual one. It was not the kind one would fill in the correct answers or select among four or five possible alternatives. It was a one question test and it lasted three hours – "Liberty, an unattainable ideal" Discuss.

I read it over and over again, I couldn't make head or tail out of it and yet I was to write on it for three hours. Since I did not grasp the central theme of what was taught in the class, I stopped worrying about what had gone. I sat down to look at the question in my own way, and I came up with several theoretical prepositions, then after that wrote my conclusion and submitted my paper.

I made up my mind to quietly stroll out of the class anytime Professor Wallace came up with the results. First week, I stood at the extreme edge of the class, on red alert, getting ready to sneak out anytime Professor Wallace came with the papers. But that week, he carried no paper. He just came in, delivered his lecture and went away. The second week, I also sat at the extreme end, alas! Professor Wallace brought nothing to the class again. Third week and fourth week, there was nothing. The class was in a buoyant mood one morning and I was the one cracking a joke when Professor Wallace surfaced, this time with the papers. I was right at the centre of the class. There was no way I could sneak out easily. Any attempt to do so would attract an unusual attention to my person. I was in trouble. I sat frozen to my seat, looking like a small child who had seen something frightening. My body went through a cauldron of racing pulses, my temperature went up as my body broke out in a sweat. Professor Wallace surveyed our faces inquiringly then beamed out a mischievous smile. I couldn't see what was funny. I stared at his face, wearing a pugnacious look, my mood highly belligerent.

"I was expecting better performances than what I have here," he said. Then he started to call out the names and the marks.

"What kind of method is this? Why should Professor Wallace adopt this unorthodox, outdated and ancient method?"

This was precisely what I was fearing. I knew my mark would be so ridiculous. It would be so poor. I never loved to share this kind of information with anyone. Why should Professor Wallace undress me before the whole class? Why must he make my disgrace a public property? Why couldn't he leave the answer sheets with the class representative or drop the papers on the table where each student could pick his own after the lecture? What was he going to gain by this approach? I stared at him. I was tensed.

Later, a rising anger began to cruise through my

veins. I prayed silently for an unknown external force to intervene and stop Professor Wallace, but no force stopped him. I had seen people seized by sudden heart attack and I wished him to experience something similar and save me from the naked ridicule he wanted to expose me to that morning, but Professor Wallace stood erect, vibrant, strong and looking radiant as ever. Finally, I resigned myself to fate.

The period of the distribution of the papers appeared long as eternity. My tension was growing and the heat was gradually becoming too much for me, but Professor Wallace appeared not to be in a hurry. He was enjoying himself. Finally, it remained just two papers. I stared at him, my tension heightened. My breathing became erratic and difficult. I was choking. I guessed that Professor Wallace had retained the worst papers for the last minutes, and I was right. The professor called the owner of the last paper but one, the mark was very poor and the entire class burst into a long, huge laughter.

My paper was the last and it was evident now that I had the worst mark
"Now, that hour of trial has come. God, give me the courage to take all the bomb shells and the ridicule - God! God!" I mumbled. I was frantic with anxiety. My heart was beating fiercely that I could hear all its beats. For the first time, my legs were trembling
"There is a particularly …"

I heard Professor Wallace up to the word "particularly" then the entire room became suddenly dark. The world stood rigid and things went blank. My face turned white with apprehension but the phrase: "excellent paper" that followed "particularly" was the thing that woke me from my daze. I tried to stabilize, listened now with all my might.

"This particular student took a completely different approach and came up with his own different set of theories which are sure to become landmarks in political science. It is an original piece of work. It is a beautiful treatise and I have asked the Departmental Secretary to produce a copy for each student because all must read it. May I invite Mayo Williams to come forward for his paper. It's a wonderful write-up." There was a deafening applause. Very many students were staring at me, wonder on their faces. I was more surprised than anyone in that room because I couldn't just know what made my paper an excellent one. There was nothing excellent about it short of the fact that Professor Wallace said so.

"Is this a dream?" I asked myself. But I could perceive it was no dream. I hastened forward and Professor Wallace gave me a warm handshake.
"A very beautiful work, keep it up," he told me.

Every member of my class was struggling now to shake my hand. I suddenly became a local celebrity. I looked up into space and said:
"God! But you know I neither worked for this nor did I deserve it." It was one beautiful, unmerited favour. It was a sweet surprise.
Two days later, I got Alero's letter

Department of International Law,
University of Lagos, Nigeria.
12th December, 1967.

My dear Mayo,
I got your letter. I am so happy that you are doing well in your studies. As I told you, I found the Department of International Law here an exciting, intellectual environment. Professor Gower, a Briton, one of our teachers, makes Law so interesting. Jovial, humorous and brilliant, he makes International Law seem as if one is eating a rich, delicious breakfast.

Daddy visited me towards the end of last session. He was not satisfied with the security arrangement in the Students' Hall of Residence here. He insisted that I should live off campus and therefore bought a two bed-room bungalow for me at Yaba, just a kilometer distance from the university. I moved into the place three weeks ago. Six security officials are here with me (three work during the day and three at night) Mayo! I am back in my usual prison again. I can't do what I like. I love to live like the daughter of an average Nigerian, just like when we were in the primary school when no one hustled around me. But that unhappy incident at Toro had destroyed all hope for my freedom. I will regularly keep you informed of all the events going on here. Direct all your mails to the Department of International Law, University of Lagos or my residential address: 777 Allen Road, Yaba, Lagos.

I have an average of four lectures per day. I only have two lectures on Friday and my weekend normally starts at 12 noon that day.

Mayo, do not forget your promise. Do not get involved with any American girl or any woman at all. Keep yourself away from such wolves. It is a dangerous zone.

Mayo, I love you.
And I will ever remain,
Your Alero.

I read Alero's letter several times. She had never reminded me of my promise in any of her several letters. "Why is she reminding me now? Is she having a premonition? If not, why now?"

Throughout that day, I was unhappy because I had let Alero down. I had broken my promise.
"But is it really my fault?"
I didn't go out of my own for another woman. Circumstances beyond my control brought me and Irene together. I looked at the matter again. I knew Irene could not constitute any danger zone to me in any form. "She has her own fiancé, Lere Adams, and both are deeply in love." I mumbled.

By making love to Irene, I had only stolen briefly what legitimately belonged to Lere Adams and Irene had stolen briefly what belonged to another woman. As long as we did not over-do it, there could be no danger. On this note, I cheered myself up.

"Boy, there is no reason to be unhappy. There is no cause for alarm," I told myself.

CHAPTER FIFTY

I t was election season and every part of George Bowen University came alive. Two very popular law students were contesting for the post of the Students' Union President that year. Teddy Wood, a fantastic footballer who had won many laurels for the university and John Wilson, the son of a popular American Senator.

Teddy Wood, 6ft 3ins tall, very handsome, he was the former captain of the university football team. He had broad bones and broad shoulders, he was a well-built man. Teddy had a sexy frame a woman would love naturally. It was no surprise that many female students liked him so much. A consummate debater, Teddy was a brilliant student and a brilliant speaker. His father was a successful farmer from the State of Georgia.

John Wilson came from a very rich home. His father was a highly successful lawyer from the State of Alabama. He had been in the Senate for the past ten years. John 6ft 4ins tall was also a brilliant student and a good speaker. Proud and snobbish, his rich family background always made him feel that whatever he wanted, he must have.

Teddy Wood and John Wilson were white and both came from the south with a long history of racial discrimination against the black. Surprisingly, Teddy loved black people with passion. He was with Dr. Martin Luther King Jnr. during his historic speech: "I had a dream."
"I love Teddy. I love his person. I love his ways," I told Irene one evening.
"John Wilson is equally good. He has many leadership qualities and these are the most important things for the post of Students' President."
"How do you come about his qualities?"
"You know we are in the same faculty. John had served in very many committees in which I was a member. I know him very well. I know his stuff. I know his ability. I know of his burning passion for students' welfare. I cannot give my vote to Teddy where there is a man like John around."
"Why not?"
"Because I prefer him to Teddy in all things. And unfortunately, there is only one post."
"People say Senator Wilson, John's father belongs to Calhoun School of thought."
"Who is Calhoun and what about his school?"
"Calhoun was a racial bigot, a fanatical hater of Negroes and the originator of the infamous philosophy that 'it is right and legitimate for the white to live on the labour of the black people so that the white might have time to exercise their higher faculties of mind and soul."

"And why must we visit the sin of the father now on the son? Is that fair?" asked Irene.

"Why shouldn't we? Doesn't your Bible read that God will visit the sin of the father on the son, and even to the fourth generation?"

"Don't you read also in the same Bible that that rule had been modified in Ezekiel 18:20 where the bible says that only the soul that sinneth shall die, that the son shall not bear the iniquity of the father, neither shall the father bear the iniquity of the son?"

Irene and I were on this issue for about one hour. Just as I raised any point, she would immediately raise a counter point. She was not one person one could easily defeat in an argument. I didn't have this against her, rather I respected her for it. Since we were different individuals, it was only natural that we might not see things the same way.

It was two days after. It was 6.30p.m. most members of Andrew Jackson's Hall, my hall of residence were having their dinner in our beautiful dining hall. I was there. We were startled by a huge, unusual noise from the direction of the main gate of the hall. A roaring crowd was drawing nearer and nearer. Soon we saw a huge mass of people trooping into the hall. They were led by a young pretty black lady. She was Irene Roberts. They were all shouting the same slogan:

"John Wilson for President! John Wilson for President!!"

Within few seconds, the crowd took over the dining hall. Its leaders: John Wilson, Irene Roberts and two other young men mounted one of the high tables which they had suddenly turned into their rostrum. And Irene Roberts, dressed in a beautiful blue jean and blue blouse addressed the crowd in an aggressive, fiery language: She radiated feminine charm and charisma.

"Great Students of Andrew Jackson's Hall!

Great Jacksonites! Great, Great and Great Jacksonites!!

I am here to present to you this evening one of the few greatest men of our time, a man of marvelous resources, a natural-born leader of men, a tested and proven manager, a scientific and talented organizer, a man who knows your aspiration and your passion, a leader you can trust and who will never let you down, a leader who has the ability to bind the students together and motivate them towards a common goal, a man who can stand up to the stress and strain of the high office of the President, a man of sound moral and high integrity, a leader that is socially and emotionally mature, a manager with diverse capabilities. Great Jacksonites, I present to you John Wilson, the man you must all vote in as your New President."

A thunderous applause rocked the hall from one end to another. John Wilson stood proudly like a victorious general. He had a lofty stature and intimidating figure. He beamed out a warm proud smile. He radiated enormous charm in his beautiful, well-tailored three-piece suit. He spoke to his audience for about ten minutes. His speech was pungent and powerful. Thereafter, John left with his crowd for another hall.

I had done a good research on John Wilson since Irene and I had the heated argument two days ago.

The research revealed that John and one other student clubbed a black colleague to a comma when he was in a high school. The case went to court but he was freed on technical ground. Another finding revealed that he was an active member of the dreaded K.K.K (Ku Klux Klan), a secret organization of the white men opposed to equal rights between black and white people.

"Why should Irene become a campaign manager for this kind of man? Why is she behaving like a blind woman who cannot see those things around her?"

Teddy Wood Campaign Team told me the previous night that their greatest headache was Irene Roberts. "She is John Wilson's Power House. She is the group strategist. No matter how you plan, she is always one step ahead. She is simply unbeatable. With her with John, we may find it difficult to win in some of the halls. She is too formidable an opponent."

I made up my mind to talk to Irene and very seriously too. I went to her immediately I finished my lectures the following day. We talked for over an hour but Irene refused to concede any ground. I told her my findings about John which she could not disprove. She only replied with just two sentences:
"It is too late in the day to change my ground on this matter. I am irrevocably committed to John."
I stared at her face in surprise.
"How much does he pay you?" I asked.
"He does not pay me anything. But you know very well that I don't need his money. On the contrary, I am one of the highest donors to his campaign funds because I

believe in him. How much can he afford to pay me? What do I need his money for?"

"It is true you may not need his money. But there is a strong rumour all over the place that he sleeps with you and that is the reason why you have a very strong passion for him."

"And you believe that, Mayo?" she now stared at my face inquisitively.

"It is no longer whether I believe or do not believe. That is not the issue. The real issue is that John as at today is the one ordering your life. He is your controller. You do what he asks you to do. Everyday, you pursue his programme. You pursue it with the aggressiveness of a hungry lion. You may not know it, you are already John's robot. With this kind of scenario – what do you expect me to believe?"

At that juncture, I felt it was no use discussing further with Irene. The whole exercise was a waste of my precious time. I left her and walked back to my room.

I was getting ready to go to the Main Library the following day around 6.30p.m. when the porter phoned me through the intercom.

"Mary James and Anna Christian want to see you."

Mary and Anna are friends of Irene. "What do they want to see me for?" I was curious.

"Kindly send them in."

"Hi, Nice to see you pretty ladies."

"It's nice seeing you too Mayo," they replied.

It was Mary who opened the talk.

"What did you do to Irene?"

"I didn't do anything to her. Did she say I did something to her?"

"Mayo! You spoke certain things to her and what you said have been making her unhappy. She has been crying since yesterday. She did not eat yesterday night and she has not eaten today either."

"And what did she say I said?"

"Mayo! That is not the issue now. We are here because Irene has been crying for two days running and we want you to see her and talk to her."

"Assuming I don't want to talk to her."

Anna cut in sharply.

"You want to kill her?"

"Why should I wish to kill her?"

"If you don't, go and see her."

"Since I don't know what is making her unhappy, what do I tell her?"

"Look at you!", exclaimed Mary.

"You spent two days together in Baltimore and Irene came back behaving as if she was love-drunk. Or you feel she would not tell us? We are her friends. We know what is going on. You spoke to her in Baltimore and she came back behaving as if she were the richest woman in America. Go and speak similar words to her. You are a man, we do not need to teach you how to handle your woman. Please, go and make her happy. Mayo! You want to promise us that you will try?"

I stared at their faces inquiringly.

"I will try," I told them.

"That is nice of you."

After they had left me, I asked myself several questions:

"What did I tell Irene that is making her unhappy?

Why is she crying?"

I was with Irene fifteen minutes later. She was still crying when I got to her. I took her in my arms and started to pet her.
"You called me a whore. You said that John Wilson is sleeping with me."
"I didn't call you a whore."
"But that was the implication of what you said."
"Irene, my dear, let's forget about the whole matter. I am deeply sorry to have made such a foolish remark."
"Do you believe I am sleeping with John Wilson?"
"Irene, I say forget about it. I am withdrawing the statement. It was a reckless remark and I am not happy about it."

I brought out my handkerchief to clean her face
"I understand that you haven't eaten since yesterday. What do you want to eat now?"
"There is bread in the kitchen. I will take bread and cocoa drink."

I went to the kitchen, boiled some water and prepared cocoa drink for Irene. She sat on my laps, there she ate her bread and drank her cocoa.

"Mayo! If you don't want me to continue as the Campaign Manager of John Wilson, I will go and resign this very night."
"No, you don't need to. It is too late to do such a thing."
"Why?"
"Because many students will read strange meanings into your action. Let's leave things as they are."

"You want to tell me that you will be happy with me if I continue?"

"I will be happy with you. You have my support."

"You are sure?"

"Very sure."

Our quarrel was over. I now took her in my arms, spun her to face me. We stared at each other lovingly, then she hugged me. I wrapped my arms round her and kissed her. My kiss ignited fire in her and she responded and kissed me fiercely. Our bodies had been very anxious to be together again. I fastened Irene possessively to my chest as I started to caress her. My caresses became more and more intense, gradually she started to shiver in excitement as my caresses were thrilling her.

"Irene, your body is a bundle of delight. It is giving me a most intoxicating feeling I have ever had," I whispered.

My kiss and my touch left her more and more breathless. And since this was a night, I wanted to please her, I tried to communicate love to her by my actions. As Irene caressed the width of my chest and shoulders, desire flared through me and I lost myself in the wonder of her warm embrace … I made love to her until she was shivering. I screwed her really hard until she screamed and screamed, and screamed again.

CHAPTER FIFTY-ONE

Teddy Wood had a romantic figure. He had huge, beautiful hair and a fine face. His campaign rallies were colorful. That year, Teddy introduced musical innovations into presidential campaigns. A band of five men played fast soul music from behind. Young, pretty ladies, about forty of them, wearing beautiful T-shirts with the picture of Teddy Wood led Teddy's rally. They moved with amazing rhythms, they danced with measured steps, the beauty was overwhelming. Teddy's team, stormed each hall of residence like a tsunami. His fiery speeches were mesmerizing.

While Teddy had strong advantage in terms of colour and arrangement, John's advertisements were unbeatable. His name was on every lip. His promos were relayed every twenty minutes on the university local radio station while he flooded everywhere with beautiful bill boards and hand bills. It was a fight between two giants. The campaign lasted three weeks, then came finally the d-day, the day of the election. It was one Saturday.

Voting started as early as 7a.m. By 2p.m., it was over. The ballot boxes were moved to the Students' Union Building and counting of votes began at 4p.m. No one was sure of the outcome of the election. The turn-out of voters was massive. The two candidates were very popular. It was the hottest election ever held in George Bowen University.

There were eight halls of residence:

Andrew Jackson Hall

George Washington Hall

John Adams Hall

Thomas Jefferson Hall

John Monroe Hall

Abraham Lincoln Hall

Anna Eleanor Hall (Women)

Ellen Louise Hall (Women)

As the counting of the votes started in the Students' Union Building, Irene phoned me:

"We have done all what we needed to do. Our monitoring team had just sent in an intelligence report that John will carry the day with a good majority."

I gave out a laugh.

"Why are you laughing?", she asked me.

"I am laughing because I haven't seen greater clowns than you and your people."

"Mayo, this is a very authentic and reliable report."

"Since your reporters did not accompany voters to their voting rooms, how did the jesters come up with their findings?"

"We have our own method. We have our special techniques. But I cannot tell you now because you belong to the camp of the enemy. We have our own joker for this election."

"When are you going to play the joker?"

"We have played it already. Our victory is as sure as death. Have you forgotten that John Wilson is a son of a famous politician? He had been in politics before he came out of the womb. He is in a familiar terrain. He is not a mere Jonny Just Come like your man."

"In spite of your joker and your so-called techniques, I am so confident that Teddy will carry the day."

"Mayo, that is a huge joke. You want to take a bet?"

"I am ready to take a bet."

"I will give you 500 dollars if Teddy wins," said Irene.

"If John Wilson wins, I will also give you 500 dollars. Is any of your friends there to act as a witness?"

"Mary is here with me. Mayo, don't waste your money."

"Irene, please, give the phone to Mary."

"Hi Mayo! I am prepared to be your witness. I will ask Irene to put down 500 dollars right away. Send 500 dollars down immediately," ordered Mary.

"Mary, I will do so."

The votes of Andrew Jackson Hall were the first to be counted. I felt that Teddy Wood would win here. My committee campaigned here vigorously, going from room to room. I was shocked when the counting ended and John Wilson won with 56 votes.

Next was George Washington Hall. Teddy told me that this was one of his strongholds. I could scarcely believe my ears when John Wilson won here by 28 votes. In John Adam's Hall, John Wilson led with a comfortable majority. With the latest victory, the members of my committee became apprehensive for the first time.

"What's happening?" I asked Henry James, the Chairman of Teddy Wood Campaign Committee.

"Mayo! There is no cause for alarm, the tide will soon change. There is nothing to worry about."

It was now the turn of Thomas Jefferson's Hall. This was the hall of Bobby Jordan, a fanatical supporter of Teddy. Here John and Teddy had the same number of votes.

"I was confident that we would win with a landslide here," said Henry James who started to show some apprehension for the first time. Then came John Monroe's Hall, this was the hall of John Wilson. John took 80 percent of the votes.

The votes of five halls had been counted and Teddy had not won a hall.

"I am afraid, Teddy had lost the election," exclaimed Henry James. I stood there, shocked and unbelieving. I was too sad.

"We did all what we could. Our campaign Committee worked so hard. Why are we having this kind of result? What went wrong?" I asked Henry.

"My friend! I don't know. This is the exact opposite of what I was expecting."

"Teddy is a nice guy. He had put in everything into this election – vigour, courage, good planning, good execution. Where did we go wrong?" I asked again and again.

"I cannot recall any particular mistake, but in a game like this, one must win and another must lose" said Henry.

"Why are we not the one winning?"

"This I cannot explain," said Henry.

The counting of the votes of Abraham Lincoln Hall which started about twenty minutes ago, had been completed. I stared at the board. Unbelievable! John Wilson won again. John was going to get a landslide victory. He was now leading by 1707 votes. His victory was a forgone conclusion. I closed my eyes and I felt as if I were going to faint. I felt so bad. I could no longer stay at the counting venue. There was no need to give myself further torture. I decided to leave for my hall. As I was about to leave, John Wilson came out from one of the side rooms into a deafening applause and cheers:

"People's President! People's President!!" a tumultuous crowd yelled. John Wilson beamed out an electrifying smile and waved to the people to acknowledge their cheers.

"Ladies and gentlemen! What are we waiting for?" he asked, then he announced proudly.

"Victory celebration has started! Let the beer and wine begin to roll out."

Just that moment, the door to one of the side rooms opened. The room was packed full with beer and assorted wine. Each person took a bottle and the victory celebration spread from the counting centre and began to go into the offices of the Students' Union Building.

I had had enough. I left the counting venue. I got to my hall, it was dinner time. I settled down to eat my fried rice and chicken. But the food tasted sour. The election result had not only affected my mood, it had affected my taste. I packed my food and headed for my room.

As I was entering my room, there was a telephone call and I rushed to the corridor. It was Irene on the line.

"Mayo! How are you?"

"I am fine."

"Well, I am happy if you are fine. Just to inform you that celebrations are already on in the Students Union Building where the votes are being counted. John Wilson is going to have a landslide victory. I will soon be there—will you love to join me?"

"No! I have just left the place."

"You never told me that you would be there to serve as one of the undertakers of Teddy's electoral failure?"

"Irene, don't be a clown."

"I told you we had a joker. I told you that Teddy did not have a chance. I told you that he was just wasting his time, next time when I speak, I hope you will take me more seriously. Now, on a more serious note, I have one important information for you."

"Is it about your John Wilson or what about?"

"No, about a different thing this time. I will be going to New York City tomorrow morning and I will return later in the day."

"What are you going there to do?"

"I want to say hello to the father of Lere Adams. He is receiving treatment in one private hospital in Manhattan. Lere told me that he might be discharged in the next few days. It will not be nice, if I don't see him before he leaves for Nigeria. Of course, it will be an opportunity to know my future father-in-law. I haven't met him before."

"Irene! It is a necessary journey. Will you let me know when you are back?"

"Sure! Mayo! I will be using your money to travel and enjoy myself. Next time you won't take unnecessary bet, at least not on a green man in politics, a lad who cannot distinguish his right from the left."

"Bye Irene. Have a nice time," I dropped the phone and walked back into my room.

"Troublesome Irene," I mumbled.

Anna Eleanor Hall named after the beautiful wife of one of the greatest American Presidents, Franklin Delano Roosevelt, had 1200 female students. Ellen Louise Hall, named after the wife of another famous American President – Woodrow Wilson, the 28th American President had 1250 students. The votes from Eleanor Hall were the first to be counted and here Teddy sprang a surprise. He won 998 votes while John Wilson got only 202 votes. John was leading now by 911 votes. Then came Ellen Louise Hall. As the counting of votes was on, so also the gap between Teddy Wood and John Wilson began to close up. Each minute, each second, the gap continued to close until it remained just 300 votes and a terrified look appeared on John Wilson's face. John gave his bottle of wine to someone. He could no longer continue with it. He stood there, rigid and unbelieving. Many of the supporters of John jumping up and celebrating with bottles of beer and wine in their hands, moved back now to the counting floor, having been informed that the tide appeared to be changing. As the counting proceeded, the tension was growing. Gradually, the tension graduated into an anxiety as it remained just 200 votes for Teddy to catch up with John.

"What kind of phenomenon is this?" asked one of the supporters of John.

Like a man watching a complicated major operation on his wife, John stayed motionless. He seemed now like one caught up in a strange enchantment. There had been noises, jubilations and cheers all over the place, now a deafening silence engulfed the counting floor and that silence was spreading into all parts of the Students' Union Building and its environs.

Now it remained only 77 votes for Teddy to catch up with John and a substantial number of votes still remained to be counted. The anxiety of John's supporters was gradually turning into an alarm and serious mental confusion. Few minutes later, the alarm turned into a shock as it remained just ten votes for Teddy to catch up with John. Three minutes later, Teddy Wood closed the gap and he and John Wilson were now at par. John's eyes turned red, he was shaking.

Two supporters of John rushed to his side, and stood by him to give him support. But counting had not finished. John's body was sweating. Those supporters taking beer and wine, looked morose and worried. They held on to their bottles but they could no longer take their drink. Some stood rigid like the door posts. Those pacing up and down seemed restless and perplexed. Those who sat down looked worried and apprehensive. When the counting was finally completed, Teddy Wood had 1151 votes in that hall of residence while John Wilson had only 99 votes. Teddy Wood had won the Presidential Election by 141 votes. The shock was more devastating than a sudden hurricane.

I was in my room preparing the speech I was going to give to console Teddy, when I heard a roaring noise. The noise rose and fell like a turbulent, angry wave, "Teddy Wins! Teddy Wins!!"

There were voices everywhere. Even the trees, the shrubs and the grasses appeared now to be talking. I first ignored the noise but it was drawing nearer. Bewildered, I gazed through my window to find out what was happening. It was as if I had woken into an alien world. I saw a huge mass of people jumping up for joy in the front of my hall. I must find out the reason and so I rushed out of the room. I first mistook the shouts - "Teddy Wins!" to be those of mischief - makers who wanted to humour Teddy and make jest of him. And there were many such clowns around. I got out to discover that a genuine victory celebration was on. Most unbelievable. It was now the turn of the victorious Teddy supporters to be shouting and celebrating while John's supporters were too downcast to talk. Some ran into hiding. I didn't look for Irene. I knew she would not be feeling fine.

"Where were the jokers she talked so much about?"

CHAPTER FIFTY-TWO

I got 1000 dollars from Mary the following Monday - my own 500 dollars and Irene's 500 dollars. Teddy Wood was sworn in that morning as the new Students' President. The ceremony was colourful.

Irene was back from New York City.
"Lere's father was discharged from the hospital an hour after my arrival at the place. He embraced me warmly. I could see enormous joy on his face. He was so happy to see me. For minutes, he stared at me admiringly - then he said:
"Lere is just like me. I like beautiful women and he has gone out to pick a beautiful woman just like the one I picked few decades ago when I married my wife," he said.

Lere's father was considerably younger than the kind of man I was expecting to meet. He seemed like a senior brother to his son. He is a lovely character," she reported.
As I left Irene, I was so happy for her. But all her reports

made me remember Alero. I just felt like seeing her.

The year 1968 started brightly, but nothing in those early months suggested that it was going to be a trying year for me. I normally got a letter from Alero every month. That January there was none. At the end of February there was still no communication from Alero and I began to wonder why. I wrote her two letters - one directed to the Department of International Law, and another to her residential address at 777 Allen Avenue, Yaba, Lagos. By the end of March there was still no reaction from her. I was dying to hear from her, yet there was no letter, there was no information. Then April crept in, I checked my mail everyday and each day I left the mail box disappointed when there was nothing from Alero.

"Has Alero become too busy that she has no time to write me? Or has she engaged in a new romance and forgotten me? Am I no longer the numero uno in her life?" Series of such questions pestered me for answers.

Then May came in, gradually, the end of June arrived, there was no letter from Alero, I knew something serious must be happening to her.

"Is she sick?" Even on her sick bed, I knew Alero would endeavour to write me "What is happening?" My anxiety had now reached a fever heat. On the first day of July, I wrote four letters: two to Alero - one directed to her university address and the other to her residential address at 777 Allen Avenue Yaba, Lagos. The third I wrote to Alero's niece living in Coker Street, Mushin Lagos. She was to look for Alero and brief me on what was happening. The fourth letter I directed to Fidelis, my friend. Fidelis was to go to the University of Lagos and look for Alero or try to visit her in her Yaba residence.

"I want to know what is going on. Is Alero sick? Fidelis, I just must hear from you before this month runs out," I wrote with a lot of emotion.

Fidelis letter was returned about a month later - with the information that he had left the address and the new one was unknown. There were no replies to the other letters.

During those critical months, something happened to Irene that made me feel so happy for her. Once in five years, one student in the Faculty of Law was always selected for the Faculty Hall of Fame. He or she must be a student who had passed out of the institution or one of the current students. The person chosen must be a brilliant student. He or she must have made outstanding contributions to the Faculty. He or she must be a role model of some sort.

Irene could not believe it when the Faculty announced her name as the person selected for the Faculty Hall of Fame that year. It was a spectacular honour. It was conferred with a great ceremony. The Dean of the Faculty read the citation, my hair rose up. It was so beautiful. Barrister Roberts. Q.C. and Lady Roberts came from Nigeria to attend the occasion.

"As a father, I feel great. I feel so proud. I feel the same way I felt the day Her Imperial Majesty, Queen Elizabeth II of Great Britain, made me a Queen's Counsel, some years back," said Barrister Roberts to the NBC Reporter interviewing him.

"I never expected it. I am still wondering why the Faculty

chose me. But it makes me so happy. I am so overwhelmed and I am so humbled," said Irene to the reporter.

Irene suddenly became a celebrity. I was so happy for her. But Irene's success made me remember Alero again that evening. It was now nine months since I heard last from Alero. Everyday, I checked my mail and each day, I consoled myself when Alero's letter refused to arrive. The next day, I would rush back to my box and go through the mail anxiously only to discover that there was nothing from her end.

However, one afternoon, I had just had my lunch and was hurrying to the lecture room where Professor R.D Stone was giving a lecture on History of Political Ideas, when Alero's letter came at last. As I held the letter, my spirit ignited fire. I was so excited. I tore open the envelope. "Whatever might be the reason for her long delay, matters no more now. At last, she has written. That is the most important thing. At last, I am going to know what is going on," I mumbled.

777 Allen Avenue,
Yaba, Lagos.
Nigeria.
20th August, 1968.

My dear Mayo,
I know you would have been wondering why I kept quiet for so long. I know you would have been so anxious to read from me. I could not write you earlier because what I did is beyond pardon. I had made series of efforts to write you but I was unable because I couldn't just gather myself together and tell you what is going on. Since it will be a great sin to hold you

445

perpetually in suspense, I finally made up my mind to write you at last and let you know that I am carrying a baby for a man. I know you will be shattered by this information. I know you will be shocked. Mayo! I don't really know what has come over me. I hope it is not enchantment. I have been too much ashamed to let you know but it won't be fair if I keep the information from you indefinitely.

I have been a great disappointment. I have been a let down. Might be this is how destiny wants it to be. Do not attempt to write me or ask for me. I am already out of Lagos. I have gone with the man even though I don't love him as I love you. Do not look for me for there is no way you can find me. I am sure you will never forgive me. I am not also sure whether I can ever forgive myself. I never expected that our relationship will end this way. I can only advise you to take heart and forget about me. The chapter about me has closed. Though it may be difficult, try to accept it as so.

Yours sincerely,
Alero.

I read the letter over and over again. The weather was cold but I was sweating. A thick perspiration enveloped me and my fingers were trembling. I first believed strongly that this was a dream. Even five to six hours after reading the letter, I still believed that it was a dream. But towards mid-night that day, the reality began to dawn on me. I was more sorrowful than an old woman who had lost her only son. Alero had been my bride right from age of seven, together we had planned and nurtured the hope of a future life of honey and ecstasy. We had always viewed the world through the same lens. We had always operated on the same frequency. We had always looked at the distant future through the same telescope. Her ways and my ways synchronized in every respect because the bond between us was deep, forged in childhood, cemented by many years of intense interaction, and fired by our newly awakened sexual need for each other. I knew no man could play my role in Alero's life. Our separation was another love tragedy, a pathetic truncation of a marvelous and exciting journey, and a sad end to a beautiful drama. For three days, I could not attend any lecture. Thank God, Irene called on me around 6.p.m., the third day. I was in a bad shape and this she could see.

"Mayo, you are looking so terrible. What is the problem? Can I phone the doctor?" she asked me.
"No, please."
"What is the problem?
"There is no problem as such. I only wish to be alone. If I am alone for sometime, I will be able to sort out some personal problems and I will be all right again."

Irene was so worried.
"But how can I leave you in this kind of condition?" I stared at Irene for a long time. I did not want to share my problem with any one. It was a personal matter and I wanted to keep it to myself. But after she had sufficiently pestered me and shown much personal concern, I decided to tell her everything.
"I have a date. Lere Adams will be coming at 7p.m. to pick me and that is about twenty five minutes from now," she told me. Irene went to the telephone booth, phoned Lere Adams and apologized that that evening

date had been cancelled because of circumstances beyond her control.

"I have told Lere Adams not to come for me at 7p.m."

"But that is most unfair," I protested.

"What is unfair? I cannot leave you in this kind of condition and go out with any man. Mayo! Do you know how much you mean to me?"

"Your man will be annoyed," I told her.

"He has no reason to. In any case, if he is annoyed because of this, that is his own private headache. I cannot but attend to you and I owe no one any apology for doing so."

"Remember, he is your fiancé,"

"Yes I know that. Should I leave in distress someone that I also love so much and go out for personal pleasure? Can that be right?"

I was surprised that Irene could show so much concern for me. She quickly rushed to her room, prepared a light dinner and within thirty-five minutes, she was back. She forced me to eat using all kinds of feminine appeals. I had not eaten anything for the past three days. I didn't just have the appetite. Irene did not leave me until 10.p.m. that day. And when she was leaving, she had done so much to cheer me up and enliven my spirit. I stood up to escort her. As we got to the door, Irene turned round to face me, put her hands round my neck.

"Mayo! You are too lovely and too good. No reasonable person would subject a man like you to any emotional stress. That is most unfair. If certain people cannot appreciate you because they are incapable of appreciating what is good, I know I

448

appreciate you because you are a wonderful guy." She drew me closer, gave me a long, deep kiss. The next moment, she disappeared into the corridor.

"Goodnight Irene."

"Goodnight Mayo! Have a wonderful night."

CHAPTER FIFTY-THREE

The following day was Thursday and Irene phoned me early in the morning.

"Mayo! Hi! How do you feel now?"

"I am feeling much better. Thank you."

"I don't want the hangover of that unhappy incident to remain with you till Monday. I want us to talk, and this time in a more conducive environment, where we won't be disturbed. Mayo, if you don't mind, I want to take you out this week-end. And we won't be back until Sunday. Will you love to go with me?"

"Where are we going?"

"We are going to Clarksburg in West Virginia, that is our neighbouring state. I am taking you at my own expense. I only want you to make yourself available."

"Irene! I appreciate your kind gesture but I am feeling better already. There is no need for such a trip. There is equally no need for such expenses. As I told you, the worst is already over."

"Mayo! I insist because I need to talk to you. You have set a wonderful academic record in this institution.

You have built a reputation, and that reputation, nothing adverse must happen to it. I want you to get everything behind you by Monday and face the future with new courage and new commitment. I don't want you to look back, rather I want you to press forward for the prize of a very beautiful future, I see ahead of you. That future is not something that can be toyed with neither is it negotiable. Therefore, we have to talk. It is important."

"Okay, you have won. I have lectures up to 12 noon tomorrow when do you want us to start off? Is 3p.m. all right with you?"

"Yes, 3p.m. is all right."

Good! I will join you then."

New Paradise, where Irene and I chose to secretly spend the weekend was opened only a year before our visit. It was a 24-room hotel, small but it had a touch of class. The food and the service were superb. It was as if Irene came there for a fashion show. Irene's father was a highly successful lawyer. He had only two daughters: Irene and Medina, her sister. They were virtually venerated and over-pampered by their parents. Irene had gone for special shopping for this outing. All what she wore during our two day stay in New Paradise were "killer" dresses, specially designed and specially tailored. Her various beautiful curves came out in the superlatives. I saw her, I went crazy. We had dinner at 7p.m. and then retired into our room. I was watching a programme on the television and Irene went to the bathroom to clean her face. When she came out, I heard her footsteps and I turned round. Our eyes collided and the world suddenly stood still. I stared at Irene, she was irresistible. She was wearing a transparent pink gown with an open back. No brassiere – her breasts: roundish, ripe, rosy shot out and were pushing against her gown. As she walked towards me, the breasts shook and trembled. They stared at me and I stared at them. Their provocative looks would melt the heart of a man of stone, but Irene knew my structure was not made of stone. Irene rolled her buttocks then her hips gyrated. Jesus! She had beautiful hips. Her eyeballs rolled in a seductive manner as Irene's face beckoned invitingly. As she moved closer, I discovered she was not wearing anything underneath.

My system suddenly ignited fire. I had promised in my mind to be gentle with Irene. I wanted to take her through the joy of love-making slowly and gently. I wanted to explore every inch of her thoroughly and methodically this time since we were keeping two days in the hotel, I was not going to do things in a rush. I was not going to be violent with her. I had decided to put my fiery passion under control and taste and suck Irene's sweetness without hurry. I was going to enjoy slowly the hot, delicious honey inside her. I was going to dig gently into the mysterious depth of her secret pleasure, savouring all the flavours and allow the aroma to last a long time. But alas! This was not to be as Irene turned my entire system on at the same time. I gripped her like a wild Alsatian dog would grip an intruder. My passion was violent. I kissed her, caressed her gorgeous breasts and screwed her hard at the same time. The three actions went on simultaneously for minutes and I couldn't believe it, Irene also hungered for me this time with voracious appetite. She wrapped her legs around me as she pressed herself violently against me, drawing me deeper and deeper, as her motion became faster and faster, then she moaned. I picked up the pace, thrusting faster, harder and deeper. As my strokes increased, she moaned loudly.

"Mayo! Please! Please! You are driving me crazy."

I left her breasts, gripped her buttocks, held them tighter and drove myself upward, exploring now every inch of her delectable interior. Those buttocks suddenly went into endless shivering. As I slid in and out of her in a terrific speed, her pelvis danced and gyrated involuntarily. My manhood plunged deeper and deeper into her and she moaned and moaned with soft cry of pleasure. A moment later, she was lost in a sea of sensation.

As I drove harder and harder into her interior, her buttocks ached in an unending tremor of pleasure.

"Mayo! Hold it! Hold it! If you don't I will bite you," she cried.

She gave me weak, delicious bites on the palm and some other caressing bites on the plate of my chest. Her bites sent a searing sensation through my system. My male root grew wild. It became now terribly energized and I screwed her hard, then harder and harder still. Irene suddenly became violent as her buttocks quivered ceaselessly beneath me. She became terribly hot in bed. The bed moved and shifted as Irene groaned and groaned. She surely did not bargain for this as I screwed her hard, much harder than anytime. Suddenly, she cried out:

"Mayo! Mayo! Please! Please!" she begged out loud. She couldn't stand the almost unbearable pleasure. But the more she cried, the more delicious she became and the more I screwed her hard. We made love over and over again until sleep came to our rescue.

I was the first person to wake up around 1a.m. I stood up slowly from the bed because I wanted to use the toilet. As I came out of the toilet, Irene too had woken up. I joined her in bed. I embraced her, then whispered:

"Honey! Why were you always screaming during the climax of our love-making, while in actual fact, you loved what I was doing to you?"

She stared at me. She was so attractive as her seductive eyes explored every curve of my face. Just being too close to her was beginning to arouse my passion again

"Mayo! I don't know how to answer your question. But I feel there is no other way a woman could express the heat of joy during the climax of love-making other than to scream. But I understand that some other women express their feeling in some other ways. But most women always scream at the heat of pleasure."

"Screaming gives the impression that you are being hurt," I told her.

"Check your dictionary, it is also an expression of excitement."

"You always screamed that I should hold it whenever you were at the heat of your pleasure but I always ignored your request. In fact, I always did the opposite."

"Why did you?"

"Because I believe that what I was doing was the best thing to do."

"How?"

"To shorten the time of the unbearable pleasure cascading through a woman's system, the man had to become cruel temporarily. He must screw her hard, atimes harder and harder still. But what seemed like a cruel act was an act of kindness – done to shorten a pleasure that was fast becoming too much for that body to bear."

"Mayo! Thank you for the lecture but I must tell you that you can run a woman crazy. Just a few minutes in your hand, all my nerves will be rioting. All my cells will become love-drunk. I don't know how you do it, you are a terrible being. Whenever I see you, I want to run away from you but just few minutes after I will be feeling crazy to see you again. I am so much in love with your love-making."

Then Irene stared at my face.

"I had thought and thought about you and I came to a conclusion that the best thing for a woman is never to know you."

"And why if I may ask?"

"Because you will sufficiently run her crazy. A woman who loves to retain her sanity must run away from you."

"Irene, even if you want to run away from me now, it is too late for I am not going to allow you." I embraced her. I kissed her again and again.

"Your lips are beautiful and sweet," I told her.

We made love to each other that early morning. While Irene immediately fell asleep shortly after, I could not sleep. I remembered Alero. I remembered what she did to me. I wanted to cry. But inside a hotel room in West Virginia could not be an appropriate place for me to be crying in the middle of the night.

"Why must you cry over spilled milk?" I asked myself

"Alero had decided to go with another man. Her father had always wished her to marry a Prince - either a son of an Alafin or a son of Oba of Benin or that of the Sultan of Sokoto. He never wished a royal blood to be polluted with the ordinary blood of a commoner. Perhaps Alero has finally done the wish of her father. Why can't you close Alero's chapter in your mind and face the future?"

I stared at Irene. She was not a Princess. She did not have the glamorous shape of Alero but she was an attractive lady all the same. Her gorgeous breasts, her thick, lustrous hair, her beautiful, round face, her sexy hips made her look quite lovely.

The African "Okin" is the Queen of the birds. But if one cannot get "Okin", one can make do with the beautiful egret.

"Now Alero is no longer available, why couldn't I marry Irene? Irene is also pretty. She is brilliant. She is fast becoming a celebrity. Even if she does not fill the position of Alero fully, she is not a poor substitute. She is also a great woman in her own right. Her qualities are different but she is also a delightful lady," I mumbled.

I stared at Irene, she was asleep. I stared at her beautiful body lying by my side. The legs were straight and beautiful. The skin was good but not as flawless as Alero's. She had more flesh than Alero but she had it in the right places. She also had a pretty face. But I must confess that I had never met any woman whose face was as lovely and as angelic as Alero's. Of all women I had come across, Alero had the sexiest eyes. But Irene was also sexy and romantic in bed. Her love-making was as good as that of Alero. Her body was sweet. It was such a bundle of pleasure. She was one of the loveliest females in my university. She had wonderful eyes and when she stared at you, your system became instantly aflame. She had nice hips and when she moved, titling the pelvis in a sexy manner, she became impossibly lovely. She was a temptress. She could dangle any part of her body tantalizingly in order to get advantage over her man. She was a lawyer-in-the-making. She was witty and brilliant. No one could easily defeat her in any argument. Irene had many qualities. She would make a good wife.

Suddenly, I remembered that the lady by my side had come to that hotel to warm me just for two nights in order to get my bearing right again. She was just my lover, she had her own man, a future Medical Doctor. She loved me in bed but that was no guarantee that she would accept me as her husband. I remembered now that many respectable wives of great men usually submitted their bodies even to the chauffeurs of their busy husbands in the private because their husbands had little time for pleasure. They could easily give out their bodies for the excursion into the delight of the flesh, but their hearts, they never gave. The hearts still remained with their husbands.

I looked at Irene. She so much loved my love-making, but would she be prepared to give me her heart as she had readily submitted her body? This question I could not answer for her.

"Can I steal her from Lere Adams?" To confess the truth, I was so determined now to steal her. "I must possess her because I also like her," I affirmed quietly.

I made up my mind to propose to her and let her say yes or no.

"What is the appropriate time to make my proposal?" I asked myself and my mind gave a reply.

"Man, go from known to unknown. Make love to her in a most wonderful way, in a way more beautiful than anything you had done so far, set all her nerves on fire, excite her cells and thrill her the way no one could ever attempt to do. After she has reached the peak of her pleasure, ask her to marry you and see what happens."

The idea looked quite good to me. I went back to bed. I didn't touch Irene anymore. We had our breakfast the following morning and we went out to see more of the town. The sun was benevolent with its rays. It was a bright, lovely day; the sky a perfect blue. We soon got to the neighbourhood park and there, we decided to while away our time. It was Saturday. The park was full of young lovers holding hands. I saw many of them under the beautiful shrubs and flowers; talking, giggling and saying sweet nothings to themselves. There were many women and their children. The children were amusing themselves; some driving toy cars, others driving toy trains. We saw elderly men and women who could scarcely walk, who also came there for fun. There were many exciting things to see.

We had refreshments around 12 noon and Irene and I sat under the shade of some beautiful shrubs to relax. I looked at Irene, she looked so adorable. My mind suddenly asked me, "why wait till evening? Why can't you propose to her now?"

I did not know when I started to speak:
"My beloved Irene!
The lovely offspring of the famous and illustrious Roberts' family.
The proud generation of barristers.
A young, articulate woman whose speech will dwarf that of Demosthenes.
An orator, Cicero would see and applaud.
A serious attorney who mesmerized judges and jurists
The youngest woman ever to qualify for GB Law Faculty Hall of Fame.
My friend and my sweetheart.
How much I love you!"
I gave Irene a most admiring gaze. I wanted my speech to serve as a tonic and it did. One corner of her mouth curved upward in what seemed like a hint of a smile. She stared at my face with a fascinating concentration, then gave me a flirtatious smile.

"Mayo! What is the reason for all this citation? How do I deserve such eulogy?"

You deserve much more than my eulogy because I have discovered that I love you and I wish to ask you to marry me."

"You want to marry me?"

"Yes, of course."

"Mayo! You are not fair to me."

"How?" I asked her.

"You know, I love you. But why are you asking me to give you what you know I am not in a position to give?"

"Why are you not?" I asked her.

"Because I am already committed to somebody else. I am already committed to Lere Adams. You know everything. I never hide the facts from you. I recently went to New York City to meet Lere's father. I have been deeply involved in the family. Going back is not only impossible, it will make me look like an irresponsible girl."

"Has Lere formally proposed to marry you?"

"No, he hasn't."

"Now, look at that! If he is serious about marrying you, why had he not made a formal proposal since all these days?"

"Mayo! You don't seem to understand."

"If I don't appear to understand, then explain the situation to me."

Irene drew a deep breath. Her eyes widened. She suddenly became sweeter and prettier than before.

"I said Lere Adams has not formally proposed, but on

460

second thought, that may not be the correct way to present it. Proposals come in different forms. Some are made formally and they are verbal. Some others are made informally, they are channeled through acts, commitment, behaviours, steadfastness etc. Such are not made verbally but the deductions are there and are so clear. So I cannot say that he had not really made a proposal. For example, when a man takes a lady to his father and introduces her to him as the woman he intends to marry, what is that, if not a proposal?"

"Have you accepted his proposal?" I asked her.

"I have neither accepted nor rejected it."

"Do you feel you love me in anyway?"

"Yes, I love you," she gazed at me now without blinking and chose her words with deliberate care.

"You are a strong, handsome, virile man, an academic wizard, a genius in your field, a far more terrible genius in love-making. Which woman will not find you attractive?"

"If your assessment is sincere, why don't you marry me then?"

"If by any chance I had met you before I knew Lere Adams, I would have preferred you to him. The issue now is that of commitment. I am already committed to him. Much as I love you, I don't see the way out."

"So Irene, you can only give me your body while you give your heart to another man?"

"Mayo! Don't say that. You should know that there is nothing on earth I can't give you, if it is within my power to give. I never think that you can one day propose to me. I have not prepared for it. I never imagine it. I know how you feel. I equally feel unhappy too that I cannot give you a positive response. I bring you here to make you happy and refocus you so that you can face the future with all your commitments. I don't want anything to distract your attention. But I never imagine that the same me who invites you here so as to increase your joy, will turn out to be an architect of something that will make you unhappy.

Mayo! Kindly reason with me. I love you. That fact you should know."

Then Irene walked towards me and embraced me. She held on to me for a long time, her face now buried in the hollow of my chest. Finally she lifted up her sober face, then stared at my face.

"Mayo! I love you. But what you are requesting of me is difficult for me to give because I had already given it out to another man."

"Irene, I will never agree with you that you've done what you said. I rather love to give you more time to think about it."

She stared at my face again. I could read emotion and sympathy in her eyes.

"Okay! I am going to think about it. Promise that you won't hurry me. Give me a good time. But remember, I am not promising anything – but just enough time to think about it."

We returned to out hotel at 5p.m. We later went for showers. We went for dinner at 7p.m. and returned to our room. Irene began to check the different channels for a movie, finally she got one. I opened a bottle of champagne and filled her cup. I also filled my cup. It was a romantic movie, it was so beautiful. As we sipped our wine and watched the movie, I was getting warmer.

"Boy! This is your last chance. Make the best use of it," something told me.

I started to plan my strategy on how best to deal with Irene that night. I was going to be different from what she had seen or known so far. I made up my mind to be gentle with her for a change. I was not going to be violent in my love-making.

When the movie finally came to an end, Irene stood up, gave me a wink and a mischievous smile. I stood up and grabbed her.

"You this stubborn girl, you have beauty, you have brains. I love you."

My arms were now tightening around her. Then I whispered into her ear:

"You are a love-portion. I am not only going to taste you, I am going to devour you tonight. You are in trouble."

She winked at me. Then she started to tease me with that funny smile of hers. I caged her in my strong arms and forced her to face me.

"Haven't I warned you not to smile at me that way?"

"You did and what do you intend to do, now that I have broken your rule?"

"I am going to punish you."

I further fastened her to myself, then kissed her, I tasted her lips in soft, slow motion. Then, I gently stroked her nipples with the thumbs over and over and over. I was touching her now in her sweet places. Soon, she began to moan. Her excitement was rising higher and higher. A few minutes later, her buttocks were shivering and her legs were shaking. I touched her in the sweetest place of all, then she moaned loudly.

"Please! Please! Please!"

"Don't plead with me. I have told you that I am going to punish you."

All through, I was gentle with Irene. I placed her on the bed. I positioned myself between her thighs. I was not going to enter into her. I placed my thick, powerful and hot man-root on her clitoris. As I moved that hot, terribly energized man-root over and over her clitoris and the same rubbed and pleasure-massaged the clitoris ceaselessly, Irene went wild within seconds. Kissing her gently but never leaving her mouth, my fingers playing now with her nipples and my man-root gently rubbing her clitoris, each movement of the tip of my man-root over her clitoris, made her shiver and shiver and shiver. Her excitement mounted up higher and higher until her hips writhed ceaselessly under me, moving now on their own volition. Gradually, her body was no longer in her control as waves and waves of pleasure flooded her. But I was not going to leave her. As the tip of my man-root and her clitoris went over each other in an erotic massage exercise that had no end, Irene shuddered and shuddered until she was now shuddering without stopping. Her excitement mounted higher and higher still until the thrilling became unbearable and Irene screamed out in a Lagosian accent: "Ye! Ye! Ye! Mi ku o!" Meaning – Ye! Ye! Ye! This is more than I can take. Oh! I am lost." For some minutes, she became delirious.

She now talked in incoherent monosyllables like a person going crazy. Her hands tightened on my back, bringing me closer, wanting more and more of me inside her. Her urgency expanded and became all-consuming. She jerked and jerked and jerked against me with soft cry of pleasure. Still, I was not violent, but I didn't leave her. If I would ever take "yes" from

Irene, I knew this was the place where it must be settled. The battle to possess her would either be lost or won here, and I was determined to win it. My kissing went on. Never had she been kissed this way before: slow, deep and fierce. My fingers continued playing their magic with her nipples and my man-root rubbed and massaged her clitoris ceaselessly, pumping into her more and more intense pleasure until her body could no longer contain it. Her buttocks ached in a tremor of pleasure. It ached and ached and ached, now very violently. Suddenly Irene went wild.

"Mayo! Please! Please! Please!" she screamed in desperation.
"Do you love me," I asked her.
"Yes! Yes!", she gasped, my man-root massaged her clitoris more and more fiercely and her hungry hips shook and shook and shook and shook until Irene went wilder with passion. I pumped more and more pleasure into her system, and then asked:
"Will you marry me?"

The thrilling had reached its climax and Irene was about to go dizzy. But I didn't leave her.
"Will you marry me?" I demanded again.
"Mayo! Mayo! I ... I will marry you. Please! Please!! Please!!!"

She shook and shook and shook deliriously as her system exploded and Irene got her peace at last.
For many minutes, she clung to me as I continued to massage the lovely, smooth skin of her back. Finally, Irene stared at my face:
"I am a lawyer, I am going to take legal action against you. You got my consent under duress."

"My dear lady! I have your tape-recorded speech here. You are the one begging me there. You are the one saying: Please! Please!! That you wanted me."

I stared at Irene's face, then whispered:
"If you are not careful, I will take you over the whole exercise again."

Irene now stared at my face admiringly, then embraced me. "Your boundless energy amazes me. Your love-making fascinates me. Your strong, handsome virile body enchants me. Your kiss electrifies my system. Your style is intoxicating, it runs me crazy all the time. My God! Can I ever do without you? Everyday, you have a different technique. It is as if you have honey in your thighs. You are an intriguing, mysterious mystery. The more I get to know you, the more I get confused."
I held Irene in my warm embrace.
"Now, that you are going to be my wife, you will surely know me in full."

At the end of her course, Irene made a First class in International Law.

CHAPTER FIFTY-FOUR

I made a first class in my first degree. I was about to complete my master's degree in 1972 when Irene and I got married. After my M.Sc, I registered for a Ph.D which I obtained in 1973. I worked for a Department of the United Nation Organization based in Washington D.C between 1973 and 1974. Immediately after our marriage, Irene proceeded to the University of London for her L.L.M degree. When she came back from London, she set up a chamber in Washington D.C and started to practise. But Irene and I lived for only few months thereafter.

Marriage during the early years always has teething problems and ours was no exception. Irene was a brilliant lawyer but a stubborn wife. Alero and I would have made a better pair because we knew each other right from childhood. Very many years of interaction made us understand each other so perfectly. With Alero, our marriage would have been so wonderful because we actually got married at the age of seven. But things never work the way one expects and fate took Alero away and Irene and I got married.

Except in love-making, we were total strangers. But I was determined to make our marriage work. Almost everyday we had one disagreement or the other. But I believed that things would ease up with the passage of time. We were young and immature. We were both very stubborn. Each wanted to have things in his or her way. We argued a lot and we disagreed a lot. Our home was like a court room where there were arguments and counter arguments. Irene was not a woman who readily submitted to the leadership of a man and her legal mind made her worse. But I believed that this period of sharp edges would soon be over. We were indeed making some progress, but they were not yet over, when something very serious happened.

Olumide, my friend based in New York City, had repeatedly requested that we should come and spend one or two days with his family and one week-end was scheduled for the trip. We were to leave home that Friday at 7.45a.m. so as to take the Greyhound Bus that would leave at 8a.m.

At 7.50a.m., Irene was not ready.
"Hurry darling, or we will miss the 8 o'clock bus."

There was nothing offensive in that sentence or might be the way I said it was not pleasant enough. I must have irritated Irene.
"If we miss 8 o'clock one, then we will take the next."
"But don't forget that Olumide will be waiting for us at the scheduled point at 12 noon. Between

Washington D.C and New York City is a four hour drive. I don't want us to keep him waiting unnecessarily."

"Mayo! I don't intend to start this morning with argument and stress. If you feel you can't wait for me, you can go. We can always go together any other time. You can also phone him, that we cannot take off at 8 o'clock as scheduled, if you like."

"Darling! What is delaying you now?"

Irene did not answer my question, I couldn't see any possible reason for her delay except that Irene wanted to frustrate the arrangement I had made.

Irene came out of the room ten minutes later, she stared at my face accusingly and then queried:

"Why are you frowning?"

"Who is frowning?" I asked her.

"You! I have asked you to go if you can't wait. There is no reason to look like an hyena. You don't need to devour me."

"My dear! I told you that Olumide would be waiting at 12 noon at the agreed point to pick us."

"If Olumide doesn't see us at 12 noon, will the world come to an end? I have told you not to stress me unnecessarily. From the look of things, I am not sure that I will go with you."

"Why?"

"I must confess to you, I am not really interested in the trip."

"But why didn't you tell me this before now?"

I knew I had to soft pedal now and do some petting in order to make sure that Irene did not drop out of the journey. Surprisingly, the more I tried to pet her the more aggressive she became that morning. In the end, I decided to leave without her.

Olumide met me at the agreed point and took me in his car to his new beautiful apartment. I had only greeted the wife and embraced the children when the phone rang.

"Hello!" said Olumide who picked up the receiver

"Mayo! Irene is on the line."

"Hello darling!"

"I just want to tell you that I am on my way to Miami, Florida. I will spend the weekend with Mary and her husband. I will be back by air on Sunday evening by 10p.m. flight."

"But you never told me."

"No, I didn't. I had no previous plan to see Mary. But I suddenly discover that the home is boring. I don't see how I can stay here for two days without a partner."

"Okay. You say you will be back on Sunday at 10p.m.?"

"Yes."

"I will pick you at the airport."

Olumide had already asked me why Irene did not accompany me and I had explained that she had to attend to one client of hers.

The following day at 5p.m., Irene phoned me; she was nervous.

"Darling! What is the problem?"

"The weather people had just announced that Miami and some coastal areas of Florida may experience hurricane in the next few hours and many people are leaving the city."

"What do you want to do now?" I asked her.

"I don't know."

"Leave the place immediately if you feel it is not safe."

"Mary and her husband have assured me that their house is safe and solid and that I have nothing to fear."

"You are the best person to decide what seems reasonable to do. But if I were you, I will quickly proceed to the airport and take the next available plane back to Washington D.C. Whichever decision you take, is okay by me."

At 7p.m., I phoned Irene and she said she would stay till the next day. There is nothing to worry about," she told me.

It was the news of a strong hurricane hitting Southern Florida that woke me from sleep at 2a.m. From the television pictures, several streets in Miami looked like an open field where they had never been buildings before. The buildings had been uprooted and carted away. I hurriedly dialed Mary's line. The line was dead. I knew trouble had come. Bewildered, I rushed to Olumide's room.

"The fact that you can't reach Mary and Irene on telephone is not an indication that they are in danger. The strong storm would have disrupted cables and broken down dishes."

I tried to calm down. By the morning, the television reported that the death toll had reached 1600 people. Throughout that day, I didn't leave the telephone booth but it was a fruitless exercise to get Irene on phone. The second day, climatologists said the hurricane was over and I rushed to the airport. I took a flight to Miami. The City looked like Rome after the Allied Forces had uprooted the Germans there. I got to Mary's place; the building was gone.

"Where are the residents here?" I asked a bystander.

"First, check the refugees centre. If you don't see them there, check the hospitals."

I took a taxi, got to the refugees centre. I was asked to go through the register. The names of Mary and David Pearson and Irene Williams were not there. My body started to shake. "Where can they be?" I asked, dismay on my face.

"Check the hospitals;" an official told me.

I checked four hospitals. There was no clue. It was the fifth hospital that I found, to my greatest shock and dismay, the dead bodies of Irene and her hosts in the morgue. I didn't know what happened to me thereafter, I was told that I collapsed and fainted.

I was in the same hospital for three days. The burial took place a week later after Irene's parents had consented that she could be buried in the USA.

This unhappy incident happened in October 1974. The shock was the type that I decided to leave the United States of America for Nigeria to take up an appointment with the University of Kano. I vowed never to have female friends. The two terrible misfortunes I had so far convinced me that I should live my life without a woman.

CHAPTER FIFTY-FIVE

For over a year after my arrival in Nigeria from the United States of America, I did not go to Toro. Though my mother came to Kano to see me, I refused to visit her. The wound that Alero inflicted on my heart was the type that I felt Toro and I would for ever be parallel lines.

"Why must I go to Toro? What is my business there?" I always asked myself.

"Your mother, father, brothers and sisters are in Toro. You friends and relatives are also there. Why wouldn't you go to Toro to see them?" something always asked me.

"But Toro will remind me of Alero. And that is a name I want to forget. Alero is an open wound that has refused to heal. Why must I go to Toro and be reminded of the betrayal of the only woman to whom I gave my heart? Why?"

I never could answer those questions satisfactorily. I therefore thought that it was in my best interest to leave Toro alone. Surprisingly, I discovered that I still loved Alero. Even when I married Irene, I remembered her everyday and every minute. Alero never left my system. My passion for her remained as strong as ever. No wonder, as days and months rolled by, I felt like seeing Toro again. My loving native land was beckoning to me. My heart yearned for my people. The love for Toro was singing in my flesh. The curiosity to find out something about Alero and how she was faring, was equally burning in my heart, no matter how much I ran away from this very fact. So, in August, 1976, I decided to visit Toro after a long period of absence.

I arrived in Toro at 4p.m. only to discover that the town was in a festive mood. There were hundreds of cars of different shapes and sizes parked on both sides of the main road that went through the town. There were banners all over the streets and few strategic roads inside the town had just been given a fresh asphalt surface.

"What is happening?" I asked somebody. He told me that Princess Alero was burying her mother and had thus made the occasion a very loud one.
I heard various sirens ushering in many State Governors. I had seen expensive limousines of many ministers. I had seen the flashy cars of many Captains of Industries and Commerce of the nation. I stood there, immobilized by surprise.
"You mean Alero is the person who brought all these powerful personalities to Toro?" I queried.
"Of course, yes."
"You mean the same Alero, the daughter of Prince Matete?"
The man stared at my face curiously, then asked me:

"Are you a stranger here sir?"

"No, I am not."

"Then you should know better. You mean you don't know that the husband of Princess Alero, is one of the most powerful men in the nation? If you don't know that, then you deserve to go back to school and do some more learning."

I felt insulted. I therefore terminated the discussion and began to move.

"Princess Alero!" I rolled the name over and over in my mouth.

Now, Alero's story was becoming clearer. It was evident to me now that the man who lured her away was one of the most powerful men of the nation.

"Is he a politician or a businessman? What are his credentials?"

I wanted to know. I would have readily sworn before any god that it was impossible for Alero to leave me for another man, no matter how rich or powerful. Alas! Alero had gone for a greener pasture.

"Everybody has a price." I had always heard this saying again and again. The saying became so evident to me now.

Since Alero was in Toro, I became anxious to see her.

"Is she still attractive and beautiful? Does she still retain her cool elegance and indescribable glamour?" I wanted to find out.

I must also confess that I was desperately curious to know the man who stole Alero, my bride. I drove slowly towards the town's square where Alero was having a great party. I had not gone more than half a kilometer when the sound of heavy music rent the air. I looked around, many of the familiar streets had changed. New roads had been constructed in several places. New buildings had replaced some of the ancient shanties. I saw some known faces.

"Mayo! How are you? Are you back finally?" asked one excited relative. I stopped to greet him.

"I am back," I told him. "Where are you now?" he asked me.

"I live in Kano."

Nice to see you again. You are looking so radiant and handsome."

"Thank you."

I had to park my car. Ahead of me was a huge crowd. I heard the sound of beautiful music. It was Afro-beat. The air was ecstatic as the music came out with electric buoyancy. Inside the great Town Square, I saw a sea of heads. The crowd was thick and from now on, I had to struggle for each inch of the ground. In the centre of the square, I saw many people dancing. And there among the dancers was Alero, "my bride". I could not mistake her. It was the same and only Alero; the very Alero that I knew. The very Alero whose love tortured me for years like worries from ten thousand demons. I had known Alero as a young girl, then as a young pretty teenager, and later as a charming attractive lady, but none of the postures I knew could compare in beauty with the one before me now: the build, the gait, the hips, the face, the beautiful eye-lashes, the attractive dress, the lovely headgear – Alero was all glamour and sunshine

I stood there motionless; I stood in a frenzy of impatience while Alero danced and danced. I had never seen such a fantastic dancer in my life. Her body kept on shaking and meandering alluringly. The way she rocked her buttocks and swung her hips ignited an instant fire of poetic eulogy from the gangan-talking-drum.

Chief Ajai stared fixedly at Alero, his wife. Looking at Alero seemed like sipping a sweet, irresistible wine and Chief Ajai soon got drunk with Alero's beauty. He first started to spray her with naira notes. As Alero's busts thrust up invitingly, drenching the Chief in the sweet sexuality of her soft, beautiful body. Chief Ajai grew crazy. He brought out his brown portfolio, opened it and rolled out huge bundles of naira notes and started to "spray" Alero with the notes.

I stared at Alero and Chief Ajai with malignant concentration. Surprise held me motionless. I stared at the scene before me in disbelief. Gradually, I started to feel a rising anger.

I didn't know when I blurted out:
"So this is the man who lured Alero away with his money. This is the man responsible for all the pains and torture, I went through. This sad story must also end here on a sad note," I hurried for my gun.
"I am going to gun down Chief Ajai here and now and make him taste the bitter fruit of his action," I vowed.

I got to my car, took out my double-barreled gun from its boot and then hurried forward; now ready to commit murder but the ground held me motionless.
"Why must you become a murderer?" something asked me

"You want to take a man's life just because of a woman? No, it is not worth it."

I stayed motionless for minutes. In the end, I changed my mind. But my inner spirit which was talking to me, continued to pester me.
"Go back to the scene. Just go there! Be a man! Watch the bitter drama to the end."

I put the gun back into the booth of my car. I decided to go back to the Square. Alero was still dancing and Chief Ajai was still spraying her with more and more currency notes. My anger was growing. Every succeeding minute, the sight before me was becoming more and more unbearable but I resolved to stay. I didn't think of it but I just saw my hand drawing out one of my business cards from the pocket of my French suit.
"Young lady, please, help me give this card to Princess Alero; that woman dancing before Chief Ajai." (pointing to Alero). The lady, who must be about 14 years, took the card from me and she was about giving it to Alero when I recovered from my stupour.
"What if the husband takes offence? What if he demands to know why I am giving my card to his wife? What for?"
I was not prepared for any ugly show. As Alero stretched out her hand to receive the card, I melted into the crowd and took my leave.

❀❀❀❀❀❀❀❀

I returned from Alero's party that evening feeling disgusted with life. A thick avalanche of sorrow weighed me down.

"Why did I come to Toro to witness this kind of show? Why couldn't I obey my inner self and stay away?" For hours, I blamed myself.

I felt so dejected because one woman I knew to be innocent had fallen a victim of the Nigerian factor. I was unhappy that the Nigerian climate had changed the morals of one woman who had once been to me the epitome of moral excellence and ideals. I was bitter because a woman who could have been a showcase to African womanhood had lost her colour. When did Alero get it wrong? I got home and bade my mother and father farewell. I couldn't stay a minute longer in Toro.

"How? You arrived only an hour ago; why are you leaving us so soon?" queried my mother.

"I am on an official trip. I only look in to see you and find out how you are faring. Thank God, you and dad are doing well. I must make Kabba City tonight. In fact, if all things go on well, I will go as far as Lokoja. I will be back in Toro again in three months to spend a good time with you."

"But you can wait till tomorrow and start off in the morning," advised my mother.

"Tomorrow is Sunday. If I start off tomorrow, I won't make Kano by 6p.m. It is too far away. There is something urgent I must attend to in the office on Monday morning. I just have to be on my way."

My parents reluctantly consented to my departure. I gave them some token and I left Toro at 5.30p.m. Even if I had nothing important to do in the office on Monday, I wouldn't have stayed in Toro that night.

The truth was that I couldn't just bear it to stay in Toro after seeing Alero and her husband, Chief Ajai. I drove for about 150 kilometres, got to Ikole-Ekiti and checked into a hotel.

I had a light dinner after which I quickly went to bed. I knew that only sleep could temporarily relieve me of the sorrow that weighed so heavily on my heart. But I found to my dismay that I could not sleep. Alero's affair simply refused to leave my system. Its memory tormented me. As I rolled on my bed from side to side, occasionally looking at the ceiling above, I discovered that I could not find rest in that room. Jealousy was flowing through my veins and it appeared as if I were looking again at Alero, and Chief Ajai doing their own things in their own way. Now, many questions were pestering me for answers:

"Why did Alero renege on her vow to me?

Why did she abandon me when I needed her most?

Why did she forget our strong union at CMS School and the bond of love that held us together?

Why did she easily forget the numerous secrets we shared?

Why did she forget our common sufferings when our lives and fate were in jeopardy in the notorious Oro Grove?

How did she lose that love, that passion which made her cling to me on the day of my departure for the USA when she wept and wept without stopping?

Why did she easily succumb to the power of money as if money is everything? Why?"

The questions kept on pouring in but alas; I had no answers to any of them. I tried to forget Alero. I tried to shut her out of my mind, but it was difficult. The painful fact was that I still loved her. The more I tried, the more I fought to forget Alero, the more my thoughts strayed back to her.

There was something in Alero that I still so much loved. There was a magnet in her which continued to attract me and refused to leave me alone. Alero was one lady, shrouded in mystery, somebody who would for ever live in my dreams, a Canaan, dwelling in the realm of sweet imagination, one woman one would for ever desire and who one would never have, a nice, beautiful, ripe fruit dangling temptingly, looking so golden and so succulent, smiling and beckoning at one, and which would for ever remain beyond one's reach.

I looked back and I saw that all through my life I had struggled so hard and I had expended so much energy to have Alero, but Alero, had remained an enigma, a mirage, a sort of shadow or a vision in the night which would for ever lay beyond my grab. And so, in my distress, I queried:
"Why is life like this?
Why is life a shadow?
A phenomenon one can see but cannot grab?
Why is life elusive and deceitful?
Why is life so cruel?"

But just that moment, I remembered the immortal words of King Solomon:
"I saw under the sun:
That the race is not to the swift

Nor the battle to the strong
Neither yet bread to the wise
Nor riches to men of understanding
Nor favour to men of skill
But time and chance happen to them all"
(Ecclesiastes 9:11)

"So it is neither the struggle nor the effort that determines what will be. What will be, will be, in spite of all human plans and efforts, and in spite of all worries and anxiety. Oh! What kind of life is this?" I asked in despair.

CHAPTER FIFTY-SIX

I did not know that Wande, my sister was in Alero's party. She had been there few hours before I arrived at the place. She watched the drama that followed after I left. As I got to Kano and entered my flat, the telephone in that room rang. Wande was on the line. She narrated to me what happened after I left Alero's party. Below is her story:

"I saw you when you sent your business card through one young lady to Alero. Alero looked at the card, took three hasty steps forward, held the young lady who gave her your card and queried:
"Where is he? Where is the man who asked you to give me this card?"

The lady looked around anxiously.
"I saw him here just now. He was standing right here by my side," she replied.
"When did he give you the card?"
"Just now."
"Then, he must certainly be in this crowd," asserted Alero. She walked quickly out of the dance floor, looked around nervously. But you were no longer in

the crowd and I wondered how. It took me some minutes before I knew you had gone. Wearing a worried look, Alero could not hide her uneasiness. Chief Ajai, her husband, hastened to her, held her by the waist.

"Darling! What is the matter?"

"My dear, somebody sent this card to me just now (showing it to him). I understand that he is in this crowd. He is a friend I have been anxious to see for some years."

"But it is wrong to leave the dance floor abruptly as you have done. Protocol does not permit you to leave your guests that way. You are the hostess, have you forgotten that?"

"How can I forget?"

"Then all other things must certainly wait till the end of the party."

"Darling! I am sorry this one cannot."

Chief Ajai then stared at her face, confused. Alero did not even wait for any further discussion. She was already on motion: still anxiously looking for you inside the crowd.

"I just must see him. I must talk to him," she asserted. Anxious and worried, she stared around, but you were no longer in the crowd. I was equally worried as to your whereabout. All this time, Chief Ajai was trailing Alero, his wife with his eyes. Finally, the husband must have got fed up as he hurried to her again:

"Darling! What do you think you are doing? You walked away in the middle of a very crucial dance without an excuse from your guests. You left everyone curious as to what is happening to you. What kind of behaviour is this?"

"My dear, please, try to understand. I just must see the man who sent this card. He is around and I must find him."

"How can the man in question suddenly take precedence over and above this party? How can he become more important than your guests?"

"Chief! You don't understand and you are not helping matters."

"How?"

"I left the dance floor and you also left the place. Is that right?

Please, go back and attend to the guests on my behalf. I will join you in a moment."

Chief Ajai still wanted to protest further but Alero had left him. The Chief walked back to the dance floor. Alero, now holding the hand of the young lady who gave her the card, searched through the crowd. After about five minutes, she was satisfied that you were not in that crowd.

"Where is he? Where has he gone to?" She stared at the young lady's face; the lady looked frustrated.

"Why must I put myself in this trouble?" the lady mumbled.

Still agitated, Alero turned to the lady again and queried:

"How did the man look like?"

"Tall, handsome with heavy hair;" she replied, looking very nervous.

"That is Mayo. He must have gone to his father's place. I will try to meet him up in the place when the party is over."

Alero walked back to the dancing floor; she was now a different woman and looked absent-minded.
"Did you see the man?" queried Chief Ajai.
"No, I didn't. But I guess where he could be and I will try to check him in the place later."
"Who is this man? And how is he to you?"
"Darling! I have already told you he is a friend that I have not seen for very many years."

By now, many of the people dancing had retired to their seats. The music had not stopped but the tempo had gone down. Guests were still being served by waiters in scarlets. Chief Ajai and Alero, his wife, started to go round the guests, thanking them for gracing the occasion with their presence. Thirty minutes later, the party was over and I left the place.

I had just spent about ten minutes at home when Alero drove into our compound in a beautiful limousine. She met mama outside the house.
"Mayo left about 20 minutes ago," mama told her.
"He said he would either sleep at Kabba City or Lokoja tonight and take off from either of the two places tomorrow morning." Mama, who was ostensibly bewildered, further explained:
"I asked him to spend the night in Toro with me but he said he could not. He explained that he had one important business to transact in the office on Monday, and for that reason, he had to leave."

Alero stared fixedly at mama's face as she exclaimed:
"That means there is no way I can see him today?"
"I really can't see the possibility, my dear," said mama.
"Thank you ma." Then Alero turned to her driver:
"The man I am looking for left only 20 minutes ago.
If we pursue him, we should be able to catch up with
him; don't you think so?"
"Not really, Madam. There are three possible routes
he could take to Kabba City; we don't really know the
particular one he took and since there is no way we
can resolve the issue here, that makes running after
him a most unrealistic venture."
"I feel I agree with you," said Alero who sighed in
frustration.

I listened to Wande's story but I could not explain
why Alero was so anxious to see me.

I left Kano City the following Monday morning for
an overseas trip. When I was back two weeks later,
Fatima, my secretary reported that one woman
called Alero phoned me from Lagos shortly after
leaving the office.

"Dr. Williams left the office five minutes ago," I told
her.
"When will he come back? Do you have any idea?"
"I am afraid he will not be back in the office in the
next two weeks. He is gone out of the country. He is
delivering a lecture at Makerere University, Kampala,
Uganda. Immediately after that, he would leave

Uganda for India where he would be delivering series of lectures at the University of Kerela."

Do you know the telephone number where he can be contacted at Makerere or Kerela?"

"No, I don't."

"Thank you very much."

"You are welcome."

CHAPTER FIFTY-SEVEN

It was my first day in the office after my overseas trip. As I sat behind my table reviewing Alero's matter, my mind suggested to me why she was so anxious to see me. Conscience had not allowed her to rest and she wished to apologize to me for all the wrongs she did.

"Do I really need her apology? What benefit will that apology serve anyway?"

I had earlier believed that Alero made a mistake. In her last letter to me, she said that she had gone with the man whose baby she was carrying even though she didn't love him. Seeing Alero and Chief Ajai, her husband, I was sure that I had never seen a more beautiful couple, living an idyllic life; filled with parties and many beautiful things. Alero had certainly gone for a greener pasture. But why did she need to deceive me? Why couldn't she tell me the truth, point blank, that she got a billionaire and had gone with him?

It was now four months since I arrived from India. I had just finished my last lecture for the day and I was hurrying to my office when the postman handed over to me a letter. On opening it, it was an invitation card from one person I least expected it. The card was from Alero, the Princess of Toro. Her younger sister, (Desola) was getting married about a fortnight and inside the card, Alero wrote:

"Mayo, I got your business card. I am so excited. Are you now in Nigeria? If so, how long have you been in the country? I am very anxious to see you. Please, do me the favour of attending this marriage ceremony."

I read the last two sentences over and over again. After her let-down and betrayal, why is Alero anxious to see me? What for? I thought and reflected on it. I could not hazard a guess. Whatever might be her reason, a fortnight later, I was back in Toro. The engagement, that is, the ceremony preceding the formal marriage of her sister, took place that evening, I was there.

Alero's figure looked so fresh and youthful. She was not as slim as before but she was so pretty. Luscious, dark, juicy and flamboyant, there is a regal air about her. Her sister: Desola, was a replica of her. She was attractive and good-looking. After the traditional ceremony in which the family of the bride-groom-to-be, presented honey, kola nuts, wine, yams, etc to the family of the bride, Alero invited me, her brother and the couple-to-be into a private session. I did not know what qualified me to be there; neither did I ask question. But I still remember now that Alero invited me, and I accepted the honour without thinking a second about it.

It was a warm, luxurious room. The paneling showed exquisite workmanship. Dele, the groom-to-be was the first to take his seat. Tall, slim with a slightly pointed nose and big eyes, he was a handsome young man. He read Law at University of Lagos and had just completed a year of National Service. Desola joined a few minutes later and they both sat staring at us.

Then, Alero suddenly turned to me, and smiled. It was one of her usual, old, disarming smiles.
"Mayo! I want you to pray for this young couple-to-be. That is why we are here."
I stared at her blankly.
"But you know I am a teacher, I am not a pastor."
"Yes, I know. But you are the one who must pray for them."
"Why?"
"Spare me that question. Just go ahead and pray."

Then, I asked Desola and Dele to kneel down, placed my hands on their heads and I blessed their marriage. All through that day, I was in Alero's place. About 9p.m., I felt it was time for me to go to my father's place and rest for the day.

As Alero escorted me out of her house, I surveyed her compound it was beautiful. The exterior of the building was a masterpiece of architecture, elegant and graceful.
"This building was completed only a week ago," she told me.
"It's very beautiful." I replied.

She held my hand, just the way she always did when

we were in love. We walked towards my car. We soon got to the car and stopped. I rested my back on the driver's side and faced Alero directly. She now stared at my face as she gave me a slow, lovely, understanding smile. I smiled back but inside, I was boiling.

I looked at this glamorous, pretty woman who betrayed my trust and messed up my life. She was terrific. I could not ignore the fact that Alero was extremely attractive. But what she did to me, I could not forgive. As I stared at her again and again, anger was surging inside me.

"Why should anyone deprive me of this one woman I laboured so hard to have? Why should Alero abandon me midstream and go for another man?" I asked myself. But much as I tried, I could not answer those questions. My internal structure was rioting, but on the surface, I maintained a cool, pregnant calm.

"Alero! I haven't seen Chief Ajai, I mean your husband since I arrived here."

"He is not around today but he will be at the marriage ceremony tomorrow. He has one business engagement in Kano State today and that is why you don't find him around."

Just that moment, I remembered the young boy I saw when I was asked to pray. I suspected that he must be Alero's son. He had a fine face. He also had large, lovely eye balls. He was very handsome.

"That would have been my son," I mumbled.

But this woman deprived me that opportunity. I remembered that blood was racing through my body all through the time the boy was around.

"Where do I begin? How do I talk to this woman who has inflicted a wound on my heart, a wound no doctor can heal?"

I was still thinking on how to begin when strangely, I found my self talking:

"Alero! I saw your son, charming little boy, just like you."

"My son?" she queried, surprise now on her face.

"Yes, your son – very beautiful boy."

"I have no son."

"What of the one I saw with you?"

"He is not my son. He is the son of my niece."

"But what about your own baby?"

"My baby?" queried Alero.

"Yes, your baby."

"I have no baby yet," replied Alero.

"What of the one you talked about in the letter you wrote to me?"

"Did I ever talk about a baby in any of my letters?"

"Yes, you did in a way. Don't you remember that you wrote to me in my third year in the university that you were carrying a baby for a man?"

Alero raised up her lovely eyebrows, stared at me fixedly and then queried:

"You said I wrote you that I was carrying a baby for a man?"

"Yes, you did."

"Which man? How?"

"How am I to know? You are the one who should tell me."

Alero stared at my face again as her eyes widened now with surprise.

"You said I wrote to you that I was carrying a baby? Why do you need to tell such a lie? What for? Since you left me and now, I had not been pregnant even for one second. How could I write you then that I was carrying a baby? How could I write you about an event that did not happen?"

I stared at Alero's face, nothing could be more amusing than her current drama. For some seconds, I did not know what to say. "Is Alero suffering from memory loss? Or what is her problem?"

"Alero! Why are you denying your own letter? Do not tell me that you can no longer remember past events very clearly? You are certainly too young to suffer from amnesia. Even that kind of excuse, I won't take. Such technique won't work with me. No, it won't."

"What technique? Who is denying her letter? And which letter? Now, look here! I am not suffering from any memory loss. My own ancestors never suffered from such a disease."

"Alero, that is okay. Really, there is nothing to quarrel about since I have the letter here. If you see your own writing, I am sure you will recognize it. When you read your own letter, you will certainly remember what I am talking about."

I hurried to the boot of my car, opened it and brought out Alero's letter out of my portfolio.

"That is your letter," I gave it to her "Since 1968, that letter had always accompanied me wherever I went."

Alero took the letter, examined it, later she started to read it. When she finished reading, she glared at me fixedly. Her eyes now glowed like red charcoals. Her hair stood on end as she bellowed in anger:

"I am not the writer of this? I don't know anything about it. Where do you get it from?"

"Alero! I won't take that from you. No, I won't. That is your writing. I can never mistake your writing even in my sleep. Why are you denying the obvious? Why are you denying your own act?"

"I am denying nothing," she screamed. She suddenly grew wild.

"Mayo! What kind of joke is this? What kind of game are you trying to play? You want to play on my intelligence? What do you take me for? A fool or a nonentity? I can guess what you have done, and I am amazed that you can do such a thing."

"What have I done?"

"Why are you asking me? However, to let you know that your game is off, I am going to show you now what you did. You impersonated me and wrote a letter to yourself that I, Alero, was carrying a baby for a man. And you still have the effrontery to bring the same letter to me. This is a strange joke, it is outrageous."

"Alero, please calm down."

" Why should I calm down? Calm down in the face of your naked mischief? Calm down and listen to more fabrications and more lies?"

I stared at Alero. Her reaction was most amazing. I knew the reaction was sheer bold face and a bravado of a pretender. It was a clever strategy to do a cover-up but I was not going to allow her to escape with it.

"Look here!" I told her firmly, but Alero bellowed:

"Hold it! I say hold it! Why must you impersonate me and write to yourself that I, Alero had gone with another man? Which man? Where is he? Where does he live? For God's sake, what are you trying to insinuate? What is your aim? Why must you fabricate such a wicked lie? Why?"

I wanted to talk but Alero screamed more loudly.
"Hold it! Your impersonation is just the least of your sins. When you made up your mind to marry another woman, why couldn't you inform me? Why didn't you show me simple courtesy and write to me that you were no longer interested in me and allow me to go my own way? Rather than do that, what did you do? You shamed me before my colleagues. You turned me into an object of ridicule. You made me a laughing stock among my fellow students."
"How? In what way?"

"You sent to me a Gossip Magazine of your university where my friends and I gathered the information that you were no longer interested in me and you were getting married that week to another girl. That was the method you chose to inform me that our friendship had come to an end. You humiliated me. You disgraced me publicly. You made me an object of derision. My affair became the subject of hot, juicy gossip throughout the entire university community. Everywhere I went to, people were always whispering behind me. For months, I hung my head in shame. I never knew that you were such a cruel, inhuman and unfeeling brute."
Alero broke down and started to cry. Her body shook and her fingers began to tremble. I moved forward quickly to hold her.

"Don't touch me!" she screamed wildly.

"Okay! That is enough. Please, calm down. You may not believe me, but the fact of the case is that I don't know anything about the magazine you are talking about. I can't remember sending to you any magazine."

"How will you remember? If you have any feelings for me, won't you remember?"

"Alero, you certainly know that I have feelings for you. I can never do anything that will either ridicule or disgrace you. That is impossible."

"What is impossible. I have the magazine I am talking about in that house. I brought it from Lagos, hoping to show you how heartless you became when you got to America."

"Can I see it?"

"Why not?"

Alero in anger left me and hurried to her house. She came back about three minutes later, holding a magazine and threw the same at me.

"That is your magazine," she told me. I looked at it, it was a copy of the Scorpion, the Gossip Magazine at George Bowen University. I glanced through it hurriedly and there at the centre page was the joint picture of Irene and myself, and below the picture - the phrase - ABOUT TO WED, and a small write up:

'Mayo Williams, a student of Political Science will be taking Irene Roberts, a Law student of this university to the altar next Saturday'

I looked at the magazine again and again, I was seeing the copy for the first time. I had never seen it before.

I was a member of the Editorial Board of the Scorpion all through my university course and I was sure that there was never an edition that carried my photograph and that of Irene. I looked at the serial number. It was not the usual Scorpion's number. The colour was slightly different from that of the normal Scorpion Magazine. This edition in my hand which said Irene and myself were getting married that week was published in August 1968 and Irene and I got married in 1972. That 1968, Irene and I were casual friends, no more. "Who is the author of this? Who is playing this prank? Who could have published the Scorpion in 1968 and indicated there that Irene and I were about to get married, when in actual fact, there was no such plan? Who did this and for what purpose?" I queried. Meanwhile, Alero stood there staring at my face, reading my eyes and reactions, an insolent grin on her face. The venom cruising through her system was growing bigger by minutes. Finally, I turned to her.

"Alero! I don't know anything about this magazine. As a matter of fact, I am seeing it for the first time. I haven't seen it before. I was definitely not the one who sent it to you. I must admit, however, that there is a Gossip Magazine called the Scorpion at George Bowen University but the colour of its cover page is different from this one. It also carries a different serial number. I suspect, and very strongly too, that this is likely to be a fake copy of the Scorpion Magazine. The layout and the arrangement lack the professionalism of the Scorpion. All these reinforce my suspicion that this is not a genuine copy of the Scorpion." I then stared at her face and asked:

"How did you get it?"

"Mayo! Do not ask me that foolish question. The magazine was posted to me from the post office of your university, George Bowen University, Washington D.C. Look at its back and look at the postage stamp. Apart from you, who else knows me in Washington D.C.? Who in Washington D.C. knows my address? Who could have posted a magazine to me from George Bowen University other than you? No one knows me there except you. Or could the magazine have dropped from the sky then? Telling me that you don't know anything about it is most insulting. I am not going to accept that. If you don't know anything about it, who then knows? You don't need to treat me like a fool. In any case, I am not one. Please, please, stop the foolery. I haven't got time for it."

"Alero! If I were the person who sent the magazine to you, I won't deny it. Believe me sincerely I don't know anything about it. I am seeing this publication for the first time. I haven't seen it before. Please, trust me on this!"

"You don't know anything about what? Jesus!" she screamed.

"Alero, I won't tell you a lie. This magazine makes me begin to suspect now that perhaps there may be a third party to this matter. I am beginning to feel that this may be a product of one mischief-maker."

"Who can that mischief-maker be other than you?"

"Alero! Please, please, exercise some patience. I smell a rat. There is something fishy going on. This letter I gave you and which I believe you wrote, you said you were not the writer. This magazine, you believe I sent to you, I am seeing it for the first time. I had never seen it before. I was not the one who sent it to you.

Something strange is going on. This is so clear and so obvious to me. Since I was not the person who sent this magazine to you and somebody else in Washington D.C. did – who was that person? Who? This is a question we must jointly find answer to. We need to find out the person who sent it to you. And if you can exercise some patience, we may have a clue."

For several minutes, I stood there rigid, confused and bewildered.

"Who could have printed a fake copy of the Scorpion in 1968, putting the joint picture of Irene and myself inside it as two people about to wed, and sent the same to Alero from Washington D.C.? And for what purpose?" I asked myself.

I tried hard to unravel the mystery, but I could not. But just the moment I wanted to tell Alero that I had no clue, I looked again at the letter written to me from Lagos, Nigeria, which claimed that Alero was carrying a baby for a man. The letter was dated August 20, 1968 and the magazine sent to Alero from Washington D.C. was also published on August 19 1968 – the same year, the same month and the same week. While the letter was posted from Lagos on August 22, the magazine was posted from Washington D.C. on August 21, just one day apart. I now asked myself:

"Why were both programmes executed the same year, the same month and the same week and almost the same day? Can there be a connection between the two?" I tried now to examine both documents more carefully.

There appeared to be a common motive in the two, and this I could see so clearly now. The fake Scorpion

Magazine was sent to Alero to deceive her and make her believe that I had married another woman. And this in 1968 when I neither had an intention nor a plan to marry. The letter which said Alero was carrying a baby for a man was also written the same time apparently to deceive me that Alero had already gone with another man. Alero claimed rigorously that she was not the writer of the letter, neither was she pregnant at any time, and I had no reasons to doubt her words. I then concluded that the letter and the magazine were carriers of false information. The letter was sent from Lagos the same week the Scorpion Magazine was sent from Washington D.C. The two were targeted at the same thing: to destroy the relationship between me and Alero. The two programmes were executed the same week. With these facts, it became so obvious to me that the same person must have been behind both dramas. "And who is the person?"

CHAPTER FIFTY-EIGHT

All through, Prince Matete, Alero's father, insisted that Alero, his daughter, must marry a prince.

"For Alero to marry someone from a lower class, that will not happen as long as I live," he vowed.

When Alero was becoming emotionally attached to me at the age of 13, the father took prompt action to send her to Ghana. When she came back from Ghana, she had blossomed into a rare, pretty lady, dazzlingly beautiful. The father told her that she must marry a powerful prince, Lo and behold! A tall, brilliant architect, a son of Oni of Ife Kingdom and a handsome young lawyer, a son of Oba of Benin Kingdom, two great princes from two famous kingdoms in Nigeria were pestering Alero for marriage. The father was so happy. But that joy was short-lived.

"I will either marry Mayo or no man," Alero insisted.

"No one here will permit you to take such a crazy decision, my girl. Never," Prince Matete ruled imperiously.

But when Oro people abducted Alero when Prince Matete was away in Lagos, and they would have killed her, but for my timely intervention, the father was compelled reluctantly to change his stand.

"A young man performed this great feat! Went to Oro Grove to free Alero! Unbelievable! Most unbelievable! Where did he get his courage from? What gave him such terrible audacity? Mayo had more than demonstrated by this unusual bravery that he deserves the hand of Alero and I concede to him that he can marry my daughter," he told his family.

I could see clearly now that that concession was a ruse. Prince Matete had kept quiet for sometime only to strike decisively later, and separate me and Alero, his daughter. I was too sure that his hand was behind both dramas. No other person could have done so.

I held the fake magazine in my right hand, and on the left, the letter which claimed that Alero was carrying a baby for a man. I had become hundred per cent convinced now that Alero was not the writer of the letter. Something told me to study both documents carefully. I knew I would soon have a clue to show to Alero that her father was the masquerade playing all the cunning games on both of us. But just that moment, my eyes wandered to the joint picture of Irene and myself at the centre page of the magazine and I recalled that moment that it was the same picture Irene and I took in a hotel room in Baltimore. Only two copies of the picture were produced. Irene took one and I took one. Since I was not the one who placed my copy in the Scorpion Magazine sent to

Alero, the only other probable person who could have done so was Irene. That moment I knew right away that I had got an important breakthrough. My suspicion was further buttressed by one other fact: in the entire George Bowen University Community, apart from me, only Irene knew anything or had heard any information about Alero. Irene was the only person in Washington D.C., I spoke to about Alero. She was the only person who knew that I had a fiancée called Alero, and who was a student of International Law, University of Lagos, Nigeria. With this additional fact, I did not need to do any further search as to who printed the fake Scorpion Magazine or who arranged the joint picture of Irene and myself to be placed in its centre page or who sent it to Alero. Irene was the person. The facts were so clear to me now.

"Alero! I have got a clue," I announced. "Irene, my late wife, is the masquerade playing all the tricks. I have got her. She was the person who sent this fake magazine to you; and I suspect very strongly that she was also the person who wrote this letter, saying you were carrying a baby for a man." I spoke calmly to Alero, but internally, I was boiling with rage. This discovery shocked me. It shook me like a violent earth-tremor. My fingers started to shake because the anger surging through me was too heavy for my body structure. That Irene could do this much, baffled me.

"Most incredible! Just incredible," I moaned. I did not know how my emotion swelled up and ran out of control as I suddenly bellowed:

"Irene had ruined me. Why did she do this to me? Why did she embark on this kind of terribly devilish game? God! Why did you allow this? Why did you allow her? What is my offence? God! I say what is my offence?" I screamed.

I broke down and started to cry. Alero first glared at me. "Isn't this another gimmick?" she must have asked herself.

But when I did not stop crying, she moved forward and held on to me:

"Mayo! You are a man, please, behave like one." I heard her. I heard her pleas. But I couldn't just stop crying. "How do I deserve this? God, I ask again – how do I deserve this?"

"Please, stop crying," pleaded Alero.

"Why must I stop crying? My entire life has been ruined. My whole career had been destroyed. My vision had been truncated. My destiny had been battered. Why must I stop crying? I am going to cry. I will cry till my head explodes Look! I have been stabbed in the back by a woman who posed as my friend. Irene had not only made a fool of me, she had made a mess of my life. Why must she do this to me? Why?" I bellowed.

"Is Irene you are talking about not this woman with you in this picture?," (pointing to the picture in the magazine).

"She is. That is Irene. That is my late wife. That is the architect of all these. She is the person behind all these dramas. She did all these in order to separate us. After that separation, she moved in to marry me. But the marriage only lasted just few years because she died shortly after."

"How? Who killed her?" Alero asked.

"Nobody killed her. It was an accident."

"O my God! What a pity. I am so sorry about it," said Alero. For several minutes, she remained silent while I kept on shedding tears of regret.

It was after a long pause that Alero spoke to me again.

"Mayo! You said Irene, your wife, was the person behind all these."

"Yes, she was. I am so sure about it now."

"How did you arrive at your conclusion? What are your proofs? And why are you so sure?"

"Alero! Kindly listen to me! The picture at the centre page of this magazine was the same picture Irene and I took when we both traveled to Baltimore, one of the major cities in USA. Only two copies of the picture were printed; Irene took one and I took one. Since I was not the one who arranged mine to be placed inside this magazine, the only other probable person who could have done so, was Irene. That is my first proof.

Irene was the only friend and the only woman close to me in George Bowen University. She was the only person I spoke to about you. She was the only person in Washington D.C. who knew your address apart from me. If a magazine was posted to you from Washington D.C. and I was not the one who posted it, naturally, Irene becomes the number one suspect. The Scorpion Magazine was sent to deceive you that I had married another woman in August 1968, when in actual fact, I did not marry anyone. The motive of the sender was to make you believe that I had married. It was a clever device to separate us and stop both of us from further communicating with each other. Only someone who probably had something to gain from our separation could have embarked on this kind of game plan. And Irene was the only person who benefitted from our separation. For immediately after our separation, Irene who was earlier on a mere, casual friend moved in quickly to strengthen our relationship. Morning, afternoon, evening, she would come to see me. She became so close and later got married to me. Apparently, she knew that she would not get me without getting rid of you. This in my view, must have necessitated this desperate technique she used.

Alero! One incident has just flashed to my memory now and it is my greatest evidence that Irene was the producer of this fake Scorpion Magazine and the one who sent it to you. I said just now that I had never seen this magazine before. That statement may not be entirely true. It just occurs to me right now that I had seen a copy of this very magazine sometime ago. As I closed this magazine in my hand and looked at its back page, I saw the name of the printer – Wesley Print. It is that name that reminds me now that I had seen a magazine exactly like this before. It is the name that reinforces my belief that Irene was the person behind this, no other person.

By the rule, all copies of the Scorpion Magazine were printed by the George Bowen University Press. It was a university policy. The day Irene was leaving Washington D.C. for University of London for her L.L.M. Degree, she brought out a big envelope from one of the shelves in her office containing many copies of the

Scorpion Magazine (I saw about 30 copies). It was not unusual for Irene to have 30 copies of the Scorpion Magazine since it was a monthly publication. But all the 30 copies before me that day were of the same edition. That seemed strange.

Why should Irene buy 30 copies of the same magazine? What for? Or had she become a Scorpion distributor? I wanted to find out.

But as I looked at the magazine more critically, I discovered that they were not recent publications. They were published in August 1968 and that year was 1972. At the back page of each magazine was the name of the printer – Wesley Print. It was that name that made me grow curious that day. As I said earlier on, George Bowen University Press was mandated to print all Scorpion editions. Why was this one handled by an external printer? And which company was Wesley Print? I was a member of the Editorial Board of the Scorpion Magazine all through 1968, and all editions that year were printed by George Bowen University Press. Where did Irene get the copies printed by Wesley Print from? Who authorized the printing? These were the questions I wanted to ask her.

But in the meantime, I picked a copy of the magazine. I wanted to scan through it. But Irene who had been staring at me anxiously, sprang forward suddenly, and seized the copy from me, then took all the remaining copies and gave them to the cleaner."

"Please go and burn them together with all the other documents I gave you. Do it right now."

"Why must he burn them? I love to read the one you

seized from me."

"What do you need a 1968 magazine for? Instead of assisting me to pack my load, you are only busy reading. Mayo! Why are you doing this to me? I must get to the airport in thirty minutes. I am already late for my flight. Please, take the key and rush me to the airport."

Whether it was a 1968 magazine or a magazine published fifty years ago, why must she ask the cleaner to burn them? I couldn't understand the basis for that strange decision. Since Irene was traveling that morning, I felt it was not an appropriate time to pick up a quarrel over a trivial issue. As husband and wife, it was necessary to part on a lovely tone. I was therefore prepared to let go. So I kept quiet over the issue, hoping that the burning might not take place before I came back from the airport. Irene's behaviour made me grow curious. I wanted to know the content of the magazine or find out more facts about it. Might be the content might give me a clue to Irene's strange reaction that morning. Immediately I came back from the airport, I looked for the cleaner.

"What of those magazines?" I asked her.

"I have burnt them. Madam directed that I should burn them. Any problem, sir?"

"No, there is no problem," I replied.

"When I saw Wesley Print at the back of this Scorpion Magazine, my mind went straight to the magazines I saw in Irene's office that morning. All the copies that I saw then, had Wesley Print on their back page like this one. This one and those that I saw then, have the same green front cover page and the same white back cover page. Those that I saw then were published on August 19, 1968. And this one was equally published on August 19, 1968. Surely, this one, is definitely one of those magazines I saw in Irene's office that day. There is no doubt about that. This is an authentic copy of the magazines that I saw. Why Irene would not let me read through a copy has just become clear to me now. She didn't want me to see this picture at the centre page. For if I had seen our joint picture at the centre page, the whole secret would have been out. To prevent this, Irene quickly seized the copy, took also the remaining copies and ordered them to be burnt. I remember now, her look suddenly became stern and fierce and I didn't know the reason why. The reason for that morning unusual behaviour is now clear to me. Irene did not want me to go through a copy of the magazine for obvious reasons.

Now, let us leave the magazine and come to this letter which claimed that you are carrying a baby. Now look at it! (showing it to Alero) the letter was written on 20th August 1968 and this magazine, sent to you from Washington D.C. was published on 19th August 1968, both were executed the same year, the same month, the same week and just one day apart. Again, the letter was posted to me from Lagos on 22nd August 1968 and the Magazine was posted to you from Washington D.C. on 21st August 1968, just one day apart. As the magazine was meant to deceive you and make you believe that I had married another woman so also this letter was written this same time to deceive me that you have gone with another man and you were infact carrying his baby. The two programmes were executed simultaneously and the objective of each was to destroy our relationship. These findings make me come to the inevitable conclusion that the same person was behind both. Irene was surely the person who sent the magazine and she also wrote this letter. She got your writing so perfectly that I did not doubt the genuineness of the letter for a second. She did an extremely convincing impersonation. Since, she was a Nigerian and a Lagosian – all she had done was to write this letter, address it to me, then proceed to the Washington D.C International Airport, send it through a relative flying to Lagos, Nigeria and ask such relative to post the letter to me from Lagos, Nigeria the following day.

Irene was a terribly intelligent woman. She was incredibly brilliant. She was, I am sure, the brain behind both schemes.

Now, Alero, one other issue has now occurred to me as I am talking, and I believe that that was what Irene made use of. In fact, it was perhaps the thing that must have made all the programmes so easy for her to execute."
"And what was that?" asked Alero.

"Irene worked for twenty hours a week in the University Post Office. I guess it was her connection with the establishment she must have utilized to carry out this diabolic plan. For example, I guess she must have seized some of the letters you wrote to me and got your address from there. She must have studied your writing from the seized letters, tried to imitate it until she became perfect and then wrote this letter which informed me that you were carrying a baby."

"Mayo! I feel that deduction is likely to be right. I buy it. It tallies hundred per cent with my own private reasoning and analysis. For about ten months in 1968, I wrote to you every fortnight. There was no reply. If you were on a sick bed, I knew you would endeavour to reply my letters. If you couldn't write and you needed to dictate your reply to someone else, I knew you would have done so. I knew it was impossible for you to get my letters and refuse to reply. I concluded therefore that the letters did not get to you. I was sure that somebody was seizing the letters along the line. That fact was so clear to me. After writing for about a year, rather than have a reply to any of the numerous letters, it was this Scorpion Magazine in your hand that arrived one day.
When the magazine showed clearly that you were getting married that week, then I felt that I must have misjudged you all along."

"You did not misjudge me. I did not marry in 1968. I married four years later. Irene sent the magazine to deceive you in order to separate us and the magazine did its job perfectly. The same thing Irene did to you, she also did to me. I wrote you more than ten letters in the year 1968, writing at least one letter every month. There was no reply from your end."

"None of the letters ever got to me," exclaimed Alero.
"They couldn't have. I guess that as Irene was seizing

your letters so was she seizing mine at the same time. She effectively made sure that our communications could not reach each other. When I waited for over ten months and there was nothing from your end, I became suspicious. I wrote Felix, my friend in Lagos to help me find out what was happening to you. Felix's letter was returned with the note that he had left his last known address and his new address was unknown.

I remember now that each evening when I went to the post office to post a letter to you, Irene was always on duty, and this must have made her job of seizing the letters so easy. Day in, day out, I kept on wondering about what was going on until one day, this letter in my hand arrived and I read through it, only to be informed that you were already carrying a baby for another man. My entire life suddenly went blank.

For three days, I could not leave my room. I was crying. I could neither eat nor sleep. But Irene was in my place in the evening of the third day, apparently to find out the effect of what she had done. She met me crying."

"Mayo! What's the problem? Why are you crying? Any bad news from home? Or what is it?" she asked me. She pestered me for over an hour.

She showed so much concern and I had to open up to her. I told her the whole story. I gave her this letter."

"Alero already carrying a baby for another man! This is a lost case," she exclaimed.

"Forget about her. Even if you don't want to forget, she is already carrying a baby. If she still loves you, she would have gotten rid of the pregnancy. And since she hasn't, then she is in love with the new man. Don't allow her to fool you around. She does not love you anymore. This is a simple fact. And the earlier you can accept this, the better," she said.

Her analysis sounded so convincing. I took to her advice. Now, with you out of my life, I was alone. And Irene, seized the opportunity to move closer to me. Of course, she soon took me over and eventually got married to me.

All through, Alero stared at my face without winking. She stared at me with such malignant concentration and heat that at a point I started to grow uncomfortable. When I finally stopped talking, she rolled out a catena of questions:

"Mayo! Why did the lady do all these? Why was she desperate to separate us? Why was she hell bent to possess you? Were you having an affair?"

Those questions caught me off guard. I stared at Alero's face, I could not answer them immediately.

"You cannot become dumb now. Tell me! Tell me the truth. Were you having an affair? For if you were not having an affair, she could not become so terribly desperate to have you."

I stared at Alero's face, then stammered:

"We were having an affair."

"Look at that! Just look at that!" she screamed.

"Why are you crying? Why are you complaining?

What is your yelling about? Didn't I warn you?"

"Yes, you warned me."

"After the warnings, why did you still walk into her trap? Why? I cannot blame the lady. She had every right to do what she did. She tasted you, you were probably so sweet, sweeter than any other man she had tasted before, then she decided to have you to herself and so devised various strategies to capture you. She saw something good, she desired it, and went for it. Where is her fault in this matter? Tell me!"

"It is my fault. I was foolish to have ignored your advice."

"I warned you. I warned you again and again because I saw it coming. And that was why I was crying that morning after spending a night with you. I had a premonition of what lay ahead. In fact that morning, I saw clearly a picture of what would happen. Just for a few minutes of pleasure, now look at the havoc you had wrecked! Look at the casualties! You said you cried for three days when you got the information that I had gone with another man, in my own case, I cried for years. I was to make a first class in my first degree. I worked really hard for it. My cumulative average did not leave first class grade until the Scorpion Magazine came and my life went into pieces. And for years, I could not gather the pieces together again.

When I was in the university, and after I had left the place, many men were pestering me to marry them. And since I had made up my mind not to marry anyone, I decided to go into the convent. I went to the Convent of Holy Maria at Ibadan and started to train as a nun."

"What? Please, come again!" I stared fixedly at

Alero's face.

"You said you went to the convent? And you want me to believe that?"

"Go to Holy Maria at Ibadan. The records are there," Alero said gently but firmly.

"You can always drive down and check when you feel like."

"Alero! Why did you need to take such an extreme action? Why? My goodness! Why?"

"If the man I intended to marry was no longer available and I did not feel like marrying anyone else, why wouldn't I go to the convent. My mom came to the convent several times to plead with me to leave the place but I refused. One time she pleaded for hours with tears on her face:

'Alero! I want you to give me a grandchild. I want to carry your baby on my back,' she pleaded. But I could not help her. That was her third visit. I was too sad to put mom in such a stressful situation. When she finally left me, she was in a terribly bad condition. She had heart disease and this matter aggravated it. She was hospitalized. The doctor said she had cardiac problem and one day my father sent an S.O.S to me: 'your mother is dying gradually. Come and save her life.'

This was the time Chief Ajai was pestering me to marry him and I felt mom's condition was being over-dramatized so that I could marry Ajai. By the time I realized it was not, mom had gone into a coma. There was a lot of hope that she would come back to consciousness. And I was told by the doctor that if she did, and learnt that I was already with a man, she might have a dramatic improvement.

"Old African women love children a lot. And if you can give your mom a grandchild, I am sure her health will improve," said the doctor. I was ready now to do anything to assist mom regain her health and so I came out of the convent. I couldn't marry Chief Ajai but I entered into one year of trial marriage with him with the proviso to go back to the convent if after a year, I discovered that I had not developed enough love for him to marry him. It was part of the arrangement that I would be living under his roof and acting as his wife publicly but there would be no connection more than that. He would not touch me. I would be living in a separate apartment. Our lawyers prepared the agreement. He signed it and I signed it. I had kept strictly to the terms and he too had not breached any of the terms. But mom that I did this for, still died along the line. She never came back to consciousness. My mom became an unfortunate casualty of what she did not really invite. For if I had not gone to the convent, perhaps her condition would not have deteriorated sharply as it did. It was a most pathetic case."

Drops of tears were running down Alero's eyes. I did not know what to say neither did I know the best way to console her. With the tears, she continued with her story.
"Chief Ajai and I were scheduled to live together for one year. I have already spent nine months with him. I still have three months more to spend. I must confess to you that he is a wonderful man. He is so caring. But his values and my values are so different. Our ways of life are also different, in fact poles apart. We are parallel lines which have no possible meeting

point. I cannot marry him. And since I had made up my mind on this, I wrote to Sister Lucia, the Head of the Convent of Holy Maria a month ago that I would be returning to the convent after four months and that she should kindly reserve my place for me. I know that this decision would pain Chief Ajai, but I am afraid I cannot do otherwise. I am going back to the convent." I stared at Alero's face. Her narration seemed like a mid-day dream. That she was not yet married, sounded most incredible. It was stranger than fiction.

"I must confess to you," Alero continued "that after tasting the convent, I fell in love with the place. I had long been searching for peace and joy, there I found both. I never knew before now that there is much joy in being married to Christ. Now, I understand better. I had tasted the love of men and the joy it could give. I have also tasted the love of Christ and the joy it can bring. I have found that all other joys outside Christ are hollow and vain. I have tasted the convent, it is sweet. It is really sweet. I must tell you that nothing in this world can separate me from the convent. There is nothing anyone can offer me anymore that can make me leave the convent. Nothing. I have just three more months to endure my present prison and agony. Then I will go back to the convent and enjoy again that abode that I really cherish and love so much."

CHAPTER FIFTY-NINE

Alero spoke for a long time. All through I stared fixedly at her face. Jesus! The lady was terrific. Her face was lovely, cool and innocent. Her figure was elegant. No one should be this good-looking. I wondered what God was thinking when He created this kind of terribly bewitching lady. There were magnets in her eye-balls that kept on attracting me. The rays from her big eye balls were sending out their usual, hypnotic spells and the same mesmerized me now with power. Alero was a delightful creature.

That she was not yet married was the greatest surprise of my life. That she had remained single all these years was a greater marvel than any of the seven wonders of the modern world. Now my problem – she was not married yet Alero was no longer available. She was still single yet I had lost her all the same.
"Why is life always playing me a cruel joke?" I asked again and again. I had got many academic laurels, but the greatest of all prizes, I had struggled all through my life to get was Alero, the Princess of Toro. Alas! An unkind providence had denied me that prize.

"Why is my life a sad music? Why is that music playing me discordant tunes all the time? Why is providence always acting contrary to my wish? Why is the current of fortune always flowing contrary to my voyage? Why?"

Alero had found a new love in Christ. She had found a new peace. She had tasted a new joy which she was no longer prepared to part with. All through, fate had stood between me and Alero and I wondered why fate had been so cruel to me.

But I still loved Alero. As I stared at her, all my cells were itching for her. I had traveled through many cities of the United States of America, I had spent a good time exploring the beauty of Europe and Asia during my holidays. I never met any woman I fancied as Alero. She was the exact woman I had been looking for all through my life.

I stared at Alero again. Goodness! She was pretty. Her figure was hot, seductive and tempting. She had never been more stunning. She had the most beautiful skin I had ever seen. As I surveyed her statistics, a mounting passion for her surged inside me. A romantic hurricane cruised through my veins. I did not know precisely what to say or how to begin. But I just found that I was talking.

"Alero! I know I have betrayed your trust and my foolish act had given you series of torture and pain but I must confess that I still love you. I never ceased to love you, not even for a second. Even though I got married to another woman briefly, you know now that it was not by design. I never planned to do such a thing. But when it became apparent to me that you had married and gone with another man, in the absence of an eagle, I had to make use of a sparrow. And after tasting the sparrow and seeing the wide difference between her and the eagle, I decided to go alone. I made up my mind that I either have you or no woman. And since you were no longer available, I decided to remain single. And for several years, I have remained in that position. For several years now, I have been alone. The fact of the case is that, no woman had ever taken your position in my heart."

I stared at Alero's face again. "How do I win her back? What are the points I must hammer to make her change her mind?" I was yet to resolve these various questions when I found myself kneeling down before her. My words were incoherent and shaking, but with quivering lips, I presented my case in a few sentences "Alero! I know it is difficult but can you forgive me? Can you trust me again? Can you give me a second chance? Can you give up the convent and marry me?"

A narrow smile lit Alero's face.
"Mayo! Your request comes rather too late. I have already crossed the Rubicon. I have got to a point of no return. I have tasted a new life in Christ. I had found that the love of the flesh is empty and vain. There is nothing in it. You may still believe that there is something there, but there is nothing there. I must therefore plead with you to forget me. Try to forget the past. Let the past remain with the past. Of course, I can see that your faults are not as deep as I earlier on

thought. You were deceived, so was I. I don't have anything against you. But to come back to you, that is impossible. I have laid my hands on the plough, I cannot look back. I have found a new friendship in Christ and there is no way I can forgo what I have now for mere fleshy lusts and earthly desires. No, I cannot. I know how you feel, but take heart. You are a man, I am sure you will soon get over the whole problem."

Her words sounded like a funeral dirge to me. They made me feel so sad. But I couldn't just take my eyes off Alero. My eyes went up and down her exquisite figure. Jesus! She was attractive. Everything about her was electric. Her cool elegance and her tantalizing look seemed to be driving me crazy. My internal structures were shivering with passion to be one with her. I knew I would never have real joy without Alero. And since my pleadings had failed and I did not know what else to say anymore, I knelt down there before her. I was desperate. And in my desperation, I tried one time more to plead with her.

"Alero! You know that my joy lies with you. Why should I live without you and without joy? I know I have offended you, but remember that you loved me before, and if you make some efforts, you can love me again."

Looking at her with pleading eyes, I stared once more at her face for a response.

"Mayo! Please, let us leave this matter alone. Regard it as a closed issue. There is no way I can come back to you. It is too late in the day. I am sorry about this. Please, try to understand," she said with a sad look on her face.

"I wished I could leave the matter alone but it is impossible for me…

Alero! Have you forgotten all we shared? Alero! Have you forgotten the covenant you made with me at the age of seven that you would for ever be mine? Have you forgotten the vow you made in your letter when you were in Ghana that if Christmas changed from December 25 and the earth changed from its orbit that you would still remain with me? Have you forgotten my pain and torture in Pa Richard's garden – all because of you? Have you forgotten the night we were returning from Zia when three men, one holding a dagger, attacked me, and nearly killed me because of you? Even if you forget all those, can't you remember again my adventure to the Oro Grove? Can't you remember when the two of us were tied to two huge stones, waiting for execution? Can't you?"

As if touched by a live wire, Alero suddenly sprang forward: "Mayo! That is enough," she screamed. She held me, raised me up from my knees and went into my arms and started to cry. For several minutes, the two of us were crying in each other's arms. After about three minutes, Alero spoke again:

"Though I had found a new life and a new joy in the convent, I feel it is time to confess to you that I too, still love you.
In spite of the various travails that I faced, in spite of the various pressures from men, in spite of the mental and physical torture I went through when you were married to another woman, in spite of the sickness of my mom which eventually led to her untimely death, in spite of the various tornadoes and hurricanes that I went through, I stood my ground. I

did not crumble. I could neither be enticed nor seduced. No man had touched me. I had kept this body holy. I had not defiled it. The covenant I made with you, I did not break. Under rain, under fire, I did not sag or waver, I had kept the faith because I made an eternal vow at the tender age of seven to be yours. And that vow I promised to keep as long as I live." Alero was still crying.

"Mayo! Even if I forget all things, I cannot forget the fact that when we were small, innocent children, you demonstrated beyond all doubts that you needed me. When I wanted to leave you, you almost went into a fit. 'Please! Never leave me,' was your plea to me. As a small child, you showed a burning passion to have me. I also made up my mind, little as I was then to be yours. Since you wanted me so much, I too did not see any reason why I should not be yours. The fact that I was a Princess did not matter to me since your passion to have me was too great, almost an obsession. When anyone desires a thing as seriously as you had demonstrated, it is only fair that he should have it, and I made up my mind that whatever it would take, I would give my heart to you. I have never changed that decision ever since.

When the Oro people abducted me and everybody abandoned me, including my mother, you were the only one I saw. You were the only person who chose to lay down his life because of me. You came, you dared the Oro lions in their dens, you did what the greatest men in history could not do. You came and fought like ten thousand men. You fought like the bravest generals of history. You stormed the conclave of Oro people like a deadly tsunami. You moved like a whirlwind, dauntless and invincible. The Oro people intended to kill me but out of the blue, you came to frustrate their plan. Like a suicide bomber, you knew you were going for a death assignment. But you did not bother about your life, you only bothered about mine. You knew you were going to die, but you still went ahead, all because of me. Everything you had, you gave because of me. You gave all ...all without holding anything back. Where is that man who can behave like you? I ask you, where is he?, if you know the direction to his house, please, show me."

Alero now stared at my face curiously and said:
"Mayo! If I don't give you my heart, who then should I give it to? If I don't give you my body, who then qualifies to have it? Who else deserves to have me more than you? If you know any other man, please tell me!"

Alero glared at my face with eyes moist with tears, then exclaimed:
"I have waited all these years because of you. I told my father that if I had to wait for forty years that I was prepared to wait. Why won't I wait for you? After all, you gave all because of me. Even more than that – one of the things God told me as a child was that He created me for you. I heard Him. I heard Him so clearly. I know God cannot lie. Since I was sure He talked to me, I was prepared to wait. I know that no matter how long, the word of God cannot but come to pass."

Alero now fastened me possessively to her chest and

with tears running in torrents down her face, she exclaimed:
"No matter how long the night, dawn is bound to
come in the morning.
No matter how long the journey,
the voyager, at last, must head for home.
No matter how interesting the trip,
Odidere, must finally head for Iwo, its abode.
No matter how lovely the adventure,
the Zulu, must in the end, head for his kraal.
No matter how long the Eskimo spends outside,
he must in the end head for his igloo.
No matter how long you spent in the arms of a strange
woman, I was sure that one day like this, you will come
back to me."

Alero now left my arms and walked into the empty
space before us. She looked up as if talking now to the
Great Creator above, as she now burst out:

"From the burning of daylight heat.
And the burden of every day.
With grief and sorrow pressing so hard.
Mocked by men and laughed at by colleagues.
Oppressed with humiliation and surrounded by
scorn.
I struggled on all the same.
Hoping that there would be a light at the end of the
tunnel.
And surely there is one.
As Mayo now finally surfaces.
To begin the journey where we ended.
The night was long.
The time seemed like a long stretch of eternity.

Furnace of affliction hit me from every direction I turned.
I looked desperately for frustration antidotes.
But there was none.
My strength seemed all but gone
As the anguish and pain pressed to almost unbearable limit.
The huge burden, I never knew I could bear.
But thank Jesus who giveth the strength.
And make me see the joy of today."

Then Alero turned round again and stared at me. She turned her beautiful eye-balls on me and suddenly burst into a huge and uncontrollable sobs. I moved quickly forward, took this angel of beauty in my arms. And for many minutes, we were crying together.

Inside Alero's house, things were no longer at ease. Melody, Alero's friend who accompanied her from Lagos was restless as she kept on muttering: "Why? Why? And why now?"

Desola, who would be getting married the next day, stood up, sat down and stood up again, now anxious and restless as she kept on muttering:
"Who will tell her? And how do we tell her?"

The Nigerian plane carrying 200 passengers and flying from Kano to Lagos with Chief Ajai on board, crashed 60 kilometres to Lagos and there was no survivor.

www.ingramcontent.com/pod-product-compliance
Lightning Source LLC
Chambersburg PA
CBHW071336020726
47502CB00001B/110